EATING PEACHES

Tara Heavey was born and raised in London, and moved to Dublin at the age of twelve. A qualified solicitor, she practised law in Co. Kilkenny and Co. Waterford for five years before turning to writing full-time. She lives in Co. Kilkenny with her partner and son.

Also by Tara Heavey

A Brush with Love

TARA HEAVEY

EATING PEACHES

TiVOLi

Tivoli
an imprint of Gill & Macmillan Ltd
Hume Avenue
Park West
Dublin 12
with associated companies throughout the world

www.gillmacmillan.ie

© Tara Heavey 2004
07171 3605 1

Print origination by Carole Lynch
Printed and bound by Nørhaven Paperback A/S, Denmark

*The paper used in this book is made from the wood pulp of
managed forests. For every tree felled, at least one is planted,
thereby renewing natural resources.*

A catalogue record is available for this book
from the British Library.

1 3 5 4 2

For Rory

Do I dare to eat a peach?

T.S. Eliot, 'The Love Song of J. Alfred Prufrock'

Prologue

Proper is my middle name. Well, it's really Bernadette. Elena Rose Bernadette Malone. My mother is a big fan of Russian ice-dancing. I got away lightly; my elder sister is called Tatiana. I used to call myself Elaine out of embarrassment. My friends call me Lainey out of kindness and affection.

Rose: that's where my beleaguered father came in. His mother's name.

Bernadette: enter the parish priest, horrified by the absence of a saint's name. If it hadn't been for the inclusion of Bernadette, he might have refused to baptise me. If not for the intercession of Saint

Bernadette, I could have been banished to the lower pits of hell for all eternity. Instead, here I stand, a good Irish Catholic girl with all the trimmings.

Malone. As in Molly.

But, anyway, Proper could have been my middle name. At least, that's what other people always seem to think. Imagine their surprise when they hear me swear for the first time. 'I never knew you cursed!' Expressions of amused shock on their faces – and a certain smugness: *Perhaps she's not perfect after all. Maybe humanity does lurk beneath that navy pinstripe and crisp white blouse.* Little do they know of the effing and blinding that goes on inside my head on an almost continuous basis. Especially when I'm talking to a client. No, I say. I can't believe your neighbour had the temerity to leave her bin out six inches over your boundary line! It's a national disgrace! Of course you shall have your day in court! The aromatic blend of curses and swear words that actually circles in my head doesn't find release until the client has been led safely down the corridor.

Because I'm a hypocrite. When you're a solicitor, being a hypocrite is an essential part of the job description. Hell, if you told the truth, you wouldn't have any clients left. Tell the punters what they want to hear and they'll come back for more. One must never burden one's client with the truth.

This attitude proved to be extremely good for business. I doubt it was very good for the soul. But, as I mentioned earlier, I had been baptised, so hopefully that earned me a few brownie points with the big guy upstairs.

Talking of the big guy upstairs, he had a few changes in store for me that I could never have anticipated.

I thought I'd always be sitting in my big, plush Dublin office, dealing with big, plush Dublin clients, and zipping around Dublin in my snazzy little sports car. Little did I know that I was due a major transformation.

Chapter One

I spun around on my new, luscious, black leather chair for what must have been the fortieth time that morning – and it wasn't even nine o'clock yet. Oh, how I loved the trappings of success! And if that made me a shallow person, so be it.

I was interrupted mid-spin by a knock on the door. I hastily readjusted my chair and picked up my fountain pen, as if poised to write something complicated and legalistic. I even furrowed my brow a little.

'Come in.'

In came Barb, my boss's secretary.

'Tyrone would like to see you, when you're ready.'

So you see, I wasn't the only one in the office with a funny name. My boss was called Tyrone Power. I kid you not. His mother, Mary, was a huge fan of the silver screen. Fifty-odd years before, she had married Michael Power of the county of Kilkenny. Tyrone maintains she married him solely so that she could inflict this terrible name on some poor unfortunate child – who happened to be him. He's always going on about changing it by deed poll, but what's the point in that when you're fifty-one years old? It would be like a man who's bald as a coot walking into the office one day sporting a thick black rug on his head.

Not that Tyrone is bald. He has a head of lush silver hair, and liquid brown eyes. He's a little on the portly side, but he's tall and carries it well. It almost suits him; he takes up more space in the courtroom. He's intense – frightening, if you don't know him. All the young secretaries are terrified of him, especially when he lets out one of his famous lion-roars. But that's just a sound effect. Gets things done.

Tyrone and I saw through each other from the outset. He baited me mercilessly when he interviewed me for my apprenticeship; cross-examined me, trying every trick in his very long book to make me lose my cool. But I could see that he was a softie deep down, and I held it all together. Hard to believe that had been almost seven years ago.

And this morning he wanted to see me about something.

I hardly dared guess that this was the moment I had been waiting for. Tyrone had been hinting for some time that partnership was imminent. I already had the plush office, the luxurious company car. I knew that he was pleased with me. Surely the next logical step....

'Come in and sit down, Lainey.'

Lainey. That was a good sign. 'Elena' was reserved for company and the odd bollocking. He swivelled his swivelly chair around to face me, leaned back and yawned. The bags under his eyes were like miniature hammocks and his shirt was crumpled. The top button was undone and his tie veered to the left. He looked like he'd put in an all-nighter.

'Have you been here all night?'

'No, just got in.'

What was wrong with this picture?

He continued to observe me until I started to fidget.

'You wanted to see me about something, Tyrone.'

'Yes, that's right, I did.'

Still nothing.

Then: 'You'll have some coffee?' He didn't wait for my reply, just buzzed the order out to Barb. I was slightly concerned. Evasive was not this man's middle name (I think it could have been Francis).

'Is there something wrong?'

He got up and stood looking out of the window, leaning like a corner boy, hands deep in his pockets.

The view was of the canal. Dublin pedestrians and cars scurried by like insects.

'I haven't been very well lately.'

A distant alarm bell started to ring.

'Oh?' I said profoundly.

'My doctor thinks I should slow down a little. No more working weekends, late nights, all that.'

'Nothing serious, I hope.'

He swatted the comment away like a pesky fly. 'No, no, not at all. Just too much stress, high blood pressure, that sort of thing.'

I nodded. That sounded all right. Didn't it?

'Can I do anything to help? Take on some of your files? You just have to ask.'

He turned to me and smiled warmly. 'Actually, I do need a favour.'

'Go on.'

'I'm thinking of moving back down the country.'

You what!

My racing thoughts were interrupted by a sharp rap on the door and the entrance of Barb. She gave me a digestive biscuit, a hot coffee and a cold stare. I noticed that Tyrone got a chocolate digestive while mine was plain. Barb didn't dislike me in particular; she just hated any female who came within a ten-foot radius of her beloved Tyrone. She was about ten years his senior, but this didn't seem to hinder her crush. The younger secretaries called her Miss Moneypenny behind her back, when they weren't calling her Barbed Wire. Tyrone just seemed oblivious. If anyone asked him for his opinion of her, he told them that she was a damn good secretary.

Tyrone sat down heavily and reached into a side drawer, pulling out a pack of Benson & Hedges and a solid gold lighter. Barb, who had been about to close the door behind her, flew back to his desk as if aided by supernatural powers (come to think of it … invisible broomstick?).

'What do you think you're doing?' She bore down on him like a Fury, hands on hips, spitting fire. Jesus, she was one scary woman. Tyrone held up his hands as if he were under arrest and let the box of cigarettes fall like an illegal firearm.

'By God, woman! Is a man to have no peace in his own office?' He tried to make a joke out of it, but his calculated rakish grin failed to dent her steely demeanour.

'Give them to me.' She held out one hand, arm rigid; the other remained firmly on her matronly hip. She reminded me of a strict schoolmistress confiscating a contraband sweet or an illicit note. Sulkily, he handed her the cigarettes.

'And the lighter.'

'Oh, come on, Barb –'

'Now! You're not to be trusted. You know well what the doctor said.'

He handed over the lighter, for all the world like an overgrown bold child.

Her voice and manner softened somewhat. 'You can have some of that special chewing gum I got you.'

'Don't want any.'

She turned on her heel, tutting and shaking her head as she went.

I waited until she had gone before I said anything. I wasn't that stupid.

'Isn't she afraid that you'll stick a piece of gum under your desk and make a terrible mess?'

'Don't start.'

'She's not in a very good mood. Did you forget to bring her in an apple this morning?'

'Yeah, yeah. Very funny, I'm sure. Now can we drop it, please? You didn't see that, okay?'

'Okay. So what else did the doctor say?' I tried to keep the concern out of my voice.

'That if I don't quit this job I'll be dead within three years.'

I was silent. Tyrone didn't say anything either; he just stared at me hard, trying to gauge my reaction. I was aware of the scrutiny and struggled not to let any emotion show. *Stay calm, Lainey.*

After a while, I said, 'But, Tyrone … this job is your life.' Okay, not very comforting, but the truth. Tyrone had no wife and no kids. He had built the practice up from scratch. Now he had fifteen solicitors working for him and was one of the most respected lawyers in the city. If it didn't sound like such a cliché I'd say that the firm was his family.

'Well, I'm not going to give it up altogether. I'm going to open a sub-office back home and run that instead. The pace of life is slower down there, and I can take it a lot easier.'

'Do you think you can be happy doing that?'

'I think so. I've been hankering for home a lot recently. In fact, I quite fancy myself as a country squire.'

I had a disturbing mental image of Tyrone in an old-fashioned tweed suit, shotgun tucked under his arm, trouser legs tucked into his socks, a couple of dead rabbits slung across his shoulder. I shuddered – especially at the vision of his matching tweed hat with flaps over the ears.

'When are you going?'

'As soon as I can. I estimate it'll take me about nine months to wind down here and hand over the reins. That's where you come in.'

He surely didn't mean that he was going to hand over the reins to me? There were plenty of more senior solicitors in the firm. I felt a knot of excitement begin to tighten in my stomach all the same.

'I need someone to head down before me, to get the ball rolling. The premises are all sorted. A new housing estate is just being completed; the auctioneer is my first cousin, and he's promised to send plenty of business my way….'

I wasn't listening any more. The knot in my stomach was unravelling. Surely he didn't mean …

'… So you'd only need to be there for about nine months….'

'What?'

'I'll need you down there for about nine months, while I honour my commitments here. You can stay in the old family home. Rent-free!'

Big swinging mickies, I thought. *What's in it for me?*

'I suppose you're wondering what's in it for you.'

'I wasn't, I –'

Tyrone laughed at me. 'It's all right. I don't blame you.' He stood and faced me, beefy hands (they were farmer's hands. Why hadn't I noticed before?) leaning on the desk. His eyes blazed into mine. The bastard was enjoying this.

'If you do this for me, there's a partnership in it for you at the end of the nine months.'

Now you're talking.

'And if I don't do it?'

'There's plenty more out there who'd jump at the opportunity.'

'All right. I get it. I'll do it. When do I have to go?'

'Two weeks' time.'

Holy shit.

'Okay. Where exactly am I going, anyway?'

'You, my dear Elena, are destined for the throbbing metropolis of Ballyknock.'

Chapter Two

I thought Christiana was going to rupture something.

'Ballymuck? You're making it up!'

'It's Ballyknock. I'm not saying it again.'

'Ballymuck!'

This time I thought she was going to explode, she was laughing so hard. I tried not to let my annoyance show. This really wasn't helping.

'This really isn't helping, you know.'

'Sorry, sorry. Just give me a minute to compose myself.' She wiped a tear from her eye with the back of her hand and made an obvious attempt to compose her features. After a while, her face lost some of its redness and returned to its normal pinky-white hue.

'Where exactly is it, then?' Hazel asked.

'In the heart of the Kilkenny countryside.'

'In the middle of nowhere, like.'

'In the middle of nowhere.'

'Cows and fields.'

'Cows and fields.'

'How far to the nearest shop?'

'Five miles.'

'How far to the nearest pub?'

'Five miles.'

'Fucking hell!' they chorused.

'You won't last two weeks,' Hazel said helpfully.

'Jesus, girls, would you give me some credit? It's only for nine months, and I'm neither a shopaholic nor an alcoholic.' I washed this sentence down with a generous gulp of Chianti.

'Nine months. That's how long it takes for a baby to grow,' Christiana informed us solemnly. Then her eyes widened in shocked excitement.

'That's it, isn't it? You're pregnant!' She pounced on the idea like a cat on a mouse. 'You don't want anyone to know, so you're going down to the arsehole of nowhere, where nobody knows you, and you're going to have the child in secret, and then it'll be adopted by a rich doctor and his kindly wife who can't have any children of their own.' The words came tumbling out.

'Yes, Chris. I'm really going to work in a laundry run by evil nuns who'll whip me if I don't wash their drawers quickly enough. Then they'll refuse

15

to let me have an epidural during labour, to punish me for my sins, and then they're going to wrench the newborn infant from my arms and give it to a God-fearing Catholic family.'

'I knew it!'

'Chris, have you been reading that book about the Magdalene Laundries again? Remind me to confiscate it,' said Hazel, rolling her eyes at me.

'The most fertile thing around here is your imagination, Chris. It's not the 1950s.'

'So you're really just going down there to work as a solicitor, then?'

'Of course.'

'Oh.' She sounded so disappointed that I was almost tempted to make up an elaborate lie for her benefit.

Hazel and Christiana were my flatmates. It was the evening after Tyrone had delivered his shock news, and we were sitting around the coffee table in what we laughingly called 'the good room'. It was only 8.30 p.m., post-*EastEnders*, but the second bottle of wine had already been opened. We three sat curled up on the overstuffed couch, engulfed in a haze of cigarette smoke and alcohol fumes. It was an all-too-common scenario.

Christiana was pretty well twisted already. This partly accounted for the excessive giggling and wild theories – but not totally. Her friends described her as 'off-beat' or 'a little off the wall'. If she'd had any enemies, which I sincerely doubted, they probably would have described her as 'completely barking'. Hazel and I were her friends – although how and why Hazel and Christiana were friends was anybody's guess. Chalk and cheese weren't in it. In fact, just to illustrate my point, I'm going to set out their differences in tabulated form. I like doing this sort of thing. It must have something to do with being a lawyer.

Christiana	Hazel
Ditzy	Salt of the earth
Too much to say	Woman of few words
Gullible	Cynical
Easily led	Leading easily
Believed in ghosts	Believed that anyone who believed in ghosts should be committed forthwith

Christiana worked 'in film'. Nobody – including Christiana herself – was quite sure what she did, but she seemed to be paid an awful lot of money for it. Hazel was an accountant by name and by nature. As the Americans would say, go figure.

Christiana fell in love with a different person every single week. She claimed she was bisexual, but I suspected this was only because it was currently fashionable in the film industry – I think it was Drew Barrymore who had started this particular trend. Quite frankly, I had difficulty keeping track. On a weekly basis, extravagant bunches of flowers

17

were delivered to the flat with her name on them. It was quite annoying, actually. They were usually from some new, up-and-coming director or from a bit-part actor or actress. These relationships tended to last roughly as long as the flowers. Either Chris blew them off because of their lack of 'Heathcliff-like qualities' (her words, not mine) or they realised in the nick of time that she had fallen off her trolley a long time ago. Hazel, on the other hand, was resolutely single. She hadn't got where she was with the aid of a man, no sirree Bob. In her opinion, a husband was a sign of weakness.

I was the only one with a steady boyfriend. Steady being the operative word.

Paul was an accountant too. He worked in the same office as Hazel, and we had hooked up at one of their work do's (or should I say work don'ts). It had been a total set-up. Paul had been taken under the wing of his best friend's newly appointed wife. Having sorted out her own love life, she turned her attention to the so-called love lives of others for her entertainment. She was Paul's social secretary. Hazel was my marketing manager. Wifey decided that I would be perfect for Paul, as I was a solicitor and therefore bound to be sensible and financially viable. How wrong can you be?

'What does Paul think?' asked Hazel.

'I haven't told him yet. I'm seeing him tomorrow night.'

Hazel nodded but was silent. I could tell that she

was worried. She suspected that all was not rosy in the Paul–Lainey garden. I guessed she was just saying nothing and keeping her fingers crossed that it would all work out. Otherwise, how was she going to take credit for our wedding?

'We'll have to have a going-away do!' It was Chris, squealing with excitement yet again.

'Oh, no. The last thing I want is a big fuss.'

'But we can't let you go off to Ballymuck without a proper send-off.'

'For the last time – Ballyknock!'

'Whatever. Go on. Say yes!'

'Oh, all right, then, if it'll get you off my back.'

'Yes!'

'But you'll have to keep it small. You, me, Hazel and Paul. You're not to invite any of your loony friends.'

'I won't, I promise. Just leave it all to me and I'll arrange everything. You're not going to regret this, Lainey.'

One small tip: whenever anyone says those words to you, start worrying.

Paul thrust inside me as if he were trying to push a boulder up a hill. I wished fervently that he'd reach the summit and hoist his flag. *How much longer?* His face hovered inches above my own, ghostly white. Beads of sweat had begun to form on his forehead. I watched in fascination as his features contorted and his body shuddered.

'Oh God!'

Thank God.

Paul collapsed on top of me. I lay beneath his sweaty bulk, waiting for a decent interval to expire before I could push him off. I judged ten seconds to be an adequate period.

'Paul,' I said gently, and patted him on the shoulder. He grunted in reply.

'Paul. I need to use the bathroom.'

'Oh, yeah, right…. Sorry.' Assisted by what I hoped seemed like a gentle shove, he rolled off me onto the other side of the bed. I leapt up enthusiastically, padded naked into the bathroom and locked the door, relieved to be on my own. I viciously spun the toilet-roll holder, releasing far more squares of toilet paper than I actually needed. *That'll teach him*, I thought unreasonably. Paul was a two-squares-only man, for both economic and environmental reasons. *Fuck the environment and fuck him.* I wiped away the meagre juices that my body had produced due to his ministrations and flushed angrily, watching with satisfaction as the toilet swallowed all evidence of our brief encounter.

As I washed my hands, I looked up into the mirror and sighed. I smoothed down my long blonde hair. We're not talking Pamela Anderson here; more Lady Helen Taylor – the type of hair that looks well adorned with an Alice band or swept back into a sleek chignon. People thought it was classy. I looked for a brush or comb in vain. Paul didn't have much use for them, being an advocate of the Phil Mitchell school of hairdressing, and I didn't dare leave my own hairbrush in his bathroom in case he thought I was dropping hints about moving in with him. He panicked at the mere presence of a carelessly discarded earring on his bedside table.

I scrutinised my face in the mirror. That was never a crow's foot at the outer corner of my left eye? It couldn't be. I was only twenty-nine and a bit. Since my last birthday I had developed an all-consuming obsession with crow's feet, laughter lines and any other facial inconsistency remotely resembling a wrinkle. I often snuck up on my reflection unexpectedly, trying to catch any lurking lines unawares. And, to add insult to injury, I still got the odd spot. Surely that wasn't on, having to worry about pimples and wrinkles simultaneously? It was like seeing a dead leaf on a glorious summer day.

There was definitely a dry patch on my right cheek. I opened the bathroom cabinet, searching for some kind of moisturiser to remedy the situation. Paul's lotions and potions were lined up like little plastic soldiers. It was most definitely a boy's bathroom. Not a hint of pink or a gently curved shape anywhere; all the containers were either dark blue or metallic grey and were shaped like phallic symbols, as if the advertisers were trying to reassure the male consumer that, no, you're not a poof if you buy exfoliator. All those little lines of plastic penises arranged with pathological neatness. Freaky.

'Lainey, are you going to be long in there? I'm dying for a pee.'

I slammed the cabinet door. I couldn't get a moment's peace.

'I'm coming.' *For the first time tonight*, I felt like adding.

Paul stood on the other side of the door, grinning sheepishly and shifting from one bare foot to the other. He was clutching his privates in one hand and holding a full condom in the other. We come bearing gifts. I was exposed in the fluorescent glare of the harsh bathroom light. I felt my dimpled thighs did not bear scrutiny. So what if I didn't know whether I fancied him any more? It was still important that he should find me attractive. I dodged Paul's kiss as I slunk by him into the safety of the dimly lit bedroom.

I would have killed for a fag, but Paul would have gone berserk if I'd lit up in his precious bedroom. The last time I had tried it he had thrown the offending item out of the open window – fully lit! How inconsiderate. He could have caused a forest fire or anything.

I could hear him banging around in the kitchen now, opening and closing presses. The kettle hissed reassuringly in the background. A few minutes later Paul emerged, clad only in a pair of gingham boxer shorts, bearing a tray heavy with teapot, milk carton

22

and plate of warm buttered toast. He smiled shyly at me as he placed the tray on the rumpled bed. He reminded me of a little boy bringing his mammy breakfast on Mothers' Day.

'I thought you might have the munchies.' He began pouring me a cup of tea, milk first, just the way I liked it. I felt sick with shame at my earlier mean thoughts. I'd forgotten how lovely he could be at times. I almost remembered why I'd gone out with him in the first place.

I examined his face as I bit into my first slice of toast. Regular, classically handsome features: light-hazel eyes, soft brown hair, strong nose, full firm mouth, and cheekbones that a supermodel would be proud of. So why did I feel so irritated every time I looked at him nowadays? He could be great when he wanted to be. And he had so obviously wanted to be tonight. It was just all the other times – when he didn't want to be great – that were the problem.

There was the excessive tidiness, for a start. It had seemed like a joke at the beginning, an endearing quirk – part of his charm, if you like. CDs arranged in alphabetical order; socks and jocks stored in colour-coordinated bundles, neatly rolled and folded. And then there was the obsession with hygiene. Germs! Everywhere! It was just so … well, it was downright anal, to tell the truth. I had reached the end of my rope with it some time ago; I had tied a knot on the end and I was hanging on for dear life.

I suppose it wouldn't have been so bad if I had also been a neat freak. It might have been a big plus. But not only was I not a neat freak, I wasn't even averagely tidy. In fact, I was a slob – albeit a secret slob. My colleagues would probably never have guessed. I kept my office in reasonably good nick. And I was always well turned out: suits regularly dry-cleaned, shoes and nails polished, hair groomed, face done. My flatmates knew all about it, though. They were as bad as me. That was why I rarely brought Paul around to the flat. I was afraid he'd faint. When left to my own devices, I could literally fester in my juices for days. My tolerance for dirt was astounding. And as for germs … you couldn't even see them, therefore they didn't exist.

And then, God help us, there was the sex – or lack thereof, as we might say in the legal world. Not that it made much difference; I could have slept through most of our sessions nowadays. There was nothing wrong with Paul's technique, as such. It was just that I was never allowed any input. Paul had to call all of the shots all of the time. I was at screaming point there, too.

My family were convinced that we were going to announce the tying of the knot any day now. They were in for a rude awakening.

I decided to bite the bullet as well as the toast.

'Paul, I have something to tell you.'

The hand bringing the mug to his lips froze in mid-air. 'You're not pregnant, are you?'

'No, I'm not pregnant!'

Relief flooded his face, and he took a sip of tea.

Jesus. Where had that come from? Had I gotten really fat lately or something? And how on earth did he think I could possibly get pregnant, what with him being so acutely careful all of the time? He wouldn't even hear of me going on the pill, probably because he didn't trust me to take it. He was the only man I knew who relished using condoms. That way he could ensure that he was in complete control. His sperm didn't stand a chance. At least it eliminated fights about who got to sleep on the wet patch.

Perverse as I knew it was, I felt secretly jealous whenever I heard of a couple getting pregnant by accident. I could only dream about the kind of passion that would result in bringing a love-child into this world – forgetting all about the tearing of condom wrappers and the balling of socks. Oh, the oblivion of torn tights!

'I have to go away for a while.'

'Define "go away".'

I told him, watching his reaction carefully. His expression remained blank. He kept his eyes down-cast throughout. Just kept right on sitting there at the edge of the bed. Topless. Five o'clock shadow – now nine o'clock shadow. Rough. My favourite version of Paul.

'Well?' The suspense was too much.

He raised his eyes slowly to mine.

'Would you like me to go with you?'

That was unexpected.

'Don't be daft. You have your job to think about; and it's only for nine months. We can still see each other at weekends – if you like.'

'Of course I like,' he said quickly. He took my hand without looking at me and stroked it gently with the ball of his thumb. He whispered something I couldn't quite catch.

'What was that?'

'I'll miss you, Lainey.'

My heart melted a little and I felt a curious mixture of affection, irritation and guilt. I thought that I should say something in return.

'Will you miss me too?'

That was it. That was what I was meant to say. 'Of course I'll miss you,' I said quickly. I almost meant it, too. In fairness, I was in shock. Paul wasn't the most demonstrative of men; this was pretty soul-revealing stuff for him.

'When did you say you were going, again?'

'In a little under two weeks.'

'So you'll be away for our anniversary.'

Another bolt from the blue. In a few weeks' time, Paul and I would have been going out for exactly one year. I remembered the date, but I was amazed that he had. We hadn't even discussed it. I fixed a smile on my face to hide the shock. 'Never mind. We can still do something special.'

Paul had stopped talking. I looked up and noticed

that he was staring at my left breast, which had popped out of its hiding-place behind the duvet. I cleared my throat uncomfortably and pulled the covers up to my chin.

'I'd better be going,' I said, hopping out of bed and quickly grabbing my clothes.

'Why don't you stay the night?'

'No. I didn't bring clean underwear, and besides, I have an early start....' I was already half-dressed.

'When will I see you again?' Paul called out to me as I was halfway out the door.

'I'll give you a call.'

I put off phoning home for as long as possible. Finally it became so uncomfortable that it was easier just to do it.

'Hi, Dad.'

'That you, Rosie?' My dad refuses on principle to call me by my first name. It infuriates my mother. It's meant to.

'Yeah, it's me. Listen, Dad, I have some news.'

'You're getting married.'

'For the last time, no!' I almost shouted.

'All right, all right. No need to get your knickers in a twist. I was only saying. You are nearly thirty now, you know.'

'Thanks for reminding me.'

'And someone has to carry on the family line. We've given up on your sister.' Tatiana (we called her Annie) was thirty-four years old and single. I didn't know which was worse, being branded as the family brood mare or as a lost cause.

'Hello, dear.' It was my mother on the other line.

'Hi, Mum. Look, I'm glad I've got you both together. Something's happened in work.'

'You've been made a partner?'

'Not exactly, but it's in the offing.' I explained the situation.

'But, Rosie, you hate the countryside.'

'Do not.'

'Yes, you do,' they exclaimed together.

Both of my parents are from the West. Childhood family holidays consisted of driving through somewhere like Connemara, past acres of fields, sheep, dry stone walls, rocks, more sheep and more rocks. The monotony was broken only by stop-offs in lay-bys, where we ate limp Calvita-and-Tayto sandwiches – which tasted to us like manna from heaven – washed down with warm, flat 7-Up and a flask of tepid tea. Then we'd examine dolmens, piles of rocks assembled by our ancient forefathers to commemorate dead chieftains. High excitement for a couple of pre-pubescent city chicklets.

'Admire the rocks!' Dad would exclaim angrily. 'They were put there by your ancestors.' And Annie and I would wonder why our ancestors couldn't have found something more productive to do with their time.

And then there was the rain, the incessant, driving rain. I shuddered, recalling weeks spent shivering in a caravan in the middle of a field in County Roscommon. The sun would refuse to come out until we got back to Dublin. My sister and I would run out of the car straight to our friends' houses, with tall tales about freckled Mayo boys who had looked at us funny, leaving our deflated parents to shake their heads at their repeated failure to educate their daughters about their cultural heritage.

But that had been years ago. I was sure I must have developed some appreciation for the countryside in the meantime. And if I hadn't, it was about time I did.

'Well, I for one think you're doing the right thing, Elena. It's a wonderful opportunity for you – and, besides, you owe it to Tyrone. He's always been very good to you.'

'Thanks, Mum.'

'Where did you say you'll be living again?' asked Dad.

'In Tyrone's old family home. It's a little cottage in the middle of nowhere, apparently.'

'When you say "middle of nowhere", what do you mean exactly? Do you have any neighbours?'

'I think there's a couple of houses close by.'

'And you're going to be living there on your own?'

'Of course.'

'Is there an alarm on the house?'

'I don't think so. Why would there be? It's in the middle of nowhere. And there's nothing to take, anyway.'

'There's *you* to take! Merciful hour, Rosie, you're not staying there on your own. You'll be murdered to death.'

'Dad!'

'You hear about it every day. Young women living in isolated country cottages, murdered in their own beds. Or worse.'

'Don't mind him, Elena. You'll be grand. You can get yourself a nice big dog to protect you.'

'But you know I don't like dogs, Mum.'

'Nonsense. You've always loved dogs. And it'll be great company for you, if nothing else. We'll go down to the pound next week and pick you out something suitable.'

'It's a dog, Mum, not a handbag.'

Oh, what was the use?

'Anyway, I've got to go. I'm only in the door and I have an early start in the morning.'

'It's ten o'clock! Where have you been all this time?'

'I was just out with the girls.' I was hardly going to admit to having unsatisfying, unmarried sex with my boyfriend. 'I'll talk to you both soon.'

'Goodbye, Elena. Sleep well.'

'Night, Rosie.'

I sighed with relief as I put down the phone. That was everyone important told.

Now I just had to get used to the idea myself.

Chapter Three

That was that, then: last day in the Dublin office for at least another nine months. It had taken me most of Saturday to tie up loose ends, so it was well after six by the time I let myself into the apartment that I'd called home for three years and three rent-hikes. I had decided to keep my room. It made sense: I was only going to be in Ballyknock temporarily, and I planned to come to Dublin every weekend anyhow. I knew I should probably do the sensible thing and look for a place of my own to buy. But I loved living there.

'Hello! Anybody home?'

No reply. Perhaps they hadn't heard me. Perhaps this was because Björk was caterwauling at the top of her lungs. Christiana was blaring her latest CD at full volume. It was her customary getting-into-the-party-mood music. She played it a lot. We'd be getting another snotty letter from the landlord if she wasn't careful.

I pushed open the door of the living room. Hazel was sitting at the table with her back to me, hunched over a bunch of official-looking papers.

'Not working weekends again?'

No response.

I went up behind her and spoke into her left ear. 'I said, you're not work–'

'Jesus Christ!' Hazel jumped as if she'd been scalded, and her Biro went flying across the room. She slumped with relief when she saw it was me.

'Lainey! You frightened the shite out of me. What are you doing here?'

'I live here, remember? God, you're on edge. Been overdosing on the caffeine again?'

'What?'

'I said it looks like –'

'Oh, hold on.' Hazel removed a lump of Blu-tac from each ear. 'For fuck's sake. A person can't hear herself think, let alone work, with that Icelandic witch wailing in the background. I've already asked Chris to turn it down twice.'

'Give her a break. She probably doesn't expect anyone to be working at home on a Saturday evening. Which brings me to my next point: what's with all the paperwork?'

32

'Don't be talking. We've got a major deal going down in work. My ass is really on the line with this one, Lainey. I wouldn't be going out tonight if it wasn't …'

'If it wasn't my going-away? Go on; you can say it. I don't mind. In fact, I'm thrilled to be the cause of you taking a break. Anyway, what about that boss of yours? I don't suppose he's working the weekend.'

'That bastard! You must be joking. Golf in Killarney again.'

'You should tell him where to go, Hazel. He's really taking the piss.'

'I know, but it's only temporary. Things will calm down once this deal is through.'

'Until the next deal. You've been saying that ever since you started working there. It's never going to calm down. Can't you see that? You work all the hours God sends, and you're never on top of things.' I peered over her shoulder at the rows and rows of minute figures. 'I don't know how you and Paul don't go cross-eyed looking at all those numbers.'

A persistent thudding was now emanating from the general direction of Christiana's bedroom.

'What *is* she up to in there?'

'God knows. Probably "creating" new dance routines. She could be committing hara-kiri for all I care.' Hazel sounded really annoyed.

'Deary me. Is she still getting on your nerves a little?'

'A little! It's like living with a cross between

Bubbles from *Ab Fab* and Samantha from *Sex and the City*. She never stops. She's driving me demented.'

'But she's always like that.'

'Yeah, I know. I just dread to think what it's going to be like with you gone all week. You're like the buffer. It's not as – I don't know – not as intense when there are three of us. I need another person to help take the strain.'

'I didn't realise you felt this way. Is it really that bad?'

'Worse. I'm thinking about looking for my own place.'

'No way!'

Hazel nodded wearily.

'But you've known each other since you were six.'

'I know.'

'You sat beside each other all through school.'

'Only because our surnames start with the same letter. It wasn't by choice.'

'But you've told me a million times how you braided each other's hair and bought gobstoppers together and swapped marbles –'

'Yeah. And then she lost her marbles.'

'But I don't understand. She lost them years ago. She's your best friend.' Along with me, I hoped.

'Used to be my best friend. I don't know, Lainey. I think we've just grown apart.'

'I'm sure it's just a phase,' I said hopefully. I didn't want our cosy little set-up to change. 'And I'll be back in a few months to help smooth things over.'

'Yeah, maybe.' Hazel didn't look or sound convinced.

Talk of the devil....

'Hazel, will you help me put my fake tan on … Lainey! You're here!' Christiana burst through the door and ran over to me, flinging her arms around my neck. 'I didn't hear you come in.'

'*Quelle surprise*,' Hazel muttered under her breath, just loud enough for us both to hear.

'I'm only here a few minutes.'

'Hazel, this is what I thought you could wear tonight.' Chris waved a wisp of shocking-pink material in front of Hazel's face. Believe it or not, this constituted an entire outfit – a skirt and top, to be precise. It wasn't exactly what I would have described as Hazel's style.

'Would you ever fuck off with yourself? I'm not wearing *that*.'

'But I wore it last week and it was lovely on me.'

'Well, *I* don't want to look like a tart.'

'Hazel!' I was shocked. I'd never heard her speak that way to Chris before. But I was ignored: Hazel stomped out of the room, roughly pushing past Chris.

Jesus! Things were worse than I'd thought.

'Don't mind Hazel,' I said gently. 'She's just been working too hard. I mean, look at that.' I gestured to the pile of papers on the table. 'On Saturday night, of all nights. I mean, it's just ridiculous.'

Christiana nodded vacantly.

'Did you say you needed some help with your fake tan?'

Chris silently handed me the bottle of Clarins spray (the best fake tan there was, in her expert opinion) that she had been clutching, and sat on one of the stools at the breakfast bar.

'Where do you want it?'

'On my back.' She pulled her top over her head and slipped out of her bra. She was as unself-conscious as a child. I started spraying the tan on her shoulders and rubbing it in.

'What are you wearing tonight, Chris?'

'My new Whistles jumper.'

I thought about this for a few seconds. 'But that means nobody will be able to see your back.'

'That doesn't matter. I'll know it's there.'

'Oh.' My friend the fake-tan junkie. 'You know, pet, if you had a baby it would come out orange.'

'Yeah? Do you think it would have ginger hair, too?'

'Most definitely.'

'That's good. I love red hair.'

She got distracted then; drifted off into one of her daydreams. Who knew what went on in that girl's head? I retreated into my own little world, and for a few minutes all was quiet between the rubber and the rubbee. Until:

'Lainey, I have something to tell you.'

I stopped rubbing. 'What?'

'You know how I said I'd arrange your going-away?'

36

'Yes.' My gut told me that this wasn't going to be good.

'And you know how you said it was just to be you, me, Haze and Paul?'

'Chris, what have you done?'

'Well – I might have invited a few extra people along by mistake.'

'How can you invite people by mistake?'

'It just sort of slipped out.'

'How many?'

'One or two.'

'How many?'

'Six.'

'Six! For pity's sake, Chris. Who are they?'

She reeled off a list of names that made me immediately lose my appetite. I could have clocked her one. Undaunted, she alighted on a new topic.

'What are you wearing tonight?'

'I hadn't really thought.'

'Oooh. You can borrow something of mine if you like.'

'No, thank you.' If I'd wanted to look like a clown I would have joined the circus.

'Oh, go on. It'll be fun.' Fun for her, maybe. Apart from inventing appalling dance routines, Christiana's main hobby was doing people up. When she was a little girl, her favourite toy had been Girl's World. The reason I knew this was that she still had it in her room. Some people might have jumped at this opportunity for a free make-over. I, however, had seen some of her previous victims.

'No, Chris. I've got plenty of perfectly good clothes of my own.'

'But your clothes are so boring. You need to use your imagination more when you dress.'

'I'm not supposed to have an imagination. I'm a solicitor.'

'You need to express yourself more.'

'By that you mean show more flesh.'

'If I had your chest I'd show it off all the time. Oh, let me pick your outfit, please! Think of it as an extra-special going-away present from me to you. Oh please, please, please!'

I looked down at her upturned little face, devoid of make-up, devoid of artifice. I thought of how hurt she must have been by Hazel's behaviour, though she had tried so hard not to show it.

'Okay. But just the top.' What was I letting myself in for?

'Oh, brilliant!' She clapped her hands gleefully, jumped off the stool and ran to the door. 'Oh – are you finished my back?'

'One back fully tanned.' I was already washing my hands at the kitchen sink, although I knew that, whatever I did, they'd be tangerine later on that night.

'You won't regret this,' I heard her calling from the hall.

I was regretting it already.

I spent the next half-hour trying on at least fifty different tops, each one more outrageous than the last. Finally we agreed on a wine-coloured angora cardigan, trimmed around the neck and down the centre with what looked like feathers in varying shades of wine and pink. It was lower-cut than I was used to, but I could live with that. Chris wanted me to wear it with all the buttons open, except for one at the chest, and nothing underneath. It was all right for her, with her toned midriff and pierced belly button; I was a mere mortal, with a roll of fat to keep in check. A matching wine camisole was debated over and decided upon.

I had to fight for the right to wear my own dressy black trousers and flat black boots. Christiana was most insistent on a pair of fake-snakeskin boots with four-inch spike heels. I won that particular dispute by giving a very convincing demonstration of my inability to walk in them. Chris herself was an expert at walking in high heels; at five foot one and three-quarters, she never wore heels lower than three inches. She was like a white, female version of The Artist Currently Known as Squiggle.

Once I had dispatched Chris to her room to complete her own extensive titivations, I rapped gingerly on Hazel's door.

'Who is it?'

'It's me.'

'Come in.'

She was sitting cross-legged on her bed, reading a book and dressed in her all-black going-out uniform. She looked up as I entered.

'She never got you to wear one of her tops!' She shook her head. 'I can't believe you were so spineless.'

'It's not a question of being spineless. I was trying to cheer her up. She was upset.'

Hazel didn't reply.

'Besides, I got away lightly. You should have seen some of the stuff she was trying to get me into.'

'I believe you.'

I sat down on the bed beside her. 'I suppose you knew about those twats coming along tonight.'

'Sorry about that. I was sworn to secrecy.'

'Are you ready, then?'

'I'm not going.'

'Well, how come you're dressed to go out?'

I could see her trying to think of an answer. 'I got dressed and then I changed my mind.'

'Well, change it back. Seriously, Hazel, surely you're not going to miss this golden opportunity to take the piss out of Chris's friends? It'll be a laugh. Besides, I'll need someone normal to talk to. You can't abandon me like this. It's like throwing a Christian to the lions.'

'I wouldn't mind throwing a Christiana to the lions. Anyway, you'll have Paul.'

'Fat lot of good he'll be. You know he'll just sit there in silence, staring at them as if they're all mad.'

'He'd be right.'

'Come on. We'll make sure we sit together. We haven't had a good chat in ages.'

'Oh, all right, then.'

'Good woman. Meet you at the front door in fifteen minutes.'

I closed her bedroom door behind me. *Phew!*

I had the distinct feeling that this was going to be a very long night.

There was no need for introductions when we arrived at the restaurant. Unfortunately, we had already met. The two separate camps eyed each other suspiciously: me, Hazel and Paul versus Oisín, Diarmuid, Fionn, Neasa, Iseult and Mona. Sure, we were outnumbered – but we were confident we could take them, being of stronger moral fibre. We nodded to each other as we took our seats. Let the Cold War commence. Christiana didn't know it, but she was Switzerland.

Chris, Hazel and I were the last to arrive. We had been delayed by Chris's last-minute nail-polish crisis: she had been torn between glittery blue and molten violet. Hazel still had a face on her as a result.

And speaking of people having faces on them…. Paul, true to form, had been the first to arrive. This meant that he had spent the last forty minutes enduring a discussion on the latest trends in men's trousers – not the type of thing he normally discussed with his soccer buddies. Judging by the cut of Diarmuid, Oisín and Fionn, brown corduroy flares appeared to be all the rage. As did blue rimless sunglasses worn on the crown of one's head.

'Hey, lads. Going on your holidays?' Hazel said cheerfully as she sat down. She was going for a pre-emptive strike.

The lads looked at one another blankly. Hazel pointed to the top of her head. 'The sunglasses. Or maybe you're expecting a sudden heat wave?'

'Actually, that's the fashion, Hazel,' said Iseult.

'Oh, is it, actually, Iseult? I didn't actually know that. Tell me more.' Hazel poured herself a massive glass of red wine. I sensed danger.

'Has anyone ordered yet?' I said.

'No, we were waiting for you,' answered Paul. Then, under his breath to me, 'Where the hell were you? You wouldn't believe the shite I've just had to listen to.'

'I'm sorry. I couldn't help it. Now please be nice. It's just a few short hours out of your life.'

'That Diarmuid has already taken years off my life. He made a pass at me, you know.'

I tried unsuccessfully not to laugh. Paul, like many red-blooded heterosexual males, had yet to be convinced that all gay men weren't after his body.

'What did you say to him?'

'What could I say? I pretended to misunderstand him.'

I was sorry I'd missed it. 'You must have said something to lead him on, Paul.'

'You're very funny, you know that?'

'Anything in trousers. You just can't be trusted.'

'Stop it.'

'He's a model, you know. I thought it was every man's dream to go out with a model.' Paul didn't find this funny at all. I, on the other hand, was cracking myself up.

'Shut up, Lainey.'

'Slut.'

He didn't dignify that with a response.

After a while he said, 'I suppose those other two are queers as well.'

'Who, Fionn and Oisín? No, they're not gay.'

'Thank God for that. I was beginning to think I was the only straight man here.'

'They're bisexual. So we might both get lucky.'

'I'm going to the jacks.'

'Careful you don't get followed,' I called after him. He glared back at me. Paul was deliciously easy to wind up.

I zoned in on the other conversation that was going on down our end of the table – between Hazel, Iseult and Diarmuid.

'So tell me, Iseult,' said Hazel, far too loudly. 'I'm dying to know. What *is* the new black?'

Iseult eyed Hazel coolly. The fashion editor of an Irish celebrity magazine, she was probably the most copped-on of the group. You could tell that she strongly suspected that she was having the piss taken out of her.

'Well, Hazel, black is always in. But I can see that you're well aware of that. I mean, just look at that *lovely* ensemble you're wearing tonight.'

'This old thing! Shucks, Iseult, I just threw this little number on as I was leaving the flat.'

'You'd never guess.' Iseult's smile rivalled Hazel's for tightness and insincerity.

'Actually, I heard that aubergine was the new black,' said Diarmuid. *For Pete's sake, don't get involved,* I felt like warning him. 'Like Lainey's cardigan.' It wasn't often that I was cast in the role of trendsetter. (I had assumed the cardigan was maroon.)

'Aubergine! Really, Diarmuid?' Hazel trilled. 'Well, what I want to know is, what's the new aubergine?'

'Um....' Poor Diarmuid was stumped.

Just then the food arrived. Saved by the starters. I had ordered deep-fried Brie; I had wanted soup, but I was afraid that somebody might be tempted to use the accompanying bread rolls as ammunition.

Paul came back and sat down.

'What's this supposed to be?' He was staring at his plate in pure disgust.

'I don't know. What did you order?'

'Pork wontons in plum sauce.'

'What's the problem? They look like wontons to me.'

'But there's only four of them!'

Sure enough, four small pork parcels sat forlornly

on a large, purple (inedible) lettuce leaf, surrounded by a trickle of brown sauce.

'Hmm. They do look a little bit lonely, all right.'

'Lonely! They're practically in quarantine. I've a good mind to send them back to the kitchen.'

'I wouldn't do that, Paul. The chef will only spit on them and send them back. Here, have some bread.' He had already asked the waitress for a new glass because of an imaginary lipstick-mark. He'd make a great health inspector.

Paul took a slice of fancy bread and bit into it viciously. After a few chews, he screwed up his face.

'What the hell is in this bread?' He inspected it suspiciously. 'It's full of green stuff. They're leaves! Lainey, somebody's put leaves in the bread.'

'They're herbs, Paul. What's wrong with you tonight? You're like a bag of cats.'

His face relaxed, and he took my hand under the table. 'I'm sorry. It's just that I get to spend so little time with you nowadays. The last people I want to share you with are this bunch of tossers.' He squeezed my hand so hard it almost hurt. 'I'm really going to miss you, Lainey.'

I gulped. 'I'll miss you, too.'

He smiled at me, for the first time that night, and kissed me lightly on the cheek. I felt a twinge of something. Regret?

I opted to put it down to indigestion.

Those of us who were having starters finished up. Diarmuid wasn't having a starter because he was on the Atkins diet. Iseult wasn't either, because she was a strict vegan. Neasa wasn't because she was dairy-intolerant, and Mona wasn't because she was following a detox programme.

'Camel!' exclaimed Diarmuid suddenly. I had no idea what he was talking about. The menu was quite unusual, but I hadn't spotted camel on there. Ostrich and shark, perhaps. (*Garçon, je voudrais camel en croute avec petits pois, s'il vous plaît.* One hump or two?)

Everybody looked at Diarmuid, who was red-faced and excited.

'The new aubergine. It's camel.'

'Did I miss something?' whispered Paul.

'Camel. Of course! Thank you so much for enlightening me, Diarmuid. Now I can shop with confidence,' Hazel said gaily. 'More wine, anyone?' Without waiting for a response, she sloshed wine into her own glass, almost up to the rim – a sure sign, as if we needed one, that she was pissed.

Diarmuid looked pleased. Luckily, he was too thick to realise that he was being made a fool of. But Hazel wasn't finished with the poor sod yet.

'Diarmuid, I must tell you what a treat it is to have this opportunity to talk to someone who's so' – she pretended to search for the right phrase – 'in the know. I mean, your hairstyle, for instance; it's so damn *stylish*! Where should someone like, say, Paul go to get a lovely do like that?'

I felt Paul stiffen beside me.

'Oh, do you really like it? Thanks. I got it done in the new hairdresser's in the Powerscourt shopping centre. Hold on, I think I still have the card….' Diarmuid started fishing around in what looked like, but couldn't possibly have been, a handbag.

'Here!' He triumphantly thrust a business card across the table at Paul, who was so dumbstruck, he forgot to say thanks.

'Although, if you ask me,' Diarmuid added, almost coyly, 'your hair is really nice the way it is.'

'I agree,' said Iseult. 'I wouldn't change a thing if I were you.' She gave Paul a predatory smile and a wink. A *wink*!

Are you hitting on my boyfriend, Missus? At least have the good manners to wait till I've gone to the loo or something. I suppose she couldn't contain herself. Paul was probably the only straight man she'd met all month.

I glanced at Paul, to gauge his reaction. He didn't seem to be having any. He was still frozen with embarrassment at Diarmuid's attentions. His cheeks were the new black.

I had been beginning to feel a little sorry for Iseult. Hazel in vicious mode was too hot for most people to handle, even though I knew from past experience that Iseult could bitch for Ireland. But that wink had extinguished my last glimmer of sympathy. *Go get her, Hazel!*

I glanced across at Iseult, who was re-applying her lippy between courses, even though she hadn't actually eaten anything yet. She was peering into a compact mirror, delicately wiping the corners of her mouth with her index finger.

'Oh, yes,' she was saying to Diarmuid, 'scarves *must* be worn long this season. It's absolutely essential.'

Essential for what? World peace? Strangling her with?

She was quite good-looking, I thought grudgingly, if you liked that sort of thing. All cheekbones and snooty expression. Kristin Scott Thomas would be a good choice to play the starring role in the movie of her life.

The main courses arrived. Paul just sat staring at his elf-sized portion of rack of lamb. I thought he might cry. He looked piteously at me. I patted his hand and promised that I'd buy him a bag of chips on the way home.

'Tell me, Lainey,' said Iseult. Warning – bomb alert! 'Where *did* you get that scrumptious cardie?'

'It's not mine. It's Chris's.'

'Ah, I see. That explains it. I thought it wasn't your usual style.'

'My usual style being?' It was a challenge.

Iseult gave a high, tinkly laugh. 'I really couldn't say.'

The wound was stinging but hardly fatal. I maintained a dignified silence. This was because I couldn't think of a suitably bitchy response. I decided to store up the insult for future reference.

Paul and I were the only people at the table having dessert, even though he didn't really like it. He knew the drill: he ordered a dessert, which I helped him pick out, and then I ate at least two-thirds of it. It was a wonderfully guilt-free method of consuming calories. Everyone else ordered their triple skinny lattes or whatever.

As we were finishing up and paying the bill (extortion, according to an outraged Paul), Chris skipped excitedly over to our side of the table. At least someone was enjoying herself.

'Hey, guys, let's all go to Manilow's!'

'God, no, Chris! Manilow's is so two weeks ago. Let's go to Mango's,' said Iseult.

I had been to Manilow's the week before, and it had seemed fine to me. I decided I'd better not admit to this for fear of being branded a social pariah.

'Are you coming, Lainey?' asked Chris.

I was about to agree until Paul shot me an urgent, pleading look.

'Um, maybe I should take Hazel home. She's a little the worse for wear.'

This was no lie. Hazel was slumped over the table, singing gently to herself.

'Are you coming out dancing with us, Hazel?' Chris shouted in her ear.

Hazel slid up and looked blearily at us from beneath her mussed-up hair. She slurred aggressively, 'I'm not going out anywhere with that bunch of wan—'

'Okay, Hazel, let's be having you.' Not allowing her to finish the sentence – although I think we all got the general gist – Paul hauled Hazel up by the elbow, simultaneously prising the wine glass from her hand and masterfully ignoring her squeaks of protest.

I turned to Chris and hugged her apologetically. 'You can see she really needs to be brought home to bed. Paul and I will look after her. You go out and enjoy yourself, and I'll see you in the morning.'

Except that I didn't see her the next morning, because she spent the night with one of the bi-sexuals. Come to think of it, I never found out which one.

Chapter Four

My first glimpse of Ballyknock was from the back of a J.J. Kavanagh bus. I was pleasantly surprised. It was a beautiful day. We were experiencing the type of Indian summer we often get in this country as compensation for the lack of an actual summer: a blazing hot day in September, when all the kids are back at school, sitting in sweltering hot classrooms, gazing longingly out of the windows. Even now, this time of year made me want to run out and buy a new geometry set. I was reminded of knees skinned on hot tarmac playgrounds. It was a time of new terms and new starts, almost like a second New Year – a second chance to make resolutions that you might actually stick to. My current

New Year's resolutions had been long forgotten. I vaguely recalled something about losing a stone in weight and breaking it off with Paul.

The bus crawled along Main Street. I remember thinking that every piss-ant little town in Ireland must have a Main Street, consisting of a church, a chipper, a newsagent-cum-family-supermarket and a boutique selling half-slips and triple packs of granny knickers. Oh, and six pubs. Ballyknock was no exception. Then there was the solicitor's office, of course. The bus moved slowly enough for me to have a good look at the new premises. Not bad. Could do with a lick of paint. And then the bus swung over the bridge.

I literally gasped with delight. The old medieval bridge, reinforced with ugly concrete and steel over time to accommodate the passing trucks, straddled a wide blue expanse of river, bordered on either side by grassy green banks. Old mill-houses, some discarded, some still in use, lined the riverbanks at intervals. The scene was completed by a pair of swans, floating regally by as if posing for a portrait. I could get used to this.

The bus stopped outside Power's pub. Power's Undertakers were next door. Padraig Power Auctioneers were across the street. Obviously Tyrone's family were the Kennedys of Ballyknock. I thanked the driver as I got off the bus, heaving my bulging rucksack behind me. He seemed to know every passenger personally, except for me, and they

52

all knew him by name: Thanks, Jimmy; see you next week, please God. I went into Power's (the pub, not the undertaker's), as per my instructions from Tyrone, to order a cab.

The bar was almost empty. There was a middle-aged man behind the counter, polishing a pint glass with an ancient-looking tea-towel. Two old lads, wearing matching cloth caps, perched on barstools opposite him. As I entered, they all stopped mid-sentence and stared at me. I thought for one terrible moment that this was one of those country pubs I'd heard of where they didn't serve women. Get back to that kitchen sink where you belong, Missus.

'Hello. I'm Elena Malone.'

More blank stares.

'Tyrone Power sent me.'

The transformation was spontaneous.

'Ah, you're Tyrone's girl. Come in and let's be having a look at you.'

I advanced slowly and uncertainly, embarrassed by the scrutiny. I felt like I was ten years old again, being inspected by elderly grand-uncles at some gruesome family function.

'Will you have a drink, love? Tom here is buying.'

'No, thanks. I'm just looking for a taxi. I have to get to …' I fished a screwed-up Post-it out of my pocket. 'Ard-ske-ha.' I pronounced the name awkwardly.

'Go 'way out of that. Sure I'll drive you there meself.'

'Do you know where it is, then?'

The three men laughed like drains. The older of the two customers – who, I later found out, was aptly known as Tom Delaney of the Rusty Teeth – erupted into an alarming fit of coughing. His companion – who went by the name of Shem – gave him a thump on the back, and he stopped coughing and re-lit his pipe. Mellow Virginia. Reminded me of my granddad.

'You could say that, love. Didn't I grow up there?' He wiped his right hand on the tea-towel and extended it. 'I'm John Power, Tyrone's brother.'

I shook his hand. 'Pleasure to meet you, Mr Power.'

'You may as well call me Johnny. Everybody else does. Besides, every second man in town is Mr Power. You'll cause terrible confusion.'

More guttural guffaws all round.

'Will you have a pint of stout, love?' This was from Tom of the Rusty Teeth, who I could have sworn winked at me, although it might just have been a twitch.

'What are you thinking of, man?' demanded Shem. 'Sure you know these young ones from Dublin drink nothing but those Bacardi Breezers. Terrible stuff. Tastes like donkey's piss. Isn't that right, love?'

'Actually, a glass of Guinness would be lovely.'

The glass of stout was placed ceremoniously before me. I picked it up and, even with my low standards of hygiene, was slightly disgusted at the way the bottom of the glass stuck to the counter. I drank deeply and gratefully, savouring the bitterness and carefully licking the line of white foam off my top lip.

I surveyed my surroundings. The pub also served as a general grocer's. Side by side with the many bottles behind the bar were packets of cornflakes, shoe polish in black and neutral, and pink butterfly slides for little girls' hair. I noticed with childish delight the three big jars of bonbons: toffee, lemon and original. I was going to have to get me some of those. But not today. I was the new solicitor in town; I had my reputation to consider. I'd have to send some little kid in to get them for me on the sly. On the wall beside me was an old black-and-white photo of a group of moustachioed men wearing old-fashioned three-piece suits and funny hats. They were standing outside a slightly – but not very – different-looking Power's pub. Previous generations of Powers, I guessed; one of the men looked spookily like Tyrone. This place was the real thing, all right. I had been in many a fake olde original pub in Dublin; this was the ambience that they had been trying to create.

A settled-looking woman, a pinny tied tightly across her ample hips, had materialised behind the bar. She was sporting a suspiciously dark head of hair for her age. She hummed to herself, swishing a bright-blue feather duster delicately along the bar, and looked at me quizzically from time to time, a half-smile on her face. I could tell she was dying to find out who I was. Finally, unable to contain herself any longer, she nudged the barman.

'Are you not going to introduce me, Johnny?'

'Elaine, this is the wife, Bridie Power. Bridie, this is Elaine, Tyrone's new girl.'

'Actually, it's Elena. But you can call me Lainey. Pleased to meet you.'

'The new solicitor, is it? Well, I never would have guessed. You don't look one bit like a solicitor – does she, Johnny? God bless us, you're very young. And you're going to be living up on top of that hill in Ardskeha all on your own?'

'Well, I am, yes.' I was from the city, for God's sake, land of joyriders, muggers and drive-by shootings; I could surely handle a few months alone in a country cottage.

'God bless us and save us – a lovely young girl like you…. Are you not married?'

'No.'

Shem made a sound that I guessed passed for a suggestive laugh in these parts. 'We won't have much trouble setting up a laying hen like you.'

'A what?'

'A laying hen. A young girl with good earning potential, like a teacher or a nurse. A solicitor, now – that's like landing the goose with the golden egg.' The three men shook with laughter and Tom had another coughing fit.

'I already have a boyfriend, thank you.' I could

feel myself getting ready to mount my high horse.

'Does he hurl?' asked Shem.

'No. He plays soccer, though.'

I might as well have told them that he was a dab hand at needlepoint, judging by the hilarity it caused.

'Don't you be minding those oul' fellas, Elaine, love. What do they know? I'm sure your boyfriend is a fine lad. But, just in case things don't work out with him, I have seven lovely lads of my own – three of them not married, even though they're getting on a bit now. I'm sure one of them would do nicely for you.'

I had a flashback of *Seven Brides for Seven Brothers*. When the brothers decide they need wives, they all go into town, kidnap the women of their choice and carry them kicking and screaming back to the homestead.

'Anyway,' Bridie continued, 'we're keeping you too long. I'm sure you must be keen to settle into your new place. I'll take over here, Johnny. You give Elaine a lift up to Ardskeha. Just wait till I give her a few bits to help her settle in.' Bridie disappeared mysteriously through a door at the back of the bar, and emerged a couple of minutes later laden down by a bulging paper bag.

'Now' – she plonked it down on the counter – 'I've put in a carton of eggs, freshly laid this morning by our own hens – what you in the city call free-range. And there's a soda bread I baked this morning – there's only a few slices gone out of it. And there's a pot of strawberry jam for you, love.'

'You'll enjoy that,' said Johnny. 'Bridie's strawberry jam won first prize at the Mivik show the other week.'

'It was the same batch, too.' Bridie smiled proudly. 'Although I suppose you'll be making your own jam soon enough. There's plenty of blackberries up around Ardskeha way, and you'll have your own crab-apple trees in the garden. They make a lovely jelly.'

I smiled politely. Why on earth would anyone bother making jam when they could buy a perfectly good pot of it in the supermarket?

'And I've put in a few teabags and a carton of milk, so as you can make yourself a nice cup of tea in your new place.'

'Thank you. How much do I owe you?'

Bridie held up her hand. 'Don't be insulting me, now, girl. Think of it as a gift to welcome you to Ballyknock. I hope you'll be very happy here.'

I thanked her profusely and followed Johnny out of the pub door. She called out to me as I left, 'Don't be a stranger, now. You know where we are if you need anything.'

I had trouble keeping up with Johnny. He moved surprisingly quickly for a man of his age; I estimated that he was about sixty, but he was lithe and wiry and seemed full of nervous energy. He had lifted the stuffed bag and the rucksack out of my arms as if they were dead leaves. He stopped beside a Peugeot 405 diesel with a 90 KK reg; it was parked high up on the narrow pavement, seemingly oblivious to the double yellow lines. It was danger-red, and the seat-covers were leopard-skin. He opened the passenger door for me with a great flourish, as if I were a movie star and he were my chauffeur helping me into my limousine. I stepped in, over a jumble of receipts, fag packets, Mars bar wrappers and a disembodied doll's head. There was a faint whiff of something that I was later able to identify as slurry.

Without a discernible glance into his mirrors, Johnny took off at high speed. The engine sounded like a lawnmower. Without indicating or slowing down, he took the first left turn we came to. I double-checked that my seat-belt was properly fastened. The car crawled up a steep hill and the engine roared painfully, as if the machine was about to take off like some old-fashioned, dilapidated fighter plane. I hoped there was a life-jacket under my seat. Can someone please pass the sick-bag?

After we had hurtled along for a while without crashing, I decided to chance opening one eye. I found that we were speeding down a narrow, tree-lined avenue. I looked to my left and realised how far up into the hills we had already climbed. Through the trees, I could see the edge of the village nestling in the valley. The river wound about the houses like a long blue ribbon. Ahead, the trees seemed to stretch into infinity. They reached out to one another across the road, forming a verdant arch; sunlight dappled through at intervals, making the leaves sparkle like so many emeralds. This wasn't half bad. It sure beat the soggy sheep and grey rocks of County Galway.

As we climbed higher and higher, the trees gave way to rolling green hills that undulated softly into the distance. We passed a field of black-and-white cows, like the scattered pieces of a jigsaw puzzle. A field of cloud-like sheep, with black faces and ears like handlebars. A field of horses in varying shades of chestnut and grey. At one point, a rabbit scuttled across the road in front of us, narrowly avoiding the bald tyres of the Peugeot. I imagined that Johnny Power was a prime suspect in a large percentage of the roadkill incidents in Ballyknock and its environs.

The man himself cleared his throat and turned to me. He yelled something that I couldn't quite make out over the roar of the engine.

'Say that again, Johnny.'

'I said, why don't you have a car?'

'I do. It's in being serviced.' I didn't like the way he kept turning to look at me every time he spoke. *Keep your eyes on the road, for God's sake, man.*

'What do you drive?'

'An Audi TT convertible.'

'Begod,' he cackled, 'Tyrone must be paying you too much.'

'You can never be paid too much,' I yelled back.

'You might be right there, love.'

'Watch out for the tractor!' I screeched as a blue tractor loomed up around the bend, directly ahead of us. The Peugeot emitted an almighty screech and skidded to a halt, just inches away from the massive back tyre of the tractor.

'Jaysus, that was a close one. The brakes are working, anyways,' said Johnny cheerfully.

I, a Catholic of the very definitely non-practising variety, uttered a silent prayer of thanksgiving.

I twisted around in my seat and peeped out through the bars of my fingers. The tractor was a 1970 reg. It was even older than me, for God's sake; no wonder it was such a wreck. My eyes travelled upwards to the cab, which was open at the back. It was a convertible! Not pleasant driving in inclement weather, I guessed; but on a fine September evening such as this, when it was hot enough for a man to drive along without a shirt on his back, I could think of no better mode of transport. Yes, I thought, as I lowered my hands from my eyes and feasted them on the broad, tanned expanse of muscle and sinew before me, I heartily approved. I watched, spellbound, as the owner of the back braked the tractor, his muscles rippling enticingly.

Johnny stuck his head out of the car window and shouted, 'Well, boy, how are you going?'

'Ah, is it yourself, Da? I'm grand.' And, with that, the godlike creature hopped out onto the roadway.

Maybe we had crashed after all. I was really dead, and this was an angel come to carry me away. I fervently wished that I had time to brush my hair.

'What do we have here?' His voice matched his torso, strong and powerful. He had ducked his head and was looking in at me through the driver's window, grinning his head off. Yes: very soft on the eye indeed.

'This is Tyrone's girl, Elaine … what did you say your last name was, again?'

'Malone. You can call me Lainey.' I extended my hand eagerly past Johnny's face, nearly whacking the poor man in the nose. 'Pleased to meet you.'

'And I'm very pleased to meet you too, Lainey. I'm Jack Power, Johnny and Bridie's favourite son.' He wiped his right hand on the leg of his overalls, which had probably once been navy blue and which made his hand even dirtier. I didn't care. He engulfed my hand in his. It was the size of a shovel.

'Would you go 'way out of that. There are no favourites in the Power household. Did you move that heifer today?'

'I did.'

'How was she looking?'

'Could've been better. I think we should get Matt to have a look at her.'

Johnny turned to me. 'Matt's another of my sons. He's a vet.'

There was another one like Jack back at the ranch! In fact, hadn't Bridie said she had seven sons?

My sense of optimism about the whole Ballyknock experiment reached a new high.

'Anyway, we'd better be off. I've to take this young lady up to Power's Cottage.'

'Is that where you're staying, Lainey?'

I nodded.

'On your own?'

'All on my own.'

'We'll have to make sure you don't feel too lonely.'

I nodded again and grinned foolishly. I hoped that meant what I thought it meant. Jack winked at me, then stood up and banged the roof of the car twice in farewell. It felt like his hand was going to come right through the rusty exterior.

We headed off again at breakneck speed. I almost felt sorry for the car; it had to put up with a lot. I closed my eyes again and braced myself for the next near miss. My foot reached for the imaginary brake half a dozen times. Every now and then I opened my eyes to try and admire the scenery. It really was stunning. Not a bad place to die, I reflected.

One thing was worrying me, though. We seemed to be driving for miles and miles, deeper and deeper into the wilderness. I hadn't noticed many houses, either. I wanted badly to ask, 'Are we there yet?' but I didn't want to risk sounding like a pathetic child.

I needn't have worried. Without warning, to me or any other drivers who happened to have the misfortune of sharing the road, Johnny made a sharp right turn into what could only be described as a boreen. This was the steepest hill we'd been on yet. The trusty Peugeot laboured up the windy road, roaring like some injured wild animal. I thought I could feel my ears popping, but surely that was just my imagination. I wouldn't have to worry about the house flooding, that was for sure.

Without bothering to change gear – sure, why would you want to be bothering with any of that oul' malarkey anyway? – Johnny brought the car, skidding and complaining, to an abrupt halt.

'Here we are. Home sweet home.'

Thank you, God! I exited the car as if it were on fire, delighted just to be alive. I felt like kissing the earth, like the Pope does when he visits a new country. And a new country it was.

Chapter Five

I was delighted to discover that my home for the coming months was a city girl's dream of the charming country cottage. Two hundred years old, but recently refurbished; oodles of character, but with all mod cons.

The cottage had been donated to the Power family by an extremely generous neighbour at the time of the Famine, when the Powers had been evicted from their former home by the archetypal evil landlord. Johnny delivered this brief potted history of the house as he carried in my bags. He made sure I was settled in before he tore back down the hill in his red chariot, no doubt causing small furry animals to run for their lives. I waved him off until the car was a red dot on the horizon, and then went back inside.

I felt very happy – even though the place was tiny. It was hard to believe that the cottage had once accommodated a family of eleven. I would barely be able to fit myself in, with all my clothes and useless knick-knacks – even though I'd planned to leave half my stuff in Dublin. But I had a good feeling about this place. *A person could be very happy here,* I thought.

I was still wrapped up in warm, positive feelings as I snuggled up in my bed that night. I had just passed a pleasant evening curled up on a very comfortable, chocolate-brown, distressed-leather two-seater in front of the modest fire that I'd lit. Some thoughtful person – I guessed that a member of the Power clan was the kind culprit – had provided a wicker basket full of briquettes, logs and firelighters.

Above the fireplace was an old framed photograph of a stern, handsome woman in old-fashioned dress. It had been taken in the days before people said 'cheese' for the camera. Her eyes had a disconcerting habit of following me around the room. It was a little creepy, to tell the truth. I'd have to find out who she was.

I had feasted on a tea of scrambled eggs – just like Mother used to make – and, for dessert, the best soda bread and strawberry jam that money couldn't buy. This was all washed down with copious mugs of steaming hot tea, accompanied by two Marlboro

Lights and the latest Stephen King. I sighed as I puffed away. This was nice. No Paul to complain.

I was blown away by the absolute silence of the place. Our flat in Dublin backed onto a major thoroughfare, and I had grown up living in the 'burbs; the lack of noise pollution – traffic, sirens, car alarms, raucous shouts from fights outside the local kippy chippy – was quite daunting. Not that I missed these sounds, any more than I missed having to listen to Hazel row on the phone with her parents, or Christiana having sex with her latest acquisition, through the paper-thin apartment walls. I supposed I'd get used to it, this weird blanket of silence.

And there was something else, too: the darkness. I had forgotten what country dark was like – that rich, deep, secret darkness that results from a total absence of street lighting. I opened the front door at one stage, captivated by the spectacle of a multitude of diamanté stars piercing the big, black, velvet sky. I stood on the two-hundred-year-old doorstep, thinking of that song, 'The Night Has a Thousand Eyes'. And then I gave myself the creeps. An unknown animal hollered into the darkness and I hurried back inside and closed the door on the night, before it could suck me in – envelop me. Maybe I should lay off the Stephen King novels for a while.

But anyway, there I was, lying snuggled up underneath my big eiderdown quilt, revelling in the feel of the crisp, clean cotton sheets. (The all-seeing mother-eye had forced me to wash up before

I retired.) The phone was beside the bed, just a hand-stretch away, and so was the bedside lamp. I had put a chair up against the inside of the bedroom door – just to make myself feel more secure, you understand. Oh, and I had placed a kitchen knife under the mattress. I laughed at my own stupidity, telling myself that it was just for the first few nights, until I got used to the alien surroundings. To the darkness. To the silence. I eventually drifted off to sleep, counting, not sheep, but the hairs on Jack Power's chest.

I woke with a start and looked around wildly. Where the fuck was I?

Realisation dawned, and I checked the time. I had been asleep for about two hours. What had woken me? I tried to remember if I'd been having some kind of strange dream. Definitely no more horror books for me; from now on I was going on a strict diet of chick-lit and the autobiographies of former Spice Girls.

What the hell … In one swift movement I leapt out of bed and flicked the switch on the bedside lamp, managing to knock it over in the process. I fumbled around for the knife under the mattress. There it was again – the noise! I stood in the middle of the bedroom floor, looking from left to right with terrified eyes, holding the knife aloft, legs planted wide apart as if I was ready to take flight or spring upon somebody. I must have looked like a bad scene from *Xena Warrior Princess*. The episode where Xena swaps her leather tunic for Marks & Sparks teddy-bear pyjamas.

I jumped again as the noise was repeated. The roof – it was coming from the roof! I looked up, terrified, at the Velux window, half-expecting to see a man's face grinning maniacally in at me. There was nobody there.

There it was again. It was a very definite scratching sound – furtive…. And again! But this time it wasn't a scratching. More like a creaking. Rhythmic. Repetitive. More like … footsteps. And it wasn't coming from the roof, I realised with a sick, heavy feeling in my stomach. It was coming from the attic.

For the second time that day and in about five years, I prayed, with sincerity and from the bottom of my heart. With a further sinking feeling, I noticed that the attic trapdoor was in the bedroom ceiling. Why hadn't I listened to my father? He had been right all along. Lone females getting murdered to death in isolated country cottages – you heard about it all the time….

'Who's there?' I asked ludicrously. My voice came out in a strangled whisper. I cleared my throat. 'Who's there?' I croaked loudly. Of course they were going to answer. *Hi, it's me. Billy the axe murderer. I've come to hack you into a million pieces. I hope tonight is convenient for you.*

'I'm calling the gardaí!' I shouted. Even I detected the dangerous note of hysteria in my voice. This time it had an effect. The footsteps broke into a run.

Omigod!

I dived on the phone and jabbed 999, barely registering that my fingers were trembling. At least the phone was working. I had half-expected it to be cut off, just like in the old horror movies.

'Hello, what service do you require?'

'Police! Quickly! There's someone trying to break in! I'm on my own!' I gibbered.

'Calm down, please. Give me your name and address.'

I did, suppressing the urge to scream at the woman. How could she be so calm? Did she not know that this was an emergency? (Presumably she did, seeing as it was her job to man the emergency phone line, and all.) As soon as she had assured me that somebody was on the way, I hung up and shouted up at the attic defiantly: 'Now, you scumbag, I've called the police and they'll be here any minute! And,' I added, as an afterthought, 'I'll have you know that I'm a solicitor!' That should do the trick, all right. What was I going to do? Send him a summons by registered post? Buy him a house?

While I waited for the gardaí to arrive, I sat like a statue at the edge of the bed, knife in my right hand, phone beside my left. I stared at the attic trapdoor for the entire time, afraid to take my eyes off it for even a second in case a murderous lunatic burst through.

At first I thought he had gone. Everything was quiet for a long time. How had he got out? How had he got *in*? I would have to get the gardaí to investigate…. But every now and then I would hear a furtive creak. He was still there, all right. Why hadn't he tried to escape? Why hadn't he attacked? And where were the gardaí? They were taking their time. It would never take this long in Dublin. Mind you, I would never have found myself in this position in Dublin, because I was never on my own at night. I was going straight back home. I would ring Tyrone first thing in the morning – if I made it through the night, that was – and tell him I couldn't do it. He'd understand when he heard what a terrifying ordeal I'd been through. Where were the bloody gardaí?

At last, I heard the sound of a car coming at considerable speed up the hill. Thanks be to God! The light of the headlights filled the bedroom and broke me out of my trance. Relief flooding my system, I jumped up from the bed and flew to the bedroom door, pulling the chair out of the way. I ran out to the front door and went weak with joy at the sight of two burly uniformed gardaí.

'Oh, thank God, you came.' I grabbed the policeman nearest to me by the arm and dragged him into the bedroom.

'You're all right, Miss. You're safe now. Did you scare him off when you woke up?'

'No, he's still here,' I hissed urgently. 'Up in the attic.' I pointed up at the attic door.

The two gardaí stood in my bedroom and looked up at the tiny trapdoor in the ceiling.

'Do you have a ladder handy?' asked the second garda.

'I don't know. There might be one in the shed.'

'I'll go check.' Garda Number Two started to leave the room. Just then, a scuffling sound came from the attic again, loud and clear. It was as if someone was crawling along on his hands and knees. I gripped Garda Number One's arm again.

'There it is again! He's still up there. We've got him trapped.' I smiled triumphantly, feeling like Nancy Drew after solving some particularly troublesome mystery.

The two gardaí exchanged a look. I couldn't interpret their expressions.

'Is that the noise you heard before, Miss?'

'Yes! Quick, get the ladder.' I was crazily glad that he'd called me 'Miss' instead of 'Madam'.

Garda Number One nodded at Garda Number Two, who went out. We could hear him rummaging around in the shed. Every now and then, a loud scuffling noise came from up above. I clung to Number One's uniformed arm harder each time, forgetting all about being proper. The garda glanced at me uncertainly. Looking back, I think he might have been a little embarrassed.

At last Number Two came back in, bearing a rusty, paint-splattered ladder. He ascended jauntily and began pushing at the attic door in a manner that I could only describe as careless.

'Watch out – he may be armed!' I hissed urgently.

72

The garda peered down at me, a bemused (or was it amused?) expression on his face. For the first time in my life, I wished fervently that Ireland had an armed police force. Then they could blow the bastard's head off and plead self-defence. It would serve him right for frightening the shite out of me.

I dug my fingers deeper into Number One's arm and shrank against him. I wanted to run out of the room, but my feet seemed rooted to their spot on the bedroom carpet. It occurred to me that the gardaí should have made sure that I was safely out of the vicinity. Surely this was negligent of them.

The upper half of Number Two's body disappeared into the attic. We could see the beam of his torch sweeping back and forth; then he swung his legs up, and we could hear him walking slowly around. He seemed to be up there for an age. *What's going on?* I felt like yelling up at him. The garda beside me seemed very relaxed. I would have thought he'd be getting ready to attack, in case Number Two needed backup.

I couldn't help uttering a short scream as a head appeared in the trapdoor. Number Two was peering down at us with something like a smirk playing about his lips.

'Well?' said Number One. Number Two nodded at him and then looked at me.

'I'm afraid you've got rats.'

This time I really screamed.

Chapter Six

The alarm drilled into my eardrums at 7.30 a.m. I jerked out of a fitful sleep and, for the second time that morning, wondered where the hell I was. After a few seconds, I recognised the blurry lines of my new bedroom, pressed the snooze button and lay back in the bed and stretched.

And then I remembered. I groaned loudly, but there was no one to hear. No one to tell me that last night had been only a nightmare. But, even if I hadn't been on my own, nobody could have performed that particular miracle for me.

After the two laughing policemen had left, I had lain awake for most of the night, ears strained for that evil scuffling. At one point, just as I was at last managing to drop off, a strand of my hair had fallen across my face and I had leapt up, shouting hysterically, convinced that a rat had just brushed past me. Sleep hadn't visited again until about half an hour before the alarm had gone off. It wasn't exactly what I would call wonderful preparation for the first day in my new office.

Rather than lie there and think of my new furry flatmates, not to mention my humiliation at having called the gardaí out to investigate the 'intruder' (I groaned again), I decided to get up. I checked my slippers carefully for signs of life and tiptoed cautiously into the bathroom. There was no way I was staying in this rat-infested dump. I was going to ring Tyrone at nine on the dot, and he could damn well arrange alternative accommodation.

I arrived outside my new office in the village of Ballyknock at five to nine precisely. I had been subjected to the hackney driver's incessant questioning for the previous ten minutes, and my foul humour had worsened. What I wouldn't have done for an O'Brien's double espresso…. I was supposed to be meeting my new secretary – with my new key – at nine. I had decided to arrive a few minutes early, just to show that I was on the ball.

At 9.15 I was still standing there. This had gone beyond a joke. I was beginning to get curious looks from passers-by. Several cars even slowed down to get a better look at me – we're not talking kerb-crawling here, just pure nosiness. I barely restrained myself from making rude hand gestures. Hardly the impression one would like to convey on one's first day in a new town in one's capacity as a solicitor.

'There you are, dear. Have you been waiting long?' A plumpish woman with rosy cheeks and short blonde hair bustled down the street towards me. She was clearly out of breath and struggling to carry several bulky plastic bags. I judged her to be in her early forties. Forty-five would hold her.

'Only half an hour,' I lied.

'Oh, you poor love. Let's go inside and get ourselves a nice cup of coffee.' She dropped a couple of her bags and held out her hand. 'I'm Patricia. I hope you're Lainey – otherwise I'm after making an awful eejit of myself.'

I took her hand, shook it in a dazed fashion and confirmed that I was indeed Lainey Malone.

'Well, Lainey, you are a pretty girl, aren't you?'

I smiled uncertainly and blushed a little. It was very nice to be called a pretty girl, but surely that wasn't the usual way to greet your new boss.

Patricia fumbled in an oversized handbag and pulled out a massive set of keys. She tried about ten of them in the lock before happening upon the right one. She kept talking the entire time.

'You'll never guess what happened to me this morning.'

I shook my head: no, I'd never guess.

'I was getting the kids ready for school, and didn't I have them all dressed and ready to go out the door, and didn't Mikey only go and spill his entire bowl of Coco Pops all the way down his clean shirt, and didn't I have to iron another one for him and wasn't I fit to hit him, and of course then we were stuck in the traffic on Main Street and I was late, and there's you, poor love, standing out on your own in the cold on your very first day in Ballyknock looking like nobody's child, but they are giving it good for next week, mind....' And on she went. I felt fit to hit little Mikey myself.

At last she found the correct key, and I entered what was to be my work-home for the next nine months. If I had thought the cottage was small....

The new premises of Tyrone Power & Co. consisted of an office for me (I could have cried, comparing it to my beautiful office back in Dublin) and an office-cum-reception-area for Patricia. This latter area housed a photocopier, a fax machine and that most essential piece of office equipment – a kettle. I watched gratefully as Patricia started fiddling around with it. My gratitude turned to consternation as she removed a large bottle of still mineral water from one of her bags and proceeded to fill the kettle with the contents.

'Is there no sink?'

'God, no, dear. Sure, how could you get a sink into this place? It's far too small.'

Silly me.

'Is there a toilet, even?'

'Not at all!' She thought this was very funny.

'Well, what do we … do?'

'The bookies upstairs have said we can use their loo.'

How kind.

Maybe I could arrange a transfer to the London office instead.

Patricia redeemed herself by making me the most righteous cup of coffee. I holed myself up in my office for the next hour and tried to organise myself. This entailed ringing and e-mailing all my friends and family members to give them my new details. Well, what if they needed to contact me urgently?

After a while, Patricia stuck her head around the door (without knocking, of course. What would have been the point, anyway? The walls were paperthin and we could hear every word the other said).

'How are you getting on?'

'Fine. And the coffee was lovely; thank you.'

'You're more than welcome, my dear. Tomorrow I'll bring in some scones. How's everything up at Power's Cottage?'

'Not great. I have a bad case of rats. I'll have to find somewhere else to stay.'

'Rats! God love you! I'll get on to the brother-in-law right away. He's into the pest control.' She made it sound as if hunting down vermin was his hobby. 'He'll have you sorted today. There'll be no need for you to move out for even one night.'

'Thanks, Patricia – that really would be terrific.'

'I'll go ring him. Then I'm off to do my grocery shopping.'

'What – now?' I glanced at the clock. It was ten to eleven.

'Well, yes. I always do my weekly shop on a Monday morning. The supermarket is nice and empty then.' Her face was full of innocent surprise. Imagine me not knowing that she always did her grocery shopping on a Monday morning.

As soon as Patricia left the building, I rang Tyrone. I was put through to Miss Moneypenny.

'Oh, hi, Barb. Can I speak to Tyrone, please?'

'Is it important? He is very busy this morning, you know.'

'Yes, it's important,' I snapped. *Cow.*

'Lainey! How goes it?' boomed Tyrone.

'Well, let's see. The house you kindly lent me is crawling with rats, you couldn't swing a kitten in the office, let alone go to the toilet, and my new secretary – who thinks I'm a pretty little thing, by the way – is off doing her grocery shopping.'

Tyrone hooted with laughter. 'So far, so good, then.'

'Whatever.'

'Never mind. You've just got off to a bad start. The office is only temporary, you know that; as soon as something better comes on the market we'll snap it up. Get Patricia onto the rat problem. Her brother-in-law –'

'I know. She already told me,' I said tersely.

'Fair enough. What do you make of her?'

'She's very nice, Tyrone, but … I don't know. Do you really think she's suitable?'

'She may seem a little unorthodox, but just you wait and see. She types up a storm, and her local knowledge is second to none.'

'You mean she's a gossip.'

'Don't knock it. You'll discover that kind of thing is very useful in the country. You're just a Dublin snob, that's your problem.'

'I beg your –'

'Ah, get over yourself, girl. I'm only pulling your leg.'

We shot the breeze, both business and personal, for another ten minutes or so; then Tyrone had to go because Barb had buzzed him a total of four times. I was willing to lay bets that it wasn't about anything important. It was fortunate for her that she managed to keep her jealousy reined in when it came to female clients; otherwise he would have had no choice but to fire her, damn good secretary or no.

My first morning on the job whizzed by. At a few minutes to one, I stuck my head into Patricia's office.

'What way will we work lunch? Do you want to go now for an hour and I'll go when you come back, or what?' (Even though she'd only been back from her shopping expedition for forty-five minutes.)

'There's no need for that. I'll just lock up and we can both go.'

'But what if somebody rings when we're both out?'

'Sure, that's what God invented answering machines for, girl. Besides, who'd be ringing anyway? All the solicitors' offices in the county close for lunch; and if it's a client and if it's that important, they can always ring back at two.'

This did have a peculiar type of logic to it.

'Right, so.' I shrugged. 'You'd better show me how to work the alarm.'

Patricia duly showed me how to activate and de-activate it, and I made a mental note of the code. As we were both leaving, she whispered confidentially to me, 'Don't worry if you forget the code and set it off accidentally. It's not connected up to the Garda station anyhow.'

You what?

'We thought about connecting it, but it'd be too much trouble. The likes of the wind or kids messing around would be setting it off all the time, and we'd keep getting calls at all hours of the night.'

'But what if somebody breaks in?'

'Sure, there's nothing to take.'

'Not yet. But soon we're going to have confidential files.'

'If any of the eejits around here broke in, they wouldn't know what to take. They might run off with the kettle, but that would be about it.'

81

'Even so, I'm not happy about that. I'm going to call Tyrone about it this afternoon.'

'You do that, love, if it makes you feel better,' said Patricia, patting me on the cheek and smiling kindly at me. (No, you didn't read that wrong: my secretary patted me – *me*, her boss – on the cheek.)

It was most definitely time for lunch.

I let myself back in at five to two. There was no sign of Patricia, but that was okay. There was no sign of her at 2.30 either. That wasn't okay. At 2.32 she breezed in through the front door and beamed at me.

'Ah, hello. Did you have a nice lunch, dear?'

'What time do you call this?' I faced her, arms folded tightly across my chest, brows knitted into what I hoped was a stern frown.

She frowned back at me. 'Is your clock not working? Don't worry, I'll have a look at it. It probably just needs new batteries.'

I looked at her face and realised that she was totally sincere.

And that was the last time I tried to be the big Boss Woman.

At about 3.30 that afternoon, from behind my closed office door, I heard the front door opening and Patricia's loud and cheerful greeting.

'Ah, is it yourself, Murt! How are you keeping?'

'Ah, you know, Patricia – draggin' the devil. Yourself?' It was an old man's voice.

'I'm grand, Murt. What can I do for you on this fine day?'

'I want to see the solicitor.'

'Hold on now, and I'll see what I can do.' She stuck her head around my office door for the tenth time that afternoon. This time she looked particularly excited.

'You've got your first client.'

'Has he got an appointment?'

Patricia was clearly taken aback. 'Well, no, he hasn't. But I thought that, since it's your first day and you're not that busy yet, you might be able to squeeze him in.'

'Who is he?'

'Murt O'Brien. His people come from Dunmore way, his mother was a Brennan from Oldtown and his father ran the local hardware store. He married one of the O'Byrne girls out of the factory and his daughter is married to Tommy Hennessy, my second cousin once removed on my mother's side – they're after building a gorgeous extension –'

'All right. Show him in,' I said, clearing a space on my desk. 'Only tell him he'll have to make an appointment next time.'

I felt quite excited, really. My first Ballyknock client!

An extremely old man wearing a shiny black suit and a fedora hat entered the room. His face looked as if it was made of old brown leather. He stopped short of my desk and executed what I guessed was his version of a double take.

'Who are you?'

I flashed him a professional smile and extended my right hand. 'Lainey Malone. Pleased to meet you.'

He didn't take it. 'Where's Tyrone Power?'

'Mr Power is going to be in Dublin for the next few months. I'm afraid you'll have to make do with me for the time being.'

'I want to see Tyrone.'

'I believe there's a train leaving for Dublin at six.'

The old man stared at me long and hard. Then something flickered behind his eyes and he sat down across from me.

'I want to buy some land.'

'Well, you've come to the right place. I'll just take your details first. Name?'

'Murt O'Brien.'

'Murt. That's unusual. Is it short for Murtagh?'

He gave me a funny look. 'You're not from around here, are you?'

'No, I'm from Dublin.'

'That would explain a lot. Murt is short for Michael.'

'Address?' I wasn't really warming to him.

'Chapel Lane, Ballyknock.'

'And that's in County Kilkenny....' I confirmed, writing it down.

'No. Outer Mongolia.' I looked up at him sharply. The ghost of what was probably a smile played about his shrunken lips.

'Does your house on Chapel Lane have a number?'

'What would I be needing a number for? Haven't I lived there all me life? Everybody knows me.'

Yes, and I'm sure everybody loves you, too, you grumpy old git. 'Now, PPS number, please.'

'What do you need that for?' he snapped.

'The Revenue has to be informed of every property transaction in the State.'

'I don't want that shower knowing my business.'

'I'm afraid you have no choice, Mr O'Brien. You can't register your ownership of the land otherwise.'

'I've never heard the like of it. I bet if Tyrone Power was here he wouldn't be looking for any social security numbers off of me.'

'I'm afraid he'd have to. It's the law, Mr O'Brien. You're not being singled out.'

'Well, in that case, I'm going to be reporting you both to the Law Society. This is outrageous carry-on.' He stood up shakily.

'You do that, Mr O'Brien.'

He glared at me and shuffled out of the room, mumbling to himself as he went.

Well, that was a good start.

At about 4.30, I heard more voices outside and Patricia poked her head around the door again.

'Are you ready for more clients?'

'Do they have an appointment?' I knew that I was wasting my breath.

'Well, no, but....'

'Sure. Show them in.' It couldn't go any worse than the last time.

Patricia ushered in what I could only describe as two sweet old ladies. They were wearing matching woollen berets and carrying matching square hand-bags.

'Please come in and take a seat, ladies.'

They both sat down, placing matching hand-bags on matching laps. Their smiles were focused on me, full beam.

'I'm Lainey Malone.'

'I'm Cissy Walsh, and this is my sister Hannah,' the old woman on the right said in a sweet, waver-ing, old-lady voice.

I took down their names. Sisters. I should have guessed. I wouldn't have been surprised to hear that they were twins – although it was hard to tell with old ladies, especially when they wore such similar hairstyles and clothes.

'And can I have your addresses, please?'

'We both live at the post office, Low Street, Ballyknock.' Cissy appeared to be the elected spokeswoman.

'Oh, do you run the post office, then?'

'That we do, and our parents before us,' said Cissy proudly. 'And where are you from, Miss Malone?'

'Oh, call me Lainey, please. I'm from Dublin.'

86

'Isn't that lovely. And are you going to be with us in Ballyknock for long?'

'Just for a few months, until Mr Power can get down.'

'Tyrone is a lovely man, isn't he?'

'You know him well, then?'

'Indeed and I do. Didn't I use to dandle him on my knee when he was still in nappies? His mother, God rest her, was a great friend of ours.'

I had a vision of Tyrone, wearing an adult diaper, sitting on Cissy's lap, squashing her and her handbag to death. I tried not to laugh.

Hannah still hadn't said a word, but, judging by her smile, she too thought that Tyrone was a lovely man.

'Have you been working for him long?'

'For about seven years. Now, what can I do for you today?'

The two women exchanged glances, their smiles faltering for a fraction of a second.

'Not a thing, my dear,' Cissy replied.

I was confused. 'Then why …'

'We just wanted to come and introduce ourselves.'

'Oh. But I was asking you for your details….'

'Is that what you were doing?' Cissy laughed. 'We thought you were just being friendly. We had to come, you see. People will be coming into the post office asking about the new solicitor, so we had to come and find out for ourselves. Don't worry' – she positively twinkled at me – 'we'll be recommending you to everybody. You're very good.'

'But I haven't done anything.'

'You're a lovely girl – isn't she, Hannah?'

Hannah's smile seemed to agree that, yes, I was indeed a lovely girl.

'We won't take up any more of your time. You must be busy. I'm sure we'll be seeing you in the post office very soon. Goodbye now, and God bless.'

And they left.

Was it time to go home yet?

Chapter Seven

It was with sweet relief that I entered the front door of Power's Cottage that evening.

And then I thought of the rats.

The first thing that caught my eye was a scruffy note on the kitchen table. It was scrawled on the back of an old delivery docket.

Vermin dealt with. Shouldn't have any more trouble. Have filled in all obvious points of entry. Traps set in attic. Radar deterrents in all rooms. Call me if any more problems. Invoice sent to Tyrone Power & Co. in Dublin.

S. Murphy

Nice one! Thank you, Mr Rat-Catcher (excuse me – Mr Pest-Controller). I could kiss you!

What was that about radar deterrents? I looked around the room and spotted a strange, grey plastic object plugged into the wall. Patricia had told me about these earlier on: they emitted a high-pitched noise, which humans couldn't hear, but which was meant to drive rodents insane and send them packing. On further inspection I discovered that there was one in every room, including the bedroom. Relieved, I threw myself onto the bed.

I was awoken some time later by a loud knocking noise. I sat bolt upright on the bed. My initial thought was that the rats had returned with a vengeance. Then I realised that someone was knocking on the front door.

A visitor? For me?

Who could it be?

It was dark outside. The clock said nine. I got up and searched groggily for my shoes, which were exactly where I had kicked them – one underneath the wardrobe and the other on top of the blanket box. I slipped them on and adjusted my skirt, which was back to front.

I could see through the glass that there was a man at the door. I didn't recognise the back that was presented to me. Perhaps it was Billy the Axe Murderer.

'Hello, who's there?'

My visitor turned around. How could I not have recognised that broad expanse of back? Jack Power smiled his devastating smile, and I was devastated.

'Oh, come in, Jack!' I simpered. (*Stop simpering!*)

Jack was laden down with an armful of logs. 'The mother sent me with wood for the fire. She reckoned you'd be cold, up here in the hills. She thought I should warm you up.'

Did he mean to be suggestive, or was it just my filthy mind?

'That was very nice of her. You can put them down here.' I gestured to a free corner beside the wood-burner. He unburdened himself and turned to face me, massive hands on narrow hips, slightly out of breath.

'Well, what do I get for my trouble?' He smiled flirtatiously.

Anything you like.

'Would you like a cup of tea?' The Queen of England couldn't have been more proper.

'Cup of tea would go down nicely, thanks. And I even brought something to go with it.'

He reached into his pocket. Instead of the packet of Toffee Pops I'd been expecting, a mostly-full bottle of Paddy emerged. Yippee!

'Do you always carry a bottle of whiskey around with you?'

He winked. 'Only for special occasions. Put the kettle on, girl, and I'll get this fire going.'

Seemed like a good trade.

91

I watched Jack furtively as he expertly built up the fire. As he squatted in front of the wood-burner, I checked for bum cleavage while pretending to check for milk in the fridge. His overalls had been replaced by relatively clean jeans and a navy fleece. His brown, wavy hair was as tousled as before. I noticed that his eyes were an intense bluey-green: *Fisherman's eyes*, I thought. As I fussed around the kitchen, organising tea and biccies, I realised that his overtly masculine presence in the house made me feel all feminine and fluffy. The big strong man comes in from a day's physical labour, bringing fuel for the fire. The man stokes the flames while the woman prepares the food. I was disturbed by how nice it felt. *Call yourself a feminist?* Maybe he had some shirts I could iron.

In no time at all, the fire blazed triumphantly in the hearth and I settled down gratefully before it; my body temperature had dropped several degrees due to my impromptu nap. Jack sat down beside me on the two-seater. Did he have to sit so close? I felt embarrassed by my proximity to this man, who was, let's face it, a total stranger. I crossed my legs away from him and tugged involuntarily at my skirt to make sure that it covered my knees. He seemed unabashed by the physical closeness – seemed to be relishing it, even. He grinned at me as he held the uncapped whiskey bottle above my mug.

'Say when.' He started to pour.

'When!' I shouted, just as my cup was about to overfloweth.

He laughed. 'Are you sure you don't just want to empty out the tea and I'll start again?'

'No, this will be fine, thank you,' I said primly.

He laughed again as he sloshed a generous measure of whiskey into his own mug. *What nice dimples you have.*

I held my mug aloft. 'Cheers.'

'Bottoms up,' Jack agreed, as he clunked my mug with his own.

There was a moment of strained silence, filled only by the merry crackling of the logs on the fire. I broke it.

'I don't suppose you happen to know who that woman in the photo is?'

'Do I what? That would be my granny, Mary Power. She used to live here.'

'Really? That's a lovely idea, keeping a photo of her in the cottage. What was she like? She looks pretty formidable.'

'Oh, by God, she was. Ruled my grandfather with an iron fist. A true matriarch.'

Hmmm, I mused. *I wouldn't mind being a matriarch myself one day.* I had a feeling I'd be very good at it. My family were always telling me how bossy I was.

'Did you know her well?'

'God, yes. I spent half my childhood here. Granny used to mind us a lot of the time. It wasn't easy for my mother, running the pub and raising seven boys.'

I bet it wasn't.

'She was great, was Granny Power. Wouldn't let you away with a thing, mind you. And she always smelt of roses. That's what I remember best about her. Every time I smell roses I think of her.' He looked away, seemingly a little embarrassed by this revelation. 'Anyway,' he said, 'what do you think of the cottage?'

'Oh, it's gorgeous,' I said enthusiastically. 'I just love the way it's been done up. I'd really like to get the name of the interior decorator.'

Jack, who had been in the process of taking a gulp of his Irish tea, spluttered it down his fleece and all over the coffee table in front of him. He narrowly missed the edge of my skirt. I jumped and stared at him in surprise. Then I realised that he was laughing. His laughter was replaced by embarrassed coughing as he leapt up to get a cloth.

'Are you all right?' I was concerned. Usually, even I didn't poison my visitors with my refreshments this early on in the proceedings.

'Fine, thanks. Jesus, that was pretty disgusting. Sorry about that. Here, lift up the tray and I'll wipe it up properly.'

I lifted objects out of his way as he cleaned up the spillage as thoroughly and efficiently as a professional housewife. I was temped to offer him a pinny (or perhaps a bib).

'Now!' He finished his clean-up with a flourish and a satisfied smile. Then he looked down at his fleece and frowned.

'I'll have to do something with this too.' He pulled the garment over his head in one swift movement, and as his T-shirt rode up I was treated to a flash of his delectable six-pack. He caught me checking him out and I looked away quickly, but not so quickly that I didn't notice a glint of satisfaction in his eyes. *He did that on purpose*, I thought.

He went over to the sink and started rinsing out his fleece, his back to me. He was wearing a plain grey T-shirt. I thought disloyally of the way the sleeves of Paul's T-shirts flapped around the tops of his arms like flags. Jack's biceps were barely contained beneath his sleeves. And those buns! Like two ripe peaches in a handkerchief. By God, I could do him some justice! I was reminded of the scripts for bad American porn movies (I'd once seen a documentary about them):

Heroine: Oh, Chip, have you been working out?

Hero: Come over here, honey, and find out for yourself!

I was still trying to come up with a cunning plan to get him out of the rest of his clothes (nudge his arm next time he took a sip, so he'd spill the rest of the tea; throw the contents of my cup into his lap while pretending to look at my watch; turn on the central heating, so that the combination of that and the blazing fire would force him to strip off;

hell, just throw him fully clothed into the shower) when the real man, having completed his ablutions, sat down beside me again. Was it my imagination or was he sitting closer this time? The hairs on his arm brushed gently against mine, making me shiver.

It was my turn to spring to my feet. 'Music! Why don't I put on a CD? What would you like to hear?'

He looked up at me and smiled a slow, lazy smile. 'Something mellow.'

Mellow, I thought as I made my way to the stereo in the bedroom. *Mellow. Does he mean something smoochy?* What did I have in my extensive (not) collection that was mellow?

Paul always jokingly called my motley selection of CDs 'the Best-of collection'. Almost every single one was a 'Greatest Hits' or 'Best of'. I reasoned that this made practical good sense: what was the point in buying an album unless you were sure you liked at least seventy-five per cent of the songs on it? Anything less was a pure waste of money. I was aware that this attitude made musical purists such as Paul shudder as if someone had just walked across their graves, but I was unapologetic. I pushed away all further uncomfortable thoughts of my boyfriend (boyfriend? what boyfriend?) and, instead, concentrated hard on my musical selection.

Tina Turner. Prince. The Beatles. The Eagles. Fleetwood Mac. *The Best Love Songs Ever* (definite no-no). *The Soppiest Lurve Songs in the Universe.*

Chaka Khan. *Hits of the Screaming Sixties. The Greatest Soul Classics of All Time. Now That's What I Call Music* 4, 6, 17 and 43. I was uncomfortably aware of just how uncool, unhip and downright middle-aged my collection was. At last I happened upon a copy of Blur's *Greatest Hits* that I had acquired accidentally on purpose from Paul (who?). It didn't occur to me at the time that it was perhaps a tad disloyal to play this in the circumstances (what circumstances? I wasn't doing anything).

I found a song I liked, about a bloke from the city who goes to live in a house in the country, and turned the volume up several notches before returning to Jack.

'That all right?'

He screwed up his face. 'I don't really like Blur.'

'Okay. Let's try something else.'

I went back into the bedroom and began calling out the names of CDs at random. He stopped me at George Michael's *Greatest Hits*, Volume I.

'Oh, that's a great collection. Play that.'

A man after my own heart! Paul always went mad when I tried to play this particular CD.

I returned to the couch and, without looking at Jack, took a swig of my 'tea'. I winced. I think my mug had received a top-up while I wasn't looking. The bad American porn movie was still running in my head:

Heroine: Are you trying to get me drunk, kind sir?
Hero: Do I need to, young miss? (Probably not.)

I took another sip. Not only did I have a very pleasant warm strip running from my throat to my heart; a nice, fuzzy sensation was also beginning to develop across the crown of my head. I looked across at Jack. I thought his eyes looked a little blurry around the edges too. There's nothing like a few home measures to get the party started.

'What were you laughing at, anyhow?' I asked him.

'Hmm?'

'When you spewed whiskey-tea all over the furniture.'

'Oh, that.' He smiled enigmatically and took another sip. 'I know the name of the interior designer.'

'Really? Who?'

'Jack Power.'

In my less-than-alert state, it actually took me a few seconds to work out who he was talking about. 'Jack Power? Oh, you mean … Oh!'

He nodded.

'You're kidding! You?'

'The one and only.'

'By yourself?'

'By my own self.'

'Wow! I mean, I don't mean to sound so amazed,' I said, sounding amazed. 'It's just that you're – well, I mean, you're a farmer.'

'A man can wear many different hats, you know.' This time he was definitely slurring his words.

I pondered this revelation for a while.

'You're not really a typical farmer, are you?'

'A typical farmer being?' His eyes seemed to lose their good-humoured haze, and he was no longer slumped but sitting upright on the edge of the sofa. Oops. Now I'd done it.

'I mean … well, you know – the usual image of a farmer is, like….'

I trailed off, unfortunately not drunk enough to be immune to embarrassment. Jack continued to look at me, long and hard.

'You mean when I came here tonight you expected me to have a piece of straw sticking out of the side of my mouth.'

'No, not at all, that's not –'

'Perhaps you'd be happier if I said "Begorrah and begob" every now and then.'

I was silent. I couldn't tell if he was joking or not. His eyes looked kind of angry to me. He got up. Without taking his eyes off me, he slowly eased off his boots. Then his socks. A shiver of fear and anticipation prickled up and down my spine. Then he started to roll up his trouser-legs. What was he doing?

Then, to my amazement, he planted his feet wide apart and gripped the material of his T-shirt just below his shoulders, as if holding on to an imaginary pair of braces. And then he started to sing.

'Old McDonald had a farm, E-I-E-I-O,

And on that farm he had a cow, E-I-E-I-O.

With a moo-moo here, and a moo-moo there,

Here a moo, there a moo, everywhere a moo-moo ...'

On every 'moo', he kicked his leg up in the air. This was so unexpected that I dissolved into a fit of giggles. *Oops, looks like our Lainey's drunk again....*

He stopped singing and joined me on the couch, laughing somewhat manically. We eventually managed to calm down. Jack leant across and wiped away the tears that had formed on the outer corners of my eyes with his left thumb. His right arm had somehow ended up across the back of the couch, practically around my shoulders. *Perhaps this would be a good time to tell him I have a boyfriend*, I thought.

'You have a lovely laugh, you know.'

Tell him!

'And lovely hair, too.' He stroked a thick strand of my hair, which had long since escaped from its sedate ponytail. I gulped. I appeared to have lost all power of speech. His face drew even nearer to mine. I was nearly knocked sideways by the hot smell of alcohol off his breath. He must have been drinking whiskey neat for some time.

Then, without warning, Jack leapt off the seat and started pulling on his socks and boots as if he was late for an urgent appointment.

'I have to go, Lainey. Thanks for the tea.' He had a strange, almost wild look in his eyes.

'That's all right. Thanks for the whiskey. And the logs.' I knew I must look and sound confused. I followed him to the front door, which he was already holding open with a strange, hunted look on his face. Had I done something wrong? Maybe he just had to be up early to feed the chickens.

'See you.' He bent to kiss me on the cheek. I moved my head at the wrong moment and he got me on the ear by mistake. Before I had the chance to consider whether to kiss him back or not, he was out the door and in his jeep. Surely he wasn't going to drive home in that state? As the car skidded on the gravel of the driveway and disappeared with a screech down the hill, I realised that, in fact, he was. I also realised that his father had probably taught him how to drive. What could I do? I could hardly invite him to stay the night.

As I staggered into the bathroom, I could have sworn that Mary Power threw me a disapproving look. *Leave me alone, Mary.* Somehow managing to stay upright, I hiked up my skirt and pulled down my tights and knickers. As I peed, I kicked the tights off my feet and sang happily to myself. 'And on that farm he had a pig, E-I-E-I-O. With an oink-oink here....' I collapsed into drunken giggles again.

I got up and flushed, then slumped over the sink and looked up into the mirror. Oh, no! Horror of horrors! I had panda eyes! I must have rubbed at them in my drunken state and smeared mascara everywhere. No wonder Jack had run off in fright. I looked like a zombie. And as for the hair … my fringe had morphed into a parody of an Elvis quiff.

For the second time that night, I went to bed without getting undressed. I knew I should probably spend some time beating myself up about my behaviour – which had been entirely inappropriate for someone who was supposed to be a girlfriend – but instead I pulled a Scarlett O'Hara and decided to think about that tomorrow.

Chapter Eight

Fortunately, I overslept, so I didn't have time to agonise about Paul the next morning. I was too busy agonising about the fact that I was going to be late for my first morning in Ballyknock District Court. Luckily, the courthouse was directly across the road from the office, so I just had time to grab the relevant summons and charge over.

What a dive! I'd been in nicer garages. The courthouse consisted of one massive, high-ceilinged room. I was to find out later that there was no heating and no toilet – lack of facilities seemed to be a common problem in Ballyknock. The judge's raised seat was high up at one end of the room, and beneath this was what looked like a giant's dining-room table. This was where the solicitors and court reporters sat. At the back of the room were a few rough benches for hoi polloi – clients, criminals, kids on school trips and nosy members of the public. To the right, another set of benches held various members of the local constabulary. The first people who caught my eye were the two gardaí who had come to my aid on the Night of the Rats. As I came in, they nudged each other and whispered to their colleagues. A few of them started to smirk.

Fantastic.

'All rise.' The court registrar entered the room, followed by the district judge – who, true to type, looked like a grumpy old bollix.

Even more fantastic.

I rushed to find myself a seat, and squeezed in at the end of the table beside a bulky, red-headed man. The judge sat down and so did everybody else. He surveyed the courtroom from his elevated throne – all the better for abusing you from a great height, my dears.

The redhead leaned over and whispered into my ear, 'Are you Tyrone's new solicitor?'

I nodded. 'Lainey Malone.'

'Brendan Ryan, the local competition.' I vaguely remembered Tyrone mentioning him. He was the only other solicitor based in Ballyknock. Judging by his friendly smile, he didn't seem too fazed by the idea of a competing firm.

He really was an odd-looking man. Did I mention his hair was red? Well, it was positively on fire. It was the type of ginger that little kids sometimes have but usually grow out of. It occurred to me that perhaps it was dyed – but no, surely nobody would dye his hair that colour on purpose? I also guessed it hadn't met with a comb in the last forty-eight hours. He hadn't grown out of his freckles, either. They were scattered all over his face and his hands; they were on his lips, on his eyelids and practically up his nose. He looked like a join-the-dots picture. He was wearing a chunky orange cardigan, buttoned up the wrong way. His wife must have knitted it for him; there could be no other explanation. The ensemble was completed by a tweed jacket that had seen better days. If he hadn't been such a hulking man, he would have been in imminent danger of being mistaken for a leprechaun.

'DPP v. Paddy Murphy,' called the registrar. That was one of mine; I had to plead guilty to a traffic offence. I jumped to my feet and rattled off my spiel, trying to sound sincere in my apology on behalf of my client. As I sat down, Brendan Ryan rose to his feet beside me.

'And I'd like to welcome Ms Lainey Malone to Ballyknock on behalf of the Kilkenny Solicitors' Association. I'm sure we're all looking forward to working with her.'

Oh, no. Tyrone had warned me about the country tradition of welcoming new solicitors on their first day in court. I'd thought I might be able to get away without it, but obviously not.

Brendan Ryan sat down and a senior-looking police officer stood up. 'And I'd like to welcome Ms Malone on behalf of the Kilkenny gardaí. We hope she'll be very happy here.'

I nodded my thanks.

And then the judge spoke. 'Yes, Miss Malone, you're very welcome. We've already heard a lot about you. I understand you're going to keep us safe from all the vermin in the town.' The judge flashed me a sarcastic smile, and explosive sniggering broke out from the garda benches. I looked quickly around the table and saw that most of my so-called colleagues were either laughing or trying not to. Even Brendan was suppressing a smile. Well, wasn't this just fan-bloody-tastic?

Welcome to Ballyfuck.

By the time I finally escaped from that damn courtroom, it was well after three. I heaved open the ugly wooden doors of the courthouse and breathed in the fresh air as if I were a lifer being released from prison. What a criminal waste of a day. At least I didn't have far to travel back to the office.

I pushed open the door of Tyrone Power & Co. and did a double take. The office seemed to have been converted into a crèche. There were children everywhere – horrible, snotty-nosed little kids tampering with the equipment. I let out an angry roar – which I didn't have to fake.

'What's going on here?'

All the little tykes (there were five of them) stopped what they were doing and turned to look at me, eyes wide with fear.

'Get out now, all of you. This is a solicitor's office. Adults only!' My voice rose several decibels. One of the little girls looked as if she was going to cry.

'Lainey! I didn't hear you come in. Were you stuck in court all this time, poor lamb?' Patricia emerged from my office bearing several reams of photocopying paper. 'Have you met my kids? Well, they're not all mine, I'm minding the two girls for a neighbour, but the boys are mine – Tommy, Christy and Mikey.'

Ah yes, Mikey. He of Coco Pops fame.

'Say hello to the nice lady.'

Silence. Patricia shoved her boys in the back and they reluctantly greeted me. It was obvious that they weren't convinced that I was a nice lady.

'I'm sorry for shouting at them, Patricia. It's just that when I came in I saw all these kids running around the office, and I didn't see you, and I thought – well, I don't know what I thought.'

'That's quite all right. I suppose it must have been a bit of a shock. The kids are doing some photocopying for their school project. I hope you don't mind.'

'No, that's just fine.' *Frankly, my dear, I don't give a shit.* I headed unenthusiastically into my inner office, feet dragging considerably.

'You take the weight off, and I'll bring you in a nice cup of coffee and one of those scones I promised you.'

'That would be heaven, Patricia. Thank you.'

She smiled and closed the door. I slumped into my chair, folded my arms on the desk and sank my head down into them, like a child taking a nap.

I'm tired, my head hurts and I want to go home – partnership or no partnership, Jack Power or no Jack Power (I've frightened him off anyhow). I missed my flat, I missed my friends, I missed my old office. I missed Paul's moaning. And now I'd just yelled at a bunch of little kids. *God, just get me out of this godforsaken shit-hole.*

I jumped and sat up straight as the door opened. Patricia placed a coffee and a scone in front of me. The scone was spread liberally with red jam.

'I hope you like raspberry jam.'

'I love it, thanks.'

I waited for her to leave, but she continued to hover expectantly at the door. I realised I was meant to sample the fare before she left. I took a bite.

'Mmm. This is just delicious.' I didn't have to lie. 'Did you make the jam too?'

'Yes. It won first prize at the Mivik show, you know.'

'Congratulations. It's lovely.'

Patricia continued to hover. Now what?

'Have you tried any of Bridie Power's jam yet?' she asked casually.

'Yes, she gave me a pot of strawberry.'

'So she didn't give you any of her raspberry, then?'

'No.'

'Hmph. Didn't think so. She only came third in the raspberry.' Patricia smiled triumphantly and left the room with a flourish. Good Lord! Get me back to Dublin, where nobody cared about prize-winning jam. What was next? Giant-marrow competitions? Quick-draw knitting-needles at dawn? I wasn't able for this. I was going to ring Tyrone and tell him I couldn't cut it. First thing in the morning.

I was still in a fouler when I got in that night. If I'd had a cat or a dog, I would have kicked it. Instead, I had to be content with kicking off my shoes and slumping onto the couch with a heavy sigh. And then I screamed. For there, sitting on the rodent-deterrent – you know, the thing that was meant to repel rodents – looking right at me, bold as brass, was a little grey mouse.

'I don't fucking believe this!' I drew my feet up onto the couch, lest a little furry creature run across them, and rooted around in my bag for my mobile. I was all for communing with nature, but this was bloody ridiculous.

'Hello. Seamus Murphy Pest Control.'

'Oh, hello. This is Elena Malone; I'm calling from Power's Cottage.'

'Ah, yes. Nice to talk to you, love. How are things?'

'Not good. I'm sitting here looking at a mouse.'

'Are you sure it's a mouse and not a rat?'

'Perfectly sure.' *Jesus Christ!*

'Well, that's great.'

'I beg your pardon?'

'You see, love, if you've got mice, that means the rats have gone.'

'And I'm meant to be pleased with that, am I?' I could feel the fury building up in my chest and getting ready to explode out of me like an alien in one of those sci-fi films. Just to annoy me even further, Seamus Murphy laughed good-naturedly.

'Don't worry. I'll come up first thing tomorrow morning and fill in a few holes for you, love, no extra charge. But do you know what I'd really recommend?'

'Surprise me.'

'A nice ferret.'

He wanted me to get a ferret! A glorified rat with extra-sharp teeth. I thought wildly about a programme I'd seen years ago, about old men in an English village competing to see which one of them could get the most live ferrets up the legs of his trousers. They would tie the ends of their trouser-legs with bits of twine so that the ferrets couldn't escape. I wanted no truck with such animals.

'I know a man who breeds them. I could get you a really good price on one.'

'I don't *want* a ferret. I'd rather have mice.' My eyes were fairly bulging out of my head at this point.

'Well, a cat, then.'

'Do you really think so?' The anger drained out of me, leaving only despair. Just then, the biggest spider I had ever seen in my entire life ran across the floor in front of me like a disembodied hand.

'Yes. You leave it with me, love. I'll have you sorted with a grand cat in no time.'

'Thanks.' I hated cats.

I hung up and sat staring into space. My eyes filled with tears of frustration. I screamed again, this time out of irritation rather than fear, and hurled my mobile across the room, where it collided with the rough plastered wall and landed with a clatter on the slate tiles. That was effective. Not only did I have mice, I now had a busted mobile too.

And I had no hope of getting any sleep tonight, either.

And it was still only bleeding Tuesday.

Roll on Friday.

Chapter Nine

The rest of the week crawled by at a snail's pace. I didn't hear a peep out of Seamus Murphy, rat-catcher extraordinaire. I didn't see hide nor hair of Jack Power, either. Looked like I'd blown that one.

I could barely contain my excitement as the train pulled into Dublin's Heuston Station that Friday evening. I was practically jumping up and down in my seat, as if I were suffering from a severe kidney problem. I was the first passenger out of her seat; I was standing at the carriage door about five minutes before the train drew to a halt.

Paul had arranged to pick me up from the station. I couldn't believe how much I was looking forward to seeing him – although I supposed that, at this point, it would be a treat for me to see any of my Dublin friends. With delight, I stepped onto the platform and walked rapidly towards the exit.

There he was.

My heart melted at the sight of him. He was standing at the end of the platform, a lone figure wearing the long black coat I had bought him for his last birthday. He didn't wear it all that much; I think he secretly disliked it. He was self-consciously clutching a bunch of white flowers. Now this *was* remarkable. Paul didn't do flowers. He thought they were impractical. Why spend all that money on a bunch of weeds that were going to be dead within a fortnight? On the few occasions I had received flowers from him, he had sent them via Interflora so that he wouldn't have to go through the mortification of being seen carrying them. As I got closer, I realised they were lilies – my favourite. As I got closer still, I could see his big soppy grin.

'Hey, you.' I reached up and hugged him close, squishing the flowers in the process. I leaned back and smiled up at him. 'Who's the lucky girl?' I asked, nodding at the bouquet.

'These are for you.' He thrust the lilies awkwardly towards me, as if I were a royal princess and he were the shy four-year-old girl who had been nominated to present them to her.

'They're gorgeous. How did you know that lilies were my favourite?'

'Is that what they are? I didn't know.'

Typical Paul, spoiling the moment with honesty. He couldn't lie to save his own life. Still, the effort had been made.

'Mmm.' I stuck my nose deep into the lilies and took a deep sniff. Of course, they had no scent. (What is it with flowers nowadays? They never have any smell. In my day....)

'They smell heavenly.' I, on the other hand, had no problem lying when I felt the occasion merited it.

'Do they really? I couldn't get any scent from them.'

'You must be getting a cold.'

'Do you think so?'

'Definitely. You should take a Lemsip before you go to bed tonight.' I could go on lying all night if necessary. It was no hardship.

'Will you make it for me?' He smiled, almost shyly.

'We'll see.'

We started to walk towards the car park. Paul had wrapped his arm around my waist, and I could feel him looking down fondly at the top of my head. I turned and smiled happily at him. His smile turned to laughter as we moved into a more brightly lit area.

'You have pollen all over your nose.'

I stopped and swiped ineffectually at my proboscis.

'Here, let me.' Paul removed a handkerchief from the top pocket of his suit jacket. It was clearly spotless and neatly pressed and folded. Anybody else would have thought that he got 'a woman' in to do his laundry for him. I, however, knew that he had done it himself.

Paul carefully folded the handkerchief into a small triangle and set about wiping the pollen off my nose. I tried not to laugh at the look of intense concentration on his face. Out of the corner of my eye, I could see passers-by staring at us. Let them stare. Paul, who usually cared so much about the opinions of others – including complete strangers – seemed oblivious.

He caught my eye and saw that I was laughing at him; he stopped rubbing my nose and looked all self-conscious and vulnerable. I couldn't resist reaching up and kissing him lightly on the mouth. He stared down at me for what seemed like the longest time. Then he cupped my face in his hands and brought his lips down on top of mine – not hard, just sweetly insistent. The barest flicker of tongue ghosted between my parted lips, causing a particular tingle that I hadn't felt in an age.

He stopped, at last appearing to remember where he was. Quite frankly, I was amazed that he had forgotten himself for so long. Usually Paul only indulged in public displays of affection when he was drunk. And I hadn't tasted alcohol on his mouth, only mint. I was further amazed at how nice this was. It was almost like one of our early dates – only better, because now I knew him.

'Is it gone?'

'Is what gone?'

'The pollen off my nose, silly.'

'Yes, all gone.' He stuffed the hanky into his coat pocket (it wouldn't do to replace a dirty, crumpled handkerchief in the top pocket of his suit jacket) and put his hand on my shoulder, propelling me towards the car park more quickly this time.

Paul had secured a late booking in The Paddy Field, my favourite Chinese restaurant – no mean feat on a Friday night. No doubt he had used the name of his firm to secure special privileges. The owners were clients.

The host was all smiles. 'Smoking or non-smoking?'

'Smoking,' I said.

'Non-smoking,' said Paul, at exactly the same moment.

We turned and looked at each other. The host looked away. I could see Paul weighing me up. Then, with an audible sigh, he turned back to the host.

'Smoking it is.'

I made sure he didn't see my triumphant smirk as I marched ahead of him towards our table. I had been prepared to stage a fake tantrum. I felt entitled. I'd had a hard week.

I settled my happy bum into my chair as Paul took off his coat.

'Jesus Christ!' he exclaimed.

'What is it?' Had he changed his mind about the smoking already?

'There's pollen everywhere.'

Sure enough, Paul's black coat was streaked with bright-orange pollen, and so was his suit jacket. He took out his trusty handkerchief and started to rub at it, which only made the stains worse. He cursed under his breath.

'Don't worry, you can get them dry-cleaned.'

'I've just got it dry-cleaned. I only put this outfit on clean today.'

This outfit. Excuse me.

'Well, we'll try to do a job on it when we go home, then.'

'It must have happened when you hugged me.' He flashed me a testy look.

'I see – so it's my fault, is it?'

'I didn't mean that.'

Yeah, right.

'It's just that – Jesus, I'll never get this crap out. That's the last time I'm getting you flowers.'

Charming!

'Oh, for God's sake, Paul. Sit down and stop making a show of yourself. Everybody's looking at you.' That usually worked. Paul looked around worriedly and sat down at last. And things had been going so well…. The honeymoon was over already.

'Let's order. I'm starved,' I said, eager to change the subject. I had that familiar heavy, weary feeling that I'd been experiencing all too often, of late, in

Paul's company. Why did we keep on having such stupid rows over nothing? It was as if we were at cross-purposes all the time. I had hoped that tonight would prove an exception – but apparently it wasn't to be.

I perused the menu as if it were a legal document. Of course, it was much more important than that. Paul looked amused (thank God).

'Surely you know that menu off by heart at this stage. You always order the same thing anyway.'

'Well, maybe I fancy a change. And don't call me Shirley.'

Good humour restored. For now.

'Shall we order a bottle of wine?'

'I can't drink, I'm driving.'

'Oh, come on, Paul, let's get hammered. I'm really in the mood. Leave the car in town tonight. We can get a taxi, and you can collect it tomorrow.'

'You know I hate doing that. It's too much hassle.'

I shrugged. The waitress approached to take our order. Her vibrant ginger hair clashed spectacularly with the scarlet kimono she was forced to wear. She looked like she knew it, too.

I went for my usual lemon chicken (Paul had been right).

'And would you like some wine with your meal?' the waitress asked in a thick Louth accent.

'Yes, please,' I said.

'No, thanks,' said Paul, at precisely the same time.

'We'll have a bottle of the Chilean red, please.' I could feel him glaring at me, but I refused to look at him; I continued to smile pleasantly at the waitress.

'I told you I was driving tonight,' Paul said, when she had gone.

'I know. You'll be able to have one glass anyway, and I'll have the rest.'

'Are you sure that's wise?'

'No, Paul, I'm not sure it's *wise*,' I spat, 'but I don't feel like being wise. I've had a shit week, and I just want to chill out and have a few drinks and a nice relaxing time with my boyfriend. Now, is there anything wrong with that?'

'No. No, of course there isn't. I'm sorry, Lainey. Tell me all about your week. I want to hear everything.'

And the thing was, he really did. That was one of the great things about Paul: he was such a good listener. He sat there with his chin on his hand, not saying much, but paying rapt attention as I waxed lyrical about all my woes and grievances. He even laughed in all the right places and asked relevant questions. At times like this, I could almost fool myself into believing that I had the perfect boyfriend. Almost.

'So,' he asked me later, as I was tucking into my slab of pecan pie (worth three million points in the Weight Watchers handbook), 'what do you want to do next weekend?'

'Oh, I don't know. Nothing special. I'll probably be knackered again. What do you want to do?'

He gave me a funny look. 'I thought I might book a weekend away somewhere. In the circumstances.'

In the circumstances. Oh, dear.

'Yes, I think it'd be a great idea to go away for our anniversary.'

'I can't believe you forgot, Elena.'

Elena. Whoops!

'I didn't forget.'

'Yes, you did.'

I reached out and placed my hand on his. It lay beneath mine like a dead fish. It was very tough at times, going out with such a sensitive man. Served me right for taking up with a Cancerian, I supposed. Paul was so easily hurt, and I was getting so tired of walking on eggshells whenever I was with him. Half the time, I really didn't understand why women wanted sensitive men. Give me an insensitive lout any day of the week.

'I'm sorry, Paul. I've just had a million and one different things on my mind, what with the move and everything…. I'd love to go away with you. How about Kerry?'

'Whatever.'

'Please don't be mad with me.'

'I'm not mad with you.'

I'd have liked to believe him, but, judging by the way he was brutally stabbing his lemon meringue pie with his fork (classic passive-aggressive behaviour), it seemed unlikely that I'd been forgiven.

'I think you've killed it.'

'What?' He looked up at me, a sulky expression on his face.

'The pie. I think it's officially dead.' I gave him a big smile, so he would know I was joking. He looked down again and put down his fork. I could tell from the way his dimples were half-showing that he was trying not to break into a grin.

'Do you want coffee?'

'No, let's just get the bill and go home.'

Ah. Home. Now, what home would that be, exactly?

'Um … did you want me to stay with you tonight, then?'

'Course I do.' Paul looked alarmed. 'You weren't thinking of going back to your flat, were you?' His eyes were wide with hurt.

'Oh, God, no!' I said quickly.

'Yes, you were,' he said accusingly. 'I can't believe you'd rather go back to Bimbo Central than stay with me.'

'Bimbo Central? Thanks very much. It's nice to know what you really think about me and my friends.'

'I wasn't talking about you and Hazel. I meant the other one.'

'Christiana has a name, you know.'

'Bloody stupid name, if you ask me.'

'That's rich, coming from someone whose girl-friend was named after a Russian ice-dancer.'

He laughed in spite of himself. Emergency averted.

'Oh, you haven't forgotten that we're having lunch with my parents on Sunday?'

'No, I haven't forgotten. I'll be there.'

Paul got on remarkably well with my parents. This freaked me out no end.

'And Annie is home from China.'

'Brilliant.' This seemed to cheer him up even more. He got on great with Annie, too.

Maybe he was just going out with the wrong sister.

Chapter Ten

Paul and I headed over to my parents' house at about one that Sunday, after staying the night in my apartment for a change. We had spent most of the evening sitting on the couch, drinking wine with Hazel and listening to her give out about Chris and her boss. She left for the office at around noon; there was no stopping her, hangover or no hangover.

I voiced my concerns to Paul on the way over. We were driving along in my beautiful car, which I'd retrieved from the garage the previous day – no more smelly hackneys for me. It felt so good to be back behind the wheel. I smiled and stroked the dashboard lovingly as I drove along. My baby!

I tore my attention away from the Audi to talk

to Paul, who was sitting stiffly in the passenger seat beside me, waiting for me to make a mistake.

'How does Hazel seem to you lately?' I asked.

'She's cracking up.'

'You think so too? Why didn't you say anything to me?'

'It's obvious to anyone with two eyes in their head. She's out of control.'

'Mm. You should have heard the way she spoke to Chris last weekend.'

'Well – I wouldn't let that worry you too much.' Paul couldn't understand how anyone could be alone with Chris for five minutes without blowing a gasket. 'Jesus, Lainey! You just went through a stop sign without stopping.'

'It's Sunday lunchtime. There's no one on the road.'

'Even so. I thought you were supposed to be an officer of the law.'

'Oh, shut up. I'm off duty.' And with that (but without indicating, as Paul kindly pointed out), I swung into the cul-de-sac where my parents lived.

Home was a four-bedroomed, two-storied, detached dwelling in the leafy suburbs of south County Dublin, distinguishable from the other houses in the estate only by the colour of the garage door and the number of shrubs in the front garden. I pulled up alongside my father's Volvo. He disapproved heartily of my choice of vehicle; something about standards, I think it was.

My mother answered the door, all floaty scarf and Yardley perfume.

'Come in, come in, you're most welcome.' She planted a resounding kiss on each of my cheeks and then held me by the shoulders and examined my face.

'It's great to see you, Elena. But you look tired. Have you been taking that tonic I gave you?'

'Yes, Mum.' *You mean that vile stuff I poured straight down the sink?*

'And Paul. Long time no see. Let me have a look at you. Handsome as ever! You've filled out a bit, too. It suits you.'

Life isn't fair. Who ever heard of a woman being told that she's filled out and that it suits her?

'Dinner will be ready in two ticks. Go into the sitting room and keep your father company.'

'Where's Annie?'

'Tatiana's only getting up now, would you believe. She says it's the time difference, but if you ask me, that's just an excuse. She was always a terror to get out of bed in the mornings.'

Everything but my father's legs was obscured by *The Sunday Times*.

'Hello, Dad.'

He peered around the side of the newspaper.

'Ah, hello.' He put the Business section to one side and rose stiffly to greet us. 'Good to see you again, Paul' – he shook his hand – 'and you too, Rosie.' He patted me on the shoulder and sat back down in his armchair. He looked so out of place in the ultra-feminine, rose-chintz living room that it was almost laughable.

'You all right, Dad?'

He sighed and shook his head. 'I was just reading about the shocking state of the economy. You two young people don't know how lucky you are to have secure jobs. Just be sure you hold on to them.'

Here we go....

'I'd give my company another six months at the most. Things are looking very bad.'

My father: the ultimate prophet of doom and gloom. For at least the last twenty years, he had been predicting the bankruptcy and closure of the firm where he worked.

'You've been saying that for ages, Dad, and nothing bad has happened yet.'

'Oh, but things have never been this serious. You mark my words.'

Words duly marked. There was no use arguing. Besides, he enjoyed talking this way; why spoil his fun?

'Lainey!'

The atmosphere in the room instantly lightened.

'Annie!'

I hadn't seen my sister for six months. We hugged each other tightly.

'You look fantastic.'

'So do you. What did you get me?' It was a time-honoured ritual.

'Don't worry, I have a pressie for you upstairs. And one for you, Paul.' She grinned at him.

Tatiana is brilliant. We're five years apart – close enough to make us close, not close enough to make us rivals. It probably helps that we look completely different: I inherited the blue-eyed, blonde looks of my father's family, while Tatiana has my mother's dark curly hair and brown eyes. She's a lot taller than me, too, with a chest like a shelf.

As soon as I was born, she took it upon herself to look out for me. She had been my mini-mammy for as long as I could remember, ever ready to beat up any kid who had the bad judgment – and bad luck – to tease or torment me.

'How's Beijing?' asked Paul.

'Overcrowded,' she smiled, 'but apart from that, it's great.'

She was taking a well-earned two-year sabbatical from teaching Home Economics to Irish teenage boys. It wasn't only the school kitchen that they had managed to burn out. Teaching English to Chinese businessmen had turned out to be a far more rewarding and civilised experience.

'It's high time you came back home and found a nice Irish boy to marry.' This was from Dad, of course.

'There's another six months to run on my contract. I might think about coming home then,' she replied good-naturedly. She had always been more patient with Dad than I had. Still, I could probably have had patience with him too if I'd lived thousands of miles away and only had to see him twice a year.

'About time, too. I need someone to look after me in my old age.'

'Don't worry, Dad. We'll find a lovely nursing home to put you in. I have one in mind already.'

You should have seen his face. We broke into peals of laughter. It was always fun, ganging up on him like this.

He muttered under his breath as he got up from his chair and went to the bay window.

'I see you're still driving that fancy car of yours, Rosie.'

'Whose car should I be driving, Dad?'

'Don't get smart with your father. Remember whose money put you through college.'

Tatiana made a face behind his back, and I bit back more giggles.

'Did you ever get that steering-wheel lock I was telling you about?'

'Um – not yet.'

'Why not?'

'Because there's already an alarm on my car.'

'Do you really think those fellas would let the likes of an alarm stop them? They can get into anything they want to nowadays. There was a documentary about it last week on the English channel. Did you see it?'

'No.'

'I saw it,' said Paul. 'It was fascinating.'

Congratulations, Paul O'Toole. You have just won yourself two hundred brownie points!

My father gave Paul an approving look. 'Don't you think she should get herself a wheel lock, son?'

'I do, yes.'

Traitor.

'You hear that, Rosie? You should listen to your young man.'

'What my "young man" doesn't know is that there hasn't been a car stolen in Ardskeha in the last ten years. I know because I checked. The locals don't even lock their car doors, for God's sake.'

'Well, you don't want to be the first in ten years, do you?' Dad nodded sagely.

'I wonder what Mum's doing in there. Dinner should be ready by now.' Tatiana the peacemaker strategically changed the subject.

I took her cue. The last thing I wanted to do was ruin Annie's homecoming by having one of my regular spats with Dad. 'I'll go see if she needs any help.' On my way out to the kitchen, I bent down and hissed in Paul's ear, 'Lickarse!'

I heard Mum before I saw her. She didn't see me; she was fully occupied in dancing and humming around the kitchen with a bowl under her left oxter and a whisk in her right hand. The kitchen was flooded with the strains of beautiful classical music, which mingled wonderfully with the pungent smell of burning. With the instinct that had been bred into me over the twenty-nine years that I had been my mother's daughter, I headed straight for the cooker and simultaneously switched it off and opened the oven door. I coughed, waving frantically in an effort to disperse the plumes of black smoke, and removed a distressed-looking chicken from the oven.

My mother didn't appear to notice. She was transfixed by the portable television that she had nagged my father into installing on top of one of the presses. I glanced up just in time to see Katarina Witt execute a particularly skilful triple toe-loop (or maybe a double axel – who knew? Mum did, of course).

'Mum,' I said gently. It didn't do to be too harsh in these situations. 'What are you doing? The dinner is getting burnt.'

The music took a dramatic turn, and Mum gripped my forearm.

'Bizet's *Carmen* on ice!' she said urgently. 'Rita lent it to me! It's fabulous, Elena – you have to see it! Just give me a minute, it's almost over.'

I looked at the tears streaking down my mother's rapt face. There were funny stripes where the salt water had come into contact with her cream blusher. She always got a bit weepy while watching ice-skating ('I could have been a contender…'). I prised the ceramic mixing bowl from underneath her left arm, noticing that one end of her floaty scarf had been trailing in it.

'Here, give that to me. You'll never get the cream to thicken if you keep crying into it like that. Why aren't you using the electric whisk that Dad bought you for your birthday?'

'Hmph! Electric whisk, indeed! The old bollix knew I wanted an aromatherapy starter kit. I'd like to tell him where he can shove his bloody whisk!'

'Mum!' I was scandalised. It was okay for me to use language like that, but she was my mother, for God's sake. A little decorum, please!

'Besides, I can't hear the music over that thing.' She wiped each eye with the corner of her apron and showed signs of starting to compose herself.

'Come on. I'll help you bring in the dinner.'

'No, no. You go inside and tell everyone to sit down at the table. I'll be quicker doing it myself.' I doubted it.

I stuck my head around the living-room door. 'Dinner's up, ladies and gentlemen. Take your seats at the table, please.'

I followed Tatiana, Paul and Dad as they filed into the dining room. The best crystal and china had been dusted off for the occasion. We all automatically sat in our allotted places, like programmed robots.

'I bet she's watching that *Carmen* tape again,' Dad said to me. I shrugged. 'I knew it. The dinner will be burnt, you mark my words.'

'I hope you all like your chicken well done,' Mum said gamely as she swished into the room, carrying a plate in each hand.

'Blackened chicken is one of my favourites, Mum,' said Tatiana. Mum smiled fondly at her and exited the room again.

'I knew it,' said Dad. 'I'm going to confiscate that bloody telly.' I noticed that he waited until Mum had gone before he said it.

Paul, who, along with Dad (the two men, don't you know), had received his food first – a dubious privilege in the circumstances – shot me a very worried look. My hidden hand patted his knee comfortingly under the table.

'Just do your best,' I whispered, smiling at him sympathetically.

Mum came back in with the rest of the plates and set them down with a flourish.

'Now, everybody – enjoy.'

We'd try. We really would.

'Would you like some gravy, Paul?' said Mum pleasantly.

I administered a swift sharp kick to Paul's ankle. *I wouldn't recommend the gravy today, sir.* Luckily for him, he got the message.

'No, thanks, Mrs Malone. I don't take gravy.'

'For the last time, call me Teresa. I won't say it again. Now, will you have some butter instead?'

I sensed Paul glancing over at me quickly. When no kick was forthcoming, he answered, 'Yes, please.'

The general rule in the Malone household was that anything that came straight from the packet and didn't require any input from my mother was safe enough.

'Well, isn't this lovely?' said Mum, beaming around at all of us. 'My whole family together.'

Except that Paul isn't one of the family, I had to restrain myself from reminding her. Although I knew she badly wanted him to be.

Down at the other end of the table, my father snorted, no doubt to convey his opinion that, no, this burnt offering wasn't lovely at all.

'Oh, Tatiana, you have to watch *Carmen* on ice. It's superb. I know you'll just love it,' my mother gushed.

Annie nodded her head affably, chewing her piece of chicken for the forty-eighth time.

Mum had been trying in vain to get us interested in ice-skating since we were old enough to stand. Tatiana, with her gangly legs that were far too long for her body, had been the first disappointment. I had disappointed approximately five years later, by delivering repeated impressions of the Sugar Plum Elephant every Saturday at the Dolphin's Barn ice rink.

'We haven't had a decent meal in this house since you got your hands on that blasted video,' snapped Dad.

'Oh, shut up, Joe.' Water off a duck's proverbial. 'Oh, Elena – don't leave the house today without taking that book I borrowed from Christiana. I've had it so long it's getting embarrassing.'

'I wouldn't worry, Mum. She's probably forgotten all about it.'

'What's the book?' Poor Paul was doing his best to make polite conversation. He never really knew what to say when confronted by mad people.

'It's about reincarnation. Fascinating! Do you believe in reincarnation, Paul?'

'Um, no. Not really.' He looked sorry he'd spoken.

'Who does Christiana think she's the reincarnation of these days?' asked Tatiana.

'Marilyn Monroe. That's why she's gone platinum-blonde again.'

'Interesting. She always goes for someone glamorous, doesn't she? Last time I was home she thought she was Kylie Minogue.'

'But Kylie isn't dead – is she?' My father sounded worried, and then looked embarrassed. He had been very taken by those gold hot pants.

'Don't worry, Dad; Kylie hasn't kicked the bucket. But that wouldn't matter to Chris.'

Dad and Paul exchanged a look. It was easy to interpret: *Women! Completely bonkers!*

Just then, Mum gave them further confirmation. 'Oh, girls, I forgot to tell you. I'm being made a Reiki Master next week!'

'Really?'

'I don't know why you're surprised. Hasn't she been bossing me around for years?' Dad had a point.

'Being a Reiki Master has nothing to do with bossing people about, as you well know, Joe

Malone. I wish you'd let me try it out on you. Your energies are all blocked, you know. No wonder you're such a grouch.'

'Paul ...' Dad determinedly changed the subject. 'Have you given any more thought to buying a property?'

'Yes, I have.' Paul smiled at my father in relief: at last, a chance to discuss a normal, sensible topic that he knew something about. His pleasure was to be short-lived, however. 'I have my eye on an apartment on the Quays.'

'No, no, no.' Dad shook his head solemnly. 'A property like that won't hold its value once the bubble bursts, you mark my words. And all those apartments were literally thrown up; they'll probably collapse at the next strong gust of wind. No, what you need to invest in, son, is a good solid property with a few years on it, down the country somewhere. Forget Dublin. I'd go for somewhere in the south-east if I were you. In fact, you know what?' He said this as if the idea had just that second popped into his head. 'The area that Rosie is living in would be perfect.'

Oh, here we go, I thought. *Why doesn't he just go the whole hog and offer Paul a dowry to take me off his hands? I'd suggest one hundred camels. They're all the rage this season, you know.*

'I'll certainly think about it.' Paul smiled politely and turned his attention back to the Brussels sprout that he had been attempting to saw in half

135

for the last five minutes.

'Mum? How long did you cook the sprouts for?'

'Oh, I don't know. Why do you ask?'

'Well, they're a bit hard.'

'They're like bloody bullets,' said Dad helpfully.

'You're not supposed to cook vegetables for a long time. It takes all the goodness out of them.'

'All the goodness in the world isn't going to benefit you if you can't bite into the damn things in the first place.'

'Mum. Dad. I have some news for you.'

All eyes were on Tatiana, sprouts forgotten.

'I'm getting married.'

She certainly knew how to pick her moment.

There were a couple of seconds of shocked silence, and then Mum squealed and ran around the table, throwing her arms around Tatiana's neck from behind and almost throttling her. She was closely followed by me.

'That's great news, Annie! Is it that guy you wrote to me about?'

Annie nodded happily, then looked over expectantly at my father. 'Dad?'

'That's great, Annie. But who are you marrying?'

'He's one of my students. I've been teaching him English.'

Dad sat like a statue. 'What's his name?'

'Chen.'

We all watched in morbid fascination as the colour drained from Dad's face.

'You mean he's a Chink.'

'He's Chinese, yes.' Tatiana's tone was cool and her expression hardened as she spoke.

'Oh, no, Annie. You can't marry a Chink.'

'Dad, please don't use that term. I'm marrying Chen and that's all there is to it.'

'But he's from a totally different culture. I bet he's not even a Catholic.'

She ignored this. 'I have another bit of news.'

We all looked at her again.

'I'm pregnant.'

My mother squealed and strangled Tatiana once more. My father sat like a thundercloud at the head of the table.

'Well, I hope for your sake that you're not expecting a girl, or you'll be forced to abort.'

'Dad!'

'Joe!'

We all glared at him angrily. He threw his napkin on the table and got up. 'I'm going to get a take-away. I've had enough of this muck.'

He stopped at the door and looked back at Tatiana.

'I hope you're proud of yourself, Miss. You're the first fallen woman in the Malone family.'

We all sat in silence until we heard the front door slam. Then Tatiana started to sob uncontrollably.

'Fallen woman!' she said between sobs. 'Where does he think he is? The Bible?'

Mum cradled her in her arms. 'Don't worry, dear. He'll calm down once he gets used to the idea. Now come into the living room and I'll give you a nice Indian head massage. It'll make you and the baby feel a whole lot better.'

I sighed. There was nothing like a good Sunday roasting.

Chapter Eleven

I was so happy to be driving my beautiful car again. I turned the top down and the radio up; it was playing a song about going to visit the countryside and eating lots of peaches. Yes, having my car back made returning to Ballyknock just about tolerable. At this rate, I might even make it to the end of the week. In fact, I was almost glad to get away from Dublin for some peace and quiet. Warring flatmates, Neanderthal fathers, hormonal sisters … after what I'd been through, handling a few mice should be a doddle.

And speaking of mice …

Patricia came into my office shortly after five on Monday evening.

'Do you have any spare boxes in here?'

I gestured to a container of flat archive boxes balancing against the far wall. She took one of them and expertly made it up. I reflected, not for the first time, that whoever invented them there boxes must be a zillionaire several times over. Wish I'd thought of them.

'I have a surprise for you,' she twinkled as she went back into the office.

What could it be? One of her famous fruit bracks? Her secret recipe for prize-winning raspberry jam? My very own pinny? I shouldn't scoff, I admonished myself; she really had been very kind to me.

I had been wrong on all counts. Approximately ten minutes later, Patricia burst through my office door holding in both hands that very same box, although this time it clearly wasn't empty.

'There you go!' She plonked it unceremoniously on top of the file I'd been working on.

I was filled with instinctual, childish delight at receiving a present, any present. 'What is it?'

'It's the answer to all your mouse problems.'

Just then, the box moved. All by itself, you understand. I noticed that the lid had been Sellotaped down on either side and that several large holes had been punched into it.

'What's in there?' Delight was turning to apprehension.

'Look through the lid and see for yourself.'

'It's not a ferret, is it?'

She laughed. 'See for yourself.'

I cautiously stood up and peered through the holes. From the depths of the box, two round green lights glowed eerily up at me. I jumped back in fright as the lights moved swiftly to the top of the box and an object like a fur and leather pin-cushion, with five pins stuck into it, shoved itself out of one of the holes.

'It's a cat, isn't it?' I said with ill-concealed disgust.

As if in reply, the box emitted a low, guttural yowl.

'It doesn't sound too friendly.'

'She's just scared, poor little cratur. So would you be if somebody took you away from your home and stuck you in a box for no good reason.'

She had a point. Still, I was confused. 'Where did she come from? I mean, did you have her hidden in your drawer all day long, or something?'

'Begod, no, child. Seamus is after bringing her around in his car. He tells me she's a feral cat that his wife – that's my sister Dorothy – has been feed-ing for the last couple of years. She's just weaned her last set of kittens.'

So the rat-catcher had come up trumps after all.

'What do I owe him?'

Patricia laughed her head off at this particular gem. 'Cats don't cost anything.'

'They do in Dublin.'

'Sure they're all half-mad up there – no offence, lovey.'

'None taken.'

'I mean, the countryside is overrun with cats; I'm certain Seamus and Dorothy are only delighted to be getting rid of this one – not that they're trying to dump her on you,' she added quickly. 'It's just that they have about thirteen cats as it is, between the house and the barns. And you're in desperate need of a cat, as far as I can tell. And they tell me that this one is a grand little killer.'

Great. 'What's her name?'

Patricia looked at me as if I were losing my mind. 'I don't think she has a name. "Cat", I suppose.'

That was original.

'Here, I'll carry her out to the car for you.'

I packed up and followed Patricia and the box out to my car. As Patricia started moving, the cat started meowing. At least, I think that's what it was doing. I didn't know much about cats, but surely that was no ordinary meow. It was more like a baby's plaintive cry – a distress signal if ever there was one.

I clicked open the doors, and Patricia went to put the box in the back seat.

'No, no, no! Not in there.'

She turned and looked at me in surprise.

'You can put it in the boot.'

She shrugged and moved to the back of the car. I shook my head in amazement. A cat, in the back of my Audi – sacrilege!

The cat kept up its pitiful mewling all the way home. If anything, the sound became louder and more insistent. There was another noise, too; a kind of knocking. I was torn between sympathy and alarm.

I finally pulled up outside Power's Cottage and approached the boot with caution. *Easy does it....* I slowly opened it. *Holy shit!*

Like a bat out of hell (or a cat out of hell), a small bundle of dark-brown fur catapulted itself past me and disappeared into the depths of the garden. I couldn't even tell in which direction she flew.

But that was the least of my problems. A second later, my nostrils were assaulted by a pungent stench. *Oh, Jesus!* I covered my nose in disgust. I might not have been the world's greatest feline expert, but I knew cat piss when I smelt it. Thank Christ I hadn't let Patricia put her in the back seat. *Horrible little animal*, I thought. *I hope she never comes back.*

I forgot all about the cat until I was leaving for work the next morning. There on the doorstep, placed dead-centre on the mat, was a decapitated mouse.

There was still no sign of her when I was getting ready for bed that night. Feeling very foolish, clad only in fleece-lined pyjamas, slippers and a torch, I advanced into the darkness.

'Cat! Where are you, Cat?'

No response.

I moved out onto the road. At times like this, I was glad I didn't have many neighbours. I wished I knew more about cats. How did one find a cat that

143

didn't want to be found? I swept the beam of the torch in random arcs about the road.

'Here, kitty, kitty!'

I hadn't told Patricia about my predicament. I was hardly going to admit to losing the creature ten minutes after she had been given into my custody. *How's the cat settling in? Oh, just fine, thank you....* If she didn't turn up soon, I'd have to pretend she'd got run over by a car or something. As far as I knew, cats were always being run over. Okay, so I lived on a road where there was, on average, one car every sixty minutes; the moggy got unlucky, that was all.

Increasingly desperate, I walked up the boreen towards the old derelict schoolhouse. It was with some effort that I quelled the impending feelings of creepiness.

'Meow,' I said quietly into the darkness.

I couldn't believe I was doing this. If only Iseult could see me now.

'Meow,' I said, louder.

Still nothing.

'Oh, this is ridiculous.' I turned on my slippered heel and headed back to the cottage.

'Meow.' This time it wasn't me.

'Meow?' I replied.

'Meow.' There it was again. I wasn't imagining things.

I nearly lost my life as something warm and soft rubbed against my left leg. In a blind panic, I dropped the torch, which began to roll down the hill, illuminating alternate patches of road and hedgerow as it went. I chased after it as if my life depended on it, scenes from *The Blair Witch Project* flashing alarmingly through my head.

I caught up with the errant torch and directed the beam uphill. Sure enough, there was the cat, eyes glowing like green candle-flames in the darkness. She was just sitting there, all casual: *What's all the fuss about?*

'Meooow,' she said as she ran towards me, tail aloft, wrapping herself around my legs again.

Relieved, I almost ran back indoors, the cat padding delicately along beside me. I placed a bowl of cat food on the kitchen floor and watched as she enthusiastically tucked into it. On impulse, I leant down and stroked her back a few times. The cat reverberated like the engine of an expensive sports car.

'You're not so bad,' I told her, and took myself off to bed.

It was the last week of September, and the Indian summer was drawing to a close. I had come to an executive decision to make the most of the few bright evenings that were left to me: I headed off on a constitutional every day after work. This evening, the sky looked uncertain. I changed into my walking gear quickly, before it could make up its mind for the worst.

There wasn't much else to do down here. Since I'd moved down to Ballyknock, my social life during the week had deteriorated dramatically. In my previous incarnation as a Dublin solicitor, there had always been someone to meet after work for a drink or a meal; even if there wasn't, there was always Paul and/or Hazel and/or Chris to hang out with. Hell, if I got really desperate, I could even visit my parents. Right then, I'd have killed for an evening in with the old dears. I was sick of watching TV; even I had a limit to how many soap operas I could follow simultaneously. In my boredom, I'd taken to having one-sided conversations with Mary Power on the wall. She hadn't started to answer back yet, but I believed it was only a matter of time.

I was so wrapped up in nostalgia for my ex-social life that I failed to notice the clouds gathering overhead. My first clue to the impending downpour was when a large raindrop landed squarely on the bridge of my nose. Then one on my hand. Then one on my forehead. Then another. And another. In sixty seconds I was soaked to the skin. A grand soft day, thank God.

Damnation. I must have been two miles or more away from the cottage – I had a bad habit of setting off on a long stroll and forgetting that I'd have to walk the same distance back again. I turned and started to run. In hindsight, this was ludicrous; I was hardly fit enough to run two metres, let alone two miles. No sooner had I begun than a large black bird, probably a crow, burst out of a hedgerow and flew directly into my path – most likely looking for shelter too. Momentarily startled, I lost my footing and fell heavily to the ground. I felt my right ankle going. *Shit!*

I must have looked a sight, sitting on the rain-sodden ground, groaning and massaging my ankle ineffectually. It really hurt. What was I going to do now?

As if on cue – in one of those rare instances of serendipity – I heard the sound of a far-off engine. It was definitely drawing closer. Thank goodness. Surely the driver would stop and be a good Samaritan. I strained my ears. Not a car; something larger. A truck? A jeep? A tractor, even?

A blue crock of a tractor emerged dramatically out of the mist and drew up beside me. Jack looked down in obvious surprise that the bedraggled lump of clothing at the side of the road was in fact a human being, and that, furthermore, it was me. He switched off the engine and jumped down lithely.

'Lainey! What are you doing out here?'

'Oh, you know. Just having a rest.' The rain was still bucketing down around us.

'Are you hurt?'

'It's my ankle.'

'Here, let me have a look.'

He knelt down in front of me and, taking my ankle firmly but gently in his hands, laid it on his knee. He undid the laces of my new state-of-the-art hiking boot and smiled.

'Thinking of going rock-climbing, were we?'

'I didn't have anything else to wear,' I replied sulkily.

Jack eased off the boot and began to manipulate my ankle up and down, left and right. At one point I let out an indignant squeal.

'Nothing broken. Probably just a sprain.'

'Just a sprain, is it? That's easy for you to say. It bloody well hurts. What makes you an expert, anyhow?'

'I'm not, but my brother gave me a few tips.'

'I didn't know you had a brother who's a doctor.'

'I don't. I have a brother who's a vet.'

'Oh, well, I'm very flattered to be compared to a heifer.'

He ignored me. 'Come on. Let's get you in out of the rain.' He hoisted me easily up into the air, like a new husband about to carry his bride over the threshold, shoved me inelegantly into the cab of the tractor and jumped in beside me.

'Now, we'll have you home in no time.' He looked over at me as he started up the engine. 'Jesus, girl, you look like a drowned rat.'

'Thanks a lot.'

'Don't mention it.'

The tractor took off at its top speed of ten miles an hour. At this rate, I might make it home by Christmas. I shivered.

'Cold? Here. Cover yourself with this.' Jack handed me a tartan blanket that stank ferociously of sheepdog. Not wanting to appear ungrateful, I draped it delicately across my knees, trying not to visualise the dog hairs and possibly even fleas that were transferring themselves to their new home – my clothes.

Despite my somewhat harsh words, I was weak with gratitude. What would I have done if he hadn't come along? I glanced slyly across at him when I thought he wasn't looking. I was wrong. He was looking. He smiled easily and openly at me.

'You all right?'

I nodded. 'Thanks.'

'Don't mention it. Maybe you can do the same for me someday.'

What? Save him in my tractor? I doubted it.

The sudden downpour had ended as abruptly as it had started. In typical perverse Irish-weather fashion, the sun had come out again. An almost perfect rainbow, in all its vivid glory, straddled the countryside before us. Everything looked beautiful after the rain – like a woman's eyes after crying: washed clean.

Jack looked good after the rain, too. I wished the wet look suited me that well.

'The view is pretty good from up here.' I meant it. I could see far more than I'd ever seen in my car or on foot. I could practically see right into people's bedroom windows, for a start. Usually, I was only able to nose into the first storey of people's houses.

'I'm telling you. People underestimate the charms of a tractor.'

'I'd say it's a real babe magnet, all right.'

Jack laughed. 'You'd be surprised. I'm not doing too bad today, anyway, am I?'

He gave me a bird's-eye tour of the countryside. To the right, a field of lazy beds – rows and rows of ridges, used for growing potatoes at the time of the Famine. To the left, the recording studio of a reclusive rock star. (Really? Rich, famous people chose to live here?) Up ahead, the gate lodge of the estate of the Master of the Hunt. I craned my neck, as instructed by Jack, to make out a herd of deer. 'And see those horses over there? See that little brown one with the bandy legs? A two-time Derby winner.' He was munching happily on a clump of grass, bathed in golden autumn sunshine. I never would have guessed. I searched for signs of security precautions, but there were none.

We reached Power's Cottage, and I wondered how on earth I was going to get down off the tractor. Without saying anything to me, as if he were a fireman and I needed rescuing from a burning building, Jack placed his left arm under my right armpit and his right arm beneath my knees, and swung me out of the tractor and onto the ground. I winced as my injured foot made contact with the earth.

'Keep your weight off it.'

He hauled me into the house and deposited me outside the bedroom door.

'You'd better get out of those wet clothes. Let me know if you need any help.'

'I'll be all right.' I closed the door, hobbled over to the bed and sat down heavily. I could hear noises coming from the kitchen: Jack filling up the kettle, Jack cleaning out the fire. I glanced at myself in the dressing-table mirror. My cheeks were flushed and my eyes were unnaturally bright. I must be getting some sort of fever.

I emerged ten minutes later, hair roughly blow-dried, dressed in pyjamas, a towelling robe and bed-socks. Oddly enough, I wasn't embarrassed by my appearance. Flames were already leaping out of the hearth.

'Here. Sit yourself down.' Jack guided me over to the couch, where I sat as instructed. He handed me a mug of tea. 'Do you mind if I go into your bedroom for a second?'

'No – but …'

He emerged from the bedroom with my duvet, which he proceeded to cover me with, tucking it right up to my chin. All that was left exposed was my face and the hand holding the mug of tea.

'Now …' He looked down at me seriously. 'Do you think you need a hot-water bottle?'

'I'm fine, Jack. Couldn't be cosier.'

He grinned. 'Never let it be said that Jack Power doesn't know how to treat a girl.'

Never let it be said, indeed. He was like some hero out of a romantic novel. Were farmers meant to be this smooth?

He was so nice. So funny. So gorgeous…. So what was he doing here with me? I banished the renegade thought immediately, before it had time to take root.

His next good deed was to bandage my ankle. He took a first-aid kit – which I hadn't even known existed – from under the kitchen sink, and wrapped my foot up like a mummy. I was relieved I'd happened to shave my legs in the shower that morning. Pity about the chipped nail-polish, though.

'You're to go to the doctor first thing tomorrow. You won't be able to drive so I'll take you.'

'What, in the tractor?'

'If you're good, I'll bring the jeep.'

So Jack Power brought me to the doctor the next morning ('a slight sprain'. Slight! The man was clearly a quack). Then he collected me from work that evening and took me home. As he was leaving (he had to bring the cows in from the field), he turned and looked at me strangely. I felt awkward in his company for the first time in the two days.

'Are you doing anything this Saturday night?' he asked.

Tell him.

'I'm going to Kerry for the weekend.'

'Oh? Whereabouts?'

Tell him.

'A hotel close to Sneem.'

'Oh. Who are you going with?'

Tell him.

'My boyfriend.'

Told him.

Jack nodded slowly, as if understanding something.

'Well … I hope you have a nice time. I'll see you soon.'

'See you next week sometime?'

He waved, without looking back at me, and sped off down the hill in the jeep.

Come back!

Chapter Twelve

The chosen location for our anniversary weekend was an elegant country-house hotel on the Ring of Kerry. I made my own way down on Saturday morning, the Audi cautiously hugging the cliff road. The spectacle of the waves rushing at the harsh coastline and flinging themselves against spiky black rocks was so awe-inspiring that I almost ended up in the ocean on two occasions.

It was mid-morning when I swung through the impressive wrought-iron gates of the hotel. I drove slowly, taking in the lush, well-kept vegetation and the ancient native trees. Paul's car was already parked in front of the hotel. He must have left his flat in Dublin at five in the morning, or some such ungodly hour. He'd probably been for a swim, had a back rub and played two rounds of golf already. All I wanted to do was sit in one of the plush reception rooms with a coffee and a smoke and read the papers. Hotels with activities were wasted on me.

I opened the door of room 101 with the key they had given me at reception – a proper key, not one of those stupid cards that never work. The room was everything I had hoped for and then some. A four-poster bed! I'd never slept in a four-poster before, but I'd always wanted to, ever since I'd read 'The Princess and the Pea' at the age of six. I sat on the edge of the bed, giggling as I bounced up and down and took in my surroundings. The décor was wine and gold, rich and royal. Original paintings of the Kerry countryside adorned the walls and each piece of furniture was an obvious antique – not that I knew much about these things, but I knew quality when I saw it; not a stick of over-varnished MDF in sight. There was even a writing desk. I kicked off my shoes, padded over and started fiddling around with all the little compartments. Hotel pencils and sheets of writing paper had been laid on. Maybe I'd even start writing that novel I was always thinking about – but later. There was still the bathroom to explore.

I turned on the light to reveal a pristine black-and-white bathroom, striking in its contrasting modernity. There was a bath with all the jacuzzi trimmings (I could be a floozy in the jacuzzi) and a shower that would comfortably fit two people (at least). But these details barely registered: I was magnetically drawn to the freebies adorning the sink. I noted with excitement the Crabtree & Evelyn shampoo, conditioner and body lotion. And then there were the shower caps, and soaps in fancy flowery boxes. Lovely. I looked around, wide-eyed, to see what else I could steal when I was leaving. There was a fluffy white bathrobe hanging on the back of the door…. No. I'd never have the nerve. I'd be glancing nervously in my rear-view mirror all the way back to Ballyknock, expecting a squad car to pull me over at any second: 'Where do you think you're going with that bathrobe?' I had always been a good, law-abiding citizen. I'd love to claim that this was for moral reasons, but actually I was just terrified of being caught.

I selected a soap, a shower cap and two body lotions and was about to transfer them to my bag when I was interrupted by the sound of a key turning in the lock. Guiltily, I threw the contraband behind me into the bathroom, where it landed with a clatter in the sink. I posed casually in the doorway, leaning my left hand against the frame, my right hand on my hip. It was Paul. I loved the way his face broke into a genuine happy smile the second he saw me.

'You're here!' He kissed me warmly.

'You're in a good mood.'

'I'm just pleased to see you. When did you get here?'

'About half an hour ago.' More like ten minutes – but who was counting?

He looked at his watch. 'What time did you leave?'

'About seven.' It had been more like eight. I'd had to wrench myself from my cherished Saturday-morning lie-in.

'Really? The traffic must have been awful.'

'Oh, it was. Terrible. I got stuck behind a tractor coming out of Ballyknock, and there was a bad pile-up just outside Cork, and, would you believe, there were loose horses on the road in Clonmel….' I trailed off as it became obvious that Paul was no longer listening to my excuses (just as well, too). He was hunkered down beside his sports bag, pulling out clean clothes.

'Were you swimming?'

'Yeah. I did about fifty lengths. The pool's fantastic. Maybe you'll come down with me tomorrow morning?'

'Yeah, maybe. Do you fancy an early lunch? I'm starved.'

'Sure. Just give me a few minutes to shower and change.'

I looked on appreciatively as Paul whipped his T-shirt over his head and stepped out of his shorts. Mmm … I'd almost forgotten about his footballer's legs. I stood in the doorway of the bathroom, watching him prepare for his shower.

'What happened here?' He was picking the body lotions out of the sink and lining them up properly again, as nature intended.

'I don't know. They must have fallen.'

As Paul turned on the jet of water and stepped into the shower, I was struck by a brilliant idea. Mentally hugging myself with excitement, I went back into the bedroom and rapidly stripped off, throwing my clothes onto the bed or wherever else was convenient. I tiptoed back into the bathroom, loosening my hair as I went, and drew back the door of the shower, startling Paul.

'What are you doing? I'm having a shower.'

'I just thought you might need your back scrubbed.' I smiled up at him in what I hoped was a suggestive fashion, and felt vaguely foolish.

Stepping into the shower, I closed the screen behind me. Paul looked at me, his brow furrowed, uncertainty clouding his eyes. I ignored this and looped my arms loosely about his neck, pressing my breasts against his chest. This, at least, had the desired effect.

'Let me wash your hair,' I said.

'What do you want to do that for?'

'I just want to. Let me wash your hair this once, Paul. Please.'

I had recently read in a well-known women's magazine that washing your partner's hair (even if he didn't have all that much of it) was a sure-fire way of establishing intimacy. I squirted a blob of

Paul's medicated, masculine-smelling shampoo into my hand and began to spread it over his head. I rubbed it in, using each and every finger to massage his scalp, until it looked like he was wearing a white foam wig. I removed the shower nozzle and started to rinse. As I did so, I accidentally dislodged Paul's shaving kit from the shelf; unfortunately, it landed slap bang on his big toe.

'For fuck's sake!' He hopped onto his other leg.

'Sorry.'

But the fun didn't end there. As he hopped, a soapy rivulet ran straight into his eye.

'Oh, Jesus!' He rubbed frantically at it.

Without saying another word, I replaced the shower-head and got out. I grabbed the nearest towel and exited the bathroom, leaving a trail of soapy footprints behind me.

An all-too-familiar phrase played once again in my mind.

Why do I even bother?

Lunch was a frosty affair – and I'm not talking about the ice-cream pie for dessert. I was in a bad mood because I felt I'd made a fool of myself. Paul was in a bad mood because I'd failed to apologise for injuring his toe/injuring his eye/ruining his shower. He could go fuck himself if he thought *I* was going to say sorry to *him*.

I think he sensed this; he was the first to thaw out.

'The food's lovely here, isn't it?'

I shrugged.

'Better than that over-priced restaurant for posers that Chris made us go to.'

He was trying to catch my eye, but I deliberately wouldn't let him. I was in a sulk.

'Will we go for a walk after lunch – explore the grounds?'

'You can do what you want. I'm going to stay here and read my book.'

We ate in silence for a couple of minutes. Then Paul said, 'I got you an anniversary present.'

'What is it?' *Damn!*

A smug smile played about his lips. 'Will I go and get it?'

'Do what you like.' I knew I was being ridiculously petulant, but I didn't seem able to stop myself.

He went out to his car and returned a minute later, carrying a large oblong box wrapped in silver paper and decorated with a bright-red bow. At first I thought it might be a dozen roses, but when he placed it in my arms I realised it was too heavy for that. A sawn-off shotgun, perhaps? A stick to beat the lovely lady with?

With that familiar Christmas-morning feeling, I ripped open the silver paper. I saw Paul wince; he hated the way I wasted wrapping paper. You could never use a piece again after I'd got my hands on it.

I finished unwrapping and stared down at the box in my lap.

'What is it?' I already knew the answer. I just didn't believe it.

'It's that steering-wheel lock your father mentioned last week. It's an amazing gadget. Look, I'll show you what it can do.' He removed it from my lap and started playing around with it, like a total fucking anorak.

My vision blurred, and for one crazy moment I thought I was going to cry. *Don't be ridiculous, Lainey. It's not as if that innocent steering-wheel lock is a symbol of everything that's wrong with your relationship....* I realised that Paul had stopped enthusing about the thing and was addressing me again.

'Don't you like it?'

'I love it, Paul. It's so romantic. I got you those cufflinks you wanted. They're in the car. I'll get them for you later. Right now, I'm going for a walk.'

'I thought you were going to stay and read.'

'There's been a change of plan.'

'Give me a second and I'll come with you.'

'I'd prefer to go on my own.' I walked out of the restaurant without looking back. There must have been something about my manner that prevented Paul from following me.

A fucking steering-wheel lock. Was I going out with my father or what?

I needed time to think.

I felt a lot better after spending a few hours on my own. The hotel grounds would have soothed the most troubled of hearts.

I met up with Paul for dinner, which was a much jollier affair than lunch. We were entertained during our meal by a pianist, who – in between beautifully played classical pieces – told the most outrageously filthy and funny jokes. The wine flowed even more beautifully than the music, and by the time we were onto our coffees I was in great form.

I had begun to talk seriously about accompanying the pianist with my superb singing voice when Paul decided it was time to go to bed. He pushed me along the corridor to our room, his hand firmly on the small of my back, guiding me when I started to veer off course. He shushed me now and then, when the strains of my marvellous rendition of 'My Way' threatened to disturb the inhabitants of the other rooms.

In room 101, I flopped down on the bed and watched the ceiling spin. I heard Paul locking the door behind us and shielded my eyes when he turned on the bedside lamp. I felt him lie down on the bed beside me. Even though my hand was still covering my eyes, I could tell he was looking at me. I felt hot breath on my neck. Gentle fingers stroked the skin of my clavicle rhythmically. I gave myself over to the sensation, stretching my supine body luxuriantly on the bed. The fingers travelled further down, tracing the outlines of my breasts and following my curves from ribcage to waist to hips. Hot, insistent lips pressed down on my mouth. I kissed them back gently, aware of the fingers starting to unbutton my top. I lay almost rigid, a knot of anticipation tightening in my stomach.

And then I heard the sound of a zipper. I looked out through my fingers; Paul was tearing open a condom and preparing to assume the position. Oh, no. Too soon. I sat up on the bed, and he looked at me in surprise.

'What?' he said to the expression on my face.

'Let's have some fun first.'

He frowned. 'I thought this was fun.'

'It is,' I said urgently, grabbing at his arm, 'but look – we have this whole hotel room at our disposal. A four-poster bed, for God's sake. When are we going to have the chance to sleep in a four-poster again?'

He shrugged.

'Not to mention the mirror in the wardrobe at the end of the bed.'

Still nothing. All I seemed to be doing was making him look uncomfortable. I pressed on regardless.

'I have a pair of silk hold-ups with me. Why don't you tie me to the bed?'

'I don't know, Lainey –'

'Oh, come on. This bed is perfect for it. You can even blindfold me if you want.'

'Why? So you can pretend that I'm somebody else?'

'Oh, don't be daft, Paul. It's nothing to do with that. It makes the sensations more intense, that's all.'

'So you've done this before, then.'

I blushed. 'Might have done.'

'Who with?'

'For God's sake, Paul. I had other boyfriends before I went out with you – you know that. Now are you going to tie me up or not?' I already knew the answer.

'We don't need all that kinky stuff, Lainey. We love each other.'

Did we?

I climbed over to the other side of the bed and got under the covers.

'What are you doing? Don't you want…?' Paul put his hand on my shoulder.

I shook it off. 'No, I don't want. I'm going to sleep.'

I lay stiffly under the covers, staring at the edge of the bedside table, until Paul eventually got under the covers himself and turned off the light. Some anniversary weekend this had turned out to be.

I lay there, wide awake, staring into the gloom, for what must have been an hour. Shortly before I fell asleep, Paul whispered my name.

'Lainey.'

I didn't answer.

'Lainey? Are you awake?'

Just pretend you're asleep.

'I love you, Lainey.'

It was two o'clock the following day, and we were having afternoon tea. This consisted of cheese,

164

ham and turkey finger sandwiches – with the crusts cut off, of course – and home-made fruit scones, still warm from the oven, served with real butter on a silver butter-dish, strawberry jam and whipped cream. I wondered how Bridie and Patricia would rate the jam; it tasted pretty good to me, but, then again, I was no expert. This was all washed down with coffee or tea, depending on your preference, served in a little antique silver pot. But the *pièce de résistance* of the entire afternoon-tea experience was the dessert of the day: strawberry mousse on a perfect, light piece of sponge, served on a silver cake-plate.

Did the people serving us not realise that we were only plebs who would have settled for a lot less?

I sat with my face obscured by the Living section of the *Sunday Independent*. I wasn't really reading it; I just wanted to avoid looking at Paul, who had his nose buried deep in the Sports section. Every now and then he would make some comment about speculation over the new manager of the Irish soccer team, and I would say 'Mmm' in response.

At one point, I looked across at him. Was he really that oblivious to what was going on in this relationship? He acted like we had no problems. Was it all a big macho show, or did he genuinely think we were doing okay?

I was considering another (solitary) walk when a shadow fell across me.

'Hello, Lainey. I thought it was you.'

I looked up to find that the owner of the shadow was an ex-boyfriend of mine.

'Oh. Hello, Eric.' I sucked in my stomach involuntarily.

Eric had been my first love. I had met him when I was nineteen and in second year at UCD, and we had been inseparable until almost the end of third year. At least, I had followed him around with puppy-like devotion, waiting for him to throw me the odd scrap of affection whenever it suited him. It tended to suit him on Saturday nights and whenever he fancied a quick blow-job. He was the type of man who takes the spark out of a woman and then dumps her because she's lost her spark. In short, he broke my hymen and my heart.

I realised he was looking expectantly at Paul.

'Eric, this is Paul. Paul – Eric. We knew each other in college.'

Paul stood up and shook hands with Eric, and the two of them sized each other up. I could tell that Paul had immediately copped who Eric was. I had told him a little bit about Eric, but not too much, as Paul had a tendency to become insanely jealous for no good reason. He knew, however, that Eric had been my first proper boyfriend and that he had been the captain of the rugby team in his last year in college. The latter fact in particular irked him no end.

'Romantic weekend away from the Big Smoke, is it?' Eric asked me.

'Something like that. You?'

'I'm down with a few of the lads. Golf.' He gestured to three men who were gathered around the bar, similarly attired in tank tops, baseball caps and stupid-looking trousers.

'Do you play, Paul?'

'I do, as a matter of fact.'

'Are you in a club?'

'Clontarf.'

'Really? Nice course.'

Paul looked pleased.

'What's your handicap?' Eric asked.

'Ten.'

'Not bad.'

'Yours?' I knew he wouldn't be able to resist.

'Three.'

Paul was crestfallen; there was no other word to describe the expression on his face. Eric smiled that smug smile that brought me back a decade in time. *So you're still a self-satisfied bastard, then.*

'What are you doing with yourself these days, Eric?'

'I'm a management consultant.'

'Really? I didn't know a degree in history and rugby qualified you for that sort of thing.'

He laughed. 'You'd be surprised what it qualifies you for.'

He'd put on a couple of stone – most of it beer, no doubt – since the last time I'd seen him. Not that I could talk: I was considerably softer around the edges

167

too. And was it my imagination, or was he already thinning on top? I sincerely hoped so. He had always been so vain about his shiny black tresses.

In college, Eric's hair had been shoulder-length. For some reason, in those disastrous romantic formative years I had been wildly and irresistibly drawn to long-haired lovers, especially if they had beards. Maybe I thought that if they resembled Jesus Christ they were less likely to use and abuse me, or maybe I'd just fancied Robert Powell when he played Jesus of Nazareth. Most of these boys were the type who would invite me up to their rooms to show me their poetry – and when they got me up there, they actually wanted to show me their poetry (always terrible angst-ridden mush). Eric, however, had wanted to show me something entirely different.

Back in the present, I tried to imagine him with a comb-over.

'Better be off. It was nice seeing you again, Lainey. We must meet up in Dublin some evening for a few scoops.'

'Yes. We must.' *Not.*

'Bye, then.'

'Bye, Eric.'

He went back to his cronies. I shook my head and resumed reading the book reviews. I wondered what I had ever seen in that prat, and it was a good feeling.

After a while, I glanced over at Paul. His face was like thunder.

'What's up with you?'

Paul continued to glower.

'Come on, spit it out.'

'You know what's wrong,' he spat.

'No, Paul, I don't know. Did Arsenal have the crap kicked out of them by Man United again?'

'I just can't believe you did that.'

'Did what?'

'He asked you out, and you said yes! Right in front of me!'

'Oh, come off it, Paul. I was just being polite – and so was he.'

'No. It was more than that. He obviously still fancies you. I suppose you used to tie each other up and have lots of showers together.'

'Oh, don't be so ridiculous.' I slapped the newspaper down on the table, picked up my bag and stalked out to the lobby. I pressed the button for the lift about fifteen times, as if that was going to make it come any quicker. At last the empty lift arrived and I got in. As the doors began to slide shut, I saw Paul running towards me.

'Hold the lift. Press the button. Elena!'

Ha! I watched the door slide shut on Paul's stunned features with satisfaction.

Back in room 101, I began to fling my possessions – which were scattered to the four corners of the room – into my overnight bag. The key sounded in the door and Paul came in.

'I hope you're proud of yourself.'

He was greeted by a stony silence.

'That was very mature – not holding the lift for me.'

That did it. I threw down the blouse I'd been holding and rounded on Paul. Looking back, I think I might even have shoved him in the chest once or twice; I was in such a blind rage, it's hard to recall. What I do remember is the expression of shock on his face.

'Mature? Don't talk to me about mature! You're the most immature, uptight, anal, sulky, annoying, pathetic son of a bitch I've ever had the misfortune to meet, and I want nothing more to do with you – nothing! Did you hear me? I'm going to walk out of this room, and I never want to see you again!'

I paused to see if my words were having the desired effect. If the desired effect had been to make a grown man cry, I had succeeded admirably.

'Paul – Paul…. I didn't mean it. I just lost my temper.'

But it was too late.

Paul walked over to the bed, as if in slow motion, and sank down heavily. His face was a distinctly unhealthy grey-white, and his eyes were wide and glistening with unshed tears that he may not even have been aware of. I felt as if I'd shot a newborn fawn at point-blank range.

In desperation, I sat down on the bed beside him and put my arm around his shoulders. He didn't respond, didn't sink comfortably into me like he usually did.

170

'You don't want to go out with me any more, do you?'

'Paul, I …'

'You don't, do you?' He turned and looked me in the eye. At that moment, the one thing I wanted to do more than anything else was to lie. But I couldn't.

'I don't think it's working out.' Why was there no better way to say it? Why did it sound like such a cliché?

He stared at me for about ten seconds, then hauled himself up off the bed as if he'd just run a marathon.

'Tell me what I need to do to change your mind.' He went to the window and looked out, his back to me, evidently trying to compose himself.

I crumpled further down onto the bed and hid my face in my hands, trying to block out this terrible scene. Maybe if I couldn't see it, it wouldn't really be happening.

'Just tell me what I have to do,' he said again.

What could I possibly say? That I wanted him to change his whole personality, become a different person entirely, be more fiery, flamboyant, challenging, passionate, dangerous? That just wasn't him. He was good, safe, kind, considerate, reliable Paul. Boring Paul. That was all there was to it. He just wasn't what I'd imagined myself ending up with. He was an accountant, for God's sake; what had I expected? Who ever heard of a dangerous accountant? But how could I tell him this?

Instead I came out with, not exactly a lie, but a half-truth.

'It's the constant rowing, Paul. Over absolutely nothing. I can't handle it any more.'

'But we can sort that out. I'll make a big effort. I promise.' He half-turned to look at me, renewed hope in his eyes.

This visible glimmer of hope alarmed me more than anything else. Because I already knew for certain that it was misplaced.

'It's not just that,' I said quickly. 'It's the jealousy and suspicion – like just now, with Eric. I need to be allowed to have a past.'

'I know, Lainey, and I'm sorry. I just can't stand the thought of you being with anyone else.'

He was facing me fully now. I found the naked truth in his expression unbearable. I had to get out of that room.

I recommenced packing. It didn't take long – two minutes at the most. (What with all the palaver, I didn't notice until I got home that I'd forgotten all the freebies.)

I stood in the centre of the room, jacket on, bag on shoulder. Paul was still staring out of the window.

'You're really going, then?' His eyes were open as wide as they could go and there was a choked-up quality to his voice.

I nodded.

'You won't even stay and try and work things out?'

'No, Paul. It's over.' And still the clichés came

thick and fast. I felt as if I were in a play. But the words were shocking to my ears, too. I hadn't intended to utter them this weekend.

I walked over to him and put my hand gently on his arm. He wouldn't look at me.

'Don't.' His voice sounded funny. Thick.

'I'll give you a call during the week to see how you are.'

He nodded out the window.

There was nothing else to be said.

I checked out.

I'd like to point out, here and now, that my decision had absolutely nothing to do with Jack Power.

Chapter Thirteen

At least the cat was pleased to see me. She was sitting on the gate, waiting for me, when I arrived back at Power's Cottage. She proceeded to wind herself around my legs at least thirty times. I knew she only wanted food, but her enthusiastic welcome helped me to feel a little better about myself. When she'd finished eating she jumped up on my knee, looked up at me in what I chose to believe was an adoring fashion and purred so loudly that I had to turn the TV volume up several notches. She dug her claws into me rhythmically, making herself a nice comfy bed, and rubbed up against me as if in ecstasy. I stroked the back of her head.

'Good Cat,' I said. 'I can't keep calling you Cat, can I? What's your name? Is it Smudge?'

The cat stared up at me solemnly. I'd seen prettier felines.

'Is it Patch? Brownie? Kitty? Sheba? Blossom? Slinky?'

As soon as I said 'Slinky', the cat upped her purring by several decibels.

'Slinky,' I said again.

This time she rolled over onto her back, paws quivering in the air, furry stomach exposed.

'Slinky it is.'

That week I was to close the sale of the first house in the new estate in Ballyknock. I was acting for the builders; Brendan Ryan – he of the mad red hair and copious freckles – was representing the buyer. He seemed to have grown several more freckles since I'd seen him last, but he was still wearing the exact same ensemble.

He led me up a dark, narrow staircase to his office. The first thing I noticed upon entering the room was a fishing-rod leaning up against the wall. The second thing I noticed was a dog sitting on an antique chaise longue in the corner.

I decided not to ask.

'Take a seat.'

I sat down on what appeared to be an ancient, gnarled dining-room chair. The dog's seat looked a damn sight comfier.

'How have you been getting on?' asked Brendan.

'Very well, thanks.'

'I've got the money here. Will I just call out the documents and you can hand them to me?'

'Fine.' He clearly wasn't going to introduce the dog. So the dog decided to introduce himself.

He jumped off his throne and made a beeline for me, tail wagging frantically. Brendan continued to ignore him. I didn't have that option: the dog placed his chin in my lap and gazed up at me imploringly with soft, droopy eyes. Any second now, he'd start to drool on the documents.

'Hello, doggy.'

His tail thumped repeatedly on the carpet.

Brendan smiled. 'So you've met my friend, then.'

'Yes. What's … I mean …'

'You want to know why I have a dog in my office.'

'Yes.'

'He's a stray. He's been wandering around Ballyknock like a lost soul for the last few weeks. He decided to attach himself to me, poor mutt. Follows me everywhere. Trouble is, I can't take him in. I've already got three Dobermans at home; they'd make mincemeat out of him.'

'What's going to happen to him?'

'I'm taking him to the dog shelter this afternoon.'

'Really? But won't they …'

'Put him down if they don't get a home for him within five days? Yes.' Brendan was looking at me carefully.

I looked down at the dog, who now had his paw on my lap. He panted up at me. He almost looked like he was smiling.

And that was how, in the space of a fortnight, I managed to achieve the following:

- Acquire one cat
- Acquire one dog
- Lose one boyfriend.

I had been putting off ringing Paul all night. It was amazing what you could find to do around the house when you were trying to avoid doing something unpleasant. The removal of dust from upper shelves suddenly became a matter of life and death. But I could stave off the evil moment no longer. It was 9.45, and Paul went to bed at about ten on weeknights. Besides, my head wouldn't get a moment's peace until I took the dreaded plunge.

Holding my breath, I speed-dialled Paul's number.

As is so often the case in life, the thing I'd wasted so much precious time worrying about never came to pass.

I got Paul's voicemail. I left a short, formal message, saying that I'd just rung to say hello and to see how he was, and that I'd call again next week if I didn't hear from him in the meantime. Not that I expected to hear from him. He was probably there, screening his calls. If I'd been him, I wouldn't have wanted to speak to me either.

I felt a strange sense of anticlimax. All that adrenaline that my body had been producing in preparation for my conversation with Paul was going to waste. I decided to ring the flat.

Hazel answered, sounding frazzled and bad-tempered.

'Hello, who is this?'

'That's a fine way to answer the phone.'

'Oh, it's you.' She sounded relieved. 'I thought it was another of Chris's idiotic friends. I'm not joking, that girl needs to hire her own receptionist.'

'Don't tell me you two still haven't made up.'

'Oh, we have – sort of. It's just those morons she surrounds herself with.'

'Well, I'm glad to hear you're friends again, because I'd like to cordially invite you both down for a weekend in the country.'

'When?'

'This weekend.'

'I can't, Lainey, I have to –'

'Don't tell me you have to work. I don't want to hear it. You can't work every weekend of your miserable life.'

'But I have a huge deal on.'

'You always have a huge deal on.'

'But –'

'I won't take no for an answer. When's the last time you went away for the weekend?'

Silence.

'You see? It's so long ago, you can't even remember.'

'Well … I suppose if I worked late on Friday night, and came in early on Monday morning, I could just about swing it.'

'Great. Now do me a favour: give Chris a shout and see if she's free.'

I heard Hazel putting the receiver down on the hall table, then knocking on what must have been Chris's bedroom door. The background music (Shakira? surely not) ended abruptly, and I heard Hazel's low, muffled tones, followed by Chris's excited squeals. A few seconds later, Hazel picked up the phone again.

'She says she'd love to come to Ballymuck this weekend.'

'Brilliant. I can't wait. Only tell her she'll get her head kicked in down here if she keeps calling it that.'

'I'll warn her. She says she's sorry she can't come to the phone, but she's meditating.'

'To Shakira?'

'Don't go there. Is Paul coming down too?'

'You haven't heard, then.'

'Heard what?'

'Haven't you spoken to Paul this week?'

There was a sharp intake of breath. 'He proposed!'

'Far from it. Didn't he tell you? We broke up.'

'No! I don't believe it. We had lunch together today in the canteen and he didn't say a word. I even asked him how you were, and he said you were fine.'

'That's Paul for you.'

'I suppose you broke it off.'

'What makes you say that?'

'You've always had the upper hand in that relationship.'

'That's ridiculous.'

'Oh, please! You've so had the upper hand it's not even funny.'

Had I? It was easy when you didn't give a toss.

'So you dumped him, then.'

'Well – yes.'

'The poor thing! He must be crushed.'

'Like you said, he seemed all right.'

'That's just Paul being Paul.'

'I suppose. You will be extra-specially nice to him for a while, won't you?'

'Of course. One of us has to be.'

'Now, that's not fair. You wouldn't want me to stay with him out of pity, would you? Keep stringing him along?'

'Yeah, yeah. You have a point. But – fuck it, anyway: you two were my only successful set-up. Now I'm down to nil again.'

'I didn't realise you were keeping score. Never mind. If you're good, I'll let you set me up with another dodgy accountant type as soon as I've got over this one.'

'Promise?'

The things I did to pacify my friends.

The dog smelt of old women's houses. I'd have given him a bath, but I didn't have the time: it was almost four o'clock, and Hazel and Chris were due to arrive any minute. They were a good three hours late already – something about Hazel having had to go into work that morning.

I looked down at the dog. The dog looked up at me, one ear pointing to the clouds, the other to the ground. He was black, apart from four mismatched white socks, a white bib and half a white face. He looked like he'd got on the wrong side of one of those machines the Corpo uses to draw white lines on the road. There was a bit of sheepdog in there, all right, and goodness knows what else; judging by his matted dreadlocks, he might have been part Rastafarian. I had spent a good part of the afternoon trying to come up with a name for him, using the same tactic I'd used for Slinky the cat, but I wasn't having much luck finding a name that he'd respond to. I had learned one thing, though, in the short time we'd spent together: he might have been a carnivore, but he had a vegetarian's soul.

He woofed at the sound of a car coming up the hill. Sure enough, I spotted Chris's new purple Beetle in the distance. Hazel called it a bubble car, and then commented cruelly, 'What kind of car would you expect a bubble-head to drive?'

When Hazel got out of the car, I was shocked at her appearance. She was still wearing her work gear and glasses – she used to wear contacts all the time, but she seldom bothered these days. She looked like she could do with a good hairbrushing – and, not meaning to be cruel, a good airbrushing. There was nothing wrong with her features; it was just that her skin was so sickly white that it was practically green, magnifying her dark shadows and blemishes. She'd probably been up all night working again. What I wouldn't have liked to say to that boss of hers, given half a chance…. Still, there was no guarantee that her unhealthy appearance wasn't due in part to Chris's driving/choice of music/ conversation on the way down.

'Your house is so dinky and *cute*!' squealed Chris. 'It's just like a little doll's house.' She caught her breath sharply, and her eyes widened as far as they could go – sure signs that she had just had a wonderful idea. 'I know! Why don't you get it thatched? It would be just like one of those perfect country cottages in the fairy tales. And you could paint it pink!'

'She'll be asking you if it's made of gingerbread next,' said Hazel.

'I'll suggest it to Tyrone next time I'm talking to him. Come and see the inside. Here, let me help you with your bags.'

Chris handed me the smallest of her set of Gucci cases and lugged the other two along on either side of her slender frame. She didn't do travelling light. Hazel, on the other hand, seemed to have brought one Superquinn plastic bag.

'Come on, Terence. We're going in.' Chris appeared to be addressing the dog, who was yelping in pure joy, his tail wagging as if it were about to come right off his body.

I put my arm around Hazel's shoulder as we walked into the house.

'You all right?'

'Yeah, fine.'

Didn't look like it.

We decided to go for an exploratory walk while it was still bright. I begged Chris to put on a pair of wellies, or at least sensible walking shoes, but she insisted on wearing the ultra-pointy-toed boots that she had purchased the previous day in Carl Scarpa. She brought her camera with her, too – a massive, professional-looking contraption that she wore around her neck. Something to do with her latest film project.

Before long, we came across a field of cows. Inevitable, really, but I thought Chris was going to have a fit.

'Oh, oh, I love cows! I haven't seen one since I was a kid.' She started taking photos, from many different angles, of a large cow that was staring at us from behind a hedge. All Hazel and I could do was look on, me in amusement and her in exasperation.

'Here. Take one of me and the cow.' Chris thrust the camera at Hazel.

'No,' Hazel said flatly, leaving no room for argument.

'Give it to me.' I took the camera and Chris lined up beside the hedge, posing prettily. 'Come on,

Terence,' she called the dog over, 'you can get in the picture too.'

'Why do you keep calling him Terence?'

'Because it's his name.'

I took several shots, until the cow started moo-ing like something out of a cartoon, causing Terence – I mean the dog – to dance in circles around Chris's feet and bark annoyingly.

'You know,' said Chris in hushed tones, as if someone might be lurking in the hedgerows, 'that cow might look innocent, but I once knew a man who was gored to death by a bull.'

'You knew him after he'd been gored to death, did you?' asked Hazel.

Chris gave her a dirty look. 'I knew *of* him.'

We headed back before long. Chris's feet were killing her. A red tractor came up the hill towards us; as we moved to the side of the road, to let it pass, Chris had the misfortune to step in a fresh, steaming pile of cow dung.

'My new boots!' she squealed.

'Don't worry, love,' shouted one of the men on the tractor as they drove by, 'it's great for the hooves!'

Three hours later, we were all three ready to go out for the night.

'How do I look?' Chris emerged from the bed-room and gave us an exaggerated twirl.

'Um … are you sure you won't be cold?'

'I never feel the cold.'

Let me start from the bottom up. Chris was wearing her new boots (which she had cleaned), Burberry tights, cut-off denim shorts, a revealing white T-shirt (no bra), a short indigo denim jacket and, to top off the ensemble, a Burberry baker-boy cap. I glanced at Hazel uncertainly, but she just looked resigned. It's not that I wasn't used to Chris's outlandish outfits; it was just that they didn't seem so out of place in Dublin. I didn't think Ballyknock was quite ready for this.

'What are we waiting for? Let's go and give those Ballymuck boys a good seeing-to.'

I gulped. 'Chrissy?'

'Yessy?'

'You know how this isn't a big city like Dublin?'

'Of course.'

'Well … things are a little different down here. It's not like Temple Bar. I'd really appreciate it if tonight you were a little bit more – how shall I say it – *restrained* than usual. Do you think you could do that for me?'

'No problem. You just point out the men you fancy, and I'll steer clear.'

'No, Chris, that's not what I mean. It's just that they all know me down here. They all know I'm the local solicitor. I can't really go mad. And you can't either.'

'Where's the fun in that?'

'I'm not asking you not to have fun. Just – well, could you just tone it down a little?' I indicated 'a little' with my thumb and forefinger.

She regarded me seriously, hands on non-child-bearing hips.

'Okay, then. Seeing as it's you.'

'Thanks, Chris.' I breathed a deep sigh of relief.

Beside me, head buried in a magazine, Hazel muttered, as if she was talking to herself, 'You'll be lucky.'

Chapter Fourteen

I couldn't get over the number of bodies crammed into Power's Select Lounge and Bar that Saturday night. Heaving, it was. I realised we might even have trouble getting seats – a problem I hadn't expected to encounter in Ballyknock.

The pub looked better at night. The dirt was less visible. A session was in full swing somewhere to our right. The musicians appeared to be in a side room, but it was hard to tell, as the entrance was obscured by several very able-bodied farmer types.

We received many a curious stare as we fought our way to the alcohol. I was relieved to see Johnny Power's friendly face behind the bar; I'd been starting to feel out of my depth. And there were Shem and Tom Delaney of the Rusty Teeth, sitting on the very same stools they'd occupied the first time I'd entered the pub. The thought that they'd been there ever since flitted across my mind. Perhaps they were Superglued to their stools by the seats of their pants. They were permanent fixtures and fittings, like the old photos and Guinness ads on the wall.

Johnny greeted me like an old friend. Any friend of Tyrone's …

'What are ye having, girls?'

'I'll get this,' piped up Chris. 'Three Cosmos, please.'

'What was that?'

'Three Cosmopolitans, please.'

'We don't sell magazines here, love. Try the newsagent's.'

Chris frowned at Johnny. It was hard to know whether he was serious or not. His expression was entirely deadpan.

I whispered into Chris's ear, 'I think you should try ordering something else.'

'Do you know how to do Sex on the Beach?'

'I do, love. Just give me a minute and I'll go and get me wellies.'

This time he *was* joking. Tom Delaney shook with gravelly laughter into his pint. Shem just stared at Chris, open-mouthed, like the little boy in the film when he sees E.T. for the first time.

Chris glanced back uncertainly at me and Hazel, who actually looked like she was starting to enjoy herself.

'Three Sexes on the Beach, please, Johnny,' I said. Or was it Sex on the Beaches?

'Why didn't you just say so in the first place?' He grinned at me as he took down the glasses, obviously enjoying this game of 'Let's make fun of the city folk'. He saw me glancing around for a seat.

'Why don't you join the missus over there? She's waiting for her pals to arrive.'

As we carried our drinks over to Bridie's table, Chris whispered to me, 'This place is very odd.'

I almost didn't recognise Bridie, resplendent as she was in a spangled top and high heels. She was seated at a small side table, with a dark-haired man.

'Well, is it yourself, Lainey? Sit down, pet.' She pulled out a chair for me.

I introduced the girls, and Bridie introduced the man at her side. 'This is my youngest, Matt.'

Matt nodded by way of greeting and smiled easily at the three of us. Not bad.

'You're the vet,' I said.

'And you're the solicitor.'

'You look very young to be a vet.' Now, that was a stupid thing to say.

'And you look too young to be a solicitor.'

'Thanks.'

My reflexes forced me to check his finger for a wedding ring. He wasn't wearing one. Still, this didn't prove anything; he might have lost it up a cow's arse.

It turned out he was twenty-seven, and two years

out of veterinary college. He wasn't unlike Jack in appearance – the same ocean-coloured eyes – but his colouring was darker: his hair was black and crinkly-looking, and he had that complexion peculiar to some Irish people, where they can have a tan and loads of freckles at the same time. (Although a tan in Ireland in October is impossible without the aid of artificial means or foreign travel.)

Bridie had the same dark colouring – although her hair was somewhat enhanced at this stage. Tonight, her eyes were emphasised by two bright-blue streaks of 70s-inspired eyeshadow.

No sooner had this thought entered my head than Chris said to Bridie, 'Are you going to an Abba tribute concert later on?' Under the table, Hazel and I kicked Chris in the right and left leg respectively. Above the table, Matt spluttered into his pint.

'Ow! What did you kick me for?' Chris looked dazed and confused.

Luckily, Bridie didn't get the reference. 'What a funny thing to say, child! I do like Abba, though. I'm going to see one of those letting-on Abba bands when they come to Kilkenny at Christmas.'

Bridie – the disco queen.

'Really?' Chris was wide-eyed. 'I'd love to go to that.'

'Well, you should get yourself a ticket and come down for it.'

'I think I will.' She looked very excited.

I heard Hazel hiss into her ear, 'Whatever you do, don't tell her you were Agnetha in a previous life.'

'I wasn't going to,' Chris replied sulkily.

Hazel changed the subject, just to be on the safe side. 'Will we go inside and listen to the music?'

So we did.

Along the way, Chris whispered to me, 'Do you think I should tell Bridie that the 70s-revival look is over? I wouldn't want her to make a fool of herself.'

I looked into her serious, frowning face.

'I think you should probably just say nothing.'

Chris led the way into the music room. The musicians and their groupies looked at her like the escaped lunatic that she was. Luckily, Bridie and Matt were with us to make the introductions and validate our presence. There was Eamonn, who played the fiddle; George, on the mandolin; Paddy, on drums and the occasional vocal. There were three accordion players, each operating at a different level of expertise. One of them, Dixie, was eighty-two years old, although he looked twenty years younger. He'd had his squeezebox since he was ten. When he played, he moved his mouth around in time to the music, as if he were sucking a toffee. An elegant blonde lady who answered to the name of Diane played the piano; then there was Conor on the bodhrán, and Margaret on the guitar. They very quickly forgot about us and turned their attention back to their reason for being there – and, very possibly, their reason for being: the music.

Without saying a word to each other, the mandolin player and one of the accordionists began to play a reel, at exactly the same moment. How did they know? Possibly they'd been playing together for so long that they knew which tune came next in the set. Perhaps they communicated by eye contact, or body language.

The music gathered momentum, growing in force as the other players joined in, each member involuntarily tapping a foot in time with the music. When the reel was finished they moved seamlessly into a jig, and then into another reel. At one point, Conor went to the bar, and Matt took his seat, picked up the bodhrán and started playing, as if it was the most natural thing in the world to do. The music leaped, whirled, galloped like a living creature. It acted like a drug or a prayer. Its cycles reminded me of ancient monks chanting: you didn't understand what they were saying, but you were sure it was something very deep and mystical and involving God in an important way.

At last the set ended, and all the spectators clapped enthusiastically. The players smiled happily at one another, their faces aglow with excitement and exertion. They knew with certainty that they were part of something good.

There was a short break for drinks, and then Paddy, the drummer, was called upon to sing. He delivered a stirring rendition of 'Red-Haired Mary'. Everyone who knew the words – which meant everyone except me, Chris and Hazel – sang along with the chorus. I badly wanted to know the words.

'Jack, you go next,' Paddy shouted towards the doorway when he'd finished.

'Yes, come on, Jackie,' several voices chorused.

My head swung towards the door. Jack was filling the doorway with his gigantic presence – he was what the locals called 'a hardy root'. Fancy Jack Power being here tonight, in Power's pub, of all places.

A feeling that might well have been glee swelled dangerously in my chest and threatened to escape from my throat in the form of a girlish giggle. I managed to quell it in the nick of time and transform it into a pleasant smile.

Look at me, I silently urged the massive figure in the doorway. *Look at me. I'm here. Waiting for you.*

You know how you can feel it when somebody is staring intently at you? You turn to look, although you don't know why; and there they are, staring. Jack's head turned slowly towards me, and we had one of those eye-locking movie moments. So I hadn't been imagining it, after all. It had been such a long time since I had experienced a frisson like this. It felt lovely. We seemed to stay like that for an age. I thought surely everyone in the room must have noticed, but they were too busy shouting out their requests. I tore my eyes away and stared at the floor. An empty pack of cigarettes and a discarded crisp packet.

'"Some Say the Divil is Dead"!'

'"Me Mother She was Orange"!'

'"Ride On"!'

'"The Men Behind the Wire"!'

'I know what I'll sing. May I?' Jack gestured to Margaret, who handed him her guitar. He pulled up a stool, sat down decisively and fiddled around with the instrument, tuning it to his satisfaction.

And then he started to sing Paul Brady's 'The Island'. You could have heard a cigarette butt drop. Every time he sang the line about making love to the sound of the ocean, he looked right at me. I swear to God!

(Where was the nearest ocean, anyway? Now probably wasn't a good time to ask.)

When he'd finished his song and the applause had died down, he squeezed onto the bench beside me. We didn't say anything, our thighs were touching.

'Mattie, you're next.'

Matt shook his head modestly.

'Come on, boy. Give us an oul' tune.'

All eyes were on Matt as the room fell silent once again. He half-closed his eyes and seemed to be focusing on a place many miles away. Then he started to sing 'Danny Boy'. I'd always hated that song – I'd associated it with the start of boxing matches. Until now.

In a voice of almost unbearable sweetness, Matt

brought his audience on an unforgetta
glen to glen and down the mountain
have heard the song hundreds of times;
I had never once noticed the poignar
lyrics? Maybe it took a talent like Matt's
them to life. As the song drew to a close, I
wiped a tear from the corner of my eye. I su
I wasn't the only one.

There were several moments of silence, fol
by a cacophony of whoops, claps and cheers.
leaned over and whispered into my left
'Talented little shit, isn't he?'

I turned and looked at him in surprise. Dic
detect a trace of bitterness?

'You're not exactly devoid of talent yourself, you
know.'

It was true. He was good – only not as good as
Matt.

'Do all your family sing, then?'

'Yeah. Either that or play an instrument.'

I was struck by an exciting idea. They could be
Ballyknock's answer to the Corrs, or the Nolan
Sisters – only with good-looking boys instead of
good-looking girls. I could be their manager! (The
Power Brothers. Haven't you heard of them?
They're huge in Turkey, you know.)

More drinks were bought all round, and somebody offered me a cigarette.

'No, thanks, I don't smoke,' I said without
missing a beat. Now why had I said that?

Who was I kidding? I knew exactly why. I'd said because Jack didn't smoke. He was the healthy, outdoorsy type. I had employed a similar tactic with Paul in the early days; it had lasted three months. The snag here was that Hazel was sitting to my right.

'Can I have a fag, Lainey?' she said.

'What are you asking *me* for? You know I don't smoke.' I shot her an urgent look.

'How come you've got a full pack of Marlboro Lights in your handbag, then?'

I whipped my head around to see if Jack was listening. Luckily, he was conversing with his number one fan – his mother.

'Give me a break, please, Hazel.'

'Why should I? It's obvious now why you dumped poor old Paul.'

'Don't know what you're talking about.'

She arched an eyebrow at me. 'Do I look stupid?'

Unfortunately for me, that was the last thing she was. *Damn! Why did I have to invite her down this weekend, anyway?*

'I'll buy you a Black Russian if you keep your mouth shut.'

'Two Black Russians.'

'Done. That's what I love about you accountants. You're so easily bribed.'

'Just one of our many sterling qualities.'

I reluctantly tore myself away from the heat of Jack Power's thigh and went to the bar. Chris was serving. How had that happened? She had removed

her Burberry cap and had haphazardly inserted about ten of the pink, little-girl hair-slides that were sold behind the bar into her wispy blonde strands. I hoped she'd paid for them. She was chatting enthusiastically to Shem, who was now wearing a Burberry baker-boy cap.

'Lainey!' she exclaimed, her face animated. 'Look at Shem. He has a Burberry coat!' She leant right across the bar, her feet no longer touching the floor, and opened Shem's overcoat to reveal the brown tartan lining.

'I bought it thirty year ago on a trip to London.'

And hadn't washed it since.

'Isn't he very stylish?'

'Oh, very.' I was sure Burberry would be using him in their next ad campaign. His was exactly the kind of image they were trying to convey.

'Did you want a drink?'

'Two Black Russians, please.'

'Are they both for Hazel?'

Now, how did she know that?

'How did you know that?'

'I'm psychic, aren't I?'

Psychotic, more like.

'I'd better make them both doubles, so.'

I didn't argue as she turned and started rattling various bottles. Shem watched, captivated; no doubt he was delighted with all the attention he was receiving from this young thing. He turned to me and grinned toothlessly.

'She pulls a grand pint, so she does.'

'That's not all she's good at pulling.'

'What was that?'

'Nothing.'

Tom of the Rusty Teeth had disappeared. I checked the floor under his stool, half-expecting to see him lying there in a pool of beer, but there was no sign of him.

'Two Black Russians.' Chris clinked the drinks down in front of me with a flourish.

'Don't you mean two outrageously camp Russians?'

The drinks were a sight to behold. The glasses were frosted, and each contained at least five cocktail umbrellas and a cocktail stick heavily laden with bits of orange and lemon and maraschino cherries. I paid Chris, anticipating my return to Jack's thigh.

'Are you coming back over, or what?' I asked her.

'Yeah, I'll come with you. See you later, Shem.'

Shem looked disappointed as Chris ducked under the counter and followed me into the music room.

The session was in full swing again, the room even more packed than before. I stood uncertainly in the doorway, a drink in either hand. I needn't have worried. Jack looked up and smiled, as if he'd been expecting me. He patted a tiny space on the bench to his right. I'd never get my backside in there. I fought my way towards the gap and plonked the drinks in front of my blackmailer.

'Two Del-Boy specials, Madam.'

Hazel didn't hear me. A red-faced man in his fifties was telling her how many head of cattle he owned. I turned my attention to manoeuvring myself back into my seat.

'You can sit on my knee if you like,' Jack said. It was a silly, flirtatious thing to say, but it still made me blush. Why didn't he ever blush? I wanted him to blush.

'You're okay.' I squeezed in – just about. I do think he could have made the effort to scooch up a little more. We were so close now that I was conscious of his every breath.

Nothing was said for the next while as everyone was carried along on the waves of the music. Only Chris and Bridie continued to natter. At one point, I heard Chris recommend sparkly blue nail-polish to Bridie, on the basis that it would exactly match her eyeshadow. She also thought it would be the perfect shade to wear to the Abba tribute concert. Bridie seemed delighted with the suggestion.

At one point, Johnny Power came in to collect empty glasses. He took one look at the piano stool, which happened to be empty just then, sat down on it and began to play. He stayed for three and a half songs. The empties piled up and there was no one serving behind the bar, but nobody seemed to care.

I wasn't a bad pianist, you know – even if I said so myself. My mother – after she had got over her initial disappointment that I wasn't going to be the next Jayne Torville – had sent me to piano lessons from an early age. Tatiana had been sent to trumpet lessons, for some strange reason. I had always been convinced that all that huffing and puffing accounted for her extraordinary chest development. All I'd got for my trouble was nimble fingers – handy if I ever decided to move over to the other side of the law and become a pickpocket, but otherwise entirely useless.

I had always quite enjoyed my piano lessons. My teacher was great – ever so slightly bonkers; unbeknownst to Mum, she rewarded me with sweets every time I did well. What I *hadn't* enjoyed was being dragged up, like a hapless heroine from a Jane Austen novel, to perform at family gatherings – a fate worse than death, to a teenager. These experiences had put me off playing for years. But tonight, I could feel my fingers itching to tinkle the ivories for the first time in ages. Maybe later on, after a few more drinks....

The set ended, to another raucous round of applause.

'Someone give us a song!'

'Me, me! I want to sing next.'

I froze. I felt Hazel freeze beside me. We exchanged a look of abject horror as Chris got up and pushed back the tables to clear a space for herself – a very bad sign. She stood excitedly within a circle of curious locals.

'Join in if you know the words.'

And then she launched into her version of Kylie's 'Can't Get You Out of My Head', complete with dance moves from the video. Chris was one of those rare people who really do dance as if no one is watching.

I couldn't look. I covered my eyes with both my hands. Okay, so she could just about hold a tune; but, my God, I'd never live this one down. I could feel Jack shaking with silent laughter beside me. About a minute into the number, I ventured to peek out between my fingers. I had to see the audience's reaction for myself. I glanced around at the incredulous expressions. Some of the men did look genuinely fascinated, but I suspected this was due to Christiana's short shorts and bra-less state more than to her musical prowess.

And then something very strange occurred. Someone started to clap. Judging from the direction of the sound, it may have been Bridie. I felt Jack join in beside me. The clapping spread like a Mexican wave. And then came the next chorus.

'La la la, la la la la la …'

This time it was definitely Bridie, singing along in her wavery old-lady voice.

'La la la, la la la la la …'

It was Matt. I took my hands away from my face and looked around the room.

'La la la, la la la la la …'

Johnny Power.

'La la la, la la la la la …'

201

Tom Delaney of the Rusty Teeth.

Then they were all singing. I could scarcely believe my eyes, or my ears. I had to hand it to her: the chick was a hit.

Eventually the night had to draw to a close. It was three in the morning, after all. For the first time in my life I had been in a lock-in, and I hadn't even noticed. The local garda sergeant, sitting congenially up at the bar, didn't seem to have noticed either.

Jack and I turned awkwardly to each other. I think I might have been more awkward than he was. I met his gaze with some difficulty.

He smiled at me. 'How long are your friends staying with you?'

'The rest of the weekend.'

'Is it okay if I call you during the week?'

Does the Pope shit in the woods? 'Yeah. Fine.'

'Talk to you then.'

'Okay. Bye.'

A swift kiss on the cheek (his lips, my cheek), and then he was gone. Just like that.

I decided I'd better go retrieve my guests.

Hazel was pissed. But it was nice pissed, not aggressive like at my going-away. She sat dozing happily in the corner of the music room – all the musicians had long since departed – a half-smile playing about her lips. The Black Russians had done the trick.

'Come on. Let's get you home to bed.' I tugged at her gently. She protested slightly before allowing herself to be shepherded towards the exit.

Now where was Chris? I asked Shem, who was up on his barstool, chatting to the sergeant.

'She left half an hour ago with young Mattie Power.'

He looked disgusted. Must have thought he was in with a chance.

Chapter Fifteen

Chris still hadn't shown up at eleven o'clock the next morning. I wasn't especially worried. I was working on my infamous mixed-grill special, the only 'meal' I could actually cook without screwing up. I was even wearing a pinny, which my mother had bought me in the vain hope that it would turn me into a cordon bleu chef by some strange feat of osmosis. She should have known better; we come from a long and illustrious line of bad cooks.

Hazel had just joined me. She was curled up on the couch reading yesterday's *Times*. She looked up suddenly and stared at the wall above the fireplace.

'Who *is* that old biddy? She keeps staring at me. It's giving me the creeps.'

I explained about Mary Power.

'Well, if I were you,' said Hazel, 'I'd stick her in a drawer. I don't know how you can bear it. Especially when you're on your own here at night.'

I didn't tell her that I sometimes chatted to the picture when I got lonely, and that I found it strangely comforting. Neither was I going to admit that I sometimes asked Mary a question before I went to bed and that, when I woke up the next morning, hey presto, I had the answer – waiting for me on my pillow, as it were. (Miraculously, this included legal advice.)

Hazel was wearing the most extraordinary pair of pyjamas. They were pink and fleecy, and the legs didn't stop at the ankles but encased her whole feet, like a giant baby-gro. I was on the verge of asking her where on earth she'd come across this item when the relative silence of the morning was disturbed by the sound of a car coming up the hill.

I looked out of the window, and my heart performed a little somersault as I recognised Jack's jeep. What was he doing here? He wasn't meant to contact me until next week. I started to panic as I visualised the state I was in. But – hold on …

The jeep pulled up outside the house. That wasn't Jack in the driver's seat; it was Matt. And out of the passenger door jumped Chris, still resplendent in last night's outfit.

'Bye, Matt! Thanks for a lovely night!' Chris waved merrily at him and ran up to the front door of the cottage. Matt grinned back at her and then gave me a wave as he spotted me peeking out of the window at him. *Damn! Busted!* How embarrassing – for me, that was; he didn't look the least bit fazed. Not an ounce of shame between the two of them! I would have been mortified.

I let Chris in. She bounded into the house, causing the dog, who had been fast asleep in his corner, to leap to his four furry paws and bark frenetically. The peace of the morning had now been officially shattered.

'Did you have a good time, then?' Was that bitterness or sarcasm in Hazel's tone? Either one was wasted on Chris. She slumped down on the couch beside Hazel, arms and legs splayed, and stretched luxuriantly like Slinky the cat.

'I,' she said, pausing for dramatic effect, 'have just had the night of my life.'

'Really?' I was suddenly extremely interested. I threw down my spatula and sat on the arm of the couch beside Chris. 'Tell us more.'

'Omigod. How can I possibly begin to describe the experience?'

'Try!'

She sat up abruptly, hands placed neatly between Burberry knees. 'Well. First of all, girls, did you know that he's the seventh son of a seventh son?'

'No!'

'Don't tell me you believe in that old baloney,' said Hazel dismissively – although, if you ask me, she looked pretty interested in spite of herself.

206

Chris ignored the remark. 'He has healing hands!' The triumphant statement hung suspended in the air. Hazel and I exchanged confused looks.

'What's that got to do with last night?'

'Well ...' She lowered her voice, drawing us in. 'He knows *just* what to do with his hands and *exactly* when to do it. I'm telling you, girls, no nook or cranny was left untouched. Every time I thought of what I wanted him to do – he just did it. It was like he could read my mind.'

I was enthralled. Hazel looked as if she might start drooling at any second.

'And as for his tongue! Every crevice licked to perfection.' Chris slumped back into the couch like a Victorian damsel swooning. 'I've never known a man to do such things with his tongue. Not ever. And I've been with quite a few men, as you know.'

We knew, all right. A cast of thousands.

'And as for his –'

'Oh, please. We really don't want to hear this. We're just about to have sausages.'

Speak for yourself, Hazel! 'I want to know.'

Chris closed her eyes and placed her hand over her heart. 'It was just beautiful. The whole experience. Simply sublime.' She sighed. 'It was like being touched by the hand of God.'

Hazel snorted. 'How can you compare a tawdry one-night stand to a religious experience? I've never heard anything so ridiculous.'

Chris studiously ignored her again. It was

becoming something of a habit. She turned to me. 'Lainey, you should give him a go. You won't regret it.'

'I will not "give him a go"!' I tried to look indignant but ended up laughing. I thought of Jack and wondered if such skills ran in the family....

'I'm telling you, you don't know what you're missing.'

'Are you seeing him again?'

'Don't be daft.'

Silly me.

'And you too, Hazel. When was the last time you had a good seeing-to?'

I looked on in horror as Hazel's features contorted in fury. 'I don't need "a good seeing-to", thank you very much.'

'If you ask me, that's exactly what you need. Stop you obsessing about that job of yours.'

'Well, I'm very sorry, but we can't *all* work in pathetic nothing jobs and get paid exorbitant sums for doing fuck-all.'

'Hazel! That's enough.'

But there was no stopping her. 'And just because you get sluttier and sluttier every day doesn't mean that we all have to act like out-and-out whores.' And with that she slammed out of the room, leaving two open-mouthed women in her wake.

Just then, a loud, insistent wailing sound erupted out of thin air. It took me a few seconds to recognise it as the smoke alarm.

That was all I needed. Burnt sausages.

208

As it turned out, neither Hazel nor Chris got to sample the charred remains of my breakfast. Hazel packed immediately and demanded that I drive her directly to the train station. Chris was gone by the time I got back. I didn't know it then, but it was the last time I was to see them together for a long time. Looking back, I should have known. It was inevitable, really.

Jack rang me on Tuesday. Perfect timing. If he had called a day later, I would have had no choice but to turn him down for that weekend. Wasn't that one of the Ten Commandments of the new dating rules? Or did the fact that the pace of life was slower in the countryside mean that he could have got away with ringing me on Wednesday? Anyway, we weren't going out at the weekend – not yet, anyway; we were going out on Wednesday night. Hold on – I had agreed to that, just one day in advance! I began to panic. He was going to think I was some desperate tart.

This kind of obsessive nonsense ran round and round in my head like a hamster on one of those wheels, never stopping, going nowhere. It had been a long time, you see, since I had 'dated' anyone. I had become so comfortable in my little routine with Paul. I tried to cast my mind back to the early days of our romance.

Paul had come along at a time when I had just started to attract men again after a long barren period. It was as if I suddenly began producing a strange and powerful pheromone. I knew love was in the air; I just didn't know who with. I had felt Paul coming. About two weeks before I met him, some mysterious force had compelled me to buy several sets of decent underwear, despite the fact that I'd had no use for such garments for well over a year.

But had I experienced this heady mixture of excitement and high anxiety with Paul? If so, I certainly couldn't recall it now. I had been happy, sure; but, right from the very beginning, it had been like wearing a comfy pair of slippers. I never worried that I was saying the wrong thing. There were no mind-games. You always knew where you were with Paul. He rang when he said he was going to ring, showed up when he said he was going to show up. Good old steady, reliable Paul.

Not that I was accusing Jack of playing mind-games. It's just that I wasn't sure how much he liked me – what he wanted from me. And it had been the longest time since I'd experienced this not entirely unpleasant out-of-control sensation. I had known from the start that Paul was in love – big-headed as that may sound. How had Hazel put it? I'd always had the upper hand.

But times had changed. Paul hadn't returned any of my calls. I was secretly relieved; what would I have said if he had? I rang and left messages on his machine when I knew he'd be in work or at soccer practice. It eased the guilt – somewhat. From time to time I asked Hazel how he was getting on. 'Fine,' she'd say.

Fine. What did that mean? Her obsession with her job had turned her into a lousy informant.

I got a 'lovely surprise' that Thursday. Mum and Dad, who had been in Cork for a few days, were going to drop in and pay me a visit on their way home. If I was 'very lucky', they might even be persuaded to stay the night.

The house was in bits. And I only had an hour to do something about it. These days, I didn't just have to contend with my own impressive capacity to make a right royal mess; Terence was even dirtier than I was.

I had discovered that, though there were many advantages to owning a dog, a clean house was not one of them. The biggest advantage was an ecstatic welcoming committee when I came home in the evening; if only I were as wonderful as he thought I was. There was also the incentive to get off my fat, blubbery arse once in a while to bring him for a walk. Then there was his uncanny ability to tell when I was down in the dumps. He would rest his chin heavily in my lap and look up at me imploringly with his brown Smartie eyes – although he did tend to do this quite a lot around dinner-time, so his motives may not have been entirely pure. He was also excellent at hoovering crumbs up off the carpet. A more dubious plus: I'd be lying on the couch, half-asleep; I would be vaguely aware of a wet, snuffly sound, but before I could sense any real danger, a sloppy wet lick would be administered to my nose and mouth. Completely disgusting, but it never failed to make me laugh. I knew that a lot of the locals, Patricia being a case in point, thought I was insane to give a dog the full run of the house; but what would be the point of having a dog for company if I was inside all the time and he was outside?

The downsides to owning a dog: hair all over the carpets, mucky paw-prints on the kitchen floor and, last but not least, the fragrance of Eau de Canine permeating the entire cottage.

I decided to tackle the smell first. I threw open every window in the house and steeled myself as the chill November air filtered in. Then I sprayed half a can of emergency air freshener through the entire building, making the cat flee in terror. Disgusting stuff, I thought as I choked, but this did qualify as an emergency.

Next job: hoover the carpet. Easier said than done; the pathetic hoover that had come with the cottage had all the power of a travel hairdryer. I attempted to vacuum up all traces of dog. In the end, I had to give this up as a bad job.

I spent the next forty-five minutes in a frenzy of scrubbing, wiping, dusting and polishing. Well, actually, I didn't really polish; I just sprayed the polish into the air to make it smell as if I had. I had read this handy household tip in a magazine once, and it sounded very clever to me. All I needed now was some of that spray that made it smell like you were baking bread, and the illusion would be complete.

I was just slipping on the last clean pillowcase, whilst simultaneously shoving junk under the bed with my foot, when Dad's Volvo pulled into the driveway. I literally wiped the sweat from my brow and surveyed my handiwork proudly. Result! Nobody would ever have known that a slob lived here.

'Elena! You look wretched, my dear. Did you have a tough day at the office?'

'Something like that, Mum.'

'Rosie.' Dad nodded at me and followed Mum into the house, carrying what looked suspiciously like an overnight bag. 'You do look a bit rough.'

Thanks. 'Cup of tea?'

'That would be lovely.'

My mother is a very generous woman. On this particular occasion, she had brought me the following presents:

- A cookbook; another to add to my pristine and rapidly growing collection
- A pot plant; yet another for me to kill. I'd give this one two weeks
- A plastic Virgin Mary key-holder that had been blessed in Medjugorje ('I'll have to check with Tyrone before I go hammering things into his

wall'). How she managed to reconcile her religious beliefs with her New Age mumbo-jumbo, I could never understand.

Dad had just brought himself. He sat in the nearest armchair and read his newspaper as Mum nattered on.

They didn't want a meal – God, no – tea and biscuits were grand. They'd stopped off for pub grub along the way. Oh, wasn't this cottage charming? So quaint, yet so tastefully decorated. The wooden ceilings were so high – very attractive feature, but, of course, so difficult to keep clean. No wonder I'd had such difficulty in reaching those old cobwebs in the corner. (*What cobwebs? Oh, shit.*) And just one more thing – I wasn't to take this the wrong way, but, next time I was expecting visitors, it really would be a good idea to hoover up the dog hair.

Talking of said dog, I let him in at my mother's request, and he immediately set about re-destroying the carpet. His attempts to ingratiate himself with his new grandparents were as shameful as they were successful, earning him four Jammie Dodgers.

'What's his name?'

'Terence.'

The dog woofed softly in approval. It was a stupid name, if you asked me, but he seemed to like it. I had tried all week to get him to answer to Jasper, but no: Terence it was.

As Mum cooed over Terence, it occurred to me that my father was being unusually quiet.

'What's up, Dad? Tired after the journey?'

'Your father's lost his job. He's been made redundant.'

Dad visibly winced, although he didn't look up – just turned another page.

'Oh, my God! I'm sorry, Dad. That's terrible.'

'Ah, it's not so bad. I'll get a good package out of it.' He still didn't look up.

Imagine. After all these years, his prophecies of doom and gloom had finally come true. I'd have to get him to help me pick this week's Lotto numbers.

'Are you going to look for another job?'

Dad was sixty.

'I haven't decided yet. I might treat it as an early retirement.' He looked up at me this time, as if seeking approval.

'That's not a bad idea,' I said.

Mum tutted. 'It's a terrible idea. What's he going to do all day long?'

I stared at her in surprise. She sounded really angry, as if it were all Dad's fault or something.

To change the subject, I launched into an account of 'my life in the country'. I wasn't long into a description of Patricia and Bridie's vicious jam war when Mum interrupted.

'Have you heard from Tatiana lately?'

'We e-mail each other about once a week.'

'Hmph. You're lucky. We haven't had so much as a phone call since your father chased her back to China.'

'I did not chase her anywhere, woman. She decided to go back early of her own accord.'

'Only because you made it clear she wasn't welcome in her own home.'

'I did no such thing. I just told her a few home truths.'

'Oh, you're impossible. You make sure you hold on to Paul, Elena. Never marry a man who'd rather make his family miserable than admit he's in the wrong. Now I'm going to bed. Elena, show me my room, please. And I'm not sharing with that man tonight.'

Since it was a two-bedroom cottage, I had no option but to let Mum bunk down with me. After ranting on about Dad for an hour, she finally fell into an exhausted stupor.

Thank God they'd be gone tomorrow when I got home from work.

I lay there for at least another hour, unable to drop off. I wasn't thinking about Mum. I wasn't thinking about Dad, or about Annie. I wasn't even thinking about Jack, for a change.

I was thinking about Paul.

I should have told my parents about our break-up. It had been the ideal opportunity. But somehow I hadn't been able to bring myself to do it. I had to come to terms with it myself first. Before that night, I'd thought I had; but evidently not. Realistically, I don't know why this surprised me. We had been together a full year. I supposed these things took time to get over, even when you were the dumper and not the dumpee.

Poor Paul.

I had made him a dumpee.

Chapter Sixteen

As I stood at the edge of the frosty hurling pitch, that Sunday morning, I forced uncomfortable thoughts of my problem parents out of my mind. I chose to focus instead on the fabulous Thai restaurant that Jack had taken me to the night before. Who knew that such a place existed in the wretched provinces?

Let's face it: I had to focus on something other than my current reality. What the hell was I doing there, anyway? I had to be mad (madly in love?). Jack had no clue what a huge compliment this was. Paul had never succeeded in dragging me along to one of his precious soccer games. I had sacrificed not only my essential Sunday-morning lie-in, but also my customary leisurely brunch accompanied by *The Sunday Times*.

Apparently this match was, and I quote, 'vital'. Vital to what, exactly, I had no idea. In my opinion, all sports were only as important – or unimportant – as you chose to make them. Despite the best efforts of a thermal vest, two jumpers, my winter coat, a scarf, a pair of gloves and a woolly hat, I was still fucking freezing.

It was official: hell had frozen over.

This had better be bloody well worth my while.

I was considering slinking back to the warm cocoon of my bed when the pitch was suddenly invaded by fifteen – twenty – twenty-five – thirty pairs of milky-white legs. They were so white as to be practically offensive. Where were my Ray-bans when I needed them? The effect was heightened by the minute 70s-inspired shorts that the players were wearing. Jack's team wore green and gold – matching socks and all; the other team was clad in red and white. Some players wore helmets; more didn't. I watched, mildly interested, as they ran around the mucky pitch, slicing the still morning air with their hurleys and hitting imaginary *sliotar*s between the posts.

Jack ran over to where I was standing. How he recognised me I'll never know; the only parts of me not buried under five inches of wool were my eyes and nose. And I was seriously considering covering them up too. Who needed to breathe? I was more concerned about frostbite. I had visions of icicles forming on my brows and lashes and the liquid part of my eyes freezing over. I kept blinking, just to be on the safe side.

Jack was all smiles, as usual. 'Lainey, you came! Thanks. I know this isn't your scene.'

I pulled the scarf down past my chin. 'Rubbish. I love hurling. Wouldn't miss this for the world.'

He looked at me doubtfully. 'See you after?'

'Definitely.'

He ran off to join the other twenty-nine masochists running half-naked about the pitch.

Just then, a gust of wind sawed right through me. *Jesus Christ!* I looked around at the other spectators. Amazingly, there were about sixty of us now, standing around the sidelines, freezing our butts off. I knew why I was there; what was their excuse? They couldn't all fancy Jack.

A man in black blew his whistle, and the battle commenced. To pass the time, I tried to work out the rules. I knew all about soccer, by osmosis; this couldn't be very different. Another load of eejits in pursuit of a differently shaped ball. I wondered if the offside rule applied to hurling too. Paul had spent many an hour trying to explain this particular piece of male nonsense to me, until I was blue in the face and he was purple.

I did my best to follow the intricacies of the game. My confusion wasn't eased by the fact that most of the players were called P.J., D.J. or J.J. –

except Jack, of course; oh, and Matt, who was playing on the same team. It was clear from the outset, even to my untrained eye, that Mr Healing Hands was the best player on the pitch. Jack had been right: he was a talented little shit. Jack was good, but Matt was better.

Jack's team – Ballymuck Rovers, or whatever they called themselves – took an early lead, largely due to Matt's striking prowess. Another thing hurling and soccer had in common: all the hugging. Jack and a large blond man jumped on each other enthusiastically, even though neither of them had scored that particular goal. Typical repressed males: sport was the only way they felt capable of expressing their affection towards one another.

The game wasn't half as boring as I'd feared. It was fast-paced and, quite frankly, alarmingly dangerous. I had played hockey in school, and that could be vicious enough at times; but at least the hockey sticks were kept relatively close to the ground. Here, every second swipe of the hurleys barely missed a head. In fact, just before half-time, one poor soul took an almighty whack on the nose. It started to pump blood, but nobody took a blind bit of notice – including the bloke with the bloody nose. It made Premiership players with their grazed eyebrows look like complete wimps.

Two male spectators standing close by commented that it was probably broken, but not to worry: that was the fifth time J.J. had got his nose broken, and it had set funny the last time, so this would probably improve the look of it anyway. So there you had it: not so much a broken nose as a blessing in disguise.

The crowd were even more entertaining than the match. The first year I qualified as a solicitor, I worked almost exclusively in criminal law. This meant I spent my days in courtrooms, police stations and prisons, often in the company of drug addicts and hardened criminals. But never in my life had I heard bad language the likes of what I heard on the side of that hurling pitch in Ballyknock.

A man who must have been a coach or a manager paced up and down the sideline next to me. The air above his head was electric blue.

'Come on, ye fuckin' little bollixes! Would ye ever get the fuckin' *sliotar* over the fuckin' bar? It's fuckin' hurlin' you're meant to be playing, not fuckin' table tennis…. Oh! Great fuckin' hurl! …'

The half-time whistle blew, and a smattering of applause broke out amongst the spectators. I clapped too – at least, I took my hands out of my pockets and brought them together several times. I couldn't actually feel them at this stage.

The two teams separated into huddles, psyching themselves up for the second half. I stamped my feet and fantasised about hot chocolate topped with fresh cream and real chocolate shavings.

Then they were off again, with renewed vigour. ('That's the ball! Great fuckin' hurl! He's a tasty player, all right! Come on, P.J., give 'em hell!') The game was just beginning to flow again when a skirmish broke out. I didn't see the incident that caused the row, but, for some reason, D.J. punched P.J. in the gob, causing him to fall backward onto the ground. D.J. then jumped on top of P.J.'s chest and attempted to throttle him. At this point, J.J. took it upon himself to intervene, trying to pull D.J. off P.J.. He got an elbow in the kidneys for his trouble, which made him crumple like an accordion. Then, all of a sudden, there were about ten players in the melée, flailing and kicking and punching. It was great – just like a barroom brawl in a Western.

It took a while for the ref to restore order. He booked five players and sent two of them off. I was about to lead a chant of 'Who's the Bastard in the Black', which was the only proper football song I knew, but I thought better of it (my reputation as a respectable local solicitor, etcetera, etcetera). One of the players sent off was P.J.. He limped forlornly off the pitch, a lone warrior, blood streaming from his mouth, holding one of his teeth tenderly in his left hand. Not to worry, said the man beside me. He still had at least four left.

Jack's team won. Of course they did. The players walked, limped and crawled off the pitch, covered in varying shades of blood and muck. Even if you had missed the whole match, all you had to do was look at their expressions to tell who had won and who had lost.

An exhilarated Jack called out to me, 'Are you coming to Power's?'

I nodded. Why not? A hot toddy was definitely in order.

Half an hour later I was happily ensconced in Power's pub, a freshly showered Jack sitting beside me. He was practically glowing with fitness after his morning's exertions. An aura of rude good health surrounded him. Me, I was just glad to have the feeling back in my extremities.

'I'm afraid I have a confession to make,' Jack said.

'What?' I was immediately on my guard.

'I brought you here today under false pretences.'

I frowned. 'Go on.'

He sighed. 'The mammy wanted me to invite you to Sunday lunch.'

'Really? Why?' I was fishing now.

'She wants to get to know my new girlfriend better.' His expression was deadly serious.

'I'd like to meet your new girlfriend too. Let me know when she gets here.'

'Don't tease. Will you come for your dinner?'

'Sure.'

He drained his pint glass and rose to his feet. 'Come on, then.'

'What – now?'

'It's two o'clock. We don't want to keep the family waiting.'

The family? Oh, no.

I nearly ran back out of the Powers' kitchen the second I walked in. Did I happen to mention that Jack was one of seven brothers? Well, they were out in force that afternoon. Along with various wives, girlfriends and partners.

'This is Paidi, the eldest, his wife Joan and their three lovely children. And this is Mickey Joe and his wife Molly – Molly's expecting in June. Jimmy and Mags. Gerry and Anne. Little Timmy ...' Timmy was a mere six foot – the runt of the litter. 'And you already know Matt.' I smiled and nodded at all and sundry. *Thanks, Jack.* Talk about the deep end.... I felt in imminent danger of drowning.

Luckily for me, after a few initial curious glances, 'the family' turned their attention back to the food. Johnny stood at the head of the table (which they must have had specially made to accommodate everyone), carving the meat like the father out of *The Waltons*. He just winked at me. Soon I was ignored completely as everyone lost themselves in the aromas and juices of Bridie's unsurpassable roast, excellent spuds and flawless gravy – a far cry from my own mother's burnt offerings. I made a mental note never to cook for Jack.

When everybody had finished, two of the wives/girlfriends automatically got up and cleared away the dirty plates, Bridie doled out generous helpings of home-made trifle from an industrial-sized bowl, and we all tucked in again.

A toddler with a snot-encrusted nose had taken a shine to me. She clung to my leg and stared up at me, finger in nostril. I tried not to let this put me off my dessert.

Her slightly elder brother was also a nosy little blighter. 'Are you Jack's girlfriend?' He gazed up at me solemnly.

My face turned the same colour as the sherry trifle – minus the custard and cream. Although the family were pretending to concentrate on their food, I could sense that every pair of ears in the room was pricked up, dying to hear my answer.

'No. I'm just his friend.'

'Then why is he holding your hand under the table?'

'Danny!' The child's mother, clearly horrified, jumped up and dragged her son away from me by the arm. 'Don't be bothering our guest. Go out and play with your new bike.'

'But he was –'

'Do what you're told. Scoot!'

The mother shot me a pained, apologetic look as she returned to the table. I, in the meantime, had invented a new shade of puce. The brothers exchanged knowing smirks. Matt audibly sniggered. I made a mental note to kill Jack, if I ever made it out of there alive.

Various women got up again to clear away the dessert bowls and make the tea. I was unsure what was expected of me – being female and all – so I started to get up to bring my bowl to the sink. Several women immediately descended upon me, removed the bowl from my hand and pinned me back down in the chair. It seemed I was getting a special dispensation because I was new. I wondered what Bridie had done before her sons' partners came along. Had she done everything herself? The idea was horrifyingly plausible: the Irish Supermammy fulfilling her sons' every need. Yet another generation of Irish men ruined. If Jack expected that kind of treatment from me, he could feck off.

At last the tea had been consumed and it was time to go. I tried not to run. Bridie saw us to the door.

'That was gorgeous, Bridie. You could open your own restaurant and charge whatever prices you wanted. Thank you for inviting me.' Sometimes I almost nauseated myself.

But it was the right thing to say. Bridie beamed with pleasure. 'Oh, not at all. You're welcome any time. Any friend of Jack's ...' She twinkled.

I turned on him as soon as we were out of earshot.

'You bastard!'

'What?' He was all fake innocence.

'That was a terrible position to put me in. I nearly died when I saw them all sitting there.'

'But you knew I had a big family.'

This was a valid point, so I decided to ignore it. 'That's not the point.' (What was the point?)

'Don't you like my family, then?'

'Don't be silly. They seem very nice. You should have given me more warning, that's all.'

'But it went really well.'

'Do you think so?'

'Yeah, absolutely. You made a great impression.'

'Really?' I was desperate to believe him. Quite pathetic.

'Yes. They all loved you.' He reached over and wrapped his massive arms around my waist.

What can I say? I was disarmed.

Chapter Seventeen

I went out with Jack twice during the following week. The chaste kisses on the cheek turned into slightly less chaste kisses on the lips. Still no tongues. Still no touchy-feely stuff. My body was a throbbing mass of frustration. It was just that I fancied Jack so much. I wanted to jump his bones every time I saw him. I suppose I should have been glad that he was so respectful, but respect was the last thing I wanted. Aretha Franklin and I would have to agree to differ.

So I decided to let him know what he was missing and go to Dublin for the weekend. Alone. It wasn't just a tactic; I felt as if I'd been neglecting Hazel and Chris lately, even though they'd only just been down. Hazel had rung a couple of times the week after they'd gone back, leaving desperate messages, begging me to come to Dublin for the weekend. I had shamefully ignored these messages, for two reasons: I needed a break from all their rowing, and I had more important, Jack-shaped fish to fry. But that couldn't be right. I wasn't the kind of woman who dumped her girlfriends the second an interesting man came along.

Was I?

It was with some trepidation that I let myself into the flat in Dublin that Friday night. A kindly neighbour had agreed to feed Slinky. Terence wasn't with me. I couldn't really visualise him in our tiny apartment; he'd knock everything over with his tail. Mum had generously agreed to have him any time I was in Dublin. My parents had a huge, old-fashioned, suburban garden; Terence was probably digging up bulbs and urinating on rosebushes that very second. I did suspect my mother of an ulterior motive. If she agreed to dog-sit, it meant I had to call in and see her – twice. Not that I resented her ploy. She already had one estranged daughter; I knew she'd never survive another one. She had tried to coax me into staying the night, but I had stubbornly refused. Any sign of clinginess tended to send me packing in the other direction.

So there I was, in the hall of the flat.

'Anybody home?' I called out as I sifted through the pile of junk mail beside the telephone. There was no reply, but I could hear strange music emanating from Chris's room. It sounded like many monks chanting. She was either meditating or engaged in a very strange orgy; you never knew with her. The pungent scent of joss sticks hit me hard in the nostrils as I passed her door. I went into the sitting room.

'Hello!'

I experienced a very funny feeling in my tummy. Something similar to the sensation of going down in a lift.

'Hello.' I couldn't see myself, but I knew the colour was draining from my cheeks.

'Long time no see.'

'How have you been?'

'Fine.' There was that stupid word again. Encompassing everything, signifying nothing.

Paul was seated on one of the high stools by the breakfast bar, nursing what looked like a mug of coffee. He seemed comfortable – physically, anyway; he had changed out of his work gear and his jacket lay slung across the couch.

What was he doing here? I searched his face for clues. Inscrutable. All I could think of was the last time we had seen each other – me the cold-hearted bitch, and him the broken man. He didn't look broken today. He just looked like ... well ... like Paul.

'How are your parents?' he asked.

That was good. Neutral topic. Talk about family. 'Fine. They ask about you all the time.'

'You haven't told them that you dumped me, then?'

Gulp!

Again, his facial expression was completely unreadable.

'No. I haven't told them.' My voice came out small. Humble.

Not that it would have made any difference if I had. They would just have gone on about him even more – what a grand, upstanding young man he was, every parent's dream son-in-law; what was I thinking of, letting him escape, when I wasn't getting any younger, or for that matter any thinner?

'How's your mum?' I asked. Resume politeness. Ignore awkwardness.

'Oh – you know. Just the same. Mad as a fruit.'

I nodded sympathetically.

Paul's mum was a religious lunatic. She went to Mass every day and twice on holy days. You couldn't move in her house without knocking over a statuette of the Blessed Virgin or a headless Child of Prague. Once a year she went on a two-week sun holiday: Lourdes one year, Fatima the next. (The year before, in Fatima, her rosary beads had turned to solid gold because of all the heavy-duty praying.) She did indulge in the odd long weekend, mind you. Lough Derg or Croagh Patrick. I suspected she flagellated herself when there was no one home, and wore dresses made out of sackcloth – whatever that was.

Paul was an only child (probably the result of the one and only time Mrs O'Toole had had sex). His father had run off with a stripper (I kid you not) when Paul was five years old. You couldn't blame the poor guy, really. It was rough on Paul, though. He hardly ever mentioned his dad. All I knew was that he lived in England and that they never saw each other.

When he was six years old, Paul had tried to crucify himself in the back garden. He had found a few bits of plywood and some rusty nails left behind by his father. He'd had to be rushed to Accident and Emergency. It was a wonder he was as sane as he was. And no wonder he was so fond of my family. Okay, they were mildly dysfunctional at times, but at least they weren't completely barking. We were what our middle-aged neighbours called 'a lovely family' – husband an executive, wife a home-maker; 2.4 daughters, one a teacher, the other a solicitor; went to Mass every Sunday…. You never know what goes on behind closed doors.

I had made a bad impression the one and only time I had been invited to Paul's mother's house for dinner. My first boo-boo had been bringing a bottle of wine with me. Alcohol was strictly for-bidden in the O'Toole household (Paul's mother still thought he was a Pioneer). I had felt like saying something sarcastic about the blood of Christ, but had managed to restrain myself. My next faux pas had been sitting down to dinner without washing my hands first ('Cleanliness is next to godliness, Elena!'). But, most heinous crime of all, I had started to eat before saying grace. I hadn't been back to the house since. This arrangement suited all parties – the mother, the son and the unholy girlfriend.

To tell the truth, I'd always been a bit miffed that I hadn't been able to charm Paul's mother. My other boyfriends' parents had all loved me – even when said boyfriends hadn't. They'd considered me a nice, sensible girl with prospects and good child-bearing hips; a little prim and proper, perhaps, but surely that was a good trait in a prospective daughter-in-law. And I came from a good family, too – whatever that meant.

But that was all in the past, and it was high time I concentrated on the present, which was sitting on a stool and staring at me in a distinctly cool manner. I wasn't accustomed to being on the receiving end of such a stare from Paul. It was disconcerting; it made him seem like a stranger. I had seen hurt in his eyes before, sure; anger, annoyance, impatience. Love. But never this cold, calculating appraisal.

I took a deep breath. 'You never returned my calls.'

'You always rang when you knew I'd be out.'

This was getting worse. Of course, I didn't blame him. I felt sorry for him, really. I'd moved on to a new and better relationship with Jack. He was all alone.

'Look, Paul, I know you're angry with me, but if you've come here tonight for a row, I'm not –'

'I haven't come for a row.'

'Then what –'

With her usual impeccable timing, Chris burst through the door. 'Oh, hi, Lainey. I didn't hear you come in. Hi, Paul. How long have you been here?'

What? Surely she had let him in?

'Is Hazel in her room, then?'

Paul and Chris exchanged a funny look.

'What is it?'

Another funny look. Then Chris said, 'Haven't you heard? She said she'd ring and let you know.'

'Let me know what?'

'Hazel moved out. She left on Monday.'

'But why?' A stupid question in the circumstances, I know, but I'd had quite a shock.

'We had another row.' Chris's tone was flat, matter-of-fact. She started to busy herself around the kitchen.

I sat in silence for a minute or so, absorbing this news.

'Where's she gone?'

'Back to her parents.'

'I suppose we'd better advertise for a new flatmate.'

'No need. It's all sorted. I've got somebody already.' Chris smiled proudly.

'Oh?' Surely we should have discussed it first. 'Anyone I know?'

As if on cue, we all heard the bathroom door opening. And then the footsteps in the hall, growing louder. And then the door slowly opening.

And in walked Iseult.

Oh. My. God.

'Hello, Elena!' She beamed.

'Hello, Iseult!' I beamed back.

I was going to fucking kill Chris.

I knew that wasn't fair. How was she supposed to know I hated Iseult? Hadn't I always pretended – for diplomatic reasons – that I liked her, that I didn't in fact think she was a shallow, vacuous, vicious carbuncle of a human being? All that had happened here was that my own hypocrisy had come back to slap me hard in the face. Still, I wished Chris had discussed it with me first.

Could this evening possibly get any worse?

Apparently it could. Iseult padded over to Paul, placed her long, elegant, lightly tanned arms about his neck, kissed him on the lips and said, 'Sorry to keep you waiting, darling.'

Darling?

My brain was performing cartwheels at this stage. A billion questions flew about inside my head, threatening to collide into one another. *How long has this been going on? What does he see in her? Why does she have to keep stroking his head? Has she met his mother yet? (Obviously not, or she wouldn't still be with him.) Has he completely lost his senses?*

Iseult was going all out to mark her territory. She

fluttered around Paul, cooing and touching him. Skinny bitch! Why didn't she just pee on his shoes and have done with it? Paul, in the meantime, was looking distinctly uncomfortable. He caught my eye on one occasion and quickly looked away. I badly wanted to retreat to my bedroom, but I wasn't going to give Iseult the satisfaction. I preferred to bite off my nose to spite my face. I resolutely sat down on the couch, turned on the TV and stared mindlessly at the screen.

'Paul….' Iseult's voice was wheedling and needlessly loud. 'Will you help me put my necklace on?'

'Sure.'

I knew I shouldn't look, but I couldn't help myself. My eyes were inextricably drawn towards them, as if to a horrific car accident.

Iseult had somehow managed to manoeuvre her body in between Paul's knees, her back to him. She held up her hair with one hand, exposing the nape of her neck. She met my eye gleefully.

Paul's face was a study in concentration. I watched him fiddling around with the delicate catch of the necklace, his brow furrowed.

'There.' He succeeded in fastening it, and Iseult let her hair fall back down over her neck. She turned and kissed him on the mouth.

'Thank you, darling.'

Paul failed to respond, either physically or verbally. I could tell he was conscious of the weight of my stare.

After what seemed like several aeons, the two lovebirds gathered up their jackets and made to leave.

'Bye, guys. Oh, hold on, Paul – I just need to pay a quick visit to the bathroom.'

What, again? I sincerely hoped that the poor girl didn't have diarrhoea.

Paul was left standing like a spare part in the centre of the room. He shifted uneasily from one foot to the other.

'Lainey?'

'What.' I didn't look up at him.

'I'm really sorry if this was awkward for you. I wanted to meet in the pub, but Iseult said she'd prefer to meet here.'

I bet she did.

'You see, she gets nervous waiting for people in pubs on her own.'

Yeah, right. That girl had never been afraid of anything in her entire life.

I looked up at him. 'Don't worry about it, Paul. You two go out and enjoy yourselves. No hard feelings on my part.' I could have won first prize in a fake-smile competition.

'Night, then. Night, Chris.'

And he was gone.

I felt Chris looking at me.

'You all right?'

'I need a drink.'

Several vodka smoothies later, I was nearly all right. It was just like old times.

Minus Hazel.

The row that had broken the camel's back sounded laughably pathetic. Chris had used the last of the milk to make a 'health drink'. When Hazel came into the kitchen to fix herself a coffee and discovered that there was no milk left, she went bananas.

'And I was just about to go down to the corner shop to replace it.'

'I'm sure you were.'

'I was!'

'I believe you, Chris. I wasn't being sarcastic.'

'Oh – sorry. Well, I was. And I told her so. I even offered her a glass of my health drink to tide her over until I came back, but she just went mental.'

I could picture the scene. Chris's health drinks were evil-smelling concoctions made of stuff like wheatgrass juice, tripe and diced frogs' legs (I made the last two up).

'So I said, "Calm down, Haze," and she went absolutely bonkers and said not to call her Haze ever again, that she wasn't a bloody air freshener. Then she stormed out. About half an hour later I heard the front door slam. I just peeked into her room, and half her clothes were gone –' She could tell this just by peeking through the bedroom door? '– and so was the suitcase she keeps on top of her wardrobe. Then, when I got home late the next evening, the room was empty and this note had been shoved under my bedroom door.'

She leaned over to the coffee table, picked up a crumpled piece of paper and handed it to me.

Gone to parents. Won't be back. Ever. One hundred euro enclosed to cover my share of upcoming bills. If more owed, please send details to parents' house.

The note was unsigned.

Was that it?

'Did you try and contact her or anything?'

'No,' Chris said. 'It was lucky Iseult could move in right away, otherwise we would have been stuck paying Hazel's share of the rent until we found a replacement.'

'Yes, I know. But it might have been better to leave it for a while – let the dust settle. Maybe we could have convinced her to come back.'

Chris shook her head vehemently. 'No way.'

I stared at her in surprise.

'I'm glad she's gone. I don't want to live with her any more. The last few months have been awful. You don't know the half of it, Lainey. I was on the verge of moving out myself.'

I was gobsmacked. This was Chris, who never got ruffled about anything – who always seemed blissfully unaffected by slights and insults.

'The only reason I lasted so long was that she

was hardly ever here. She worked late every single night – she was never in before nine – and she'd go into the office every Saturday and Sunday morning. When she *was* here, she'd go round the place slamming doors and biting the head off me every time I opened my mouth. And that's not all. Remember how fussy she used to be about her appearance?'

I nodded. I remembered, all right. Although she dressed even more conservatively than I did, Hazel was fastidious when it came to her looks. She got her hair trimmed and the colour touched up every six to eight weeks, without fail, and she got a monthly manicure, facial and eyebrow-pluck. Her clothes were always immaculate – there was never a stray hair or a speck of dust on the black trouser suits she wore for work. Her morning preparations had frequently had Chris and me banging on the bathroom door in frustration.

'Now she only seems to shower every few days,' Chris told me, 'and she hardly ever bothers to wash her hair. As for make-up – forget it.' And this was a woman who used to get a Christmas card every year from her beauty therapist.

I shook my head silently. I had known things were bad, but I hadn't realised they were *this* bad. Of course, I should have known. If I were a proper friend I *would* have known. But I had been wrapped up in my rapturous thoughts of Jack. I thought of the frantic phone messages that I'd ignored, and cringed.

'I'll ring her first thing in the morning.'

Chris shrugged. It seemed that the treatment she had suffered at Hazel's hands over the last few months had deadened any sympathetic feelings she might have had. And they'd been so close!

I felt compelled to remind Chris of how warm and witty and fun Hazel had once been. 'Do you remember our holiday in Majorca?'

Chris smiled faintly at the memory.

'We had such a brilliant time,' I said. 'Remember that night Hazel got high and took over the karaoke bar? She wouldn't let anyone else have the microphone.' The poor girl didn't have a note in her head.

'She wasn't so uptight in those days, either,' said Chris. 'She had it away with two different Spanish waiters that fortnight.'

'Oh, yes! What were their names again?'

Chris frowned. 'I think they were both called José.'

'I think you're right.'

Maybe all Spanish waiters called themselves José, to avoid complications and future identification.

'Talking of having it away, have you given Matt a go yet?'

'No, I have not. And will you stop talking about him as if he were a fairground ride?'

'He's the best ride I've ever had.'

'Well, it won't be happening. Remember his brother Jack?' I smiled shyly. 'I've been seeing him.'

'Really?' Her face was a study in amazement.

'Yes, really. What's so strange about that?'

'Nothing, I suppose. I wouldn't have thought he was your type, that's all.'

Not my type! Since when was a kind, funny, muscle-bound love-god not my type?

'Lainey?' Chris's voice was childlike as she changed the subject. 'Am I very difficult to live with?'

'Well – you play your music too loud sometimes. But, apart from that, no.'

'Hazel says I am. She says I'd try the patience of Job.'

'That's not true. You're a brilliant flatmate. Hazel's just not herself at the moment. I wouldn't take anything she says right now to heart.'

After a few moments' silence: 'Who's Job?'

'Bloke in the Bible.'

'Was he very patient, then?'

'Must have been.'

I was silent again. And worried. Very worried.

I sighed. 'What are we going to do?'

'I think we should have one more vodka smoothie and go to bed.'

Chapter Eighteen

I rang Hazel's home number first thing in the morning. Her dad answered. No, Hazel wasn't there, she'd gone into the office. There was no point talking to him – he was a big eejit; I asked for Hazel's mum, but she was out shopping.

I rang Hazel's office number and got her voicemail. Then I tried her mobile and got her voicemail. Sometimes I hated technology. I even went into town and tried to go to her office, but the security guard – jobsworth bastard – wouldn't let me in.

I tried to contact her again on Sunday but got nowhere. Frustrated, I decided to go and spend some quality time with my parents. Anything was better than hanging around the flat, waiting to be assaulted by Iseult. I got the hell out of Dodge.

My mother was literally bursting with news and gossip. Not only had my first cousin in the States given birth to twins (Shawn and Shannen. Eek!), but – wait for it – Tatiana and Chen were coming home for Christmas.

I greeted this piece of information with mixed feelings. Sure, it would be great to see Annie again, and I couldn't wait to meet her new man; but I hoped he knew his kung fu. He'd need it when Dad got his hands on him. It wasn't every day that one of Dad's precious daughters became a fallen woman.

I didn't voice my concerns to Mum. It would have been mean, when she was so elated by the news. She was already planning to enlist Chen's help to feng shui the entire house. (That should improve Dad's mood no end.) She was also swotting up on Chinese medicine so she'd have something to talk to him about. I felt sorry for the poor bloke already.

I asked how Terence had got on for the last two nights.

'Oh, famously! He was a bit excitable after you left, but I gave him a shiatsu massage and he was grand after that. And you're not to take this the wrong way, now, but he was a little mucky, being a country dog and all, so I gave him a good shampoo and he's all the better for it.' She let Terence in from the back garden and he charged into the sitting room, tail and legs and tongue flying. He was euphoric at the sight of me, even though I say so myself. The mutt smelt like the perfume counter in Boots. He was wearing a tiny green bow above his right ear. It wasn't Mum's fault. She was only used to dressing girls. I'd remove the bow as soon as we got back to Ballyknock. I didn't want the other doggies to make fun of him.

I entered the working week feeling as if I'd had no break. The weekend's revelations had taken their toll. I knew it wasn't reasonable to be so affected by Paul's new relationship – I mean, he had the right to go out with whomever he wanted; I had relinquished my claim. No doubt it was just a reflex reaction to feel so rotten. We'd only been apart a wet week. That Iseult certainly couldn't be accused of letting the grass grow under her feet. Come to think of it, neither could Paul. It had hardly been a decent mourning period.

Luckily, I had Jack's attentions to look forward to. I was keener on him than ever and felt an urgent desire to see him again – to make sure he still liked me; to have my worth affirmed. It must have been the weekend away that did it. Absence *did* make the heart grow fonder, after all.

I hoped it made the dick grow harder too.

I decided to give him one more opportunity to make his move. If he didn't, I was going to make it for him.

When a pleasant Tuesday evening ended with no more than a polite kiss, I resolved that Thursday night was going to be The Night. My very limited stockpile of patience had exhausted itself.

I invited Jack to dinner at 'my place'. Why, I hear you wonder, did I do that, when a) I couldn't cook and b) I had sampled his mother's amazing food?

Well. Apart from desperation, the reason was that I'd temporarily forgotten that I no longer lived in Dublin and, as a result, was no longer within spitting distance of Marks & Sparks. Preparations for previous dinner parties had involved a swift trip to Marks, after which I bunged everything I'd bought into the oven for however long it said on the packet. Pretty foolproof – even for me. Now what was I going to do? Mild panic started to set in. I even considered taking a half-day on Thursday so I could drive up to Dublin, stock up on provisions and make it back down to Ballymuck in time for dinner. That was Plan A. Too stupid, even for me. Plan B involved a mixed grill ... no. I couldn't possibly do that. But if he was still around for breakfast the next morning ... I decided to stock up on rashers and sausages, just in case.

Eventually, a café in town saved the day. I discovered in the nick of time that they sold some of their delicious produce. I emerged on Thursday evening with a lasagna, a quiche and a cheesecake. I could just about handle salad and garlic bread myself – with the aid of Superquinn.

So that was the food sorted. What about me? I rushed home to commence preparations. By the time I'd bathed in rose-scented bubbles and sprinkled myself with matching rose talc, I felt like a Turkish delight – hopefully, good enough to eat. Good enough to melt in Jack Power's mouth. I dressed, made up my face and pinned up my hair with more care than usual. I decided on a messy chignon kind of affair, with a few carefully contrived tendrils escaping at the side. That way, he could fantasise about taking it down. Maybe I should wear my reading glasses so that he could take them off too (But, Miss Malone, I had no idea you were so beautiful…).

I smiled at the result in the mirror. 'Tonight's the night, honey child.'

As I peered at my reflection, checking for flaws, I caught Mary Power's eye in the mirror. I turned to face her – her dark, mysterious eyes staring right into me, as usual; that enigmatic Mona Lisa half-smile.

'I suppose you don't approve of this kind of behaviour, do you?'

Funnily enough, she didn't reply. Encouraged, I continued.

'I'm not a slag, you know. I really like your grandson. I might even marry him someday. But times have changed and people don't wait until they're married any more. He's being a bit slow off the starter's block, and I'm just giving him a little push in the right direction. A woman has her needs – you know that.' It sounded daft, but I felt like I owed her an explanation. It was her house, after all.

If Mary Power was unhappy with this, she certainly wasn't letting on. Satisfied, I resumed my attempts to make the house look respectable. I had just removed the worst of the dog hair from the carpet – and dimmed the lights so that the rest of it wasn't too visible – when the jeep pulled into the driveway. Jack made his entrance, a bottle of wine in each hand.

'I'm starved. Let's eat!' he proclaimed loudly.

I couldn't argue with that.

You may have heard women of a certain age say of a man, 'He made me feel like a teenager again.' Well, that goes a little way towards describing how I felt about Jack Power that night. (Not that I was a certain age, you understand. Only twenty-nine and a half. A mere pup!) For the first time, I felt uneasy in his presence – tongue-tied, unable to be myself. I don't know if he noticed. He kept the conversation going, in any case, with that easy charm of his.

Finally, dinner demolished, I bit the bullet and suggested that we adjourn to the couch. He agreed without any hint of awkwardness. He'd probably been in this situation a zillion times before.

At this stage, we'd managed to polish off both bottles of wine. I offered him an Irish coffee, which he accepted. That part of the plan was going okay, anyway – the part where I got him so sozzled that even *he* wouldn't consider driving home. There wasn't exactly a taxi rank in the vicinity. However, the other part of the plan, which involved me remaining relatively sober so that I could be in control of the situation and my faculties, had gone horribly pear-shaped. Obviously, a big, rebel part of me had decided I needed double-Dutch courage.

We curled up on the couch with our coffees. The log fire crackled comfortingly before us, and Mary Power looked down imperiously from above. I had to congratulate myself at least on the setting of the scene. You could almost imagine you were in a log cabin in the Canadian wilderness. All that was missing was the sheepskin (mooseskin?) rug – something upon which Jack could throw me and make mad passionate love to me.

After a while, he took the glass out of my hand and placed it on the floor beside him. 'Here. Snuggle up properly.' He grabbed my legs by the knees and swung them up so that they rested across his legs.

'Now. Isn't this cosy?' he said, handing me back my glass.

Yes, it was. Very cosy. And very nice. In ordinary circumstances I would have been delighted with this result. But tonight was no ordinary circumstance. Did I mention that tonight was The Night?

I sat quietly, only half-listening, as he chatted away. I was conscious of the rain rattling against the Velux, the wind whipping around the corners of the cottage, Jack's proximity and body heat…. It took me a few moments to notice that he'd stopped talking.

I tore my mesmerised gaze away from the fire and looked into his ocean-coloured eyes. The flames were reflected in them, lending them an eerie, flickering glow. All at once I felt afraid. Jack looked deadly serious.

In what seemed like an agonisingly slow movement, he leant over and brushed my lips with his. That one feathery touch sent sensations shooting around my whole body. Several tortuous seconds passed, in which I was aware of nothing but his hot breath on my face. Please, sir, can I have some more?

I wasn't disappointed. He brought his lips down onto mine again. This time the kiss was long and soft and deep. He pulled away again – but only for the briefest moment. Then he brought his hand up and cupped my face, kissing me again and again and again. All the time the kisses grew stronger. Longer. More probing. In no time, his massive hands were on my neck – my shoulders – on my breasts, moulding their shape. I arched my body into his, making strange little whimpering noises.

I pulled away without warning.

'What is it?' His voice was husky and urgent.

Without saying a word, I pulled my top over my head and unhooked my bra. He stared for a few seconds and then pounced, alternately feasting his hands and his mouth on my breasts. All sorts of feelings were surging through me. I writhed on the couch beneath him, thinking I was about to explode.

When I couldn't take any more, I wriggled free and stood up. Looking down at him, I held out my hand.

'Let's go inside.'

Jack hesitated. Something strange flitted across his features. It might have been fear, but I couldn't be sure.

'What's wrong?' I said. 'Don't you want to?'

'No, it's not that.' He took my hand and allowed me to lead him into the bedroom.

Once inside, I closed the door, grateful that I'd fixed the lighting earlier so that it was soft and flattering. I hastily removed the rest of my clothes and jumped under the covers to hide my naked body. Jack stood at the end of the bed. He looked uncertain. I patted the space of duvet beside me in what I hoped was an inviting manner.

He put his hands on his hips and looked at the floor. 'I don't know, Lainey.'

I sat upright in the bed. 'What don't you know?'

'Is this a good idea? I don't want to rush you.'

I relaxed. 'Is that all? Don't worry. You're not rushing me. I'm ready.' And had been for the last month. I patted the bed again.

Jack removed his shoes slowly and – I hoped this was only my imagination – almost reluctantly. He lay down beside me, on top of the covers. He was flat on his back, one hand behind his head, his eyes fixed on the ceiling. I leant over and rained soft kisses all over his face. No response. I tenderly unbuttoned his shirt, exposing his flawless torso. I gently kissed his chest and treated it to feather-light strokes. He didn't stir. I unbuckled his belt. He was motionless. It was clear that he didn't have a gun in his pocket, and neither was he pleased to see me.

'Jack … what is it?'

I draped myself across his body in what I hoped was a seductive manner, my thigh pressing against his thigh, my nipples brushing against his. I kissed him on the mouth, hopefully – desperately.

'Jack,' I whispered. His name hung in the air. Still he wouldn't look at me. With an exasperated sigh, I rolled over onto my own back so that our bodies were no longer touching. What was going on? I didn't understand.

We lay beside each other in mutual silence. The inches that separated us could have been miles. Eventually, Jack made his move: he kissed me lightly on the cheek and got up off the bed. I watched impassively as he dressed himself. When he was fully clothed, he turned and looked down at me.

'Lainey.'

I didn't reply.

'Lainey, answer me.'

'What.' I hadn't meant the word to emerge from my mouth in a vicious hiss, but it did.

'I'm sorry, but that was just too soon for me.'

Oh, you poor delicate flower.

'I would have been happy with just a snog tonight, and then we could have met up for lunch tomorrow, or something.'

My apologies for being such a slut.

'I mean, it's not as if you don't have quite a nice body....'

Quite a nice body? Don't do me any favours.

'I didn't have a condom, anyway.'

I did. Thanks for asking.

'And I have a very early start tomorrow. I'd be much better off sleeping in my own bed tonight.'

Don't let me stop you.

Jack paused for a few seconds.

'Good night, then.'

I didn't reply.

'Lainey. I said good night.' He sounded almost angry. Accusing. As if it was I who had ruined everything.

'Good night,' I said tersely.

He seemed satisfied with this. He left.

I listened for the desolate sound of the front door opening and closing; then the door of his jeep, the slam echoing into the night; then the jeep taking off down the hill, the noise of the engine growing fainter and fainter. Then I pulled the covers up to my chin, turned my face to the wall and cried my eyes out.

Chapter Nineteen

I didn't sleep much that night. Neither was I afforded those few moments' grace you sometimes get when you wake the next morning, as yet blissfully unaware of your problems. I recollected last night's debacle the second I regained consciousness. I groaned inwardly and curled up into the foetal position, wishing I were a tiny infant again with no problems or responsibilities.

I felt sick to my stomach when I thought about the events of the previous night. It wasn't just the humiliation — although, God knows, that was acute enough. It was also the utter demise of hope. I hadn't realised until now that I'd had my hopes pinned on Jack to such an extent. I'd really thought that this was It. That he was The One. I shook my head at my own stupidity – imagine still believing in The One at my age. *You're nearly thirty, Lainey. For God's sake, cop on to yourself. You're meant to be sensible, together, pragmatic....* The thing was, up until that point, I had assumed that I was all these things. But no. It transpired that, when it came to the male species, I was as clueless now as I had been at eighteen.

Grey light filtered in through the curtains. I heaved myself out of bed, even though it was still too early to get ready for work. I couldn't stand to lie there any longer with just my self-destructive thoughts for company. I dragged myself into the kitchen – carefully avoiding Mary Power's gaze – and cursed loudly at the sight of the flotsam and jetsam of the night before. It was like returning to the scene of a crime, seeing the telling evidence of the disaster that had occurred in that very room. Maybe I shouldn't touch anything, just cordon off the whole area until the love police arrived and carried out their investigation. They could draw a chalk line around my body: the victim. Verdict: crime of no passion.

Unable to bear looking at the scene any longer, I rapidly began to clear away the dirty plates and glasses. Seldom had I felt such enthusiasm for a cleaning task that didn't have a deadline attached to it (imminent arrival of visitors, for example). But how else was I to start the process of putting it behind me?

This task accomplished – you'd never have guessed he'd been there – I made myself an almost solid cup of coffee and forced myself to drink several glasses of water in order to counteract the damage I'd inflicted on my thumping head. I was sure I was having some kind of minor brain haemorrhage. The coffee was comforting and revived me somewhat.

Next, I took a long hot shower to wash off his scent, such as it was. I was about to dress myself when I decided, in my infinite wisdom, that I hadn't yet been tortured enough. I walked slowly towards my full-length mirror. Gazing directly into my own bleary eyes, I let the blue towel I was wrapped in fall into a cloth puddle at my feet. Then I began the delicate process of dissecting my body, inch by inch, to work out which particular part of me had so disgusted Jack.

Jack.

I could barely bring myself to think – let alone say – his name.

It's never an easy thing to do, stare at one's naked body in the mirror, with nothing to hide behind. The unflattering early-morning light flowed through the window and added to the horror. Every flaw was laid bare, exposed in all its glory: the stretch marks on my breasts; the slackness of my stomach muscles; my dimpled buttocks; and, worst of all, my raw-sausage-meat thighs. As I pummelled the mottled flesh, I reached levels of self-hatred that I hadn't thought possible. I resolved never to let a chip or a morsel of cream bun pass my lips ever again. The next time Jack Power laid eyes on me, I'd be a svelte supermodel. Then he'd be sorry. I'd have him crying into his beer.

When I'd finished putting myself down, I got dressed for work. I considered ringing in sick, but what was the point? The last thing I needed was to hang around the house all day with nothing to do but think. So I braved the cold. I braved the wind. I braved the driving sheets of rain. And I went into the office and tried to be brave.

When I look back on those few weeks leading up to Christmas, I don't remember all that much — just a kind of Ground Zero of the soul. What I do remember is that the bright, crisp, promising days of early December had given way to a deluge of almost biblical proportions. The whole country-side was afloat, the sky was on the ground and my walks with Terence had become few and far between. Sunny south-east, my arse.

Work was manic — young couples anxious to get into their new homes by Christmas. Normally this attitude irritated me somewhat, but this year, I was almost pathetically grateful for it. I threw myself headlong into my work; I came home most evenings feeling as if my brain had been sizzled on a frying-pan, sunny side down. And my eyes felt sore and overheated, like overworked electrical appliances. But this suited me just fine. Work I knew. Work I could do. Work I was good at.

Men, I clearly wasn't good at.

Disastrous relationships from my past that I hadn't dwelt upon for years came back to haunt me, like ghosts of Christmas past. I wasn't even going to try any more. From now on, it was lesbianism or the nunhood for me.

In all this time, I didn't see hide nor hair of Jack Power.

And then, all of a sudden, it was Christmas. Thank God for Christmas.

I didn't really care if Dad murdered Chen. I was just happy to be away from Power's Cottage and Ballyknock and all its associations. To be in familiar surroundings with the people I'd known since birth was strangely comforting.

I buried myself in Christmas preparations. Mum was delirious with excitement at the prospect of Annie's homecoming, and I allowed myself to be carried along on her wave. Let's face it, I had nothing else to get excited about.

Since each of my parents had asked me approximately twelve times if Paul would be coming over for Christmas, I had no choice but to finally tell them the terrible truth. They were both devastated. You'd think I'd dumped them too. Of course, I could hear the subtext in their heads: I was as good as thirty now, and ne'er a suitable match in sight.

Even though they had the good sense not to voice this concern, I was as indignant as if they had said it to my face. Did I have a sell-by date stamped on my forehead or something? Invisible, indelible: *Consume this woman before the thirtieth or she'll start to go off, begin to smell.* That was me – over-ripe. Soon young men would offer me their seats on the bus. I'd start buying bumper packs of Mass cards.

Mum bombarded me with endless questions about the whys and wherefores of the break-up. 'Why don't you invite him around anyway?' she suggested. I could see the plotting and scheming going on behind her eyes. I silenced her by telling her that Paul had a new girlfriend and that she was a very glamorous fashion editor. That shut her up.

Dad's only comment was a barely audible mumble to the effect that he supposed that now I was going to take up with some foreigner too. Mum turned on him fiercely and warned him once again that if he caused any trouble while Chen was a guest in their house, she'd divorce him. Dad hid behind his newspaper for protection. I didn't blame him. My mother could be pretty terrifying when it came to the protection of her children.

At least now that Annie was paired off and knocked up, some of the pressure would be taken off me. Mum and Dad's thoughts would be distracted from my impending spinsterhood. I considered telling them about Jack (not all the gory details, you understand), just to prove that there was life in the old dog yet, but they were disappointed enough already.

We went unashamedly overboard with the decorations. This year we had many new additions to our usual tacky streamers, baubles and twenty-plus-year-old decorations that Annie and I had made in primary school (sections of egg carton sprinkled with glitter. I think they were meant to be bells). My parents had been to Long Island earlier that year, to visit the then-expectant mother of twins Shawn and Shannen (eek!); while they were there, they'd stocked up on all kinds of out-door lights, including a sparkling reindeer and an illuminated plastic Santa. Mum and I were ludicrously proud of our efforts and fully believed that our house resembled the famous Budweiser ad. Dad, however, informed us that our home was in danger of being mistaken for South County Dublin's answer to Amsterdam's red-light district.

So we were all set. The excitement had nearly reached fever pitch by Christmas Eve, when Annie and Chen were due to arrive. Dad went to the airport to meet them, in his newly hoovered Volvo. Terence was wearing his reindeer-antlers headband. Mum and I busied ourselves putting out little bowls of peanuts and crisps, to the accompaniment of *Christmas with the Rat Pack*. The aroma of mince pies and mulled wine filled the air. (You must be able to get a spray for that too.)

By the time we heard the car pulling into the drive, we had been waiting for such a long time that I'd begun to worry that Dad had taken a detour into the Dublin mountains to kill Chen and bury his finely chopped body. But no: there was Chen, strolling through the front door, smiling easily at everyone. At least, I thought it must be him.

'Lainey, this is Chen.'

It was.

I hugged Annie fiercely. Chen was instantly overpowered by Mum, who started clucking all over him: 'Let me take your coat.... You must find it dreadfully cold over here.... Are you tired after your journey? ... Would you like a drink? A nice pint of sake, perhaps?'

'Mum, sake is a Japanese drink,' said Annie, in amused exasperation.

I was in the process of following them into the sitting room when Annie grabbed me urgently by the elbow and dragged me back into the hall.

'Has Dad said anything to you about Chen?'

'Not really. He's been warned to be on his best behaviour, on pain of divorce.'

She let out a deep breath. 'Thank goodness for that.'

'How was he just now in the car?'

'Silent.'

'Better than violent.'

She nodded. Just then, Dad brushed past us carrying two suitcases. We both automatically flashed him a smile.

'What are you two up to?'

'Nothing.' A reflex response that dated back to our teenage years.

Christmas Eve that year in our house was something of a success. Dad behaved impeccably – the super-civil host – while Mum kept the conversation going by firing round after round of ever more probing questions at the travellers. Poor Chen looked quite overwhelmed – so much so that, after only a couple of hours, Annie suggested that they should go to bed because of the jet lag. If you ask me, they were only trying to get out of the game of charades.

I had convinced my mother to let the visitors sleep in the same bedroom. She had agonised about it until I'd pointed out that Annie was already up the duff, so what harm could it possibly do?

She stopped her future son-in-law as he was about to climb the wooden hill to bed.

'Chen, if you don't mind, tomorrow after dinner I'd love to get your expert opinion on a few ideas I have up my sleeve. I want to re-design the kitchen so that it's auspicious from a feng shui point of view.'

'Okay. But only one problem …'

'Yes?'

'I think that feng shui is … How you say?' He glanced at Annie for help. 'A lot of bollix.'

There were a few moments of silence; everyone was frozen to the spot. Then, from the deep recesses of the living room, came the sound of Dad's roaring laughter. Then we all started to laugh, like at the end of an episode of *Scooby Doo*. I knew then with certainty that everything was going to be all right.

My mother went into paroxysms of delight upon discovering that Chen was Catholic (she had been too afraid to ask before) and would be only too delighted to accompany the family to Christmas-morning Mass. So, after the great annual present-opening ceremony around the tree (Chen's presents were impressively apt – and expensive), we all trotted down to the usual half-past-eleven service.

The church was packed. Everyone was in good form and showing off their new clothes. The sermon was light on the fire and brimstone, as befitted the day that was in it. But still I couldn't help thinking that the priest spoke too slowly. You'd think I could be patient for one hour out of my life, but the truth was, Mass bored me to tears. The fact that I hadn't been since last Christmas hadn't boosted the novelty factor. The choir, however, were superb and performed a wonderful rendition of 'A Spaceman Came Travelling' – again. It was like Christmas déjà vu. Apart from the Chinese bloke standing to my left. And apart from Annie's burgeoning bump.

The night before, when Dad was out of the room, she had shyly shown us the five-month-old swelling, which she was keeping discreetly hidden beneath voluminous jumpers. It was weird, in a nice sort of way. Her boobs, which I hadn't thought could possibly get any bigger, were even more enormous than usual. She confided that she now had to order her bras off the Internet (I'd long suspected that breasts that big only existed in cyberspace).

Christmas dinner was the traditional roast turkey with all the trimmings. Surprisingly, it didn't come out burnt. This was due in no small part to the mysterious disappearance of the remote control to the kitchen TV. It had taken all my skills as a lawyer to convince my mother not to attempt aromatic duck as an alternative Christmas dinner. I couldn't, however, stop her from putting a bottle of soy sauce on the table along with the gravy. When she brought out two bowls of prawn crackers, purchased from the local Chinese take-away, for the starter, Annic, Chen and Dad collapsed into fits of giggles. This was very interesting for me; I'd never seen my father giggle before and hadn't thought he was capable of it. Chortling, maybe; chuckling, perhaps; but giggling?

After dinner, Mum caused further hilarity by suggesting that Chen entertain us all with 'some origami tricks'. He politely declined, after explaining that origami was in fact an ancient Japanese art.

'Chen isn't at all what I expected,' Mum confided as we stacked the dishwasher.

'What were you expecting?'

She paused, a dirty plate suspended in mid-air. 'I

don't know. Just something … different.' She sounded disappointed.

I knew exactly what she had been expecting. I had seen the copy of *Shogun* on her bedside table. She had expected Chen to arrive at the door in full samurai costume, sporting a long ponytail, like Richard Chamberlain in the mini-series. Never mind that the samurai were Japanese; that was what had been in her head.

Mum's disappointment was in direct proportion to Dad's approval. I was quite proud of the way he was handling himself. Here was a man who had envisaged his daughters marrying nice, respectable Irish lads, preferably professionals, preferably with parents who came from the West – a pair of doctors from Sligo would have been ideal – yet here he was, taking his exotic future son-in-law to his bosom. Mind you, it didn't hurt that Chen was a rampant sports fanatic. He was especially fond of Manchester United. Normally Dad wasn't too fond of Man U fans, accusing them of jumping onto the bandwagon of success. He supported West Bromwich Albion himself – out of sheer bloody-mindedness, I suspected. He may well have been their only supporter in the entire country. But his surprise and delight that Chen knew anything at all about soccer more than made up for Chen's support of the Red Devils.

And, furthermore, Chen was just *dying* to learn all about the rules of Gaelic football. The two men disappeared off into Dad's study for an hour and a half after dinner (while the dishes were being done). I was eventually told to go 'rescue' Chen and fetch them both in for a game of charades, but he didn't look in the slightest need of rescuing to me. Some Gaelic match was playing, unnoticed, in the background. Chen and Dad were well into their second six-pack and, heads close together, were loudly discussing the current Middle East crisis. They both looked as if they were enjoying themselves no end.

'What are you watching?'

They looked up at me in surprise, and I felt as though I was intruding.

'A video of the last time Galway won the All-Ireland.'

'I didn't know they had colour in those days. Anyway, come on; you're wanted for charades.'

Chen hadn't played before, but he picked up the rules quickly enough. Dad went first. He stood up, in his new Debenham's jumper and Farrah slacks ('slacks' – a word second only to 'gusset' in ugliness). He may have been staggering a little. He held up five fingers.

'Five words,' we all roared.

He made a motion as if he were reeling in a fishing-line.

'Film,' we all shouted.

He held up one finger.

'First word.'

He made a 'T' sign.

'*The Day of the Triffids.*'

Dad was visibly crushed. 'How did you know?'

''Cause you do that one every year,' said Annie. 'Now it's my turn.'

So she hoisted herself up and acted out 'the Battle of the Bulge', pointing to her stomach for the final word. Dad in particular found this hysterical. Then we played Trivial Pursuit, boys against girls. They thrashed us, due to Chen's superior knowledge of – well, everything, really. Then he taught us how to play five-card stud poker. The stakes were high: the pool was five euro. Dad was the biggest winner of the night, happily raking in his shiny one- and two-euro coins as if they were real Las Vegas chips. I'd seldom seen him so happy. I almost felt sorry for the memory of Paul. Even in his heyday, he had never made such an impression.

I wondered what he was doing right now.

It was well into the wee hours by the time we all went to bed – a little drunk, a little tired, but a lot happy.

Chapter Twenty

That family get-together was exactly the tonic I needed. The only snag was that I had to return to Ballyknock sooner or later. Christmas was over; the glitter had long since been washed away by the rain, the fairy lights extinguished. I felt like a discarded Christmas tree put out for the bin-men.

My charming little cottage in the country had never seemed bleaker. I was sick with longing for the comparatively bright lights of Dublin. I even rang Tyrone and begged him to let me come back. But he convinced me to stay. It was only for another six months – no time at all; and the spring wouldn't be long coming; and he needed me down there; and he'd make it worth my while.

So I stayed.

January can be the most unforgiving of months. The prospect of spending the remainder of the winter in Ballymuck seemed to me that year to be the worst kind of endurance test. My walks with Terence had become more or less non-existent; most days I couldn't bring myself to step outside the relative safety and warmth of the cottage into the harsh, hostile winter landscape. Everything seemed so – dead. I just battened down the hatches and prayed for the early onset of spring.

Then there was the danger of bumping into Jack at any moment. I didn't think I had the strength right then to handle the mortification. But I kept a constant lookout for him. Every time a car sped up the hill, my and Terence's ears pricked up simultaneously. Whenever I turned my trolley into the next aisle in the local supermarket, I expected him to be there, peering at me from amongst the vegetables. But he never was.

You see, I still held out some hope for him, in a teeny-weeny corner of my heart. Surely all the good times we'd had couldn't be obliterated by that one unfortunate night? I knew, deep down, that I'd give him another chance if he'd have me.

But I needn't have worried my little head about running into Jack Power. I was in the office one afternoon in mid-January. My concentration was broken by Patricia, who had been hovering around for some time now. She was fiddling around with the filing cabinet in a manner I recognised as meaning that she wasn't actually looking for a file but had something on her mind.

'Can I help you with anything, Patricia?'

'Oh, no, love. I've just this second found what I was looking for.' She plucked a file arbitrarily out of the cabinet. She moved towards the door and then, as if struck by a sudden thought, turned to face me.

'By the way …'

'Yes?'

'I was wondering if you'd heard how Jack Power was getting on in New York.'

'Excuse me?'

'Bridie was telling me at Christmas that he'd gone to New York for six months, and I just thought that since you and he were very … close….' She trailed off in a kind of fascinated embarrassment.

I stared blindly at the file in front of me. I didn't even have the wherewithal to cover up and pretend I'd known all about it. I thought I might be sick.

'I'm sorry if I spoke out of turn, love.'

Patricia closed the door gently behind her and left me alone with my racing thoughts. She might have been nosy, but she wasn't mean; she wasn't the type to revel in another person's discomfort.

New York? Why? For what? With whom? When had this been decided? He'd never once mentioned it to me. Had my thighs been so off-putting that he'd had no choice but to quit the country forthwith?

271

New York.

Six months.

Well, that was that, then, wasn't it? Gloom descended on me like a heavy grey blanket.

Then, one night in February, Paul phoned. Surprised? Me too.

'Hi, Lainey.'

'Paul!' I was so lonely that it was lovely to hear his familiar voice.

'Am I disturbing you?'

'No, not at all.'

'I checked *EastEnders* was over before I rang.'

I laughed. He remembered my addiction. He ought to; he'd suffered it for long enough.

'Do you still watch it?'

'Of course.'

'Thought so.'

There were a few moments of silence.

'Look, I won't beat about the bush. I'm ringing about Hazel.'

'What about her?'

'She's been admitted to St Catherine's Hospital.'

My blood turned to ice.

'Has she been in an accident?'

'No, St Catherine's. It's a psychiatric hospital.'

'Oh, Jesus Christ. What happened?'

'I'm not sure. Some sort of breakdown, I think.'

When I failed to reply, he continued, 'Have you spoken to her recently?'

'No.'

Hazel had made it abundantly clear that she wanted nothing to do with me. My initial worries for her had soon turned to hurt and feelings of rejection. I had only managed to get her on the phone once. Before she'd speak to me, I'd had to go through the ordeal of listening to her mother coercing her into taking the call. Even then, she'd been cold and evasive and had cut the conversation short. I had sent her a Christmas card, asking her to contact me over the holidays, but she hadn't even sent one back.

'Lainey – you all right?'

Paul's voice pulled me back from my thoughts. I realised I must have been silent for at least a minute.

'Yes, I'm fine.' Which was more than could be said for Hazel. 'Is she allowed visitors?'

'Yes. I'm going to see her on Sunday –'

'Can I come with you?' I interrupted.

'Course you can.' He sounded pleased.

'It's just that I'm afraid I'd bottle out if I had to go on my own.'

'You don't have to explain. I didn't much fancy going on my own either.'

'Does Chris know?'

'I don't think so. I haven't told her, anyway. I thought it'd be better coming from you.'

We arranged a time and a place to meet on Sunday. The second he hung up, I dialled the number for the flat. Iseult picked up.

'Hello.'

'Hi, Iseult, it's Elena.'

'Sorry – who?'

'You know – your flatmate.' *Bitch!*

'Oh, Elena! I'm so sorry!'

Yeah, so am I. Sorry I have to share a flat with a snobby cow like you. 'Can I speak to Chris, please? It's important.'

'I don't know. I'll just check and see if she's available.'

Who did she think she was?

'Christiana!' I heard her call out. Iseult was in the habit of calling everyone by their full names. This suited me fine, as I only liked my friends to call me Lainey.

'Lainey!' Chris sounded out of breath.

'Chris, I'm ringing about Hazel.'

'What about her?' Her tone instantly became cool and hard.

'You haven't heard, then.'

'Heard what?'

'Chris, she's in a mental hospital.'

There was a long silence, on the other end of the phone, which I didn't try to interrupt.

'When can we go and see her?'

Paul, Chris and I met outside the gates of St Catherine's that Sunday morning. I felt ill with nerves, as if I were about to go into a very important exam. My jitters weren't calmed by the sight of St

Catherine's. Gothic wasn't in it. It was like something out of Mary Shelley's *Frankenstein* – an ugly, sprawling old building dominated by a tall, sinister tower. Was that where they kept the worst of the loonies?

Was Hazel up there?

The sense of desolation was compounded by the waves crashing angrily against the shoreline. St Catherine's was situated right on the brink of the sea. Land's end. The colour of the waves reflected the sludgy grey sky. I was reminded of Alcatraz. I looked around suspiciously, expecting to see men in uniform patrolling high barbed-wire fences with vicious-looking Alsatian dogs. Strangely enough, there were none. There was just an imposing wrought-iron gate, which we went through without so much as giving a password.

It was weird, but we were all dressed in black. You'd think we'd planned it. Paul was wearing the black coat I'd bought him for his last birthday – bright-orange pollen stains long gone. We all had matching white faces, too.

We asked for Hazel at Reception. We were given directions – there was nobody available to escort us – by a pretty, smiling girl who seemed totally out of place in her surroundings. Where was Nurse Ratched?

Halfway down an impossibly long corridor, we came across an obstruction. Up ahead was a stationary vehicle – it looked a little like a golf buggy, but it was laden down with various domestic supplies – driven by a man who was clearly an employee. He was talking to someone we couldn't yet see.

'Ah, come on now, John. Be a good man and get up out of the way. You're always doing this.'

'No,' said another voice. 'Not until all my demands are met.'

'Come on, man. You have to let me by. They're totally out of bog roll on Ward 3.'

We drew close enough to see that there was a man – presumably an inmate and not another employee – sprawled across the floor, impeding the progress of the buggy. He saw us, too.

'Halt! Who goes there?'

Luckily we had reached our stairwell and didn't have to get past him. We all ducked in through the door and burst out laughing like a gaggle of silly schoolkids. I felt terrible, laughing at the afflicted – but it was funny. And God knows we all needed something to laugh about just then.

We ascended the stairs to the second floor. Was it my imagination or were our footsteps becoming slower?

We saw the sign for Hazel's ward up ahead. Thank God. But – oh, God ... what would we find in there?

Paul was about to push the door open.

'Stop!' It was Chris. 'I'm sorry, but I don't think I can go in.'

'It'll be okay. It's only Hazel.'

'I know. But I'm sorry, I really can't.'

I looked at her white, pinched face.

'Okay. You don't have to. Just stay here and wait for us.'

I pushed open the door.

'No!' Chris almost shrieked. 'I'm not staying out here on my own.'

So we all three went into Ward 4. It was a long, narrow room with beds on either side. Thankfully, all was peaceful – perhaps the inmates had just received their meds. We scanned all the faces, looking for a familiar one, half-hoping not to find it.

I was beginning to think we were in the wrong place when Chris exclaimed, 'Over there!' and pointed to the very last bed on the left.

Sure enough, there was Hazel. A little paler and thinner than usual, but Hazel just the same. Her bed was beside a grubby-looking window out of which she was staring. *That'll suit her,* I thought ludicrously. *She always likes the window seat on planes.* She was sitting quietly, knees up, covers half off. She wasn't rocking to and fro. She wasn't wailing. She wasn't wearing a straitjacket. She was just Hazel.

As we reached her bed, she turned towards us and gave a little start.

'Hello,' I said.

A mixture of emotions fought for precedence on her face: pleasure, anger, shame.

'What are you lot doing here?'

'We've come to see you, silly.'

There was an awkward silence, which we filled by presenting her with our ridiculous gifts. I had brought along a bag of fruit. Well, that was what I normally brought to patients in hospital. Was it the done thing to bring fruit to someone in a mental hospital? Could they cause injury to themselves or others with a finely sharpened banana? Paul presented her with a gossip magazine and a packet of Mikado biscuits (10% extra free). Chris bore a big white plastic bag, which I discovered – too late – contained her top ten self-help books. This gift seemed woefully tactless, somehow. I steeled myself for a vicious reaction, but I needn't have worried: Hazel accepted each gift with an almost eerie absence of emotion. I got the impression I could have handed her a live lobster and she wouldn't have batted an eyelid. With monumental effort, I blinked back tears. It was like a light had gone out inside her; as if the Hazel I knew had been taken by body-snatchers and replaced by this insipid stranger.

It was Paul who broke the silence.

'What happened to you, Hazel?'

I stiffened. Surely that was too direct. But, quietly and calmly, she began to tell us what had happened.

Hazel had got to the point where she was working every single weekend. She hadn't had a day off in three months. Her working day began at seven and ended at eight. In the final weeks, things had got very hairy indeed. Her first glimpse of the office building each morning reduced her to tears. She knew she was in real trouble when she was in a department store one lunchtime, buying tights for work, and went to the toilet; they happened to use the same hand soap that was in the office toilets, and the smell made her vomit.

It had all come to a head one morning when her boss had summoned her into his office and given her a right bollocking in front of two of her colleagues. She hadn't answered back. She hadn't responded at all. She'd just turned and walked out of his office and out of the building, stopping only to collect her bag and coat. She'd kept on walking until she reached her parents' house, six miles away. There she'd walked straight up the stairs to her room, got into the bed of her childhood and slept for eighteen hours. When she woke, her distraught mother, unable to get any sense out of her, had called the family GP, who had sent her straight to St Catherine's.

'So here I am,' Hazel concluded flatly.

It was lucky a nurse approached just as she was finishing her story, because not one of us had the first clue what to say. The nurse silently handed Hazel a tablet and a small plastic cup half-filled with water, then plumped up the pillows and left as silently as she had arrived. Hazel swallowed the pill and looked at me defiantly.

'It's only an antidepressant.'

I nodded.

'I'm not mad, you know.'

'Oh, I know.'

She stared at me long and hard, trying to work out whether she could believe me. Seemingly satisfied, she tore her eyes away and went back to looking out of the window. A sea view. How nice.

Paul and I exchanged glances.

'How long will you be … staying here?' he asked.

'I can leave whenever I like,' she said sharply.

'Oh, I know – I didn't mean –'

'The doc thinks I should stay for another week.'

We all nodded sagely.

'Maybe we could all meet up when you're back home,' I ventured. 'I mean – as soon as you're feeling up to it.'

She shrugged. 'Maybe.'

Paul looked at me again. 'I guess we'll be going now.'

I nodded. She certainly didn't seem keen on having us there any more.

'What'll you do for the rest of the day?' It was the first time Chris had spoken.

'Oh, I have a very full afternoon ahead of me. First an hour of basket-weaving, followed by a spot of finger-painting. Then I have my electric shock therapy to look forward to.'

Chris looked horrified.

'She's only joking.' I dragged her gently away from the bed. Optimism reared its pretty but naïve head. The old Hazel was still in there somewhere.

'I'll give you a ring at home in a week or so.'

'Whatever.'

As we moved away she lay down, presented her back to us and pulled the covers up to her ears.

The collective relief as we left the ward was palpable. Walking considerably faster than we had on the way in, we managed to reach the corridor leading to the exit without further mishap. Just as we were about to reach the light at the end of the tunnel, a chilling scream rang out. I thought it came from the tower. Mrs Rochester! Chris ran the final few yards. It took all my willpower not to run after her.

Fifteen minutes later we were seated in a coffee shop, close to St Catherine's but mercifully out of sight of the tower. We sipped our lattes as if they contained the elixir of life. Nothing much was said for some time; we were all caught up in our private thoughts. Then Chris spoke.

'Imagine,' she said, 'all along, everyone thought that I was the mad one.'

We didn't try to deny it.

Right then, Chris seemed to be the sanest person I knew.

Chapter Twenty-one

After what seemed an eternity, the harsh days of winter softened into the sky-blue days of spring. It didn't take as much effort on Terence's part to get me tramping the roads of Ballyknock of an evening. In fact, these walks proved to be the perfect antidote to a busy day at the office.

It was the end of March. The clocks were just about to go forward or back or whatever it is they do at that time of year. I luxuriated in the gentle spring sunshine as it bathed my eyelids. It felt like a long-lost friend that had been away on an extended trip, possibly to Australia.

The hedgerows around Ardskeha were studded with wild violets and little, yellow, star-like flowers (what were they? I'd have to look them up) – Easter colours. The Easter bunnies abounded, too; a young rabbit seemed to appear around every bend to torment Terence. Luckily he was too dumb or too slow to catch any of them, although he put up a great show of delirious barking and chasing each time. He probably ignored them when I wasn't there.

As I ambled contentedly, I was aware of an old, familiar scent intermingling with the usual sweet aroma of fresh cow-pat. An unmistakable green smell.

It was growth. New growth. The countryside was coming alive before my very eyes.

Trees that, a couple of short months ago, had appeared gnarled and close to death, hunched and bent against the wind like ancient folk, were now covered in sticky, lime-green buds. I had never before been so viscerally aware of the changing of the seasons, the renewal of life. The natural world had only been sleeping.

I was happy to let Terence lollop up ahead. A lead seemed mean and unnecessary in the circumstances. I spotted him every so often, excitedly sniffing a rock or a clump of grass and then cocking his leg against it in ecstasy. I was marvelling at his doggy world, filled with a myriad of scents that I was totally unaware of, when I heard the harsh sound of an engine up ahead. At first I thought it was a piece of agricultural machinery in a nearby field – the sound was raucous enough – but it was getting louder all the time, coming closer. Obviously a vehicle of some kind. I shouted several times at Terence to come back, but he studiously ignored me, intent on some new, exciting smell. He continued to stand stock-still in the middle of the road up ahead. The vehicle drew closer and closer. In a panic, I began to run towards him.

'Terence!' I yelled.

But I was too late. A red Peugeot careered around the corner and connected with Terence's vulnerable little body. There was a terrifying yelp and a sickening thud as he was catapulted into the air, to land in a crumpled heap at the side of the road.

There was a rushing sound in my ears. After being glued to the spot for a few interminable seconds, I began to run again, but this time I seemed to be running in slow motion, each leg weighing a tonne, feeling like I was trapped in one of those bad dreams where you're being chased by a monster and your legs betray you by refusing to work properly.

As I reached the scene of the accident, Johnny Power emerged from the driver's seat and ran over to where Terence lay.

'This your dog?'

The only response he got was incoherent babbling. But it told him everything he needed to know.

'You should have had him on a lead.'

I felt a surge of fury. 'And you shouldn't have been driving like a bloody lunatic!' It came out as a screech.

He looked at me in alarm, then took off his jacket. 'He's still alive, anyhow. We'll take him to Mattie. He'll know what to do.'

I looked down fearfully at Terence. He was alive, all right – for the time being. His bewildered eye stared skywards, like that of a dying fish on a trawler.

I looked on uselessly as Johnny wrapped Terence tenderly in his anorak and placed him on the back seat.

'Get in beside him and I'll drop ye down to the surgery.'

In a slightly less maniacal fashion – although this difference would not have been discernible to the untrained eye – Johnny drove back down the hill to the village. In the surgery, he masterfully bypassed the queue, Terence in his arms, a distressed me in tow.

'Sorry, lads,' he said by way of explanation, 'but you can see he's in a bad way.' The motley collection of cat, gerbil and budgie owners nodded their heads in concerned unison.

Johnny marched straight through a door marked 'Surgery', and I followed him. Matt was inside, finishing up with his last patient. He didn't appear at all surprised by our impromptu appearance.

'Put him down here.' He gestured to an examination table. 'Gently does it.'

He began to poke and prod at Terence's limp body.

'Hmmm … lost a lot of blood.'

I noticed with horror a rapidly expanding dark stain on Johnny's anorak.

'Can you make him better, please?' I sobbed.

The two men turned to look at me, somewhat embarrassed by my tears. I was too far gone to care.

'I'm going to have to operate. Do you have pet insurance?'

I shook my head. I'd never even heard of it.

'Don't worry about the cost. I'll look after it,' said Johnny.

As the kindly veterinary nurse led me gently out of the room, I heard Matt say, 'Jesus, Da. Not another one.'

The next forty-eight hours were crucial. Isn't that what they always say? They were nightmarish, in any case. I was amazed at how tightly and how quickly that scruffy little creature with the lopsided ears and crooked arse had wrapped himself around my heart. The thought of Terence experiencing distress or pain was unbearable to me.

But somebody up there had been looking down on us. A few days later he was well enough to come home, sporting a large bald spot on his side, in the centre of which was a scar. Around his neck was one of those ridiculous-looking upside-down-lampshade contraptions, meant to prevent him from pulling at his stitches. He also wore a bewildered expression and carried with him a prescription for plenty of TLC.

He went to the kitchen, whimpered pathetically and circled three times before settling onto his cushion in the corner and promptly falling asleep. Slinky – who normally regarded him with the disdain that her naturally superior species reserves for canines – crept up to the sleeping Terence, sniffed delicately at his stitches, licked them a few times, and then curled up beside him and fell asleep herself, all the while purring loudly. I took the opportunity to pop down to the supermarket.

Paul had a theory that you could tell a lot about a person by the contents of his shopping basket: whether or not he's a keen cook, for instance, or how healthy his lifestyle is. That was why I was concerned to find that I'd bought one bottle of vodka, one packet of chocolate biscuits and five cans of gourmet dog food. I knew what impression this must have given my fellow shoppers: that I was a sad, lonely, alcoholic spinster, with an eating disorder and only an animal to keep me company.

As I drove home, I had a vision of myself as an old woman. My hair was still long, but now it was pure grey and straggly. I was unmarried and childless, with fifty cats – all descendants of Slinky. My neighbours shunned me, and their kids called me 'the mad old cat woman' and performed knickknacks on my door. I was still living in Power's Cottage.

But that was ridiculous. I'd be back in Dublin in four months' time – back to the vibrancy and the hectic social whirl of my former existence. I had already passed the halfway point in my time of incarceration in the Irish countryside. It was downhill all the way from now on. I had another, altogether more pleasant vision, this time of myself (in present times) on a high nelly bicycle with a basket attached to the handlebars. The basket overflowed with fragrant wild flowers. I wore a long summer dress and open-toed sandals. My hair fanned out behind me and the cool breeze caressed my tanned face as I freewheeled down the hills of Ardskeha.

My pleasant reverie was interrupted by the realisation that a car was looming up ahead. I felt immediate irritation. It was a particularly narrow strip of road; I knew from experience that, if the driver of the other car failed to pull in sufficiently, my beautiful baby's paintwork would be badly scratched by the scrub growing in the ditch. It was a jeep; good – that meant the driver had no excuse not to pull in good and far.

Except he didn't. With great annoyance, I registered the angry scraping noise as the branches made lethal contact with my left wing. As I drew alongside the jeep, I prepared to give the driver a dirty look at the very least. But my anger immediately dissipated when I saw that it was Matt, local hero and saviour of dogs. We lowered our windows simultaneously.

'How's it going?' he called.

'Good, thanks. How are you?'

'Great form. I've just been up at Power's Cottage. I was in the area, and I thought I'd call in and see how Terence was doing.'

'Sorry we missed you.'

'I can come back with you now, if you like.'

'Well – okay, then.'

An excuse to refuse him had been on the tip of my tongue, but I could see that would have been churlish. It was nice of him to take the trouble of calling in on Terence. And, apart from the fact that I owed him the hospitality, it would do me good to have the company. I'd been spending far too much time on my own lately; if I wasn't careful, I'd end up a bona fide recluse and my fantasy of being a wild-haired old crone would come true. Besides, if I didn't invite him back (although, come to think of it, he'd invited himself), I'd only end up eating all the biscuits by myself.

Matt executed a highly illegal U-turn on a hairpin bend and followed me back home. Once inside, he made a beeline for Terence, who was still curled up in the corner, looking woebegone. When he saw Matt, however, he began to thump his tail feebly against the floor and rolled onto his back to have his tummy tickled. Even Slinky – who normally fled when a stranger came into the house – stayed in her curled-up position beside Terence and purred like a motorbike when Matt rubbed her head.

I made Matt a mug of tea and he sat back on the couch, crossed his legs casually and smiled at me. I smiled back.

'I really can't thank you enough for everything you've done for Terence.'

'My pleasure.'

'I heard you stayed up all night with him after the operation.'

He shrugged. 'It was the least I could do. I couldn't let another animal be sacrificed on the altar of my father's Peugeot.'

'Does he send a lot of business your way, then?'

'Like you wouldn't believe. The man's lethal once he gets behind the wheel of that rust-bucket.'

I settled back comfortably in the armchair, tucking one foot up beneath me. 'Anyway, I just wanted to let you know how grateful I am.'

'Really? How grateful would that be, then?' He was still leaning back on the sofa, his body totally relaxed, his eyes intent.

I frowned. 'Very grateful, of course.'

'Grateful enough to come to the races with me next week?'

'What?'

'You heard.'

'But … No – I'm sorry, next week isn't good for me.'

The cheek of him! What did he think I was – some sort of prostitute who paid for services rendered with sexual favours? What did that make Terence? My pimp?

'Ah, come on. You must get lonely up here on your own all the time.'

'No,' I lied. I could hear the temperature of my voice drop by several degrees. 'And I don't need your pity, either.'

'Who said anything about pity? I'm merely trying to extend the hand of friendship.'

Yeah, right. I was willing to bet that wasn't all he wanted to extend.

'Look, Matt … no offence, but I'd feel weird going out with you, after being with Jack.'

The mere mention of his name made me blush deeply, and it occurred to me that maybe Matt knew all the intimate and embarrassing details of our last night together – although that didn't compute: he'd hardly have asked me out if he were aware of the full horror of my thighs.

'I don't see what Jack's got to do with it. He fecked off to the States, didn't he? I wouldn't feel any loyalty to him if I were you.'

'It's not a question of loyalty. It's a question of … of morality.' I alighted on the word triumphantly.

Matt gave a small laugh and settled even more comfortably into the sofa. 'Is that all?'

'Yes. That's all,' I said coldly. He uncrossed his legs and began munching a chocolate biscuit. He didn't seem perturbed in the slightest. If I'd been him, I'd have been cringing with embarrassment; in fact, I would have been out the door minutes ago. To add insult to injury, the traitorous Slinky leapt up onto his lap and proceeded to make a little nest for herself. It had taken me a fortnight to get her to sit on my knee. He was like St Francis of Assisi – although, as far as I knew, St Francis hadn't had a reputation as a womaniser.

Maybe I was being a little unfair.

'Look, Matt, I'm not trying to be a bitch here. It's just that – two brothers … it just seems a little sick to me. And then there's Chris.'

He looked at me blankly.

'Chris,' I said. 'You know, Christiana. Small, blonde, bonkers – that night in Power's….'

'Oh, Christiana!' he exclaimed, the penny dropping. 'Why didn't you say so in the first place?'

'My name's Elena, by the way.'

He grinned. 'I know your name. And I promise I'll still remember it next week when we come back from the races.'

I looked at him disdainfully, I hoped, but by now he was staring off into the middle distance and chomping on another biscuit.

'How is Chris, anyway?'

'Why? Do you miss her?'

'Does she miss me?'

'I doubt she even remembers your name.'

He laughed, drained his mug and leaned forward, his hands clasped loosely between his knees, a discommoded Slinky mewing in disapproval.

'Look,' he said, 'if it makes you feel any better, I can state categorically, as my Granny Mary is my witness –' He gestured to the great lady above the fireplace. '– that, if you come to the races with me, it won't be a date.'

'No strings attached?'

'There'll be no sex on the cards whatsoever. I give you my word. Even if you beg for it.'

I couldn't help laughing at that. I was won over.

'Oh, all right, then – since you put it like that … I'd love to go to the races with you.'

Matt fell back into his seat as if exhausted. 'Jaysus. I had no idea lawyers were such hard work.'

He got up to leave, taking one more biscuit for the road. 'I've got to go and see a man about a cow. You keep a good eye on Terence, and give the surgery a ring if you have any concerns. I'd hate to think I'd missed a good night's sleep for nothing.'

He paused at the front door. 'I suppose a good-bye kiss is out of the question?'

'Get out,' I laughed.

When his jeep was no more than a tiny dark-green dot at the bottom of the hill, I closed the door and went back inside.

Incorrigible.

Still, I didn't feel quite so lonely any more. The crone fantasy now seemed a distant memory, and I was speeding down the hill on my bike again.

Chapter Twenty-two

It was a pet day.

I'd never been to the races before. Did I have to wear a hat? I researched the matter extensively by asking Patricia, fount of all knowledge on things local.

'A hat is optional, lovey. It's nice to wear one, but they still let you in if you don't. And it doesn't have to be too formal, either; you don't need to look as if you're going to a wedding.'

I took the information as gospel. Tyrone had been right: there was nothing – but nothing – that Patricia didn't know about local custom, and it came in very handy on the most unexpected occasions.

My millinery choice was made considerably easier by the fact that I only had one hat. It was a wide-brimmed, floppy straw affair, very Pimms and lemonade on the lawn. I usually just plonked it on my head when I was sunning myself in the garden; but I had a long, pink, raw-silk scarf that I could tie around it in a floppy bow, which would be perfect on this occasion. Since the day was so gorgeous, I decided to wear with it a long, pink summer dress, which was getting its first outing of the year, and strappy sandals with two-inch heels – quite high for me. I tied my hair back into a loose ponytail at the nape of my neck and applied light make-up. I was as pleased as I could be with the result.

Matt picked me up at the allotted time and complimented me excessively. Proceedings were already in full swing when we arrived at the racecourse. I couldn't get over the throngs of people milling about. Styles ranged from smart casual to elegant formal. I was relieved not to feel out of place.

Like his brother, Matt seemed to know everyone – although, among the people greeting him, the ratio of women to men was quite worryingly high. Some of these women kissed him on the cheek before eyeing me up and down speculatively. *No,* I felt like shouting at them, *I'm not his latest bit of fluff!*

But I was glad to have him with me, just the same. I felt woefully unqualified to place bets on my own. The bookies were all in one area, a bewildering array of men of various ages in varying styles of caps and overcoats, all willing and able to take your money off your hands. They all kept their takings in what looked like oversized handbags that were made of battered leather, as if the men and their bags had been on the circuit for years. They each had a child-size blackboard on which they wrote mysterious figures – they might as well have been hieroglyphics, for all the sense they made to me. Every so often, one of the men would look at something through a pair of binoculars and change one of his figures. It was baffling yet fascinating.

I allowed Matt to place my bets for me, but I insisted on picking my own horses. He suggested that we study the form first. I pretended to know what this meant. I soon found out that it involved, in part, watching the animals being led around a paddock prior to the race. I chose my first horse on the basis of its sweet expression and a charming white blaze on its nose. Matt gave me a strange look.

'You can't pick a horse just because it's pretty.'

I stuck my nose haughtily in the air. 'That's not the only reason. I have a feeling about this horse.'

He shook his head before selecting an ugly, vicious-looking brute that I'd never have chosen in a million years.

His horse galloped to an easy victory. Mine took a tumble at the first fence.

'Was that the feeling you had, then?' Matt inquired.

'What?'

'That the pretty horse was going to fall at the first fence.'

'Oh, shut up!' Smart-arse. I'd show him.

For the next race, I decided on Serena's Lad. I chose him because I'd once owned a guinea pig called Serena, but I pretended to Matt that it was because he had good, strong-looking legs.

'Strong-looking legs, eh?' He looked at me doubtfully. 'Are you sure you won't go for that chestnut filly – number eight? I'd say she could do the business all right.'

'No.' I shook my head firmly. 'Serena's Lad it is.'

'Have it your way.'

I had it my way.

I had considerably more success this time. Serena's lovely Lad soared athletically over the first two fences before refusing at the third, sending his jockey flying. Meanwhile, number eight, the chestnut filly, flew home to a decisive victory.

'Two out of two,' said Matt as we went to collect his winnings – again. Was there nothing that this man did not excel at?

I took his advice from then on and finished the day with a tidy little profit. I got so caught up in the cycle of studying form, placing bets, watching races, going to the winners' enclosure – where the steam rose off the horses' bodies like smoke – and eventually winning, that I forgot all about lunch. Most uncharacteristic. It wasn't until late afternoon, as I was standing behind a woman who was wearing a hat made of a manipulated wire coat-hanger and pink and white marshmallows, that I realised how hungry I was.

'Hungry?' It was Matt, reading minds as usual.

I thought we'd head to one of the many food tents, but no; Matt had a surprise in store.

'Wait here and prepare to be impressed,' he instructed me.

He disappeared off in the direction of the car park, and reappeared five minutes later carrying a gigantic basket.

'I hope you like picnics.'

Did I what! I followed him to a pleasant green area, a little way from the general noise and mayhem. We settled down in the shade of a massive copper beech, the sunlight dappling over us through the leaves.

The picnic hamper contained one bottle of Moët & Chandon champagne (lightly chilled), one bottle of freshly squeezed orange juice, one large bowl of green salad, one cheese board comprised of five different types of cheese, four swans made of choux pastry and fresh cream, and one punnet of peaches. Matt had also brought along two champagne flutes, cutlery, napkins, paper plates and a blanket to sit on.

We clinked glasses that were bubbling over with Buck's Fizz.

'I don't know what to say, Matt. You've outdone yourself.'

'As long as you enjoy it.'

I did. What is it about eating outdoors? The food somehow tastes so much better. I helped myself to salad, cheese and two swans. The combination of late lunch and early-summer sunshine ensured that the champagne bubbles went straight to my head, stopping off on the way only to tickle the inside of my nose. I took my hat off and let the sun beat down on my face. My eyes began to close.

'Here, lie down,' said Matt. He gently pulled me back until my head was resting in his lap. (You've heard the expression 'like putty in his hands'?) He began to stroke the hair around my brow. After a while, I felt him loosening my ponytail and pulling it out of its bobbin.

'That's better,' he said quietly, as he started to run his fingers through my emancipated mane.

I knew I should stop him, but I simply didn't have the willpower. The combination of his rhythmic fingers grazing my cheek and neck, the twittering birds, the buzzing bees, the scent of fresh-cut grass, the sunshine, the champagne … I seemed powerless to resist. I comforted myself with the thought that, if he expected me to behave like Chris, he had another think coming.

It was a few minutes before he spoke.

'We forgot the peaches, Elena.'

'I'm stuffed.'

'Have one. They'll only go to waste.'

I made to get up, but he pressed me down again. 'I'll get it for you.'

Eyes still closed tightly against the sun, I listened to Matt rummaging around for the peaches. When the rustling noises stopped, I held out my hand; but nothing materialised in it. Instead, the warm, sweet-smelling, fuzzy skin of the peach was held lightly against my lips.

I took a bite. The skin yielded easily and my mouth was filled with intense softness and sweetness. The flesh of the peach melted onto my tongue and the juices slid down my throat. Once I'd swallowed, I felt the fruit pressed against my lips once more. I took another bite. This time, some juice squirted out and landed on my cheek; I could feel it dribbling down my face towards my chin. I reached my hand up to wipe it away, but Matt caught it.

A shadow fell across my face and I felt hot breath, then a peculiar sensation as his tongue delicately licked the juice from my face. I froze. When the peach was held to my lips for the third time, I hesitated for a long moment before sinking my teeth into the flesh again. No sooner had I swallowed than Matt brought his lips down on top of mine. I responded urgently and hungrily, drawing his tongue into my mouth.

He stopped abruptly and offered me more peach. Then more kisses. More peach. More kisses. Soon there was no peach left.

'You want another one?'

I nodded greedily and we did it all again,

although this time the bites of peach were smaller and the kisses longer.

When I caught myself silently willing Matt to take off my dress, I pulled myself together and moved away. I sat up and looked around, as if I'd forgotten where I was. Just to recap, I was in a field, contemplating fornication.

The sun momentarily popped its head behind a cloud, and this was enough to fully break the spell. I stood up and brushed the crumbs off my dress, then busied myself tidying up the plates and glasses, too embarrassed to look Matt in the eye; but soon everything was cleared up, and I had no choice but to look at him. He hadn't moved. He was half-lying, half-sitting, his weight resting on his elbows, his ankles crossed. He stared up at me intensely, his eyes like rockpools.

We were both startled by the sudden sound of a giggle. I gasped and whipped my head around, just in time to see two young girls run off from behind the copper beech.

'Hey, you two!' Matt called after them. 'Lizzie O'Donnell and Kate Murphy! I'm going to tell your mothers on you – spying on people like that!'

This just sent the girls into further kinks of laughter. We watched them sprint off until they had disappeared into the crowd.

'You know them?'

'Lizzie's a cousin of mine and Kate is Patricia's niece – you know, Patricia who works in your office.'

Patricia's niece! That was all I needed. The details of my illicit affair would be all over Ballyknock by sundown.

But what was so illicit about it? We were both free agents, consenting adults, etcetera, etcetera. If I hadn't recently broken up with Matt's brother, everything would have been marvellous.

'Shall we go and put a few more bets on?' I was keen to disrupt the highly charged atmosphere.

'The last race finished fifteen minutes ago. Didn't you hear the announcement?' His voice was ever so faintly mocking.

No, I hadn't heard it. I wonder why.

'We could go down the local,' Matt said. 'That's what most people do when the races finish. Should be a laugh.'

I scratched my cheek, twiddled the buttons on the front of my dress, fiddled with the ribbon on my hat. Then I retrieved my bobbin from where it lay on the picnic blanket and tied my hair back into the most formal ponytail I could manage in the circumstances.

'No offence, Matt. Thanks for everything. I've had a lovely day – the races and the picnic and everything …' I trailed off momentarily. 'But I'm pretty tired now, and I really don't feel like going to the pub. Could you drive me home?'

That sounded very sensible, didn't it? Reasonable and polite, too. I knew Matt was studying me carefully. I half-expected him to object, but he didn't.

'Right you are. Let's go.' He climbed to his feet, bundled up the last of the gear and held out his hand to me. I took it shyly, hoping that nobody would see us as we walked back to the car – ironic, considering what we'd just been up to.

Back in the jeep, I had the worrying thought that Matt might be reading more into my request to be brought home than there was to be read. He wasn't expecting a night of squelching passion, was he? Just to be sure, I kept my arms and legs tightly crossed for the entire journey and directed my knees pointedly away from him. I gazed resolutely out of my window, ostensibly to admire the gorse as it blazed against the sky and clashed magnificently with the grass. I spoke only when spoken to, and my replies were as polite and as proper as I could possibly manage.

Power's Cottage. I glanced nervously at the man in the driver's seat. *Please don't make this difficult....*

Matt smiled and leaned his forearm across the back of my headrest.

'I'm not going to be invited in, am I?'

'Um ... well, as I said, I had a lovely day, but I'm –'

'I know. You're tired.'

'Yes.'

'I'll give you a call.'

I nodded in response, got out of the car and watched as he drove down the hill. Then, feeling as if I'd had some sort of lucky escape, I went into the cottage and shut the door behind me.

Chapter Twenty-three

Sleep came more easily than I had anticipated. I still felt half-drugged. It wasn't until the next morning that I attempted a full post-match analysis. It wasn't easy. Where was Johnny Giles when you needed him?

To backtrack a little, I woke early – early for a Sunday morning, that is – and, struggling into my dressing-gown, wandered barefoot into the small conservatory. It was already sauna-hot in there. Another glorious day loomed ahead, and I had nothing to fill it with. But that was okay. I had always had an infinite capacity for doing nothing – a generous navel to contemplate. If I were ever to write an honest CV, I'd list 'doing nothing' as my main hobby. I'd probably dress it up, call it meditation or something.

I drove down to the shop and returned with a blueberry muffin and the Sunday papers. I made proper coffee and settled down for a morning of complete rest and relaxation. Only my mind had another agenda. That was when the analysis began.

What was it about these Power men? There had been a time – not so long ago – when I'd had complete control in all my relationships; when I hadn't felt like a tiny, insignificant feather being blown along by every gust of wind life sent my way. I hated this feeling – but I was surprised by the realisation that I loved it too.

I also realised, that morning, that I was still smarting badly from the humiliation I'd suffered at Jack's hands. I'd never before been so thoroughly rejected by a man, and now I saw that it had shaken my confidence to the core. Any belief I might have had in my own physical attractiveness had been diminished significantly. It would be nice to tell you that I had too much self-esteem to be adversely affected by the insensitive actions of one man, but that didn't appear to be the case.

And surely Matt knew about that awful night. Men talk about these things as much as women do, and the two brothers were close. Several times, yesterday, I'd only just managed to stop myself from asking Matt how Jack was getting on. I badly needed to know why he'd done what he'd done.

Embarrassment and pride were the only things that had stopped me from asking outright.

But there was something else holding me back – from Matt, that is. I felt as if I was on the brink of something – what, I wasn't sure; as if I was about to take a plunge into dark and mysterious waters, like a mermaid who would never be able to go back to living on dry land. I didn't know whether I was ready to burst out of my safe mould. It wasn't foreboding I felt; only fear.

So I did what I always did when confronted with a perplexing situation. I made a list. I can't remember all the details now, but it went something like this:

Title: *The Continuation of My Relationship with Matthew Power*
Subtitle: *Provided, of course, he wants to pursue a relationship with me*

Pro
- *Chris says he's great in the scratcher*
- *Less likely to end up as sad old crone*
- *Could be fun*
- *Got nothing better to do*
- *He's a spectacular kisser*
- *He saved Terence's life*

Con
- *He slept with Chris*
- *Polite Ballyknock society will be scandalised*

- *I strongly suspect that he may only be after one thing*
- *He gets around a lot – what if I catch something?*
- *I don't know if I could face another rejection*
- *He's Jack's brother*

Usually, such an exercise served to clarify the situation; but this time, as both lists were precisely the same length, it merely added to my consternation. Maybe I was looking at this from the wrong angle. A little comparing and contrasting might be in order.

Matt
- *Exciting*
- *Fun*
- *Good-looking*
- *Puts together an amazing picnic*
- *Chris says he's great in the scratcher*

Paul
- *Kind*
- *Fun (when he wants to be)*
- *Reliable*
- *Good-looking*
- *Down-to-earth*
- *Honourable*

I immediately scribbled out the list in frustration. This was getting me precisely nowhere. What was the point in comparing the two men, anyway? Paul was part of my past now. I threw down my pen and took a sip of my lukewarm coffee. I idly watched a pair of bluetits collecting strands of Terence's fur with which to line their nests. How cute – and how strange, that little bits of Terence should be up goodness knows how many trees in Ardskeha.

My pleasant musings were rudely interrupted by the telephone.

'Hello?'

'Morning, Lainey.'

'Morning, Matt.'

'What are you up to today?'

'Don't know yet.'

'Fancy a walk?'

Hmmm ... what to do? If only my lists had produced a more conclusive result.... Oh, feck the lists. It was a beautiful day. Why let it get away?

'All right. What time?'

Another summer dress, this one in shades of blue and lilac, was resurrected. No hat or heels required today.

It was a walk. Just an innocent walk. Then why did I feel so guilty – as if I were betraying someone?

Matt arrived at ten past two. White T-shirt, dark canvas jeans; crinkly black hair, tanned, freckly face and forearms; knowing blue-green eyes. He wasn't as tall as Jack, nor as well built. He was more lithe – wiry. He moved with a cat-like grace. I'd never come across a man so comfortable in his own skin.

We decided to walk around Ardskeha. There seemed little point in going elsewhere when you'd be hard pushed to find scenery that stunning. Hand in hand – as if we were a couple – we walked up and down the boreens. Matt helped me over stiles into fields where he'd played as a child. I walked barefoot on the grass. He pointed out the tracks the foxes used. He showed me a badger's den and a rabbit warren. He told me the names of all the wild flowers and trees I'd been wondering about, and which insignificant-looking weeds were hiding cures for common ailments. He seemed so perfectly at home, so totally in synch with his environment.

We were back at Power's Cottage before I knew it. Matt looked at me expectantly. How on earth was I going to avoid asking him in this time? The truth was, it just felt too dangerous to have me, Matt and a double bed in close proximity.

I had a brainwave.

'Why don't we sit outside? If you set up the tables and chairs, I'll sort the drinks.'

'Sure. Where do you want them?'

'Over by the cherry tree.'

Down at the bottom of the old-fashioned garden of Power's Cottage was a massive old cherry tree. In full bloom, as it was now, it resembled a giant, fluffy pink canopy. The blossom wouldn't last much longer; even now, the slightest breeze made pink petals rain down like confetti.

Luckily, I had some old-style lemonade in the fridge (alcohol was a definite no-no today). I made up a pitcher, with plenty of ice and fresh lemon slices, and carried it out to the garden, along with two glasses. Matt had set up two wrought-iron garden chairs and the matching table just beyond the shade of the cherry tree. He was staring up into the branches.

'I have a lot of happy memories of this tree,' he said as I set down the pitcher. 'I spent a lot of time in this garden when I was a kid. My granny used to mind me and Jack after school. We spent hours up in that tree – playing *Star Trek*, mainly. Jack always got to be Captain Kirk because he was the eldest. See that funny lump in the bark?'

I nodded.

'That was the throttle. You could get up to warp speed nine if you pressed it hard enough.'

I merely nodded again. To be honest, I was a little uncomfortable at the casual mention of Jack's name.

Matt had stopped talking, and his attention was fully focused on me once again. 'You know, I'm sure he didn't mean it.'

'You're sure who didn't mean what?' I knew exactly who and what he was talking about.

'Jack. Whatever he did or said to you. I'm sure it was nothing personal.'

'What do you know about it?'

'Nothing. But I do know that Jack has a lot of issues he needs to sort out.'

'Issues'? What manner of psychobabble was this? Did Jack's 'issues' excuse his shoddy behaviour that night? His intimations that I had dragged him to bed against his will? His comment that my body was 'quite' nice?

Matt must have recognised the cynicism in my face. 'Don't be too hard on him, that's all. He's a nice guy really.'

I used to think that too.

As the sun shone down on our heads, we each drifted off into our own silent reverie. It was almost too hot to make conversation on this lazy, sunshiny Sunday afternoon. I watched drowsily as two butterflies performed a mating dance. They were like free-floating petals come to life. They teased and chased each other for a full minute before disappearing over the wall into the neighbouring field.

At one point, I offered Matt some food.

'No, thanks. I'm not that hungry yet.'

Yet? How long was he planning to stay? He didn't expect me to cook for him – did he? But my alarm was soon dispersed by the sun's rays, and I drifted off pleasantly again.

After a while, I felt Matt move his chair closer to mine. Then, without a word, he gently lifted my lower legs by the calves and laid them across his lap. Next, he eased off my sandals and began to massage my feet, one at a time. I didn't object, because a) I'd just got a pedicure and b) it felt like heaven. Like the floozy I was so obviously becoming, I let him continue. I decided I liked being a floozy. I didn't even get worried when his hands travelled up past my ankles and onto my shins, and then my knees.

But my eyelids did jerk open when I felt his hands slide under the hem of my dress and onto my lower thighs. I looked at him and gulped.

'What …' I had to clear my throat before I could continue. 'What are you doing?'

His eyes were frighteningly intense. And then he spoke the sweetest words that have ever been spoken by a man to a woman. Words that, without even realising it, I had been waiting to hear from a man all my adult life.

'Anything you want, Lainey. I'll do anything you want.'

My pulse racing in my ears, I stood up and held out my hand. Matt silently took it and allowed me to lead him under the heavy pink branches of the cherry tree. I leaned my back against the trunk and pulled his body in to mine. Our kisses continued from where they had left off the day before, although they were more frenzied this time. I took both of his hands in mine, kissed them passionately and then placed them at the top of my dress. He instantly got the message and began urgently opening the buttons down the front.

I had a glorious feeling of being exposed and liberated, all at once. We were outdoors, yet hidden; in danger of being caught, yet safe. The only things now separating Matt's naked hands from my naked body were a front-loading white bra and a cotton white thong. These barriers were soon disposed of. What followed was a flurry of physical sensations, of an intensity I'd never experienced before. Wherever I arched my body, Matt's fingers or mouth or delicious tongue followed. The rough bark of the tree against the skin of my back. The sunlight dappling through the branches against my front. The petals falling down onto my bare breasts. I almost felt at one with the universe. I certainly felt at one with the tree.

As soon as Matt was as naked as I was, I coiled my legs around him. Instinctively knowing what I wanted, as I had known he would, he hoisted me up off the earth, and I wrapped my legs around his waist.

With each thrust, a shower of pink petals rained down on our pink bodies. The tree would soon be as naked as we were. I felt like I was in a scene in a Bollywood movie – only X-rated. And then the pink explosions went off in my body and my head.

So, you see, I needn't have worried about Matt trying to get me into bed after all.

Chapter Twenty-four

I didn't go to work the next day. I wasn't sick; I was in a daze. I would have been a liability in the office, staring into space and making stupid mistakes that I'd only have had to rectify the next day.

So I stared into space at home instead. I took a break from staring at lunchtime, for a sandwich and the Ricki Lake show. Tabloid TV – the modern-day version of throwing Christians to the lions. The title of today's show was 'Get Your Hands Off My Brother, Mother'. It featured a selection of tarts and hos who had taken liberties with more than one male member of the same family. A black colossus of a woman in the audience shook her chubby finger at one of these women and called her a 'hoochie mama'. Was that me? Was I a hoochie mama? I wasn't exactly sure what it entailed, but I could tell by the woman's tone that it was no compliment. I began to get the heebie-jeebies. What had seemed so right yesterday now seemed so wrong....

I switched channels and watched an appalling Australian medical drama instead, but I couldn't get the chilling thought that my life was turning into an episode of *Ricki* out of my head. I might as well up sticks and move to a trailer park in Sweet Home Alabama. And how weird that that show should be broadcast today, of all days. There was definitely a message in there somewhere.

I looked up at Mary Power, who regarded me sternly.

'Oh, shut up,' I said loudly, making Terence jump. 'It's your fault for having such attractive grandsons.'

I felt marginally better for having pinned the blame on somebody else. But blame for what, exactly? I was single. Matt was single. Jack was in New York. Chris wouldn't give a toss. She'd just want to compare notes.

My guilt magically evaporated when Matt picked me up that evening. Later on that night, at twilight, with a brook babbling beside me and bats swooping low overhead, I became at one with a large, flat rock.

I honoured the office with my presence the next morning. I strolled in at about half past nine. My hair was down and still wringing wet after my long and luxurious shower. I'd decided to let it dry naturally for a change. Pity I couldn't have another day off and let it dry in the sun. Sun-dried hair – almost as delicious as sun-dried tomatoes. My face was ever so slightly tanned and free of make-up. I wore a navy skirt and a white linen blouse, open at the neck; I'd noticed in the car that I'd forgotten to iron one of the sleeves, so I'd just rolled them up. My legs were bare; I just couldn't face tights today.

I cherished the look on Patricia's face: amazement tempered with disapproval, overshadowed by burning curiosity. It was the first morning I'd been in the office later than her since I'd started work in Ballyknock. Oh, she was polite enough. She even told me my hair was nice down. But I noticed she didn't bring in scones for at least three weeks.

Mid-afternoon, I had a call from Tyrone. As usual, he was introduced by the nasal and noxious tones of Barbed Wire.

'Can you hold for Mr Power, please?'

'Yes, Barb.'

For goodness' sake, how long had I worked for him? And that cold bitch still announced him as if I were a stranger.

Tyrone came on the line, voice booming as usual. I instinctively held the receiver several inches away from my ear.

'Lainey! How's the form?'

'I'm in great form, Tyrone, thanks for asking.'

'Delighted to hear it. You sound it, too. Listen, I'm coming down to pay the Ballyknock office a visit.'

'When?'

'Tomorrow.'

Holy shit! 'Thanks for the notice. You wouldn't be coming down to check up on me, by any chance?'

'Lainey Malone! What a question. Don't you know I have the utmost faith in you?'

'Do you, now? Sorry for insulting you, so.'

'Apology accepted. I just feel the urge to visit the furthest outpost of my empire.'

'Your empire? Excuse me!'

'So I'll see you tomorrow at nine. Oh, hold on – Barb wants a word.'

'With me? About what?'

'How would I know? See you.'

He put me through to his illustrious secretary.

'Barb. What can I do for you?' She was probably going to warn me to stay away from her man.

'Actually, Elena, it's a little awkward….'

What was this I was hearing? Was the great Barbed Wire unsure of herself?

'It's about Tyrone.'

I thought so.

'He puts on a good show, but he's been very unwell lately.'

'Really?'

'Yes. He's been working his fingers to the bone, trying to get everything sorted so he can move down to the country. He's overdoing it. He won't listen to me any more. Maybe you'd have a word with him – see if you can convince him to slow down a little.'

'I'll certainly try.'

'And another thing....'

'Yes?'

'Don't let him smoke. He tells me he's off them, but I know he sneaks the odd fag every now and then.'

'I promise I'll keep an eye on him.'

'Okay, so. Bye.'

'See you.'

'Oh, Elena?'

'Yes?'

'Thank you.'

'You're welcome, Barb.'

How about that? Not so cold after all.

Patricia and I spent the rest of the afternoon in a frenzy of tidying and organising. Bins were emptied, desks were cleared, miscellaneous post was filed – Patricia was even keener to impress the boss than I was. I completed several odious legal tasks I'd been putting off, astounding myself with my new-found motivation.

Tyrone arrived at quarter to nine the next morning and began a frighteningly thorough investigation of every file in the office. Equally frightening was his appearance. He had aged an unnatural amount since I'd seen him last. Gone were the chubby, prosperous, fat-cat cheeks; the skin was pulled taut over every contour of his face. I didn't say anything until we were at lunch. He'd taken me out for posh nosh in the local golf club. He couldn't wait to begin exercising his membership rights.

'You've lost weight,' I blurted out over coffee.

'Thanks. I'm thinking of giving up this solicitor lark and becoming a model. What do you think? They say it's never too late for a change of career.'

I purposefully kept my expression stern. 'I don't mean it in a good way. You look gaunt – sick, even.'

'Well, the doctor told me to cut out the fatty foods, so I did.'

'Are you sure that's all it is? You're not working too hard?'

'Have you been discussing me with Barb?'

'Don't be so paranoid. It's as obvious as the nose on your face. You've been pushing yourself too hard, as usual. You know what the doctor said: you have to start taking things easier.'

He shrugged my comments away. 'The harder I work now, the quicker I can get down here and relax. And the quicker you can move back to Dublin. That is what you want – isn't it?'

'I suppose. But I don't want you half-killing yourself in the process. That would defeat the whole purpose.'

319

Tyrone fished around in his pocket and pulled out a pack of Benson & Hedges.

'No!' I almost yelled. 'You're not allowed.' He looked at me oddly and I quickly amended, 'I mean, you can't smoke in here. It's a no-smoking area.'

'Then why is there an ashtray on the table?'

I was momentarily stumped.

'Well, it's just that I've given up and it's too much of a temptation to be around anyone else smoking.'

'But you still have an ashtray in your office.'

'It's for clients,' I said, thinking quickly. 'In case they get stressed or upset and need to light up.'

He scanned my face. I made sure I didn't look too triumphant as he put the cigarettes back in his pocket.

'You *have* been talking to Barb, haven't you? That's why she asked me to put you back on to her yesterday on the phone.'

'She might have said something.'

I waited for the legendary Tyrone Power temper to flare up, but he just grinned at me. 'Amn't I the lucky man, to have two such gorgeous women looking out for me?'

I breathed a sigh of relief. I hadn't made him angry.

'Because you're looking great, Lainey. I've never seen you look so well. Country living must agree with you.'

I considered this new concept in surprise. Maybe it did suit me. Although I'd also recommend regular sessions with Matt Power to induce a sense of total well-being.

'As a matter of fact, you look like the cat that got the cream.'

'Do I really?' I smiled. Like the cat that got the cream.

'Wouldn't be anything to do with Mattie Power, by any chance?'

That wiped the smile off my face. I hadn't realised that the Ballyknock grapevine swung all the way to Dublin.

'How did you know about that?' I couldn't play it cool.

He laughed at me. 'A little Bridie told me.' He was enjoying this, evidently getting his own back.

'Whatever happened to poor old Jack? I heard you were seeing him before Christmas.'

Had he, now? He'd never let on before.

'Bridie's terrified you're going to send another of her sons off packing to the States.'

The cheek!

'What are you doing – working your way through the whole lot of them?'

'No!'

'And what about that Dublin lad you were seeing – Peter, wasn't it? You brought him along to the company barbecue that time.'

'Paul.'

'Paul, that's it. Nice lad. What did you do with him?'

I shifted uncomfortably in my chair. When was this barrage of personal questions going to end? This was the one drawback of being on good terms with your boss.

Tyrone sensed my discomfort and took pity on me. 'All right, all right, I'll shut up now. But seriously, Lainey ... can I give *you* a bit of advice?'

'What?' I was wary.

'Just be careful with young Mattie. I mean, don't get me wrong, he's a grand chap and I'm awful fond of him; but – well – he's a bit of a lad, if you get what I'm saying. All right for a good time, but don't get too hung up on him.'

I blushed furiously. 'Don't worry, I won't.'

'Glad to hear it. Now come on – back to the office. We've got work to do.'

Chapter Twenty-five

Tyrone returned to Dublin, and I did my best to return to some semblance of normality. Easier said than done, with Matt on the scene. I mean, one-night stands are so demeaning. That's why it was so imperative that I should see Matt again. And again. And again.

We took full advantage of the long, mild spring days and dined *al fresco* most evenings. Over the coming weeks, I became at one with a meadow (Matt made daisy chains for my ankles, wrists, neck and waist), a deep green forest (on the forest floor amongst the bluebells), a hay-shed (it was raining. Fun but a bit prickly), a tree-house (he was the type of man who would try to get you up a tree rather than into bed), a waterfall (highly recommended) and the back of his jeep (reminiscent of teenage years. It was quite chilly that night).

You might wonder how – with all this excitement going on – I could drag myself away to Dublin for a weekend. I had two reasons for going. The first one was that Tatiana had given birth to a baby girl. No, she hadn't been forced to abort when they had found out that she was expecting a girl; no, Chen hadn't insisted that the child be deposited in the nearest orphanage while they tried to conceive a son and heir; no, Annie hadn't been forcibly sterilised so she couldn't have another child. When I rang and spoke to Chen, he wept tears of pure joy.

My parents, too, were beside themselves with happiness. They were travelling to Beijing on Monday to visit mother and child. I wanted to see them before they left, and to give them presents for Annie and my new niece – LuLing. I was now Auntie Elena. How strange.

The family home was in uproar. Cases were packed, unpacked and repacked. Piles of ironing loomed high on the kitchen counter. My mother rushed around in a blind panic, crossing items off lists with a red Biro and adding new items with a blue Biro. My father sat in his armchair, quietly reading a book entitled *How to Survive an Aeroplane Crash: One Hundred Tips*. I gently pointed out that his choice of reading material could hardly alleviate his fear of flying, but he just said, in a very solemn voice, 'There's no harm in being prepared, Rosie.' The eternal Boy Scout.

My mother reported that he was driving her demented. I thought it best to refrain from commenting that she'd been demented for years, probably since long before she had met him. It wasn't just his failure to assist in the holiday preparations that was driving her to distraction – although he probably thought he was preparing, in his own special way.

Since he'd retired, his mission had been to find himself the perfect hobby. First there had been bridge. Mum didn't mind that – it got him out of the house and meeting new people – but his interest waned after a few short weeks. Then there had been the photography. Dad had reportedly bought thousands of pounds' worth of equipment ('Think of it as an investment, Teresa') – and that obsession had lasted exactly twelve days (she'd been keeping count). I meekly pointed out that this would come in handy to take pictures of LuLing, but Mum was not to be dissuaded from her frustration. Then he'd been all set to take up wood-turning ('It's something I've wanted to do my whole life, Teresa'); Mum couldn't even get the car into the garage any more, what with all the equipment; and had he produced so much as one bowl? I think you know the answer. His latest passion was for home brew. You couldn't get near the airing cupboard for pipes and bubbling cauldrons. It was the last straw when Mum discovered that all her clean knickers smelt of beer.

Of course, she just wanted him to go back to work. He was clearly invading her territory.

After about an hour, I couldn't wait to vacate the premises. Before I left, I fed Terence and shut him out in the back garden. It was for his own good. Witnessing such a high level of domestic un-bliss couldn't be good for him.

This brings me to my second reason for travelling to Dublin on this particular weekend. It seemed that Hazel was finally ready to face the world again. Chris, Paul and I were meeting her for lunch.

I was the second person to arrive. Hazel was sitting alone in a booth at the back of the café. I tried to quell my nerves as I walked towards her. The last time I'd seen her, she'd been in St Catherine's.

Hazel looked up from her menu just as I reached the booth. She smiled weakly.

'Hi, Lainey. It's good to see you.'

I struggled to control my emotions as we embraced. It felt like squeezing a bag of bones. As I settled in opposite her, I tried not to make it too obvious that I was scrutinising her face for clues. Was this the old Hazel? The new Hazel? (The mad Hazel?) She was wearing her glasses. Her hair was down and unadorned, but freshly washed; her face was devoid of make-up, but she'd lost her deathly pallor. She was wearing jeans and a pale-grey top, simple and pristine. In other words, vintage Hazel.

'You're looking well,' I told her, relieved that I didn't have to lie.

'So are you. I love your hair.'

'Thanks.' I was bashful. I'd decided to leave my hair loose again today. It now extended halfway down my back. A few days before, I'd taken a few strands on the left-hand side and worked them into a plait. Matt had liked it. Now the hairstyle was making its maiden voyage to Dublin.

I was about to ask her how she *really* was, when the others arrived – or, I should say, the others plus one. Whose bright idea had it been to bring Iseult along? Hazel's first foray back onto the Dublin social scene, and somebody had to bring along her nemesis. I glared at Paul and he looked away, embarrassed. There was no point glaring at Iseult, because she was talking shrilly into her mobile phone, and there was no point glaring at Chris because – well, because she was Chris.

Paul and Chris hugged Hazel as if she were breakable. Then Chris turned her attention to me.

'Lainey! What have you done to yourself? You look amazing. Let me have a look at you.'

Had I really looked that bad before? And was the fact that Chris thought I looked amazing actually a good thing? Before I could decide, Chris – much to my embarrassment – forced me to get out of my seat and give her a twirl.

I was wearing a long, floaty skirt that contained all the colours of the universe in a vivid haze, and a simple white linen top with ruched sleeves and a lace-up neck. My boots were tan suède, and my short, fitted jacket matched them. I wore giant gypsy-style earrings and colourful bangles. Chris heartily approved.

'I've never seen you looking so good. If you were showing a bit more leg, you'd be perfect.'

Showing plenty of leg herself, she clambered into the seat beside me.

I was aware of Iseult, still talking loudly into her phone, looking me up and down. She was speaking at her assistant.

'No, no, no, Samantha. I told you not to listen to that one; she wouldn't know Prada from Primark. You should always do what *I* tell you. The whole thing will have to be re-shot. The hippy-chick look went out with the Ark.' She snapped her mobile shut.

'Hi, Elena.' She bared her teeth at me; it was probably meant to be a smile, but it reminded me of a programme about sharks I'd recently seen on the National Geographic channel. She proceeded to kiss everyone, once on each cheek. What was all this continental-style kissing? I must have missed its introduction. Had it been brought in with the euro? Irish people couldn't be doing with all this kissing stuff. It wasn't natural.

Paul sat next to Hazel, opposite Chris and me, and Iseult squashed in beside him. As Hazel, Chris, Paul and I ordered coffees and sandwiches, Iseult ordered salad and mineral water and loudly informed us that she'd just returned from a photo shoot in the Caribbean. Puke!

A situation that could have been horribly awkward was made less so by Chris's blessed aimless chatter. She was very excited because the company she worked for was going to allow her to direct her first short film. She was undaunted by the prospect, despite the fact that she had not the first clue what the film would be about. She did have ideas, however – plenty of them, each more outlandish than the last.

Hazel was unusually quiet – although who knew what was usual in these circumstances? She seemed afraid of the crowds of people in the restaurant. Maybe we should have picked somewhere quieter. But it was Grafton Street on a Saturday afternoon; quieter didn't exist. Her body language was different, too. She sat holding her coffee mug in front of her face, gripping it tightly in both hands, her eyes darting from side to side. She was aeons away from the cool, calm, collected Hazel I knew so well – the girl who could sum up a person in one succinct phrase, thereby reducing me and Chris to tears of laughter. At least her eyes had lost that eerie, faraway look.

The East European waitress brought over Iseult's order. Iseult held up the bottle of water that had been placed before her and shook it from side to side, pinky finger extended.

'Excuse me. What's this?'

'You ordered a bottle of water, did you not?'

'I ordered a bottle of still water, dear. As in no bubbles. *Capiche?*'

'I am very sorry. I will get you another bottle right away.'

Iseult rolled her eyes in despair. One just couldn't get the staff nowadays.

'That kind of thing drives me mad. Oops – sorry, Hazel.' She held her hand up to her mouth and tittered.

Hazel and I exchanged a look that was just like old times. I glanced at Paul, but he was concentrating hard on his sandwich. He appeared oblivious, but I knew him and I knew he must be uncomfortable, to say the least.

How could he stand being with her? Okay, she was good-looking. And, God knows, not an ounce of fat clung to her taut thighs. But, really, was that adequate compensation for everything else he must have to put up with? And, even more worrying, what did that say about me? A lot of men routinely go for a certain type – just look at Rod Stewart. Was I the same type as Iseult? I knew we didn't look alike, but…. What a horrifying thought. I'd have to ask Hazel when she got a little better. I could hardly ask Chris. (Hey, Chris? You know your friend, the complete pain in the arse? Please tell me I'm nothing like her.)

I wasn't mad about the effect she was having on

Paul, either. He'd barely acknowledged me since they'd arrived. The odd thing was, I kept catching him looking at me; but every time I tried to meet his gaze, he looked away a split second too soon. Was he not allowed to so much as look at other women any more?

Why did he have to bring her along, anyway? The more I thought about it, the more annoyed I got. How on earth were we supposed to have a heart-to-heart with Hazel when Cruella DeVil was breathing down our necks?

As soon as there was a lull in the conversation (Chris had taken the first bite of her sandwich), I said impulsively, 'Paul, how are things with you?' I was determined to draw him out.

'Um … like what things?'

'Well – work. How's work? Not doing crazy hours, I hope.' That was very tactful of me in the circumstances, wasn't it?

'No more than usual. Although I've had a few late nights recently.'

'You'd need to watch that,' said Hazel quietly. It was one of the first times she'd spoken. 'You don't want to end up like me.'

This silenced everyone – everyone, that is, except Iseult.

'Well, I think Paul is absolutely right to work hard at his career. You don't get anywhere these days without ambition. And it's especially important for someone in Paul's position.'

What position was that, exactly? Under her thumb?

As Iseult uttered her words of wisdom, one of her arms went around Paul's neck and the other travelled under the table to his knee (I hoped). She snuggled up against him coquettishly, staring at me. *Oh, stick it up your swiss, you stupid bitch!* I had a good mind to mention Matt. I probably would have done, if Hazel hadn't known that he'd already shagged Chris. And there was no guessing what Chris herself might come up with. No, I was better off keeping schtum.

We finished up our sandwiches amidst much mindless small talk, the blander the better.

'Coffee, Paul,' said Iseult.

'Yes, please. I'd love another cup.'

'No. Coffee, Paul. I want a decaf. And get me two sachets of sweetener.'

Nobody moved.

Then Paul turned his head slowly towards her and said, 'I'm sure the waitress will be around any minute to take your order.' His face was set like stone.

Iseult started to say something else, but thought better of it and closed her mouth. I resisted the urge to raise my clenched fist in the air and shout, 'Yes!'

They left not long after that. Iseult didn't really say goodbye; she was too busy barking orders at the long-suffering Samantha again. Paul trailed behind her, fury and embarrassment intermingling on his features.

'I'll give you a call next week, Hazel. Bye, Lainey, Chris.'

Chris had to go too. She had an urgent jam-and-funk-dance class to attend. I got out of my seat to let her pass. As she moved out of Hazel's earshot, she said to me, 'He's good, isn't he?'

I reddened. 'What are you talking about?'

'We both know who I'm talking about. Told you he was exceptional. And I'm glad to see you using that hair and those tits at last. High time. It's a sin to waste such God-given talents.' She smirked at me, and pranced off to go jamming and funking for the afternoon. Flabbergasted, I returned to my seat.

'What was all that about?' asked Hazel.

'Oh, nothing. Just Chris being Chris. Anyway … alone at last. We can talk properly now.'

Except the thing was, I couldn't think of a darn thing to say. I wanted to act normally, I really did. But things *weren't* normal, and there was no denying it.

'Are you going to keep living at home for the time being?' I tried.

'Yes. It's the best place for me right now, I think. Mum and Dad have been brilliant.' She stared off into the blue yonder, as if recalling how great her parents had been.

'And how about work? You're hardly going back to that hellhole.'

'God, no. Not that they'd have me back.'

'Their loss.'

Hazel laughed without humour. 'It's nice of you to say so. But I don't think they'd see it that way.'

'Well, they should. You worked damn hard for that miserable shower of shites.'

She took a sip of coffee. 'It doesn't matter any more. It's in the past. I have a job interview next weekend, anyway.'

'Really? For where?'

She had applied for a position as a part-time bookkeeper in a small, family-run firm. Of course, she was completely over-qualified for the post, but her therapist thought it would be good for her. Imagine – sane, logical, sensible Hazel had a therapist.

'You see,' she explained to me, after a while, 'like I was saying to Laura – that's my therapist – the other day, I feel like I've been lied to all my life.'

'By who?'

'Oh, I don't know. Nobody. Everybody. Society, I suppose. I mean, I've played by the rules all my life – and look where it's got me. I was told to work hard in school, so I did. "Keep at the books," my father used to say. So I did. And I got a good Leaving Cert and I went to college, and my parents were so proud…. I was the first in our family to go to college. Did you know that?'

I nodded encouragingly.

'So I decided to study accountancy. I was always good at maths, and it seemed like a sensible, practical option. I mean, people will always need accountants. And it meant I'd be considered a professional. Me! So I worked really hard and got all my exams. I came third highest in my class. Did you know that?'

I shook my head. No, I hadn't known that.

'So then I get my first proper job, and it's damned hard work, but I don't mind. I'm prepared to put in the long hours, you see, because I want to do well. And I do. I get promoted. Then I decide to move on to that last dump of a place. Worst move I ever made. But I kept working hard, and at first I didn't mind. I thought I could cope. I sacrificed everything for that job – my social life, my health, my relationships. Do you know how long it's been since I've had a proper boyfriend?'

'How long?' Actually, I knew, but at this point her questions were purely rhetorical. I didn't like to interrupt her when she was on a roll.

'Five years.' She held up her open hand for emphasis. 'Five – long – years. Do you remember that idiot Dinny?'

'Yes.'

'Well, he was my last boyfriend. Just think of it – that fool! And what were they for? All those sacrifices?'

I shook my head.

'For nothing, that's what. Study hard. Go to college. Get a good job. Work hard. Lick the boss's arse. Put off getting married. Put off having kids. And for what? Fuck all. I tell you, Lainey, it's all a load of bollix. I would have been better off pissing around in secondary school for five years and then working as a checkout girl. Or going to Australia for a year. Most of my friends did that. Why didn't I? Will I tell you why?'

She banged her fist on the table.

I nodded, fearful now that the floodgates had been opened. The couple at the next table had stopped talking and were eavesdropping avidly.

'Because I thought I was being the smart one, that's why. I thought, *I know! I'll stay home, work hard and get ahead while those other poor fools backpack around Australia. They'll never get on in their careers.* That's what I thought. I mean, how smug can you get? Look at them now – thriving. And look at me. I've fucked up my life good and proper.'

'No, you haven't, Hazel. Don't say that.'

'But I have. What accountancy firm would have me now? I just walked out on my last job. I didn't even give notice. I'd be afraid to ask them for a reference – God knows what they'd say about me. And what man's going to want me now? I've been in the nuthouse, for God's sake.'

'Any man would be lucky to have you.'

'You must be kidding. Besides, it wouldn't be fair of me to inflict myself on a fellow human being at this time. And that's the other thing.'

There was another thing?

'I'm almost thirty-one. What chance do I have of ever becoming a mother?'

'Hazel! You have loads of time. Look at Annie. She didn't meet Chen until she was thirty-four, and she didn't have LuLing until she was thirty-five.'

'I suppose so.' This pacified her somewhat. But then: 'That's the feminist movement for you.'

What did the feminists have to do with it?

'They con you into believing that you're going to be completely fulfilled by a career, and that you can put off motherhood forever. But it's all damn lies. Look at all those women in their thirties on IVF programmes. They were lied to as well.'

The couple at the next table were preparing to leave. The woman was looking at Hazel strangely. All of a sudden, she came over to us and said rapidly, 'I couldn't help overhearing, and I agree with everything you've said. The best of luck to you.' She held out her hand.

Hazel shook it, a bemused expression on her face. Then the woman practically ran out of the café, seemingly overwhelmed by her own impulsive behaviour. Her boyfriend scampered after her, looking equally self-conscious. Hazel and I looked at each other and burst out laughing.

'What was all that about?' she said.

'Well, it was a vote of confidence, anyway.'

'Why didn't you tell me I was talking so loudly?' She looked sheepishly around at the rest of the punters sitting close by, but they were all ignoring us.

'There's an alternative career for you. You can become a motivational speaker.'

Still laughing, we ordered more coffee. I stirred my latte thoughtfully.

'That Iseult is a piece of work, isn't she?'

'You can say that again.'

'What on earth does Paul see in her? She treats him like a child.'

'And I suppose *you* never treated him like a child.' Hazel was smirking at me, one eyebrow raised.

Who? *Moi*?

'I didn't. Did I?'

She shrugged her bony shoulders, almost apologetically. 'Well, yes, you did. Some of the time.'

I stirred another packet of sugar into my coffee. Was that true? It had to be, or why would she say it?

'Anyway' – she patted my hand encouragingly – 'I wouldn't worry about it. He's only with her because he can't be with you.'

I stopped stirring.

'That's rubbish.'

''S'obvious.'

'But he practically ignored me earlier.'

'Only because she was there. I'm telling you, he's still carrying a big, flaming torch.'

I didn't quite know what to do with this piece of information.

But I did feel something inside of me soar.

When we were in imminent danger of overdosing on caffeine, we finally left the café. I cajoled Hazel into coming to the cinema with me. She wasn't up to browsing around the shops – too many people for her to cope with just then, she explained. She also apologised for ignoring my phone calls before Christmas. She said she just hadn't been able to cope with talking to anyone – and she still found it tough. Getting through today's lunch unscathed had been a personal triumph for her. Hell – if you could cope with Iseult, you could cope with anything.

But the cinema was the perfect place for her. Because it was mid-afternoon, the Savoy was half-empty. I love going to the cinema in the daytime; it always makes me feel like I'm playing hooky. We chose the least highbrow film there was. Think of the most mindless action movie ever, combine it with the cheesiest chick-flick you've ever seen, and multiply that by ten. It was much worse than that.

We both loved it. Arms cradling massive tubs of popcorn, feet illegally up on the seats in front of us, we hugged ourselves in anticipation. I loved the whole spectacle – the curtains edging back from the screen, the larger-than-life ads, the trailers, even the warning to turn off your mobile phone.... They all heralded the start of two hours of escapism and fantasy. We forgot ourselves, forgot the world around us and lost ourselves in the magic of Hollywood.

Chapter Twenty-six

I left Dublin at half-two the next day. I had planned to stay longer, but there's only so much one daughter can take. And, besides, I couldn't wait to get back to Ballyknock.

Matt had arranged to call around at eight. But I got back at five, and there was no way I was waiting three hours. I decided to call to his surgery instead. As I pulled up outside, I could hardly suppress the excitement that was threatening to burst right through my chest. Lucky I had an airbag. I smiled goofily at myself in the rear-view mirror as I hastily brushed my hair and applied a coat of lipstick. It was a new, cutting-edge, shimmery shade that the woman in the shop had talked me into buying. It was really me, apparently. She must have seen me coming a mile off.

At the sight of the surgery, Terence began to shake and whimper in the back seat. He hadn't relished getting his stitches out.

'It's all right, boy,' I told him. 'It's not your turn this time.'

I stepped out of the car and ran lightly across the gravel and up the steps. The waiting room was empty. There was one other car outside; Matt was hopefully finishing up with his last patient. Even the receptionist had gone home. I sat down in one of the plastic chairs, crossed my legs and admired the fake tan I'd oh-so-professionally applied to my legs that morning. For once, it didn't look as if somebody had poured Bisto haphazardly down my shins. The toenails were looking good, too – new hot-pink shade I'd also been conned into buying. And I was wearing the new underwear I'd furtively bought in Knickerbox the day before. Even though I'd entered the shop wishing I were wearing shades and a fake beard – you'd have thought I was buying a giant dildo, going by the embarrassment I'd caused myself – I had emerged triumphant, head held high, bearing a pretty little bag brimming over with frothy pink lace. I couldn't wait to take my matching bra-and-knickers set for a test drive and see if Matt liked it too. For years, I'd been a slave to white cotton briefs and sensible matching bras; now that seemed like eating vanilla ice-cream all your life, when there were so many other flavours to choose from.

The door to the surgery was slightly ajar, and I could hear the conversation within. It sounded like it was winding up.

'So give him one of these tablets twice a day.'

'Thank you so much, Mr Power.' A woman's voice.

'Oh, please – call me Matt.'

'How much do I owe you – Matt?'

'Tell you what – let's forget about it, since it's your first visit. If the tablets don't work and he needs more treatment, we can talk about payment then.'

'That's very decent of you, Matt. I'm really grateful.'

'Yeah? How grateful?'

My leg froze mid-swing.

A high-pitched giggle. 'Oh, very.'

'Enough to come on a picnic with me next week?'

'Maybe.'

I'd heard enough. I ran out of the waiting room, down the steps, across the gravel and towards my car. I fumbled around with my car keys, which no longer seemed to fit the lock. I dropped the bunch of keys on the ground with a clatter.

'Shit!' I couldn't help exclaiming loudly. Finally, I was in my car. I slammed the door shut and turned the key in the ignition. The engine revved angrily.

The last thing I saw as I swung out of the driveway was Matt's face, a picture of horror,

342

freeze-framed in the surgery window. So I did what every woman worth her salt would do in the circumstances.

I gave him the finger.

Back at the ranch, I waited for the deluge of tears. I waited in vain. I must have been shell-shocked.

So I tried indignation instead. How could he? I'd just wasted the best six weeks of my life on him (mind you, he was the reason they had been the best six weeks of my life). And the very minute my back was turned – the first weekend I went to Dublin – he'd asked another girl out! And maybe she wasn't even the first. There could have been a new girl each week, for all I knew.

'No offence, but your grandson is a right dick-head,' I told Mary Power. She stared back at me impassively.

But, try as I might, I couldn't work up a good head of steam on my anger. I had got a shock, all right; but, behind it all, if I was entirely honest with myself, I wasn't all that surprised. Deep down, I knew the deal. I wasn't in love with Matt any more than he was in love with me. All my life, I'd been taught that you couldn't have good sex without being in love. Well, Matt had blown that particular myth out of the water. Why I'd ever bought into the concept in the first place was beyond me now. It had never proved to be true in my own life.

I had let myself be played, by a player of virtuoso

standard, and I had enjoyed every note. I had used him as much as he'd used me. But 'used' wasn't really the right word. We had *enjoyed* each other – taken pleasure from each other's company, not to mention each other's body. There had been genuine respect and affection. I knew there had been.

As my feelings came into focus, I realised that my overwhelming emotions were disappointment and a sense of loss. I'd so enjoyed our little trysts, and now they were over. Our fling had been flung. Even if Matt wanted to carry on regardless, it wasn't in my nature to share a man with goodness knew how many other women. And it would have been selfish to try to keep him all to myself. A talent like his should be shared. No doubt he felt the same way.

The phone rang. Anticipating this, I had put it on answerphone.

'Lainey, are you there? If you are, will you pick up, please? … Lainey, it's me – Matt. Look … I'm very sorry you had to hear what I think you heard. Give me a ring if you like, and we can discuss it. Bye, then.' He hung up.

I sat in silence for a few minutes, thinking how much I'd miss him. Then I got to my feet and started unpacking my overnight bag. Enough moping. I had things to do and stuff to get ready for work in the morning. I comforted myself with the thought that at last I'd found the one thing at which Matt Power didn't excel: monogamy.

And then I thought of someone who'd never treat me like that in a million years.

At times like this, I found there was only one thing to do: throw myself into my work. It was the one constant that could always be relied upon in an ever-shifting universe. There was always work, and plenty of it.

That Monday was district court day in Ballyknock. Brendan Ryan and I were on opposing sides of a case – a ludicrous traffic accident that had been caused in equal parts by the stupidity of both of our clients. The judge clearly agreed; he made an order for fifty-fifty liability. Couldn't say fairer than that. Having convinced our respective clients that we were mortal enemies, Brendan and I went for lunch together.

'How are you getting on with that dog?' he asked me as we were waiting for our food.

'Great. I called him Terence.'

'Terence? Really? That's unusual.'

'Brendan, remember that day in your office, when you told me that you were going to bring him to the pound and that he'd probably be put down?'

'Yes.'

'Well, did you mean that?'

'Of course not.'

Didn't think so.

Was it just me, or were all men lying bastards?

Talking of lying bastards, I was relaxing at home one evening the following week when there was a knock on the front door. I was understandably irritated, as there were still ten minutes of *EastEnders* left to run. Who could be calling at such an inconvenient hour?

The last person in the world I expected to see, that's who. If Elvis Presley himself had turned up at my front door, sporting a white sparkly jumpsuit and singing 'Heartbreak Hotel', I couldn't have been more surprised.

I didn't recognise him at first. His hair was transformed, for a start: dyed blond, shaved at the sides, gelled into a disorganised peak at the top. He seemed sleeker, less chunky. He was wearing dark-grey flared trousers and a tight-fitting black polo-neck.

He looked like a hairdresser.

'Come in.' What else could I say?

Jack nodded at me and sheepishly entered the house. Hands deep in pockets, he looked around as if seeing the place for the first time. He sat on the couch, his tense body leaning forward. I tried not to think about the last time he'd sat there.

'I'll put the kettle on,' I said. Well, it always worked on *EastEnders*. When in doubt, make a nice cup of tea.

I handed him his mug, taking special care not to touch his hand with my own. Then I sat down next to him, balancing precariously on the edge of the couch.

'How have you been?' I asked.

'Fine. You?'

'Fine.' There was that word again.

There followed about thirty seconds of the most uncomfortable silence I'd ever endured. When I couldn't stand it any more, I said, 'Did you cut your trip short?'

He nodded. 'By about a month. I needed to come home and sort a few things out. I might be going back. I haven't decided yet.'

'How was New York?'

'Brilliant. Loved every second of it. I was only there for a couple of months, though; I spent the rest of the time in San Francisco.'

Oh. I took several sips of reviving tea, which luckily was hot and sweet.

'Lainey … I have something to tell you.'

'Go on.' I looked up at him and our eyes locked. He gazed at me imploringly. He looked as if he was about to speak, several times, but the words always seemed to get jammed in his throat.

'Oh, Jesus. This doesn't get any easier.' He hid his face in his hands.

'Just say it, Jack.'

A pair of turquoise eyes looked searchingly into my own.

'I'm gay.'

I nodded and took another sip of tea. I had already known. I'd just needed him to come out and say it. I could feel his eyes burning into the side of my face, but all I could do was stare at the floor.

'For Christ's sake, Lainey, say something – please.'

'Do your parents know?'

He slumped back into the couch. 'I told them last night. Not long after I got in.'

'How did they take it?'

'Mum was great. I mean, she cried a little at first. But, as she said to me, it's not as if I'm her one shot at having a grandchild.'

'You're her favourite son anyhow. Now you can be the daughter she never had.'

Jack checked to see whether or not I was being bitchy. Then we both started to laugh.

'Another cup?'

'Yes, please.'

I boiled up the kettle again.

'How about your dad?'

'Not so good.'

I gathered from the pained expression on his face that this was an understatement.

'Maybe he just needs some time to get used to the idea.'

'Maybe. But I don't think either of us will live that long.' He sounded utterly miserable.

My own mood, however, was becoming more jubilant by the second. You may find this strange; but, you see, for five months I'd thought that Jack had rejected me because I was physically repulsive. But his rejection had had nothing to do with me at all. He couldn't have fancied me if he'd tried. Not even if I'd had the body of Naomi Campbell. Unless …

'You're not bi, are you?'

'Nope. I'm afraid I'm a one-hundred-per-cent bona-fide poof.'

Hooray! He was gay! That meant I was okay!

He was queer. A shirt-lifter. A woolly woofter. An arse-bandit. A sausage-jockey.

What fantastic news!

'You know, you're taking this very calmly. I thought you'd freak.' Jack was studying me carefully.

'I'm just glad you didn't run off to America because of my disgusting thighs.'

'Is that what you thought? I'm so, so sorry.' He took my hands in both of his. 'I felt so terrible after the way I left things that night. And then just leaving the country without any explanation … what must you have thought of me?'

'I thought you were a right prick.'

'Of course you did. You had every right to. But I never meant to hurt you, Lainey.'

'But you did. I just wish you'd told me the truth. I would have understood, you know.'

'I know, I know. I'm sorry.'

'What did you think you were at, anyway?'

'Oh, I don't know. I was in denial, I suppose. And I was under a lot of family pressure to get a girlfriend.'

'You mean you went out with me to keep your mammy off your back?'

'Something like that. I suppose you think that's terrible.'

'I do, as it happens.'

'I don't blame you. But look at things from my point of view. Do you think it's easy being a gay farmer in Ballyknock?'

No, I didn't suppose it was.

'So can we get over this and be friends?'

'I don't know, Jack…. It all feels very weird.'

'It's bound to. You've only just found out. But in time you might feel differently. I mean, we always got on great, didn't we?'

This was true.

'And if I was straight, I'd definitely choose a girl-friend like you.'

I wasn't sure about this one. 'Is there something masculine about me, then?'

'God, no! Just the opposite. That's another reason I thought you'd be the perfect cover. You've got long blonde hair and – if you don't mind me saying – quite a large chest.'

He should know. He'd seen it in all its glory.

'You reminded me of the women I used to pre-tend to fancy in the girly magazines that the lads would pass around in school.'

I didn't know how to take that. Did I really look like a Page Three tart? The perfect cover for a gay boyfriend? Maybe I could hire myself out.

'You've gone all quiet again. Say something – please,' said Jack.

'I was just wondering….'

'What?'

'When you went to San Francisco – did you wear flowers in your hair?'

'Only on special occasions.'

Jack stayed for a few hours. He didn't seem to be in a big hurry to go home. It was odd, but kind of nice at the same time. He told me about this man he'd met in California. Jack liked him a lot, but he wasn't sure how serious the other guy, Chuck (no, honestly), was about him. It was a typical girly chat, really.

As he was leaving, he asked me, 'Will you come to the pub with me tomorrow night?'

'Which pub?'

'Power's. Where else?'

'I'm not sure if that's a good idea.'

'Ah, come on. I need the moral support.'

'Well, the thing is, I'm kind of trying to avoid Matt.'

'What's wrong with Matt?'

'Nothing. It's just …'

'Oh, no. Don't tell me you and him …'

''Fraid so.'

'How could you? And me barely cold in the grave.' He was smirking at me.

'I needed someone to help me get over you.'

'So you picked my own brother? Shame on you!' Jack was enjoying occupying the moral high ground for the first time that night.

'Actually, he picked me.'

'I don't doubt it. He's like a bitch in heat, that lad. But you needn't worry about bumping into Matt. He's probably forgotten all about you by now and moved on to the next blonde.'

'Thanks a lot.'

'Oh, you know what I mean. He doesn't have a faithful bone in his body. If you were the last woman on earth and he were the last man, he'd still find some way to cheat on you. Granny Mary was right about him. "That Mattie would flirt with a gatepost," she used to say. But I shouldn't be hard on him. He took my news very well – said he'd known all along.'

'I wish he'd told me,' I said.

'I wish he'd told me, too. Would have saved us both a lot of bother. So, anyhow, you needn't worry about him.'

'Well, it's not just Matt. It's your mother too.'

'What's wrong with Mam?'

'Nothing. I'm afraid she'll blame me for turning you.'

Jack laughed raucously. 'Don't be daft, woman.'

'I'm not being daft. I know that's what she thinks.'

'Trust me. She doesn't. Please say you'll come.'

'Oh, all right. Anything to shut you up.'

He turned to me one more time before getting into the jeep.

'And you never know – you might get lucky. My brother Timmy will be there, and he's single.'

'Do you really think I'd touch another Power man with a bargepole?'

He bellowed with laughter again. He was sounding more and more like the old Jack I used to love – still loved, really.

'I'll pick you up at nine.'

Chapter Twenty-seven

'Wow! I can see I'm not the only one who's changed. You look gorgeous. I love your hair; it really suits you down.'

'Are you going to keep commenting on my appearance all the time, now that you're a poof?'

'Might do. I'll even give you a makeover if you like.'

'Not just now, thanks.'

I looked him up and down. Tight black T-shirt. Black PVC trousers. Diamond stud in his ear.

'Jack, I hope you're not going to act like a gigantic cliché now that you've come out. I mean, look what you're wearing. I'm not saying that you don't look well – because you do – but, seriously, aren't things going to be hard enough for you tonight? Do you really want to walk into the pub dressed like that?'

'I figured, why not? Give them something to really talk about. I've been hiding my light under a bushel for far too long.'

'Fair enough,' I said. I guessed that it was probably just a phase he was going through, that once he got used to his new identity he'd start dressing normally again. I hoped. I clambered into the passenger seat. 'Just try not to drive like a maniac, please.'

'Just try not to be the passenger from hell, please.'

'Oh, shut up.'

'You shut up.' He grinned, leaned across and kissed me on the cheek. Then he drove off down the hill like a maniac.

I turned and looked at him from time to time, marvelling at how I'd been fooled for so long. It seemed so obvious now. Of course he was gay. He was virtually the perfect man in every way; how could he possibly be heterosexual?

It was like George Michael in the 80s. A generation of girls had fallen head over heels in love. And did any of us so much as suspect he was gay? Not one. We were too busy obsessing about that dazzling smile, that orange tan, those muscular calves, those nifty dance moves, the dashing white shorts, the highlights. There was a time when

George's mug shot graced the wall of every unisex hair salon in the country. And still we didn't cop. Looking back, it seemed surreal.

I was the first to walk into the pub, as Jack was having difficulty finding a parking space. It was Thursday night – music night – and the place was already packed.

Shem was the first to see me. 'Ah, here she comes. Lock up your sons.'

'What's that supposed to mean?' I was in no mood.

'Nothing,' said Shem, alarmed and back-pedalling furiously. 'I didn't mean a thing by it. Just a turn of phrase, that's all. Can I buy you a drink?'

I must have seriously rattled him. Shem never offered to buy anybody a drink.

'I'll have two bottles of Miller, please.'

'Two!'

I nodded. 'I'm very thirsty tonight.'

A woebegone expression on his face, Shem turned to Johnny. 'Two bottles of Miller for the lady.'

Johnny nodded curtly at me and got the drinks with his trademark rapid-fire movements.

I made space for Tom Delaney, who was returning to his barstool from the jacks – at least, I assumed that was where he was coming from; it would explain why his fly was undone. Away from his barstool, he was revealed as a big, shambling wreck of a man. He climbed back onto his throne and regarded me curiously, the stem of his pipe rattling between his few remaining teeth.

The sudden draught on my back told me that somebody had just walked in behind me. The looks on Shem's and Tom's faces told me that person was Jack. He came up and stood beside me.

'Shem! Long time no see. How are you going?'

Jack held out his massive hand for Shem to shake. Shem took it silently and moved his own hand feebly up and down before letting it drop.

'Tom! Good to see you.'

Tom couldn't or wouldn't take Jack's proffered hand. His mouth hung open, revealing the full magnificence of a lifetime lacking in oral hygiene. Jack patted him on the shoulder instead. Whether he actively meant it as an insult, or whether it was a reflex reaction, I couldn't be sure; either way, Tom swiped at his shoulder as if he'd just been injected with a deadly virus. Johnny was watching all this like a hawk.

Furious with the men, I snatched up the two bottles of beer, handed one to Jack and steered him away from the two old farts. 'Come on. Let's find a seat.'

The hurt was evident in Jack's features. He'd known Shem and Tom his whole life.

'Don't worry,' I whispered into his ear, 'he probably thinks you're after his body.' This raised the ghost of a smile.

Our next problem was to find somewhere to park ourselves. The music room itself was jammed.

The strange looks we were getting from all and sundry made the prospect of asking anyone if we could join them at their table seem quite daunting.

'Over here, Jack!' came a familiar voice from the far recesses of the room.

Matt Power and a blonde girl were sitting in a dark corner booth.

Jack gave me a look. 'Would you mind?'

'It doesn't look as if we have much choice.'

So we went over and sat down with Matt and this week's totty.

'How are you, Lainey?' He actually winked at me. The nerve!

'Couldn't be better. You?' I eyed him coldly. Okay, so I hadn't been mortally wounded by his conduct, but that didn't mean he should get off scot-free.

'Great form. This is Anita.'

He clearly had a type, anyway – although this latest model was younger, skinnier and blonder than me. Every woman's worst nightmare – I'd been replaced by a younger blonde! Anita gave me a suspicious look, which I decided to ignore.

Matt turned his attention to his brother. 'Jesus, Jack. What the *fuck* are you wearing?'

'What's wrong with it?'

'You're asking for trouble, mate. Could you not tone it down a little, for your own sake?'

'This is me, Matt. I'm not hiding it any more. I did that for far too long.'

'All right. On your own head be it.'

Anita was clearly smitten with Matt. She was glued to his arm, gazing continually into his eyes and giggling at everything he said. She didn't go unrewarded: he paid her plenty of attention. Matt had the knack of making a girl feel as if she were the only person in the room/field/tree. I should know. I admit I felt the odd pang of jealousy, but mostly I felt sorry for her. She was young and even more foolish than I was. I wondered if she had been the one in the surgery the week before. If I got drunk enough, I might ask her.

Jack put on a great show, being entertaining and expansive as usual, making sure Anita felt included. It couldn't have been easy for him, but he made it look like it was.

A mass exodus from the music room, as the musicians took a break, was our cue to move in. We received a mixed reception from the remaining inhabitants. Some nodded; some gaped, wide-eyed, at Jack and then quickly looked away again; some of them greeted Matt warmly. None of them greeted Jack warmly. But we were in. When we were seated, I squeezed Jack's knee in support.

'Careful,' he said. 'Someone might start a rumour that I'm straight.'

The musicians returned, and the session recommenced. I was relieved; it made the fact that none of the locals were talking to Jack less obvious. They played a selection of tunes, the music transforming the plain, box-shaped little room into an aural paradise. As usual, Johnny entered the room midway into the session, set down the glasses he was collecting and sat down at the piano, joining in seamlessly. Then the call was made for people to sing.

A woman called Jackie, who was home from England, murdered two Mary Black numbers in quick succession. She was a musical serial killer. She suffered further from comparison when Matt sang 'Raglan Road' directly after her. If Anita hadn't been impressed enough beforehand, she now looked ready to lay down her body and soul for Matt – and she probably would, in a few hours' time.

Next, Dixie, the most ancient of the accordion players, sang 'Don't Forget Your Shovel'. Never mind the shovel, he forgot most of the words. He got through by making up a lot of them and inserting a few well-placed 'la-la-la's. He was still better than Jackie.

'Okay, who's next to give us an oul' tune?' Johnny shouted enthusiastically, fingers poised above the piano keys, raring to go.

'I'll go.'

The room fell prey to the most deafening silence in the history of deafening silences. I wanted the ground to open up and swallow me whole – and I wasn't even the one who had offered to sing. *What is Jack thinking?* I thought. I looked across at Matt. His face had the same expression I could feel on my own.

There was an ominous scraping sound as Johnny pushed back his stool, got up from the piano, picked up the empties and walked back to the bar. Nobody said a word.

'Will one of you accompany me?' There was a desperate, fake cheeriness to Jack's voice.

Silence. Then: 'I will.'

This time it *was* me that had spoken, although I scarcely believed it myself.

'Thanks, Lainey.' Jack squeezed my arm as I stood up and walked shakily across to the piano.

'Don't thank me yet,' I hissed back. 'I'm a tad rusty.'

I sat down on the piano stool and looked down at the alien keys. *What was I thinking?* The musicians and locals alike looked alarmed as Jack rose from his seat and stood in the centre of the room, a giant, PVC-clad figure. This was not the custom in Power's Select Lounge and Bar; people were meant to remain sedately in their seats whilst singing.

I held my breath as Jack began. His voice strong and clear, he sang the opening lines of Gloria Gaynor's 'I Will Survive'. The ultimate gay anthem. You go, girl!

He made it through the first verse unaccompanied. I played a few faltering notes; then a few more. By the time he got to the chorus, we were sucking diesel!

Jack started to clap his hands in time to the music, gesturing to his audience to do the same.

Matt and Anita began to clap enthusiastically. I would have too, if my hands hadn't been otherwise occupied. Behind me, I could discern a few half-hearted clapping noises.

When the song ended, Jack got just enough applause that he announced he was going to sing another song.

'This one is especially for the mammy,' he declared. He bent his head towards me and hissed, '"Dancing Queen".'

'Come on, Jack. Would you ever sit back down? How am I supposed to know how to play "Dancing Queen"? And you never liked Abba before. Don't tell me your taste in music has gone the same way as your taste in clothes.'

'Come on, Lainey. It'll be a laugh. Give it your best shot.'

I gave it my best shot.

Someone must have gone to get Bridie, because she appeared at the door during the second verse, looking proud as punch. And well she might. Not only was her son a fine figure of a man, he was a damn good singer, too – not to mention a pretty decent performer. He confessed to me later on that he'd taken singing lessons in San Francisco.

My relief at the end of 'Dancing Queen' was short-lived: Jack announced his intention of singing 'just one more'. By the time he finished 'I Am What I Am', you couldn't get in the door of the music room. You couldn't see out of it, either; it was too crowded with bodies. The round of applause that followed fairly lifted the roof.

Jack dragged me to my feet and forced me to take a bow with him. I stopped laughing long enough to tell him how proud I was of him.

'I'm proud of you, too,' he said. 'You're the best fag-hag I've ever had.'

'Oh, shut up, you great big raving queen.'

Chapter Twenty-eight

It had been two weeks since that memorable night in the pub. It was mid-May, and the weather was still uncommonly good.

A lot had happened. My parents had returned from Beijing, bursting with the news that Tatiana, Chen and LuLing were coming home to live in Dublin at the end of the year. My mother was now an expert on all things Oriental ('Imagine not knowing that the samurai were an ancient Japanese warrior caste'). Hazel had got that job she'd been telling me about. She'd already started and was loving every minute of it. Her working day began at quarter past nine, she had a twenty-minute coffee break at eleven, an hour and a quarter for lunch and more coffee at four, and she went home at half-five on the dot. And she did this only three days a week. No wonder she loved it. Where did I sign up?

Things had improved considerably for Jack at home, too. Bridie had summoned the whole family – including Johnny – and given them a stern lecture concerning their behaviour towards Jack. Jack said the grand finale of her speech had been when she told the assembled throng, 'He's here, he's queer, get used to it.'

Apparently, she was a huge fan of *The Ellen Show*.

Jack and I laughed solidly for about ten minutes when he told me this. Then we spent the next ten minutes making up alternative slogans: 'He's here, he's queer, so have another beer,' 'He's here, he's queer, he's got a pierced ear' and – Jack's personal favourite – 'He's here, he's queer, and what a great rear.'

But I knew that Jack's laughter was partly a cover-up. It would take more than a good sound telling-off from Bridie, undisputed boss of the household though she was, to sway Johnny and a couple of Jack's elder brothers. The harsh truth had to be faced: it might never happen.

I put these thoughts out of my head. It was far too nice a day. I had absconded from work early – one advantage of being your own boss. And that's what I had become since I'd moved down to Ballyknock.

'My own boss.' I said the words out loud. They did have a lovely ring to them. As long as I got my work done, I could come and go as I pleased. I had settled into a nice little routine of 9.30 to 5.30 – a far cry from crazy Dublin working hours. There were a few disadvantages, sure. The facilities weren't so hot and my office wasn't exactly luxurious; but we got by. Then there was the drawback of being apprehended by clients in the local supermarket and pumped for free legal advice. At least I didn't have to worry about clients approaching me after Mass; I avoided this by not going to Mass. But, all in all, I had few complaints.

I strolled along the now-familiar roads around Ardskeha. Terence scampered a few yards ahead. The only sign of his recent ordeal was a funny patch on his left side where the fur hadn't fully grown back yet after his operation. He turned and looked back at me, as if telling me to step on it. He had a piece of wood in his mouth. It stuck straight out like a single, giant, rotten tooth.

I'd lately come to the realisation that Terence and I had a lot in common. We both needed a pat on the head every now and then, and someone to feed us biscuits.

The sun shone pleasantly on our respective heads, and the birds were in fine voice; it was like having our own private concert. The hedgerows were lush with bluebells, buttercups, cow parsley and clusters of small, white, as yet unidentified flowers, which I intended to look up in my new wildflower book when I got home. But the undisputed winner of Flower of the Day had to be the hawthorn – masses of white, sweetly scented blooms, hanging overhead like heavy clusters of precious gems. Who needed Aladdin's Cave? Everything was so beautiful, so fertile, so alive. I was reminded of that passage from the Bible – I couldn't recall the exact words: something about lilies in the field not having to toil, yet Solomon in all his glory was never clothed as beautifully. That day, I felt as if I fully understood those words for the first time. Maybe I'd resign and sit around in a hedgerow all day long. Nice work if you could get it.

I was so lost in the joys of nature that I didn't realise I'd walked further down this road than I'd ever walked before. The views were familiar – the river valley still to my left, the fields still rolling uphill to my right – yet different. Terence seemed more excited than ever. He hadn't been here before either. We crossed a small, ancient-looking stone bridge, the river beneath it reduced to a mere trickle by the unusually dry weather.

I rounded a bend, and my eye was caught by a flash of vivid blue. It was in a small raised area at the corner of a crossroads. As I drew closer, I saw that it was a tiny old graveyard carpeted with bluebells. I'd never seen such a stunning mass of wildflowers. It was as if the bluebells were on steroids. Well, I reasoned, they *were* well fertilised. I hoped that, when I died, I would get the opportunity to nourish such beautiful flowers.

The entrance to the graveyard consisted of a small wrought-iron gate set into a high, rough stone wall. I looked around, but there was nobody there. With some difficulty, I managed to draw back the rusty bolt and let myself in.

I called Terence, who bounded in behind me and cocked his leg against the nearest headstone before I could stop him. The stone – like many of the others – was clearly very old; any words that hadn't been eroded over time were concealed by moss. They weren't all like that, though. Some were newer. I carried out a swift survey and found that the most recent date was 1986.

I sat down companionably beside this flat tombstone. Looking back, it seems like a strange thing to have done; but, at the time, the place was so peaceful – magical, even – that I just wanted to stay and absorb the feeling for as long as possible. It was as if the emotional turmoil of the last few months had never existed – or, if it had, it simply didn't matter any more.

I examined the tombstone beside me more carefully. It might have been the most recent, but it hadn't escaped the ravages of time. Trailing ivy obscured most of the wording and the stone was dappled with moss. There appeared to be a verse on it. I tugged at the ivy to reveal the first words:

> *Gather ye rosebuds while ye may,*
> *Old Time is still a-flying;*

I pulled away the remaining ivy to reveal the rest of the verse.

> *And this same flower that smiles today*
> *Tomorrow will be dying.*

It seemed like an odd choice of verse for a tombstone. Who did the grave belong to? I scraped away the moss at the top of the stone.

> *Mary Power*
> *of Power's Cottage, Ardskeha, Ballyknock*
> *Died 16 May 1986, aged 84*
> *R.I.P.*

> *And her daughter*
> *Ellen Power*
> *Died 10 January 1940, aged 6 weeks*
> *R.I.P.*

'Happy anniversary, Mary,' I whispered. It seemed important not to talk too loudly. Somehow, I wasn't rattled; I was just overcome with sympathy. Poor Mary, to lose a child like that. I felt I should say a prayer or something. I blessed myself and said a quick Hail Mary. Then I just sat for a long time.

The sun beating down on my head seemed to be willing me to stay. So did the birds, the trees, the bluebells – the silent inhabitants of the cemetery. I felt as if I was melting into my surroundings. And it was at that precise moment that I admitted to myself the knowledge that had been building up inside me for some time now. I had been feeling it every time I looked at Terence, or Slinky. Or the other day, when I'd been planting flower seeds in the garden of Power's Cottage and had seen that they wouldn't bloom until September, when I'd be long gone. When I caught my first glimpse of the cottage every time I drove up the hill. When I looked across at the rolling hills, the river valley, the mares and foals in the fields. Even when I tasted Patricia's jam or sat in on the sessions in the pub.

I didn't want to go back to the city. I wanted to stay here – to make this place my home.

The thought, once acknowledged, didn't overwhelm me as I would have expected. Rather, it was a relief to get it out in the open.

I must have been sitting very still, thinking these thoughts: a butterfly that had been flitting around the graveyard alighted delicately on my knee. I felt that she was staring at me, but that was ridiculous. I stayed still as a statue for several minutes until she flew away. My eyelids heavy from the unrelenting sun, I lay down on a bed of moss and bluebells and closed my eyes.

I'm not sure how long I slept, but when I awoke, the sun had travelled right across the sky and was beginning to drop. I shivered. The cold must have woken me up. I sat up and rubbed my eyes. Terence was lying beside me, panting lightly, looking at me intently and waiting for my next move.

'Why didn't you wake me?'

He sat up and licked my hand in response, then looked at me again, head cocked to one side. The downward tilt of his eye, the upward tilt of his ear ... I could have sworn that he was smiling at me.

'Come on, boy,' I said, struggling to my feet, 'let's go home.'

Slinky was there to greet us when we arrived back at Power's Cottage. She ran along the fence like a gymnast on a beam and made a perfect dismount, before wrapping herself around my legs and meowing hungrily up at me. It was way past her dinner-time.

I'd only intended to be out for half an hour, so I'd left every window in the house wide open – something else I couldn't do in Dublin. I opened the front door and went inside, the two animals hot on my heels. The gust of wind I brought in with me made the wind chimes inside the door jangle. In fact, the whole house felt breezy, as if the inside had become the outside. And it smelt so fresh, so fragrant – although it wasn't just fresh air; there was some sort of flowery scent.... I inhaled deeply. Roses.

Up ahead, Slinky stood motionless in the door-way to the sitting room. Then she arched her back, her fur standing on end, and spat viciously.

'What is it, Slinky?'

She flew between my legs and back out the half-open front door.

'Who's there?' I called out.

I advanced slowly and peeked into the sitting room. Terence whimpered and hid behind me, his tail between his legs. There was nobody there, but the scent of roses was more intense. I moved cautiously into the room and glanced above the fireplace for Mary Power's reassuring image. The picture was crooked – as if someone had taken it off the wall and failed to replace it properly.

I went over and adjusted it. Mary Power and I smiled at each other.

'Thank you,' I said – or did I just think it?

Because now I knew exactly what I had to do.

Chapter Twenty-nine

I didn't arrive in Dublin until well after eight that Friday evening. I had called the office, but there was no reply. Tyrone wasn't answering his mobile, either, so I chanced calling around to his house.

Tyrone lived in Ranelagh, in an elegant red-brick building with a well-established, well-manicured front garden. It was a shame he didn't have someone to share it with. I felt an unexpected wave of pity towards my boss. For all I knew, that pity was misplaced. He chose to live this way; maybe he liked it. And, besides, what was I doing wasting my sympathy on a man who lived in a house worth over two million? It was amazing that he and his money hadn't been snapped up by some manipulative minx a long time ago. There was no way he was short of offers. Much to his amusement, his name often cropped up on 'Most Eligible Bachelor' lists.

As luck would have it, he appeared to be in. At least, the light was on in the front room. I rang the doorbell and peered in at the bay window; I could just make out a shadow moving behind the heavy curtains.

Tyrone opened the door a few seconds later. He was still wearing his work shirt and suit trousers; his jacket and tie had been replaced by an enormous, grey, hand-knitted cardigan. He was holding a crystal tumbler containing dark-orange liquid and ice. I was sure he wasn't meant to be drinking scotch, but tonight wasn't the night to bring it up.

'Hi. Nice cardie.'

'Lainey? What are you doing here?' His unkempt silver eyebrows were raised in surprise.

'I thought I'd check up on you. Find out what you *really* get up to on a Friday night.'

'Is something wrong?'

'No.'

'You'd better come in.'

He held the door open wider for me and I entered the long, dark hallway. On the rare occasions when I had visited Tyrone at home, I had always got the same feeling. It wasn't anything I could put my finger on, exactly, but the place needed a woman's touch. Not a woman like me, obviously. I meant one with proper home-making skills. Personally, I wouldn't have had a clue where to start.

Tyrone hurried ahead of me into the living room. I followed him in, just in time to catch him hiding something behind a stack of books. Judging by the aroma in the room, it was probably a dirty ashtray. But I wasn't going to say anything about that either.

'Drink?'

'Got any whiskey?'

'Um ... don't know. I'll have to check.'

'I'll have a whiskey and 7-up, if you have it.'

This made him wince, as I had known it would; I knew how much it irked him to dilute his precious firewater. But I couldn't resist. He went off to fix my drink, turning the volume down on the stereo on his way out of the room.

Not for the first time, I was struck by the similarity between my boss and Inspector Morse – although, while Morse had ice-blue eyes, Tyrone's were molten brown; and, while Morse listened to opera, Tyrone existed on a strict musical diet of diddly-eye. You could take the man out of the bog....

He returned. 'There.' He pressed the drink into my hand. 'Enjoy – although I don't know how that's possible. Anyway, cheers.'

We clinked glasses and he sat down opposite me in his armchair, a quizzical look on his face. 'Are you planning on telling me what this is about, or am I going to have to guess?'

'Can't a girl pay her boss a friendly visit once in a while?'

'Come off it. What have you done? Have you sold somebody the wrong house?'

'No!'

'You called the district court judge a grumpy old bastard and he held you in contempt?'

'No.' I was laughing now.

'What, then?'

'Tyrone, I've been thinking.'

'This should be good.' He leaned back in his armchair and took a large gulp of his drink, as if steeling himself.

'Well, you know I've been in Ballyknock for about seven months now –'

'Let me stop you there. I think I know what you're going to say. I understand you must be dying to get back to your life in Dublin; but I swear to you, I only need you there for a couple more months. And I won't forget what you've done.'

'It's not that at all.'

'What, then?'

'Well, the thing is … I really like it down there. I was thinking I might like to stay.'

Tyrone blinked at me a couple of times. I took the opportunity to keep babbling.

'I mean, business has been booming – there's plenty of work for two solicitors. And you wanted to cut back on work; I'd be there to take the pressure off whenever you needed me. You'd be able to take lots of afternoons off to play golf or go fishing.'

He interrupted, 'I was planning on doing that anyway.'

'I know. I mean, obviously, you're the boss and you're entitled to do whatever you want. But me being there would make it easier for you to get out and about. What do you think?'

Tyrone took another gulp of scotch and stared off into space. I sat there, breath bated. I couldn't tell whether or not he was trying to make me sweat.

When I couldn't stand it any more, I said, 'Will you even consider it?'

'No. I won't consider it –'

'Oh, Tyrone, why?'

'Because I don't need to. You're hired.'

'Really! Oh, thank you!' I jumped out of my seat and clapped my hands. 'Can I hug you?'

'Best not. An old fogey like me might get funny ideas.'

'Oh, Tyrone, this is brilliant! I can't thank you enough.'

'There's no need to thank me. A girl like you might come in useful around the office. You can make my coffee and type up my letters when Patricia's off sick.'

'Very funny. Seriously, though, you won't regret this.'

'I know I won't. I only hope that *you* don't.'

'Don't worry about me. I'll be fine.'

377

I had decided to stay with my parents that night, on the basis that I couldn't stomach Iseult. It was near ten when I arrived home. The house was in darkness and the driveway was empty. *Shit*. I'd forgotten my key. I fumbled around in the rockery in the front garden.... Bingo. Mum still kept a spare key under the ornamental Buddha.

I let myself in, turned on all the lights and looked around for clues to my parents' whereabouts. I was filled with childish indignation that they weren't home when it suited me. So what if they didn't know I was coming? Where were they, anyway, at this hour on a Friday night? My parents never went out any more. They were far too old for that sort of thing.

It wasn't until the next morning that the mystery was solved. I stumbled into the kitchen, bleary-eyed and dishevelled, at about half past nine, wearing a white towelling robe that I'd owned since the age of sixteen. My mother was already up and about – showered, dressed, made up and clattering about the kitchen. She was humming a tune I didn't recognise.

'Morning, Elena. Sit down and I'll make you a nice healthy breakfast.'

I didn't like the sound of that. Past experience indicated that this would involve lots of bran. I'd munch on a few spoonfuls to keep her happy, then buy a Danish on the way out.

'Aren't you surprised to see me?' I asked.

'No. Sure, isn't that fancy car of yours parked right outside?'

'So where were you last night? I didn't even hear you come in.'

She beamed at me as she busily opened and closed presses. 'We went ballroom dancing. It's your father's new hobby.'

Dad? Ballroom dancing? Never! 'Was it his idea?'

'No, it was mine. Last night was his first night, but I really think he's taken to it already.'

The image of Dad doing the foxtrot, wearing a monkey suit and a snooty expression, was too bizarre to contemplate. I'd only seen him dance once before – when he'd got pissed at my cousin Eileen's wedding. He'd forced the mother of the bride to jive with him, humiliating her thoroughly before putting his back out. I hoped Mum wouldn't be too disappointed when this particular hobby fizzled out after a couple of weeks.

'Now! Get that down you. Wait till you see all the photos we took in Beijing.'

She all but ran out of the room, but not before handing me a bowl full of something that looked as if it should have been served in a nosebag. She returned seconds later, smiling broadly and carrying no less than five packs of photos.

'Someone was busy.'

'It was your father with his new photographic equipment. You know, we had to pay a fine at Heathrow – two hundred and fifty euros for excess baggage, just because of him and all his gear. I don't know – that man!' Mum shook her head. But I knew her, and she didn't sound the tiniest bit annoyed to me.

And so for the next hour – or so it seemed – we looked at baby photos. I had to admit that my niece was adorable, even though I said so myself. I could claim no connection to the jet-black spiky hair, the cinnamon skin, the massive brown eyes; but the nose…. Was it possible that she had my nose? There were a variety of poses: LuLing sleeping; LuLing crying; LuLing smiling (wind, apparently); LuLing staring at the ceiling; Tatiana and LuLing; Chen and LuLing; Tatiana, Chen and LuLing; proud granny with LuLing; proud grand-dad with LuLing…. Need I continue?

I chose a few photos to take back with me. They weren't bad. Maybe Dad had a latent talent. Then I stood up. Enough was enough.

'Where are you going?' Mum looked disappointed.

'Upstairs, to get dressed. Then I'm going into town to meet the girls for lunch.'

'So soon! I was hoping you could help me put the photos into albums. I bought ten new ones, you know.'

'I'd love to, but I promised to meet them and I can't let them down. I'll help you with the photos later on.'

'You've hardly touched your breakfast.'

'Ah, Mum. You know I don't eat that mush.'

'It's not mush. It's a nutritious, high-energy cereal, packed with fibre.'

I gave her a look.

'Oh, have an apple, then.' She knew she wasn't going to win this particular argument.

To appease her, I grabbed an apple, rubbed it a couple of times against my ragged bathrobe and took a bite.

'Are you regular these days, Elena?'

'Mum, please!'

It was nearing midday when I pulled up outside the end-of-terrace house in Sallynoggin. The only remarkable thing about the grey, pebble-dashed building was its southside address, which lent it a market value of six times its true worth.

It felt weird being here again after all this time; strange, yet familiar. The Child of Prague – head intact – still stood sentry in the downstairs window. The front door was slightly ajar, held open by a thick green wire that led to an extension lead on the front path. I rang the doorbell a couple of times, but there was no reply. After a while, I tentatively pushed open the door.

'Anybody home?'

The only person who appeared to be home was Pope John Paul II, who smiled benignly at me from his ornate gilt frame on the wall. I followed the green wire along the narrow hallway and through the galley kitchen. It disappeared out the back door. As I followed it, an electrical whirring noise grew louder. I pushed open the back door.

Paul was strimming the hedge, his ears encased in bright orange muffs. I couldn't figure out a way of getting his attention without risking him cutting off an arm, so I sat down on the step outside the back door to wait for him. I was prepared to be patient, but, as it turned out, I didn't have to be; a few seconds later, Paul inexplicably turned and looked right at me. After a puzzled stare, he turned off the machine, pulled the earmuffs down around his neck and walked slowly towards me. He was wearing a pair of old combats and a U2 T-shirt that I happened to know he'd owned since he was seventeen.

He didn't stop walking until he literally loomed over me. I had to crane my neck and shade my eyes in order to look at him properly. Not that this helped me any. His expression was illegible.

'What are you doing here?'

I was being asked that question a lot lately. I was going to have to stop popping up unannounced all over the place.

'I was in the area, and I thought I'd call in and see how you were doing.'

'What were you doing in the area?' Still the stony countenance.

I didn't blame him for being suspicious. He of all people knew what a consummate liar I was. But

I wasn't worried: I had my story learnt off pat, as usual.

'I was at the hairdresser's I used to go to – you know, the one above the Spar in the village. I wanted to see if they could fit me in.'

'And could they?'

'No.'

'Maybe I can help you out.' He held the strimmer above his head and revved it theatrically.

I laughed. 'You're okay. It was a wash and blow-dry I was after, not a full decapitation.'

To my immense relief, Paul smiled and sat down on the step beside me.

The truth, for those of you who are interested, was that I'd remembered that his mother routinely got him to come around on Saturday mornings to do various odd jobs ('The devil makes work for idle hands, Paul').

I watched Paul shyly as he made small talk. The veins in his hands and forearms were protruding in the heat. A rivulet of sweat ran down his forehead, his temple, his cheekbone, his jawline, his sinewy neck, before disappearing in a trickle down the frayed neck of his T-shirt.

'Would you like a cool drink?' I said, interrupting whatever it was he had been saying.

'Um … yeah, that'd be nice.'

I went back into the kitchen and rooted around in the fridge and presses. All I could find was Ribena. And it wasn't even Toothkind. I remembered Paul's mother serving it to me in a wineglass, the one and only time I'd been to dinner at the house – as if that was fooling anybody.

I could do better than that. I slipped out of the house and around the corner to the off-licence. What a wonderful thing to have right on your doorstep! Completely wasted on Paul's mum, of course. I purchased a six-pack straight from the fridge and fairly skipped back to the house, delighted by my own ingenuity. I triumphantly handed Paul a beer.

'There you go. What every working man needs after a hard day's graft.'

'What's your excuse, then?'

'I don't need one. Does your mother not object to living around the corner from an offie?'

'You know her. She objects to anything that might possibly lead to somebody somewhere having some fun.'

'Where is she, anyhow?'

Paul took a large gulp of beer and sighed. 'Mass. Where else?'

'Is it a holy day, then?'

He looked at me solemnly. 'Lainey, don't you know that every day is a holy day in the O'Toole household?'

We both giggled, savouring the cool, bitter tang of the beer and the contrasting hot, sweet caress of the sun.

'I could help you, if you like,' I said.

'With what?'

'The gardening.'

'What, *you*?' Paul found this extremely funny.

'Yes, me. What's so funny about that?'

'Nothing. It's just that manual labour has never been your thing.'

'How do you know? You've never seen me doing manual work.' I was quite indignant.

'Exactly.'

'Well, the offer stands.'

'Thanks.'

'You're welcome.'

I wasn't looking at him, but I could tell he was still smiling to himself. Oh, well; let him. Wasn't it better than having him annoyed with me? I really hadn't been sure what kind of reception I'd get. I should have known. Paul could never be mean to anyone for any length of time.

I still didn't fully understand what I was doing there. And I still wasn't sure what I wanted to say to him. All I knew was that I'd had to come.

'When are you expecting your mother back?'

'Any time now. Why? Are you afraid she'll kick you out?'

'She wouldn't – would she?'

'I don't know.' He smiled. 'Maybe if she sees the beer.'

'Tell you what. Why don't I help you finish up here, and then we can go out for lunch? My treat.'

Paul looked doubtfully at me.

'That's if you don't have other plans,' I said. *Involving Iseult*, I thought.

'No,' he said slowly, 'I don't have plans. It's not that. I'm just concerned about your clothes getting wrecked.'

'Is that all? Don't worry about my clothes. That's what God invented washing machines for. Come on – the sooner we get started, the sooner we finish.'

Chapter Thirty

For the next hour, Paul strimmed while I collected branches and dumped them on the compost heap. It was all I was qualified to do, really. Paul was by far the more expert gardener.

Watching him when he wasn't looking, I decided I liked him with his gardening hat on. It suited him better than the stuffy accountant look. He almost reminded me of that gardener bloke off the telly whom I fancied. Come to think of it, I fancied nearly all the gardeners on the telly, even the overtly gay ones. I didn't know what it was. There was just something so *earthy* about what they did for a living. Some occupations were just more attractive than others. Photographers – I liked those, too; but they had to be proper ones, mind, not amateur photographers like my father who wore slacks. Building labourers, especially on hot days when they removed their checked shirts and performed daredevil stunts on scaffolding. Mechanics – all that oil. And cowboys…. What can I say? The ultimate in masculinity.

Accountants didn't feature too high on the list.

By the time we'd finished the garden, my pristine white top wasn't all that pristine any more. I didn't care. I was happy. We decided that we each deserved another tinny after all our hard work. We were just cracking into them when the back door flew open and the Wicked Witch of the Southside stuck her head out. We instinctively hid our cans behind our backs like bold children.

'Elena.' Her greeting was cool.

'Hello, Mrs O'Toole.'

'Paul, what about that fruit tree? It needs pruning.' I'd forgotten what an annoying, high-pitched, nasal Cork accent she had.

'I'll do it later. Me and Lainey are just heading out for a spot of lunch.'

She sniffed. 'But I'm just after buying us a couple of lovely chops.'

'I'll have mine for my tea.'

'Okay, so.' She slammed the door shut, her face like a slapped arse.

'Oops,' I said. I looked searchingly into Paul's face. 'We don't have to go out for lunch, you know.

I could piss off and leave you both here to enjoy your chops.'

'No! Don't mind her. I'm just going to run upstairs and have a quick shower – five minutes at the most, I promise. Will you be okay?'

'Yeah, fine. Go ahead.'

I watched as he hid the remaining cans in the shed and then disappeared into the kitchen. He flashed me an encouraging smile as he left. I could see his mother quizzing him inside. 'What's *she* doing here?'

I tried to see things from her point of view. She was probably lonely. And the one day of the week when she got to see her only son, I – brazen hussy that I was – spirited him away for the afternoon. I could see her moving around in the kitchen. I supposed I should go in and talk to her. I could hardly stand out here when she was only a few feet away, behind the door, and there was no way she was going to make the first move. It was up to me. Time to make nice.

I knocked gently and opened the door into the kitchen. I gave Mrs O'Toole my best conciliatory smile, but all she did was look me up and down disapprovingly. The top I was wearing, which had seemed perfectly acceptable two minutes earlier, suddenly felt obscenely low-cut and tight-fitting. Mrs O'Toole herself could easily have been mistaken for a plain-clothes nun. She was wearing what could only be described as a smock – grey –

and she had a plain gold crucifix around her neck. Her hair was atrocious. It was as if she'd gone to the hairdresser's and said, 'Make me look as unattractive as possible.' And as for make-up – forget it. She was poles apart from my own mother, who wouldn't be seen dead without her lipstick. (I'm serious. She'd literally given me instructions as to the exact shade and brand of lippy she wanted to wear when she was being laid out. Dad had told me that she'd tried to include this in her will, but that the family solicitor wasn't having any of it. I think he might have been having me on.)

It was a pity about Mrs O'Toole, because you could tell she was pretty, deep down. Her features were regular and her bone structure good. Her waist was still tiny, too – must have been all that fasting and clean living. I mentally sifted through the selection of oul' fellas I knew in Ballymuck, bachelor clients and Power's regulars alike. There had to be somebody I could set her up with.

'Cup of tea, Elena?'

'Yes, please!' I said this as if she'd just offered me a free week in the Algarve. A breakthrough!

I did my best to make desperate small talk, as the red light of the Sacred Heart shone down on my head. Had she been away recently? Oh, yes; she'd just come back from ten days in Lourdes. And had she had a good time? Oh, yes. She'd had a lovely time pushing wheelchairs around and attending candlelight vigils. (I prefer candlelight dinners, myself.) She'd even bought a brand spanking new holy-water font for the hall. She showed it to me. Blue and white plastic. 'Isn't it gorgeous!' I said. Honestly, I made myself sick sometimes. I was going straight to hell, I had no doubt about it.

When I had run out of things to say – after about two minutes – Mrs O'Toole said, 'So how long have you been back on the scene, then?'

I was taken aback. 'What? … Oh, no – Paul and I aren't together. I just called by to say hello. As a friend.'

She shot me an incredulous look and said, 'I was wondering why that skinny girl hadn't been around much lately.'

Skinny girl? It had to be Iseult. Did that make me the fat girl?

I was just about to reiterate that I was no longer her son's girlfriend when said son burst through the door. That had to have been the quickest shower in history. There were clearly advantages to having little or no hair. Paul was most likely terrified of leaving me and his mother alone in the same room for any significant length of time. He'd probably been imagining all manner of carnage while he was upstairs.

'Ready?'

As ready as I'll ever be.

Half an hour later, we were sitting in a hotel in Dalkey. The lunchtime rush was over, so we managed to get a table by the window, overlooking the sea. The waves lapped indolently against the rocks and the horizon disappeared into the haze. I broke the habit of a lifetime and ordered a salad, shocking us both.

It came to light, in the course of the conversation, that Paul had the next two weeks off work.

'Are you going away?'

'No.'

'What are you going to do, then?'

'Don't know, really. Just hang about.'

'That's a bit of a waste of your annual leave, surely?'

He shrugged. 'There are a lot of jobs to be done in my mother's house – painting, tiling, that sort of thing. It'll be good to get them out of the way.'

'Two weeks with your mother? You'll go nuts.'

'Will you just drop it, please?'

I looked at him in surprise. 'Take the head off me, why don't you?'

'Sorry. I didn't mean to snap.'

'But you did.'

'Look, if you must know, I was supposed to be going on holiday with Iseult. Today.' He glanced at his watch. 'I should have been landing in Ibiza about now.'

That shut me up. The great unmentionable had finally been mentioned. I speared a piece of cucumber with my fork and chewed it solemnly, keeping my focus on my plate.

'Well?' said Paul.

'Well what?'

'Don't you want to know why I'm in Dalkey instead of Ibiza?'

'Only if you want to tell me.'

'We broke up last week. It was too late for me to swap my leave with anyone else. So here I am – two weeks on my hands, and nothing to do with them.'

So many questions were buzzing around in my head. What had gone wrong? Who had dumped who? Why hadn't Chris told me? Who had dumped who?

'Did you – I mean, I'm very sorry to hear that.'

'Are you really?'

'Of course.'

'I finished with her, by the way.'

'Did you?' I tried to keep my tone as neutral – and as sincere – as possible. 'Poor Iseult. Was she very upset?'

'Hardly. She's brought her new boyfriend to Ibiza with her.'

'No! You mean they've gone on *your* holiday together?'

'I don't mind. She paid me back my half, so she can do what she likes.'

'Who is he?'

'Some hot new actor. She met him while he was being interviewed for the magazine.'

'What's his name?'

'Dylan Mayberry.'

'Never heard of him. He must be crap.'

'He's got a bit part in the new James Bond.'

'Everyone knows you don't have to be able to act to be in a Bond movie. I'm telling you, he's probably crap.'

Paul was laughing. 'You don't have to do this, Lainey. I'm not upset.'

'You sure?'

'Positive.'

He played around with his food for a bit. 'I thought you'd have heard already.'

'How would I hear?'

'From Chris.'

'That one? You know what she's like. It wouldn't even occur to her to let me know. Although, of course,' I added quickly, 'why would she?'

'Yes, of course. Why would she?' he answered equally quickly.

We both ate silently for a while. It occurred to me that Paul must have thought I knew about his single status when I'd turned up at his house that morning. I tried to work out what that told me, and came to the conclusion that it told me absolutely nothing.

I couldn't resist asking the next question.

'Paul, can I ask you something? Just one final thing about Iseult, and then I promise I'll shut up.'

'Shoot.'

'Why on earth did you go out with her in the first place?'

Paul sat back in his chair, folded his arms and laughed. 'So it wasn't my imagination. You really *didn't* like her.'

'Oh, I'm sure she would be lovely if she weren't so horrible. I wasn't exactly her favourite person either, was I?'

'Oh, I don't know. Sometimes I used to think she was jealous of you.'

'Of me? Why?'

'Can't think of a good reason.'

'Thanks.'

He grinned at me. 'No, she was always pumping me for information about you.'

'You still haven't answered my question.'

'Why did I go out with her?'

'Yes. You'd want to have a pretty good explanation.'

'If I tell you why, you have to promise not to tell another soul.'

I moved forward in my seat. This sounded gripping.

'I won't tell anyone. Brownie's honour.'

'Why do you always say that?'

'It's a long story. Now, come on. Spit it out.'

'Okay. The night we got together, I was out with the lads after soccer practice. We went to this poxy new bar that we normally wouldn't be caught dead in. But we couldn't get into O'Brien's, and we had to watch the Arsenal match somewhere.'

'Naturally.'

'So there I was, minding my own business, watching the match, when who walks in but Chris and a bunch of her noisy mates. Iseult was there, and so were all those losers that were at your going-away. At half-time, Iseult comes and sits down next to me. She's sidling up to me and doing those things that girls do when they're interested.'

'Like what?'

'You know – smiling too much, giggling, hair-flicking, touching your hand all the time … that sort of shit.'

'Do I do that?'

'No, you're different.'

'Well, don't say it's the kind of thing "girls" do, then.'

'All right. Point taken.'

'Go on.'

'I will if you'll let me. So the second half starts, and she's still sitting there. And I'm thinking, *What's she playing at? The match is back on. Why doesn't she feck off back to her friends?* But she just sits. And you'll never guess what happens next.'

'What?'

'Do you remember that guy Diarmuid, who was hitting on me that night in the restaurant?'

'The model.'

'That's him. Well, doesn't he come over to join us? Lainey – he starts to come on to me. Right in front of my mates.'

'No!'

'Lainey, he touched my knee.'

'No!'

'I'm not joking. I didn't know where to look. It's not funny, you know.'

'I never said it was.'

'Then why are you laughing?'

'I'm not. Come on, tell the story.'

'So, anyway, all my mates are looking at me. No one's even watching the match any more. I had to do something. So I pretended to be into Iseult. I mean, what else could I do? I was mortified. To cut a long story short, I ended up kissing Iseult, and Diarmuid went off in a huff. Next thing I know, we're a couple and she's organising dinner parties at my flat and inviting all my friends.'

'Poor Diarmuid.'

'Fuck Diarmuid. I didn't even get to see the second half. And that match was crucial.'

I couldn't contain the laughter any more. Poor Paul. Caught between Diarmuid and Iseult. Between a rock and a hard place. Between a pair of rocks and a hard-faced bitch.

Paul watched me laughing, the ghost of a smile on his lips, his dimples coming out to play.

'Did you like my little story, then?'

'Yes, thank you. Highly entertaining.' I was wiping the corners of my eyes with my napkin.

'Will I order coffees?'

'Please.'

I attempted to size him up as he played with his cappuccino, chatting amiably on and off, the rest of the time staring unselfconsciously out to sea.

This was my opportunity.

My reason for coming here seemed so clear now. I took a deep breath.

'Paul?'

'Yes?' He tore his eyes away from the ocean and smiled deeply and warmly into mine.

'Since you have all this time off and nothing to do with it, why don't you come and stay with me in Ballyknock? I mean, not for the whole two weeks, obviously; just for a few days, at first, and you can see how you get on – not that you're not welcome to stay for the two weeks if you like. I have a spare room. You could stay there and I could show you around. There's loads to see and do, and people to meet, and you could see where I work, and there'd be no strings – honestly.'

I finally ran out of breath. I sat looking at him looking at me, feeling totally exposed.

At last he spoke.

'I'd love to.'

Chapter Thirty-one

I drove us back down to Ballyknock that Sunday. The journey was a little like that scene at the end of *The Graduate*, when Dustin Hoffman and Katherine Ross – still in her wedding dress – are sitting at the back of the bus. He's just burst in on her wedding to another man, and they've run off together. Then they both comprehend, at the same time, the full enormity of what they've done. And they can't think of anything to say to each other.

It was a bit like that with me and Paul. We had both made what felt like a momentous decision, and neither of us knew what to say next. I turned on the car radio to ease the awkwardness, and began to wonder if I had made a huge mistake.

We had to pick up Terence on the way home –
Patricia had graciously agreed to mind him for the
weekend. She nearly caused herself an injury at her
own front door, craning her neck to make out who
was in the car with me. If she did hurt herself,
I knew the name of a good solicitor…. I had a
feeling she'd be in my office first thing the next
morning, searching for phantom files. I decided to
save her the bother.

'Patricia, I have somebody here I'd like you to
meet.'

She followed me like a novice nun about to have
an audience with the Pope.

'Patricia, this is Paul. Paul – Patricia.'

They shook hands through the open car
window.

'Paul is my ex-boyfriend. He'll be staying with me
for a little while. He's on his holidays.' Best to be
upfront right away.

'Hello, Paul. Lovely to meet you. Are you a
solicitor too?'

'No, I'm an accountant.'

'Really? Isn't that lovely! And how long do you
think you'll be staying with us for?'

'Probably just a few days.'

'Is that all? We'll have to do our best to convince
you to stay longer, won't we, Lainey?'

'We will, Patricia.'

'And how long did you say you two were going
out for?'

'We didn't. Look, we're pretty tired after our journey; we'd better be off. Thanks again for looking after the dog.'

'Not at all. He was no trouble. See you bright and early tomorrow morning.' What – she was planning on coming in before ten, for a change?

'God, she's nosy. Are they all like that down here?' asked Paul as we pulled away from Patricia's house. I could see her receding figure, waving at us enthusiastically, in the rear-view mirror.

'No, she's the nosiest I've met. But she's very nice. And wait until you taste her jam.'

I found that I wanted him to love everything about Ballyknock and everyone in it.

Slinky – intrepid little explorer; she had been missing for the best part of a week – was waiting for us back at the cottage. Having feared the worst, I scooped her up and hugged her tiny, purring body before letting us both into the house. She licked my hand with her little sandpaper tongue.

'Um … you don't let the cat indoors, do you?' said Paul.

'Of course I do.'

'What about toxoplasmosis?'

'Toxoplas-what?'

'Toxoplasmosis. You get it from handling cat shit.'

'Funnily enough, fondling cat turds has never been a major hobby of mine.'

It probably wasn't the best time to mention Slinky's endearing habit of making a little nook for herself on my unmade duvet. The story made us both look bad.

Paul followed me into the house, and I gave him a quick guided tour.

'What do you think?'

'I'm impressed. It's not what I expected. I thought it would be more basic. But it's like something out of an *Ideal Homes* magazine.'

I beamed with pleasure, as if I'd designed and built the cottage myself. Terence, who had joined the tour halfway, wagged his whole body with delight at being home and at the prospect of having an extra playmate. He gazed up at Paul expectantly.

'Um … you keep the dog in the house, too?'

'Yes. Where else would I keep him?'

'I just assumed he'd be chained up outside.'

Chained up outside! How would *he* have liked to be chained up outside? I was a little annoyed, but I decided not to mention for the time being that Terence slept at the foot of my bed.

Talking of bed, we retired soon after that. I showed Paul to his room and exited rapidly, muttering 'Good night' to his feet before closing the door firmly between us.

As luck would have it, it poured with rain all day Monday. The spectacular views that I'd been raving about were virtually non-existent. I sped home from work that evening torn between eagerness to see Paul and anxiety that the first day of his holiday had been a complete washout.

He was waiting for me in the kitchen, wooden spoon in one hand, tea-towel in the other. It was lovely having someone to come home to. I almost asked him then and there to be my wife.

'What did you get up to today?'

'Well,' he began primly, 'I cleaned the kitchen from top to bottom.'

'But I only cleaned it last week.'

Paul gave me a look that said, *Call that cleaning?*

'Are you casting aspersions on my housekeeping skills?'

'What housekeeping skills?'

'I resent that,' I said – although privately I felt it was fair comment.

'I don't know how you haven't contracted salmonella.'

'I don't eat salmon.'

'If you were a hotel, they'd close you down.'

'But this isn't a hotel, Paul.'

'If it were, at least I'd be able to sue you if I got food poisoning.'

'Oh, give it a rest. What's for dinner? I'm starved.'

'Is chicken stir-fry all right for Madam?'

'Yes, thanks. Smells great. Where did you get the wok? Did you bring it with you?'

'No, Lainey. It was in the press under the cooker.'

Really? Fancy that.

I did know where he'd got the ingredients. I usually had plenty of healthy food in my kitchen. This was because only the unhealthy stuff actually got eaten. Maybe with Paul here, I wouldn't have to keep throwing my veggies out all the time.

Dinner was amazing. I contributed by opening a bottle of wine and clearing up afterwards. *Quid pro quo*.

At about eight, I noticed that Slinky hadn't come home for her tea. 'Did you see the cat today?'

Paul pursed up his lips like – well, like Slinky's arse, actually. 'Yes, I did, as it happens. You'll never guess what he did.'

'She.'

'Whatever. I was taking in the washing off the line –' What washing? Oh, yes … I vaguely remembered hanging out a load sometime last week. 'And I had it all neatly folded and ready to iron, and I turned my back for two minutes – and wasn't the cat fast asleep on top of the pile!'

No! What scandalous feline behaviour.

'So I had to wash it all again.'

'That was a tad extreme.'

'Lainey! You'd never know what you might catch.'

You never knew. Toxoplas-whatdoyoucallit or anything.

Slinky did little to redeem herself the next day by jumping in through the open window with an almost-dead baby rabbit in her mouth. I tried my best to explain to Paul that this was probably intended as a welcome gift to him, but he wasn't having any of it.

It had bucketed down all day long again. Paul hadn't had a very good day. He had broken the fridge whilst attempting to defrost it with a blow-torch ('It was a disgrace, there was a yoghurt in there that was older than me,' yadda yadda yadda). I was beginning to despair. At this rate, he'd be gone by Thursday.

But, on Wednesday, the heavens stopped conspiring against me. The day dawned bright and clear and stayed that way. I drove home at lunchtime to say hello, but there was no sign of Paul or Terence. When I got home that evening, the first thing I saw was a bunch of wild flowers sitting in the middle of the dining-room table.

'Where did they come from?'

Paul emerged from the kitchen, grinning. He looked thoroughly at home in a pair of biodegradable trousers and a lived-in T-shirt. I'd rarely seen him look so relaxed. Or so scruffy.

'Do you like them?'

'They're gorgeous.'

'I picked them while I was out on a walk.'

He described to me where he had been. It was more like a hike than a walk.

'While I was picking them, a guy on a red tractor stopped and asked me why I was weeding along the side of the road.'

'Where did the vase come from?'

'The cupboard under the sink. Lainey, did you open *any* of the presses before I got here?'

I ignored this. 'Did you bring Terence with you?'

'It wasn't so much that I brought him as that he decided to come along. I told him to stay, but he wouldn't. You're not very obedient, are you, Terence?'

Terence sat between us, looking from one face to the other with adoring doggy eyes. He woofed softly at the sound of his name. If Paul really hadn't wanted to bring him, he could have locked him in the house, but I decided not to point this out.

Paul enthused about the countryside for about an hour that night. He didn't say a thing about going home.

On Thursday evening, I came home to an even more elated Paul.

'The local priest called around to welcome us to the community.'

'Us?'

'He assumed I was your husband.'

'Did you put him right?'

'I told him I was just a houseguest. He knew all about you, though – that you were the local solicitor, and that you worked for Tyrone and came from Dublin.'

I was still confused. 'What's so great about a priest calling round? Was he very nice?'

'Far from it. He was a complete bastard. He sat there for half an hour, drinking your tea and eating your biscuits and giving out about solicitors. According to him, it's your lot's fault that all those priests have been done for sexual abuse. He particularly hates Tyrone, by the way.'

Tyrone had handled a few such high-profile cases.

'I hope you stuck up for me.'

'No.'

'Thanks a bunch.'

'But Terence did. While the priest was ranting on, I was watching Terence out in the garden. He got sick and then ate it.'

'Charming.'

'So I let him in, and he went straight over to the priest and licked his hand.'

'Did you, Terence? Good boy!'

'He shed a shitload of fur onto the bottom of your man's trousers, too.'

'Oh, did you? You're such a good boy.'

We petted Terence profusely and promised him extra treats for his supper that night.

'Lainey….'

'Yes?'

'Is it all right if I stay till the end of the week?'

'You can if you like.'

The end of the week came and went, and neither one of us said a word about Paul going home. I took a few days off work and we toured the countryside. I brought him to hot spots that Jack and Matt had shown me. I didn't tell him that, of course. What do you take me for? Have you forgotten that I'm a lawyer and therefore used to being flexible with the truth? We even went out for a drink in Power's with Jack one night. I was a little nervous, but the two men got on great. It seemed that Paul only had a problem with gay men when they tried to chat him up.

We were sitting in the conservatory one evening towards the end of the second week, in total silence, watching the sun sink down into the river valley. A spider spun a silken palace in the corner of the room. We watched the birds having their final feed before bedtime, singing their sweet incantations. Paul had made me a little birdhouse, using pieces of wood and old tools that he'd found in the shed.

We had just had a long conversation about his father. It was the first time Paul had ever really talked to me about him. He sat motionless, glass of wine in hand. Slinky was curled up fast asleep in his lap and Terence lay across his feet. He turned his head slowly towards me.

'You're going to find it hard to leave all this behind.'

'Hmmm?' I was so relaxed that at first I didn't register what he was saying.

'When you come back to Dublin; you're going to miss this place. When are you coming back, again?'

'I'm not.'

Paul sat up, and Slinky poured off his lap like hot oil.

'What do you mean, you're not?'

I forced myself out of my drowsy haze. 'I've decided to stay here.'

'Forever?'

'Well, I don't know about that. For the foreseeable future, anyway. Sorry I didn't say anything before. I've been meaning to tell you.'

Nothing was said for a while.

I finally broke the deadlock. 'Could you ever see yourself living somewhere like this?'

Paul smiled at me gently. 'I suppose so. If the circumstances were right.'

It was Saturday. Already. Paul was due back in the office that Monday. The atmosphere was strained, for the first time since his arrival.

He had insisted on cooking a special meal, to thank me for letting him stay. While the preparations were in full swing, I went out for a walk – partly to get out of the way, and partly to clear my head. So many thoughts were whirling around inside it. The two weeks had gone so well … only not as well as I had hoped.

Paul was still my ex-boyfriend.

The delicious cooking aromas wafted down the hill to greet me on my return.

'Mmm. What *is* that?'

'Thai chicken curry.'

'No, that other smell. Something sweet.'

Paul smiled proudly. 'Peach pie. There were all

these peaches in the fruit bowl, just going to waste, so I thought we could use them up tonight.'

I couldn't help but notice Paul's edginess throughout the meal. Even when we were sitting on the sofa afterwards, he seemed ill at ease.

'Paul, what's wrong?'

He rested his forehead in his hand, covering his eyes. 'I have some things I want to say to you.'

I swallowed. 'Go on.'

It took him a while to get going.

'Well … first of all, I can't thank you enough for letting me stay with you these past two weeks. I've had a brilliant time, and it was just what I needed.'

'I had a great time too.'

'Did you really?' His voice was sharp.

'Yes, really,' I said softly, admiring the curls that were starting to develop at the nape of his neck. I'd never known he had curly hair.

'Because I don't know why you invited me down. Let's face it, I was a crap boyfriend.'

'You weren't –'

'Yes, I was. Let me finish, please, Lainey. I was petty, jealous, insecure, controlling –'

'Paul –'

'Don't try and deny it.'

'Well, okay; it's partly true. But it's not as if I'm without fault, and it didn't stop us from having fun a lot of the time – did it?'

'I suppose not.'

'And we've had fun these last two weeks.'

He nodded.

'There you are, then.'

But Paul wasn't planning to forgive himself that easily. 'I was such an idiot, though – that time in the hotel in Kerry. I can't believe the way I acted. Like with Eric – how could I have been so stupid? I'm so sorry, Lainey. I don't blame you for dumping me. I deserved it.'

'Paul! There's no need to be sorry.'

'There's every need.' He startled me by gripping my hand urgently. It was the closest physical contact we'd had since he'd got there. I swallowed again. Paul's hazel eyes were fairly glowing.

'I'd do anything for another chance, Lainey – a chance to show you how much I've changed. Anything.'

It was all I could do to breathe.

'Hold on. Don't say anything yet.' He stood up abruptly, went into his room and returned carrying a book.

'Is that for me?'

'For both of us, really. If you want.'

He handed me the book.

Tantric Sex. I could feel myself blushing as I flicked through the pages.

'I bought it a few days ago.'

'Did you, now?'

'Yes. I've been reading it while you were in work. There are some things in it I thought we could try … but only if you want to. I'll understand if you're not interested.'

I took a deep breath.

'Well, seeing as how it *is* Saturday night … this position on page fifty-five looks interesting.' I showed him the page. 'If you think your thigh muscles are up to it.'

As I led him by the hand to the bedroom, he said to me, 'Would it be okay if I stayed for another week?'

Epilogue

It was the perfect day for a wedding – Midsummer Day. It was also two years to the day since Paul had decided to hand in his notice and move permanently to Ballyknock.

A marquee had been erected in the garden of Power's Cottage. Festooned with flowers and fairy lights, it ran from the gable end of the house right down to the cherry tree. Beautiful though the marquee undoubtedly was, none of us could bring ourselves to go inside just yet. The glorious evening was too enticing. Instead, we all sat and chatted at wooden picnic tables.

My father and Chen had turned their newly dry-cleaned suit jackets into goalposts and were trying to teach LuLing how to play soccer. Like any woman worth her salt, she couldn't see the point. Every time the ball came near her, she picked it up and ran with it, giggling hysterically as her daddy and granddad gave chase, her chubby little legs going like pistons. Dad and Chen discussed it and came to the conclusion that she might be more suited to Gaelic football.

But everybody else knew that ice-skating was her thing. Mum had insisted that Tatiana bring LuLing skating the moment she could walk – and LuLing, in her custom-made skates, had taken off across the ice as if she was born to it. She now went twice a week, and her mammy and granny had excessively high hopes involving Olympic gold medals.

Annie sat down on the fragrant lawn beside me and called out to her husband, 'Don't come running to me when you've got grass stains all over your jacket.' Chen grinned at her and continued chasing LuLing around the garden.

'How are you feeling?' Annie asked, looking searchingly into my face.

'Like Humpty Dumpty's sister.'

'And the ankles?'

'Up like puddings.'

'You poor thing. I was the same with the twins.'

Annie had given birth to twin girls three months previously, thereby making Chen the proudest father in Ireland. Before that, she had worked part-time as a secretary in Tyrone's Dublin office; upon returning to Ireland, she had discovered that she didn't have the heart to return to secondary-school teaching. Tabitha and Thomasina, she had called the twins. I had pleaded with her to give them plainer names – had she forgotten what it was like to be teased in school? all those years of being called Tatty or Titty-Anna? But she now claimed that this had been a character-building experience. Maybe she was right, but I wasn't taking any chances myself. If I had a little girl, I was going to call her Ellen.

We were joined by Paul, who handed me my seventh sparkling mineral water of the evening. He had added a strawberry and a chunk of lime, in an effort to make this one more exciting. He sat down behind me and tried to put his arms around my waist; finding none, he instead placed his arms as far as they could go around my distended belly.

I often wondered what he thought of me now – this big mound of leaks and rumbles that had once been his girlfriend. Sometimes I felt that he was waiting for me to go into labour like a scientist waited for a volcano to erupt – wanting to be there, but afraid of getting caught in the lava flow. I felt afraid sometimes, too. But there was no escaping my own body.

'You look lovely,' he whispered into my ear, and kissed my jawline.

I appreciated his efforts, I really did. But they didn't stop me from feeling like Demis Roussos in my party dress.

'How do you feel?' It was a question I was being asked a lot of late.

'Great.'

It was true. I did feel great most of the time – like a big, fat, happy Buddha, or a placid, well-tended sacred cow.

The pregnancy had been an accident – a happy accident. It's amazing how the simple process of weeing on a stick can change the course of your whole life. It was almost time to test out my allegedly child-bearing hips. Not to mention Paul's paternal skills.

Paul was a transformed man since he'd moved from the city. It wasn't just his hair, which was now wavy and curled about his shirt collar (he looked like the gardener off the telly), and it wasn't just his new casual style of dressing. He'd given up accountancy and was working as an organic farmer. He spent most of his days happily up to his armpits in muck. When he wasn't working, he was growing lilies in the back garden of our new home, a few miles away, or making organic crab-apple jelly from a recipe Bridie Power had given him. It had been passed down from Granny Power.

Healing the rift between his father and himself had been a real turning point for Paul. His own impending fatherhood had spurred him into making contact. Relations had been awkward at first, and it had been hard for Paul to forgive and forget. But his father's explanation that he had been repeatedly warned off by Paul's mother rang true, somehow. Of course, they were unlikely ever to have the ideal father-son relationship – it was too late for that; but perhaps Mr O'Toole could repair some of the damage by treating his grandchild the way he should have treated his own little boy. He had already visited us for a week that spring, and he was due to fly over again the second his first grandchild was born.

As for Mrs O'Toole, she had so far refused to visit us in our 'house of sin' or to acknowledge our baby, conceived as he or she had been outside holy matrimony. As far as I was concerned, this made life even more perfect. Paul still held out hope that she'd have a change of heart once the child was born. But, even if she didn't, he had his own family now.

Brendan Ryan – local solicitor extraordinaire – emerged from the mouth of the marquee.

'Can we have everyone in for the tango demonstration?' he roared.

He was wearing a new fireman-red cardigan that his wife had knitted for the occasion, together with a white shirt, a scarlet tie, black trousers and shoes, and shocking-pink socks. The effect was striking, to say the least. He gave me a freckly grin before disappearing back inside.

Relations between our firms continued to be good. If a mad client came to Brendan's office looking for advice, he sent him directly over the road to us. We would often return the favour. It balanced out and everyone was happy with this arrangement. We still had good-natured spats in Ballyknock district court, which had become even more enjoyable since the previous judge had been forced to retire on the grounds of ill temper.

Paul hauled me to my feet, and we followed the scatterings of people making their way into the tent. I couldn't wait to see this: my parents, the award-winning dancers Mr and Mrs Joe and Teresa Malone, giving a tango demonstration. Once, years ago, I'd asked my father if he regretted not having a son. He'd told me not to be daft – that, if my mother had given birth to a son, she would probably have christened him Rudolf and packed him off to ballet lessons. Dad had said he wouldn't wish such a fate on any young lad. And look at him now – Twinkle-Toes himself.

We scanned the room for prime seats.

'Over here!' It was Hazel, looking radiant. She was wearing a sky-blue trouser suit, an all-over St Tropez tan and perfectly sculpted eyebrows.

Of course, I knew one of the reasons for this radiance. Rumour had it that she was getting a good seeing-to from Mattie Power on a regular basis. (True, she wasn't blonde, but he didn't seem to mind.) But he couldn't claim all the credit. Hazel was a new woman since she'd taken a year out to travel the world. She'd returned six months ago and set up her own accountancy practice – in Ballyknock village. Her poky (so far) office was upstairs from the new premises of Power, Malone & Co. Solicitors. The entire population of Dublin would be living down here soon.

Unfortunately, she and Chris had never regained that closeness they'd had before Hazel's meltdown. For some reason not even fully understood by Hazel herself, she had taken out the worst of her frustrations on Chris. The wounds she'd inflicted had never fully healed, and both of them accepted that perhaps they never would. Sometimes you can't go back. Other friends had flowed into their lives, filling the void that each of them had left in the other.

Chris had been fired by the film company when her first short film turned out to be a spectacular flop. Undeterred, she'd moved over to Essex for six months to do a diploma in interior design (and to give the Essex girls a run for their money). Shortly after her return, she and Jack Power had set up their own interior design consultancy firm in Dublin.

Of course, Chris claimed to have known all along that Jack was gay. Nice of her to fill me in, as usual. Jack, in turn, claimed that Chris was the ultimate gay icon. I'd always known she'd find her niche sooner or later.

I sat down beside Hazel, who was sharing a table with Jack, his partner Chuck – whom he'd wasted no time in importing from San Francisco – Bridie and, last but not least, Johnny. Jack pulled his seat up beside mine.

'How's it going?' I whispered into his pierced ear. The earring was the only discernible sign of his gayness – other than Chuck, of course. These days, Jack mostly dressed like a boring, straight, old fart.

'Could be worse. No blood spilled yet.'

I glanced over at Chuck, who was chatting to Bridie. Johnny sat on the other side of his wife, sipping a pint and looking distinctly uncomfortable.

Jack had discovered that Ballyknock wasn't quite ready for him. One of the brothers had taken over the running of the farm, and Jack now lived in a stylish apartment off Dublin's South Great George's Street, with Chuck. Both his career and his personal life were going swimmingly. He sang in a gay nightclub every second Saturday night. I sometimes went up to see him – usually on the nights he was in drag, because they were the best. He had confessed to me recently that it was his greatest regret that he was too old to audition for boy bands.

I decided this would be a good time to ask him.

'Jack, I have a favour to ask you.'

'How could I refuse anything to a woman in your delicate condition?'

'That's why I'm asking you now.'

'Sounds scary. What is it?'

I took a deep breath. 'Will you be the baby's godfather?'

His face broke slowly into a grin. 'Don't you mean godmother?'

'I'm afraid Annie's already got that gig.'

'You could have two. I could be its fairy godmother.'

I pretended to consider this for a moment. 'All right, then. Will you do it?'

'I'd be delighted.'

Sorted.

The remainder of the Power clan, including Matt – current holder of the title of Ballyknock Bachelor of the Year – and the various little snot-nosed baby Powers, were distributed around the nearby tables. Amongst them sat Shem and Tom Delaney of the Rusty Teeth. Shem had been widowed about a year before. He'd recently started doing a line with Cissy Walsh from the post office. Patricia and the other matrons of Ballyknock were scandalised by his behaviour – the poor woman barely cold.... I suppose nobody likes to feel that they're dispensable.

As the applause following my parents' tango petered out, the bride and the groom took the floor. Tyrone took his blushing, blooming, blissful, blossoming bride in his arms for their first waltz as a married couple. Barbed Wire – who, we'd learnt today, had been christened Barbara Ann after the song – looked up lovingly into her new husband's face and smiled a smile that made her look ten years his junior rather than his senior. She had moved down to Ballyknock with him to continue as his secretary, and the rest, as they say, was history.

As for me, it had been a while since anyone had accused me of being proper. I'd long since found the thing that had been missing from my relationship with Paul the first time around.

It had been me all along.

I noticed that the champagne reserves were running low. I went into the kitchen of Power's Cottage, where I knew the extra bottles were being kept. I felt another twinge as I got up. I'd been having contractions for almost an hour now. Lucky they hadn't come any earlier; I had only ticked the last item off my 'Baby – to do' list that very morning. The contractions were still weak enough and far enough apart not to be a worry. But I'd have to tell Paul soon. He was having such a good time that I was reluctant to spoil his fun. And, besides, why would I want to sit around in a hospital when I could be here, amongst family and friends?

Feeling surprisingly calm, I uncorked a bottle of champagne and poured myself a glass. It was the first time alcohol had touched my lips in eight months – it could hardly do the baby any harm at this stage. I glanced up at Mary Power, who smiled regally at me from her place of honour above the fireplace.

'Well, Mary,' I said, raising my glass to her, 'things haven't turned out too badly after all. Cheers.'

I clinked my glass against her glassy frame.

Then I stepped back out into the sunshine.

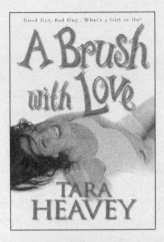